THE SLEEPING
KING

LAUREL COLLESS

BALBOA.
PRESS

A DIVISION OF HAY HOUSE

Balboa Press books may be ordered through booksellers or by contacting:

Balboa Press
A Division of Hay House
1663 Liberty Drive
Bloomington, IN 47403
www.balboapress.com
1 (877) 407-4847

Because of the dynamic nature of the Internet, any web addresses or links contained in this book may have changed since publication and may no longer be valid. The views expressed in this work are solely those of the author and do not necessarily reflect the views of the publisher, and the publisher hereby disclaims any responsibility for them.

The author of this book does not dispense medical advice or prescribe the use of any technique as a form of treatment for physical, emotional, or medical problems without the advice of a physician, either directly or indirectly. The intent of the author is only to offer information of a general nature to help you in your quest for emotional and spiritual well-being. In the event you use any of the information in this book for yourself, which is your constitutional right, the author and the publisher assume no responsibility for your actions.

Any people depicted in stock imagery provided by Thinkstock are models, and such images are being used for illustrative purposes only.
Certain stock imagery © Thinkstock.

Print information available on the last page.

ISBN: 978-1-5043-8864-1 (sc)
ISBN: 978-1-5043-8865-8 (hc)
ISBN: 978-1-5043-8910-5 (e)

Library of Congress Control Number: 2017914611

Balboa Press rev. date: 10/25/2017

For my mother Helen (1937 – 2014)

CONTENTS

BOOK VIII
Spiral Hall

For I am inclined to believe that my beloved Arthur of the future is sitting at this very moment among his learned friends, in the Combination Room at the College of Life, and that they are thinking away in there for all they are worth, about the best means to help our curious species: and I for one hope that some day, when not only England but the World has need of them, and when it is ready to listen to reason, if it ever is, they will issue from their rath in joy and power ...

T. H. White
The Once and Future King

BOOK I

The Wake-Up

Let Me Sleep

eter Blue swiped at the air around the ottoman sofa.

"Let me sleep!"

But the gentle jabbing of bony fingers on his ribs continued. Peter opened his eyes and was surprised to see a very old man staring down at him. Peter shouldn't have been that surprised, since he was an only child living in an old people's home. In fact, he was surrounded by them now in the day room, snoozing in their chairs. But this old man was not one of the residents of the Gum Tree Rest Home. He had a very long beard and was dressed in what looked like an old sack.

"It's time to wake up," the man whispered hoarsely.

"I am awake!" Peter said moodily. "But I was trying to sleep."

The old man smiled patiently. "Very well; sleep if you want to."

Rolling over on the narrow sofa, Peter's eyes settled on a slanting shaft of sun that had broken through the blinds. Suddenly, the light seemed to flatten out like a sheet across the floor, and then fold inwards like origami paper. The whole floor was falling away beneath him. Peter gripped the edges of the ottoman sofa. There wasn't even time to shout. He clenched his eyes shut; his stomach was in free fall. The sofa then thudded to a halt.

Peter opened his eyes. It was dark except for a yellow light that bobbed towards him.

As the light got closer and Peter's eyes adjusted, he saw it was the old man again, holding a candle and wearing a high hat.

The old man spoke in a voice surprisingly rich and full. "There now! That settles it – we've both got what we wanted."

"What did *you* want?" Peter asked, rubbing his eyes.

"I wanted you to wake up."

"Well, what about what *I* wanted?"

"You wanted to sleep," the old man said kindly. "And now, here you are, wide awake in just the right dream."

Peter was about to ask how you could be wide awake in a dream, when his attention was drawn to the old man's chest pocket, where a tiny green-brown frog stared out at him. The frog opened its mouth in a gaping way, and, instead of making a croaking sound, its voice came out in a series of squeaks. It took Peter a moment to realise the frog was actually speaking.

"Is that him? Is that the king?" the frog squeaked. It sounded disappointed.

"*Shh!*" The old man gave the frog a stern look, then turned to Peter. "Don't worry about Rani, she gets a bit above herself."

Peter nodded, unsure.

"It's because I'm the seven-times great-granddaughter of a famous frog," Rani explained, her voice filled with importance. "Quercus Croak was his name ... maybe you've heard of him."

Peter pretended to search his mind. "No, I don't think so," he mumbled. He turned to the old man. "Where did the day room go? Are you some kind of wizard or something?"

The old man laughed roundly but didn't reply.

"His name's Tollen," Rani said squeakily. "He's Tollen of the Forest and Frogs – don't you know anybody?"

"Be polite now," Tollen warned.

Rani was quiet for a moment, still staring at Peter. Then she bowed her curved head regally.

"You can pat me if you like."

Even though the frog was annoying, Peter couldn't resist reaching over to stroke her greenish-brown skin.

"It feels so real," he told Tollen. "Quite dry and rough, even though it looks slimy."

"Slimy?!" protested Rani.

"Well, what I mean is," Peter faltered, "it's hard to believe this is a dream."

"Well, never mind that now," Tollen said. "We need a sign."

Tollen sneezed loudly, making the candle flame sputter.

"Was that the sign?" asked Peter.

"No, a cold; the weather has its hold on me."

"The weather? How?"

"Ask the frogs; they suffer the most."

"Suffer from what?"

"The consequences."

"Of what?"

Tollen shrugged crossly. "People raising the seas, sinking the rivers, and poisoning the skies."

The little frog coughed squeakily to demonstrate the suffering of her kind.

"And what are the consequences?" asked Peter.

"Great floods, superstorms, wildfires. ..."

"Fire?" Peter shuddered.

"*Shh.* ... Don't fret child!" Tollen handed Peter the candle. "Hold this!"

Stepping off the sofa, Peter waved the candle flame about curiously.

"Where are we, by the way? It looks like the inside of a tree or something."

"Very good," Tollen said approvingly. "Genus *Quercus,* the common oak."

"Am I still in Australia?"

"Well, yes and no. You're everywhere and nowhere – if you know what I mean."

Peter shook his head nervously. "Actually, I think I need to get back."

"Well, we'll soon have you home again," the old man muttered.

Tollen pointed to a circular opening in the tree and said, "But first, look outside, and tell me if the ravens still circle the mountaintop."

Peter poked his head through the small opening. "It's kind of dark out here. I can't see much."

"Or was it falcons or pelicans?" mumbled Tollen.

Rani the frog laughed.

"Could it be kookaburras?" Peter pulled his head back inside.

"I don't think so ... but according to the prophecy, there's a bird that no longer flies when the Sleeping King must rise."

"Oh well," said Peter knowledgeably. "Lots of bird species are getting extinct every day."

"That's right!" Rani squeaked self-importantly.

"Frogs too," said Peter, fighting a smile as Rani edged backwards into Tollen's pocket.

"Well, then, it must be time," Tollen said in a grumbly voice."

"Time for what?" asked Peter.

"Time for you to wake up and start your quest; the old ones can't mind you forever."

Peter frowned deeply.

"You're going to have to leave soon. ... A little too soon ... maybe." Tollen surveyed Peter's thin boyish frame gravely. "But then, the dark ones do still fear you; fear your legacy at least."

Tollen fixed his gaze on the candle flame, which sputtered unsteadily in Peter's hand. A rush of paddy paws on Peter's shoulder made the candle lurch.

"Hold still the candle!" Tollen scolded, "I'm trying to get a vision going."

Peter glared after the frog, now swinging wide circles from a jutting tree root. But he couldn't resist asking, "How can you swing like that without falling off?"

"I'm a tree frog. *Whee-e-e ...!* I've got opposable fingers that work like your thumbs."

"*Shh!*" The old man was becoming misty eyed. "Ah, well now! I see you here with many such ones as you – children, their hopeful breath mingling with a gentle afternoon wind." He paused. "You must find them, Peter Blue ... and lead them."

Peter gaped uncomprehendingly.

Tollen smiled. "You look just the same ... it could have been yesterday."

He was gazing not at Peter but the candle.

"Together, we can raise your light anew."

"What light?" Peter asked nervously.

"What light?" mimicked the frog, annoyingly.

Peter glared at Rani again. "I don't know what anyone here is talking about. And besides, frogs can't talk. They're only supposed to say *ribbet!"*

Nobody replied.

Then, suddenly, Peter relaxed again. "Oh, I get it; this is all just part of the dream, isn't it?"

"I assure you it is not!" Tollen interjected.

"But he *is* dreaming," Rani screeched. "You said so!"

"Yes, all right this is a dream," Tollen conceded.

"A *ribbeting* dream," interrupted Rani, widening her mouth into what might have been an attempt at smiling.

Peter took a step forward. "So, is this real or not?"

"It doesn't matter; your quest is real."

"But I can't lead people!" protested Peter. "If I ever have to make a speech or something, my voice goes all squeaky."

"What's wrong with squeaky?" interrupted Rani.

"It's no matter," Tollen said. "You're a philosopher type; you'll find a way."

"A philosopher?" Peter's voice rose.

"You're a thinker, a boy with ideas."

"But I never—"

Tollen raised a long bony hand to interrupt him.

"Now don't fret ... although, ..." he remarked, looking doubtfully at Peter. "You will need extra protection. Now where did I put that?"

Tollen scoured the titles on the spines of his book-laden shelves.

"Ah. ... *The Wayfinder.*" He thumped a big book down onto a desk table. Dust flew.

"Are you sure that's the *Wayfinder* book?" queried the frog, squinting down at the cover. "I think it's the old telephone directory."

Tollen placed a pair of wire-rimmed glasses at the end of his nose and checked the title. "It's hard enough remembering all these mind maps without having to memorise telephone numbers," he joked.

"Well, why do you need it?" Rani squeaked.

"To get Peter Blue back to his right *where* and *when*. Navigating these inner worlds is always much more difficult on the way back."

Peter felt his stomach tighten, but he didn't say anything.

"Plus, this book makes the loudest bang when I shut it," added Tollen.

Peter watched warily while the old man consulted its pages.

Next, Rani was somersaulting through the air towards Peter. His arms flew to protect his face, but the frog made a perfect landing, feet first, into Peter's thick red hair.

"I'm also learning to croak," Rani told him proudly.

The old man shifted his gaze back to them.

"That should do it," he said. "Now lie down again, Peter, and when I shut the book, you'll be ready to wake up and start your quest."

"Wait!" protested Peter. "What about my new protection? Weren't you just looking for something?"

"Oh right, yes." The old man shuffled his bony fingers through the steep rise of pages. "I was using it as a bookmark some years back! ..."

He plucked out a thin reed of yellowy paper and studied it. "Good! This will do nicely."

Tollen folded the paper lengthwise three times, chanting, "Once, twice, and thrice."

The paper now was the length of straw, and Tollen tucked it between the frame and cushion of Peter's sofa.

"Don't forget this," Tollen warned.

Peter wondered how a piece of paper was going to protect him, but he was too polite to ask.

"Right. Ready, boy?" Tollen asked.

"No, not yet. Can you first get this frog off my head?"

"Hop down, dear one, and say goodbye," the old man coaxed.

"I haven't said hello yet!" Rani landed with a *thump* in Peter's lap.

"It's time," said Tollen softly.

"Wait!" Peter objected. "I like it here."

"He likes it here!" screeched the frog.

"Of course he likes it here." Tollen held the boy with a gaze softer than before. "In many ways, this is home."

He'd spoken kindly, too kindly. Peter's cheeks were suddenly damp with some strange mixture of sadness and longing.

When the old man spoke again, he made it a point of being much gruffer. "Now, you must go!"

"Wait! Can I come back?"

"Yes! But you have to find your own way."

"But—"

"You must!" said Tollen, even more gruffly. "That is your quest!"

And then, the heavy book slammed shut.

Getting Home

A strong spiralling wind blew up around him, pulling Peter and the sofa into a vortex of white. Peter closed his eyes and clung to the sofa's metal-rimmed edges as it lurched into a slow spin. As the spinning sofa gathered speed, the whiteness grew thicker, and chattering voices seemed to rise in volume and then fade again in the air around him.

Then, as quickly as the spinning started, it ground to a silent halt.

Rani the frog's high-pitched squeal pierced the silence. "*Ow!* My opposable finger ... it's stuck in the book!"

Silence again.

Peter didn't know how long the silence lasted. He became aware of a lick of warm sunshine on his face. Strong hands were pulling him up, raising him high into a wide sky. It was Dad. He was wearing his blue GAIA jacket, and he wasn't dead.

As Dad hugged Peter's face close to his chest, Peter spotted something white and plump, like a marshmallow, on Dad's jacket shoulder. When he reached for it the little marshmallow disappeared. He reached again and saw it wasn't a marshmallow but a tiny white clenched fist. It was his own fist. A thin wail rose from Peter's mouth and into Dad's ear.

"Shh!" Dad hugged him closer.

The wailing stopped.

The GAIA jacket hummed.

Tollen's voice, impatient, came through. "Oh, thunder and lightning! We've got the wrong *where* and the wrong *when*."

Peter wanted to tell Tollen not to worry; he would stay here with Dad, and everything would be all right again. But when he moved his mouth, he found that he didn't know how to form words.

A voice whispered behind him. Was it Mum? Peter strained his neck around to see her.

"I'm so close now, Byron. It could be just months."

But Dad was impatient. "Thelma, you scientists have no idea of time. Even here, at the end of the earth, you must know they're going to find us soon."

"I know, sweetheart, but if I could finish this formula, it could make all the difference for Peter, and even the future of the earth itself."

"Look, I've told you what we have to do, Thelma."

"Oh, Byron, not this again!"

Peter could feel Mum's hand nervously patting at his hair.

Dad said, "Well, it's time to take control of the situation! We're sitting ducks."

"But, Byron, it's too risky."

"It's our best hope, Thelma. We bring them here, then we finish this thing forever."

Peter's chubby little legs began to kick and squirm. Suddenly, he wanted to try them out. When Dad lowered him to the ground, he was off, charging bow-legged across the grassy clearing.

"I'll get him!" cried Mum.

Mum made a dive for him, and missed.

"If you can catch him!" Dad chuckled.

Peter made it all the way to the research cabin. It hadn't burnt down. Behind him, Mum was laughing, then scooping him up and pulling him close. It felt good. Peter wished he could speak. He saw bubbles floating out of his mouth and into the air. They weren't bubbles, he realised; they were giggles, his giggles.

Mum was gently spinning him round in her arms. Then it started getting too fast. He was caught in the spiralling wind from before. The world went white again. Thankfully, Peter's hands found the narrow edge of the sofa as it floated passed; he pressed his belly against it, as if it were a surfboard, and then he was in free fall again.

The sofa landed with a jolt. The misty whiteness cleared, and Peter saw that he was back in the Gum Tree day room. The chairs where the residents usually slept were all empty, but Peter was not alone. Beside him on the sofa was Tollen, staring out the window into the bush. And the bush was on fire.

Peter looked down at his legs and was shocked to see smuts of black soot and red welts covering the skin. Also, his legs looked shorter than they should. He tried standing up but, instead, fell face forward onto the day room floor.

Luckily, his grandmother, Nonna LaRosa, was there to pick him up.

"These aren't my legs!" Peter told her in a voice that didn't sound like his own.

"*Shh!* Don't try to talk." Nonna looked younger than usual. Her straight, shoulder-length hair was a darker grey than Peter remembered. Her eyes through her thick oval-rimmed glasses were red from crying.

"We're all just glad you're alive." Nonna lifted him back onto the sofa next to Tollen and began dispensing small sips of water over Peter's blistery lips.

Peter saw that Tollen also looked younger, though still very old.

Then, Rani's frog voice came through. "You've got the right *where*, but still the wrong *when!* And by the way, my opposable finger still hurts!"

Peter wasn't sure if Tollen could hear the frog. He was deep in conversation with Nonna.

"We must build a moat around this place." Tollen gestured with a wide sweep of his robe sleeve.

"A moat?" Nonna looked surprised. "What about the water shortages, and ... well ... the fact that the Gum Tree Rest Home isn't exactly a castle."

Tollen coughed politely. "It will be a dry moat, wide and shallow; call it a firestop, if you will. When the moat is done, I'll do my best to protect the space within, if you can do your part by keeping the boy from crossing beyond it."

Nonna nodded uncertainly. Matron was beside her now, taking notes.

"But for how much time?" Nonna asked.

"Time?" repeated Tollen. "Time is an illusion that cannot easily be brought into this discussion."

"Why not?" protested Nonna. "The boy's five, and I'm not going to live forever."

"I understand," the old man said, nodding softly. "It's only that, as you probably know, when one begins to tamper with space, it will necessarily have an impact on time."

Nonna looked back at him blankly.

"And yet," the old man added, raising a finger instructively, "one thing I am certain of in this case is that time *will* tell."

Matron nodded solemnly. "Everything will be arranged just as you suggest."

"Good." The old man was suddenly all business. "I'll provide the blueprint and supervise the works, and GAIA will naturally shoulder the costs."

Peter felt his attention wandering.

Soon Angel the cook was there smiling and offering the old man one of her homemade oatmeal biscuits.

I should warn him, thought Peter.

But it was too late.

Tollen was groaning and clutching his jaw in pain. Peter saw him secretly slide the biscuit remains into his hip pocket.

Peter couldn't resist peeping into the pocket to see if Rani was there. She wasn't; instead, he spotted a different frog with speckled brown skin. Peter couldn't pull his eyes away from the frog's unblinking stare.

In an instant, the spiralling wind was back, along with the white vortex. Peter clung to the ottoman's metal-rimmed cushiony edges, just waiting for everything to stop.

CHAPTER

Greed with a Capital G

W hen Peter woke up, the day room was empty and he could smell burning.

Matron was pushing open the large double doors. "Come on, Peter Blue, you're late!"

"Has the fire …?"

"No, not fire. Angel burnt dinner again," Matron said matter-of-factly.

"Why can't I go across the moat?" Peter asked as he hurried to match Matron's quick strides down the dimly lit corridor.

Matron stopped and swung round on the heel of her white nursing shoe. "Do you want to cross it, to leave Gum Tree?"

"No!" Peter replied truthfully."

"Well, then." Matron patted his shoulder briskly. "Let's get you to dinner."

The dream sat like a ball of intact memory in a place at the back of Peter's head that he couldn't quite reach. There'd been something in the dream that he wasn't supposed to forget. When he tugged gently at the ball of memory, its edges began to dissolve. The more he tried to pull at it, the quicker he felt it melting away. …

By the time Matron pushed open the dining room door, the dream was gone.

Angel was there, though.

"Here comes Peter Blue, the youngest but the slowest!" she called good-humouredly.

Peter smiled but kept his eyes to the floor, trying to scuttle unnoticed across to Nonna's table. It wasn't easy being the only kid living in an old people's rest home.

"Late again, Peter!" Mrs Weakes waved her blue notebook from her wheelchair. "I'll have to write you down for a demerit."

Peter smiled unworriedly as he hopped into his regular seat between Nonna and Mr Biggs.

Nonna peered over at him through her thick oval-rimmed glasses.

"You were so deeply asleep, we couldn't wake you," she said worriedly. "What are we going to do with you?"

"He sleeps more than we do!" observed Mrs Weakes, "and we're all over eighty!"

"Don't sleep your life away, Peter," Nonna La Rosa told him.

"Well, he doesn't have that much to live for really, does he?" sniffed Mrs Millet.

"Shush!" Nonna told her.

"Oh, I wouldn't worry," said Mr Biggs, folding away his newspaper. "He's just practising for when he's teenager. Isn't that right, Peter?"

Peter smiled at him, then turned back to Nonna.

"Why can't I go to the other side of the moat?" he asked her.

She looked surprised. "Well, Peter, it's not that you *can't* go; it's just more of a precaution … for your safety, really."

"But my safety from what?"

Everyone seated at Nonna's table stayed silent, waiting for Nonna to reply.

"Well. …" Nonna shifted her pear-shaped body uneasily in the wooden dining chair. "That's the annoying thing, Peter. I'm afraid I can't remember. …"

Nonna turned to Mr Biggs seated beside her, seeking his support.

He was like his name: a big man with a big heart.

"It's to keep Peter safe from the bush fires, surely," he said. "After all, it is a firepit."

"Yes, I suppose that's it," agreed Nonna doubtfully.

Mrs Millet reached across the table to pat Peter's arm. "Don't be in too much of a hurry to cross the moat, Peter. Life on the other side brings so much disappointment!"

They were interrupted by the rattle of Angel's dinner trolley.

"Beef Wellington with Béarnaise sauce," Angel announced. She began doling out dinner plates of inedible-looking food.

"Something to eat?" asked Mr Witherspoon, reaching for Mrs Weakes's handbag. Mrs Weakes snatched it back sharply and stowed it in her lap.

"Have to keep a tight watch on your belongings with Mr Witherspoon around," she told Peter. "Look! He thought my beige leather handbag was the beef!"

"He can't help it if he's delusional," said Peter, using Matron's big word for describing Mr Witherspoon. Anyway, Peter also secretly thought that the burnt meat wrapped in soggy pastry looked a lot like the beige leather handbag.

At the end of the table, one of the Trelawney sisters said brightly, "I'll just pop a bit more Béarnaise sauce on mine."

"Did you say she burnt the sauce too?" asked the other Trelawney sister.

"Oh, honestly!" Mrs Millet clanged down her fork. "I left my husband of fifty years to come here, just so I could eat a few meals before I died that I didn't have to cook myself. And this is what I get: beef Wellington like rubber boots!"

"Actually, it's beef Wellington like the duke," corrected Nonna LaRosa, winking at Peter through her thick glasses.

"Never mind," said Mr Biggs. "The Duke of Wellington probably had better teeth than we do."

"Impossible," Mrs Millet objected. "Look, even Peter's eleven-year-old teeth can't bite their way through this lot."

"Peter's not eleven till tomorrow." Nonna interrupted her own chewing to correct Mrs Millet again.

Further down the table, Mrs Worthington Smith-Jones pushing aside her untouched dinner and raised her powdery face to Mr Biggs. "Have you been home lately?" she asked in her fake British accent.

"Ah no, not lately, Mrs WSJ, no. ..."

Even though the British had settled in Australia more than two hundred years earlier, Mrs Worthington Smith-Jones still believed England to be the rightful home of Australians.

"England's so green this time of year." She sighed wistfully, then turned to Mrs Millet. "What about you, Vera, have you been home?"

"Australia's my home," Mrs Millet told her snippily. "Anyway, you meet me here at this table every night, so when do you think I'd have had time to fly to England and back?"

Peter suppressed a giggle. Then he saw with alarm that Mrs WSJ was now looking at him.

"Have you been home lately, Peter?"

"Ah. ..." Peter blushed and glanced nervously at Nonna. "I've never been to England."

Pop Olsen and the two skinny men who looked like stick insects were staring vacantly across the table at him.

"But you will one day, won't you?" interrupted Mrs Millet. "Go to London to live with your aunty and uncle? After Nonna, you know. ..." She made a cutting motion at her throat.

Peter held his breath, but Nonna just laughed.

"Don't get ahead of yourself, Vera. I've still got a pulse."

"Well, as much as we love Peter, we've always said that an old-folks home is no place for a young boy," said one of the Trelawney sisters in a worried voice.

"He needs children his own age to play with, not us old wrinklies," advised the other sister.

"Well, the most important issue is his *ed-ew-cation*," interrupted Ms Moth.

The Moth, as Peter called her in the privacy of his own head, had long grey hair, which she wore tightly combed up into a bun. It made her seem more severe than she really was. Like Matron, the Moth was bossy, but in a different way. While Matron had strict rules, the Moth had strict opinions. For example, if Peter didn't get all his homework or his required reading done, she would waive the offence away carelessly, saying. "But what did you think of it, Peter? Think, Peter, think. Tell me your ideas."

Peter watched her now, dabbing her handkerchief at the corners of her mouth.

"Delicious!" she pronounced.

"What did you have?" asked Peter, hoping to move the subject away from his *ed-ew-cation* to her vegetarian dinner.

She stared a moment at her empty plate. "Let's just say that while you were dining on the Duke of Wellington, I was feasting on the Earl of Sandwich."

Peter laughed encouragingly, hoping to start a new conversation on the earl, but there seemed to be no more appetite for British nobles.

This left Nonna an opening to push forward on the subject of Peter moving to England to live with Aunty Surla and Uncle Gorrman.

"Peter won't be going to London just yet," Nonna said, and then she mouthed something across the table when she thought Peter wasn't looking.

"What?" Mrs Millet stopped chewing and leant forward. "They don't want him ...?"

"Shush!" Nonna insisted.

Reluctantly, Mrs Millet went back to her chewing.

Peter pretended he hadn't heard. He didn't want to stay with his aunt and uncle either, so they were all even. Nonna would just have to stay healthy. He glanced over at her. She didn't look like she was going to die, but you could never tell with old people. One man last week had fallen face first into his soup. "A weak heart," Matron had said, so Angel had decided not to take it personally.

Mr Witherspoon, whose plate was already clean, was eyeing the half-eaten dinners of Pop Olsen and the stick insects.

Nonna caught Peter looking longingly towards the door.

"Clear your plate first, Peter," Nonna cautioned.

In the interest of haste, Peter began sawing the beef Wellington into cubes and inserting piece after piece into his mouth. He wanted to get back to the ottoman for another nap, to find that dream again.

Angel returned and smiled round hopefully, showing her two perfect dimples, one in each cheek.

"How's everyone going over here?"

"Oh lovely ... lovely, thank you," mumbled Mr Biggs politely.

"Still working," said Mrs Weakes through gritted teeth.

"Oh, you ate everything Peter!" Angel praised.

Peter's mouth was so full, he could only nod.

"Perhaps we might try a French dish tomorrow," suggested Mrs Millet. "This English food is so. ..." With a grimace, she left her sentence hanging.

"I'll see what I can do." Angel sniffed and moved on.

For a few moments, Nonna's table occupants chewed silently.

Then, peering out the window into the half-light, Ms Moth said, "No sign of fire yet, then?"

"The bush is still recovering from the last fire," said Mr Biggs disapprovingly.

The residents stared out at the lines of charred and broken trees on the far side of the moat. Only the one great jarrah gum tree still rose up to fill the sky, as it always had.

"A magic tree," Angel had once told Peter. "Should have been burnt to the ground many times over, but it just refused to go."

"A tower of strength," Mr Biggs had called it, after the last fire had circled it hungrily for three days before finally pulling back, deprived of its prey.

"I heard the whole town of Jarra Jarra's evacuating," Nonna told Mr Biggs worriedly. "They say it's going to be another Black Sunday Fire."

"Well, it's only Friday, so let's not get ahead of ourselves," said Mr Biggs mildly. "Although there's no great cause to be hopeful. All we seem to get is weather disasters nowadays."

"He's right," said Ms Moth. "And look at the bush: dry as dust."

Nonna sighed. "Even the dew dries up before it has a chance to reach the ground."

"How many days without rain has it been now, Peter?" Ms Moth asked.

Peter frowned and tried to shift the big ball of meat to the side of his mouth. "Humbred and forfy-wum."

"One hundred and forty-one," Ms Moth said, interpreting Peter's speech while frowning at his disappointing table manners.

Mrs Worthington Smith-Jones raised a lace handkerchief theatrically to her forehead, "Oh, dear Mr Biggs, what's happening to our weather?"

"Too many greedy people! That's what's happening to the weather. They're all so greedy for more and more stuff that the earth can't cope with the pollution and the waste." Mr Biggs replied staunchly, pushing away his plate and pulling out his tobacco pipe. "Today's generation of power is characterised by greed with a capital G."

"As was the last one," Ms Moth interrupted. "And the one before that. People are always greedy for more than they need, and greedy for whatever anyone else has."

Mr Biggs nodded sadly.

"Greed!" repeated Ms Moth. "It drives nations and their leaders to conquer each other."

"Well," said Mrs Worthington Smith-Jones, "I'm sure the Duke of Wellington was a lovely man. He beat that nasty Napoleon, didn't he?"

"And for what?" asked Ms Moth.

Mrs Worthington Smith-Jones looked back blankly at her.

"And for what?" Ms Moth relaunched her question at Peter.

"Um. ..."

"Let me put it another way: Why did Napoleon have to invade England at Waterloo in the first place?"

"Ah. ..." Peter wasn't very strong on history. He looked with alarm around the table for help, but Nonna and Mr Biggs only nodded back encouragingly, while Mrs Millet gazed down at her uneaten dinner.

"Why?" Ms Moth persisted.

"Um. ..." Peter pushed the lump of meat back into his cheek. "Ah ... greed ... with a capital G," he said, guessing it was the answer she sought.

"Exactly!" the Moth slapped the table with her small hand "Greed! For power, in the case of Napoleon."

"Not greed for the English food," suggested Peter, surprised when the grown-ups exploded with laughter.

"Well," said Mr Biggs, wiping it eyes, "it'll have to be someone from the new generation to step up and fix things."

"Someone like Peter," suggested Ms Moth.

"Me?" Peter gagged on his ball of beef.

"Well, it doesn't have to be you exactly," giggled Nonna reassuringly. "Just someone like you."

"Why not Peter?" chorused the Trelawney sisters. "He can do it."

"Yes, of course. You're right. Why not Peter? He's as good as anyone!" Nonna acknowledged hurriedly.

All heads turned towards Peter.

"Um … I was actually planning to spend my life here at the rest home," he said. "Maybe when I'm older, I'll get my own room … one with a veranda like Mr Biggs's."

"Well, my room will be free soon if this cough keeps up," said Mr Biggs good-humouredly.

"Oh, shush that silly talk, both of you," said Nonna.

They were interrupted by a screech of car brakes coming from the gravel driveway at the front, and then the sound of men's voices – angry men's voices.

CHAPTER

Devlin Dean

M atron was pulling open the heavy front door when Peter slid through the shadows and into the narrow cloakroom next to the entrance. He was curious to see the angry men, but he wanted to keep hidden because their shouting scared him. It smelt dank and mouldy in the cloakroom, but the view through the narrow open window was good.

Out on the driveway, taxi headlights lit up two figures: a short man, who appeared to be the taxi driver; and a tall old one, who seemed to be balancing a pile of jackets and shirts in his arms.

"I said, 'I need my fare!'" the driver was shouting. "Give me my taxi fare!"

"And I told you, if you want money, go ask the bank – they stole all my money and my house!" the old man barked back at him.

"Don't tell me your problems! Just give me my fare, or I'm calling the police."

Peter chewed nervously on the ball of meat still in his mouth. He wondered what would happen next. Would they fight? Would it be dangerous?

The two had almost reached the veranda when Matron stepped briskly out from the shadows in front of them.

"You can't come in here!" she told the tall man holding the jackets.

"Try and stop me," he said rudely.

Peter watched as Matron crunched athletically from side to side to stop him from dodging past her. Her white nursing pumps glistened in the car lights.

The tall man paused and sighed.

Matron spoke to the taxi driver in the same soft but firm voice that she used with her residents. "Now, you will take your customer and his travelling wardrobe to his correct destination at once."

"This is my correct destination," interrupted the tall man angrily.

"I assure you it's not; visiting hours have long finished."

"Well, I'm not a visitor!" For a moment, the old man looked beaten. "I'm a new resident."

At the window, Peter felt his heart lurch with a mixture of fear and excitement. This angry man was moving into Gum Tree?

"Well," Matron intoned, "there's far too much paperwork for this late hour, and no room has been prepared for you, so I suggest you go to a hotel and come back tomorrow."

"The hotel's closed – with the bush-fire alert," interrupted the taxi driver.

"Do you think I'd have come to this dump if the hotel was open?" interrupted the tall man.

Peter could see by the light from the porch that, although the man's hair was jet black, his face was heavily lined.

"Well, then, stay with a friend, and come back tomorrow," Matron said with finality.

"Nah, no friends."

Somehow, this didn't surprise Peter.

"So, it looks like, tonight, I'll be the guest of Her Majesty's government." With that, the tall man dodged past Matron, taking the steps up to the veranda two at a time.

"Not without your paperwork, you won't." She hurried after him.

The taxi driver followed, and Peter had to pin his head flat to the wall in order to keep watching them.

"For the last time, please take this man away!" Matron told the taxi driver.

"I don't want him!" the driver snapped back. "I just want the old fossil to pay his fare."

"Who are you calling old?"

The tall man had roared with such unexpected savagery that the driver leapt backwards down the steps.

Matron, on the other hand, stood firm, tapping her foot.

"Well?" she said staunchly. "Aren't you going to give this poor driver his fare?"

Peter watched as the tall man, sighing all the while, unloaded his great pile of suits and ties onto the wicker chair by the door. He pulled out a pen and notepad from the top pocket of his white shirt.

"What's that?" asked the taxi driver suspiciously. "Because if you're going to write me an IOU, don't—"

"It's not an IOU," snapped the tall man. "it's something much better."

Peter watched the tall man curl his pen with a flourish on the paper, then slap it into the driver's open hand.

The driver looked down at it blankly.

"It's a share," explained the tall man. "One share in Devlin Dean Holdings."

Although Peter had never heard of Devlin Dean Holdings, the taxi driver clearly had.

But, still, the driver seemed unsure. "How can you issue a share in that …?"

"Because I am he – I am Devlin Dean."

"But how can Devlin Dean, a multimillionaire, not have taxi fare?"

Devlin Dean seemed to consider this a worthy question. "Let's just say I've had a few very bad afternoons in the markets."

Peter heard plodding footsteps. It was Mr Biggs opening the front door and stepping out onto the porch.

"Need any help, Matron?"

Devlin Dean must have seen his chance because, in an instant, he scooped up his clothes, dodged past Mr Biggs, and rushed into the building.

Peter felt the cloakroom floor shudder as the new man charged past, in the direction of the old south wing.

"Mr Dean!" Matron's voice, now anything but calm, rose up. "There are no vacant bedrooms down there, Mr Dean!"

Peter waited at the cloakroom door, listening. Outside, there was a scrunch of gravel as the taxi retreated into the night. Then, Peter thought he heard a gentle bumping sound coming from inside the large floor-to-ceiling wardrobe behind him. Were there rats? He tiptoed over and slid the door open.

Too late, Peter remembered this was where Matron kept the dead people's coats. He was hit by a rush of cold wind that seemed to circle the inside of the wardrobe, bumping along the battalion of old coats and rattling the wood-panel walls. How could a breeze be blowing inside? Peter could only think of one possibility.

"Ghost!" he hollered, stumbling backwards. "Help! Ghost in the jackets!"

The ghost seemed to swirl all around him as Peter yanked open the cloakroom door and fled down the south corridor.

The residents, who'd gathered outside the dining room to get a look at Devlin Dean, now had the added attraction of watching Peter Blue screaming past.

"Ghost! Ghost! In the jackets!" he cried.

One of the Trelawney sisters tried to catch Peter's arm.

"It's not a ghost in a jacket," she called after him. "It's just a rude man who's carrying a lot of jackets."

Mrs Millet stood patting her platinum-blonde hair hopefully.

"Have you seen the new resident, then, Peter?"

Peter's breath was coming out in quick bursts.

"He's not a new resident!" interrupted Matron from the other end of the corridor. "Not without his papers!"

Peter fled off in the other direction, looking for Nonna. But as he rounded the corner, he hit smack into the tall, striding upper body of Mr Devlin Dean. With the impact of the collision, Peter delivered the remaining meaty contents of his mouth right onto the millionaire's clean white shirt.

"Oh, stone the crows! Did you spit on me?" Devlin Dean seized Peter by both elbows. "Did you spit on my shirt?"

Devlin Dean gripped Peter in a way that left him staring face first into the angry brown stain.

"Sorry," managed Peter.

Peter tried to wipe at the stain, but Mr Dean pushed him out to arm's length.

"What are you doing here, anyway? I was told visiting hours were over?" Mr Dean raised his eyebrows tellingly at Matron, who'd just pulled up beside them.

Mr Biggs arrived a moment later, carrying all of Mr Dean's jackets and shirts.

"I live here," mumbled Peter.

"What ... here? Where are your parents?"

"Dead. ..."

"Oh. ..."

Mr Dean released Peter's arms.

"Well, what were you eating?" Mr Dean asked, a little less irritably.

Peter didn't reply.

The stain was growing larger, seeping across the whiteness of the shirt. Mr Dean rubbed at it, making it worse.

"I asked you a question," Mr Dean persisted. "What were you eating?"

"Um. ..."

"Tell me!" the angry man barked.

"Ah ... it was the Duke of Wellington!" Peter said, hoping to make the mark sound more important than a regular meat-and-gravy stain.

"The Duke of Wellington?" repeated Mr Dean.

Peter nodded.

Mr Dean seemed to be holding his breath. Then, the corners of his mouth twitched. He gave a small chuckle, which grew into a loud, choking laugh.

"The Duke of Wellington?" he said again. More laughter rose from him, sounding like a high-pitched whine. "And I suppose you've just got back from the Battle of Waterloo!"

Peter didn't dare reply. He was more frightened by the laughing than the shouting.

Devlin Dean's shoulders then began to shake, and the laughs started to sound more like sobs.

The group of residents who'd gathered round them stood silent and staring.

Finally, Matron interceded, speaking in a kindlier tone now. "All right, all right. Come with me now, Mr Dean. You've obviously had a long day."

She led him off, gripping him by the elbow.

Mr Biggs followed, bowed beneath the weight of Devlin Dean's wardrobe.

"We do have one empty room in the new wing, Mr Dean," Matron said soothingly.

Peter stood, watching them go, and felt amazed that he'd been the one to make such an angry man laugh – laugh until he almost cried.

5

French Toast

Peter scanned the breakfast room but saw no sign of Nonna or the others. Instead, sitting straight-backed in Nonna's chair, with his laptop in the place where Mr Biggs usually laid his newspaper, was Devlin Dean. His straight back and stiff white shirt and business suit looked out of place among the cotton leisure suits of the Gum Tree residents who sat bowed over their breakfast trays.

At the centre of the room with her trolley of trays, Angel was announcing the menu: "French toast with cinnamon on homemade bread," she called, flashing her dimples about the room.

Peter caught the lingering smell of burnt toast in his nostrils. He was hungry but not that hungry.

In the kitchen, Peter found Nonna, Mrs Millet, and Mr Biggs. The warm smell of baking filled the air.

"Happy birthday, sweet Peter Blue," said Nonna in a sing-song voice.

Peter had forgotten all about his birthday.

"We're getting ready for cake and tea this afternoon in your honour," Nonna added.

"Thanks, but who's making the cake?" Peter asked nervously.

"I am," confirmed Nonna, pointing a wooden spoon at three enormous golden cake mounds rising in the large industrial oven.

"Not Angel?"

"No. Angel's making the tea."

"I don't drink tea," said Peter, relieved.

"Have you been to see your ghost this morning?" Mr Biggs teased.

"It was just my imagination," said Peter, sitting down at the wooden table beside him.

"Well, Cora and Edna Trelawney keep the coats of five dead husbands in there," Mrs Millet told him. "They've got photos of them all over their room. I couldn't stand living with all those ghosts."

"Well, your husband's still alive," said Peter. "And you can't stand to live with him either."

"That's different," Mrs Millet told him huffily.

Angel pushed open the door and jumped at the sight of them all in her kitchen.

"Who's that new man out there?" she asked. "He didn't so much as thank me when I served him breakfast!"

"That would be Devlin Dean, the multimillionaire," said Mr Biggs. "The Deans are the last of the big-money families from around these parts; got that big mansion up on the hill."

Mr Biggs pointed with his fork towards the western hills.

"The family got rich on logging the jarrah gum trees," continued Mr Biggs. "The ancestors of our friend out there, the Great Gum."

Peter stared into the distance at the magic tree.

"The last jarrah gum standing for miles around here," said Mr Biggs.

"Cutting down primeval forests for profit," said Nonna. "Shame on them!"

"Plenty of people are still getting rich by plundering our ancient forests – at least those that the bush fires don't get to first," said Mr Biggs, adding a prolonged sigh to the end of his sentence.

"Well, if he's so rich, what's he doing here at Gum Tree?" asked Angel.

"Locked out of his mansion," Mr Biggs replied.

"Doesn't he have a spare key?" Peter asked.

"Not that simple," explained Mr Biggs patiently. "The bank has taken over his house and all his belongings – he's lost all his money, and a lot of theirs as well, I imagine."

"But why would a millionaire come here? Why wouldn't he just stay with a rich friend or something?" Angel persisted.

Mr Biggs cleared his throat meaningfully.

"You haven't seen him in action," interrupted Nonna LaRosa, rolling her eyes.

"Down at the newspaper office, we used to call him Mean Dean," recalled Mr Biggs. "That's how he's known by the investors on Wall Street too."

Mrs Millet patted her blonde hair thoughtfully. "Actually, I thought he was rather charming."

"Well, I'm sure he must have some redeeming qualities," said Angel.

At that moment, Mean Dean himself pushed open the swing door, causing Angel to jump again.

"What do you call this?" he growled, pushing his uneaten breakfast plate towards Angel.

"French toast." Angel glanced over at Mrs Millet. "I had a request for something French."

"And you call this French toast? I can barely cut through it with a knife, let alone chew it!" Mean Dean exclaimed.

Mr Biggs stood up slowly and affected a friendly laugh. "Never mind. The French probably have better teeth than we do."

"What utter rubbish!" scoffed Mean Dean. "The Aussies have much better fangs than the Frogs."

He banged his burnt breakfast on the bench and turned towards Angel. "Anyway, you're missing the point. You can't call yourself a chef if you're not able to pull off a simple recipe like this."

Nonna jumped to Angel's defence. "Well, she's not actually a chef. So, it's not her fault if she's always burning the food."

"I'm not *always* burning the food," protested Angel.

Nonna continued, "Well, anyway, what I meant is she's not trained as a cook. She's a nurse, but she needed the job."

Mean Dean briefly digested this information and then said mockingly, "Well, if she's a nurse, you'd think the one thing she'd be good at with the food is checking its temperature."

Angel strode huffily to the other side of the kitchen and rattled some dishes while Mean Dean turned his attention to Peter.

"Hey, you! Duke of Wellington! Do you want me to make you some real French toast?"

Peter nodded uneasily.

"Right!" Mean Dean snatched up one of Angel's aprons from the hook and looped it over his head.

"Now, you always want your French toast to be slightly crisp around the edges. And I emphasise the word *slightly,*" he said, looking pointedly at Angel. "But the trick, at the same time, is to keep it soft in the middle."

Mean Dean fired up a few frying pans, then began pacing the kitchen – from the fridge to the bread bin, to the spice counter, and back.

"Cinnamon and a little nutmeg – just a dash. ..." He spoke as though everyone had been placed there in the kitchen just to listen to him.

Angel stayed at a distance, pouting and pretending to look the other way.

"You want to whisk your milk, egg, and spices well enough," Devlin Dean continued, and then, lowering his voice, he added. "But there's a secret."

Gesturing towards a bowl of fruit next to Angel, he said, "Quick, give us an orange."

"I'm not at your beck and call," Angel told him through pinched lips that kept her dimples well hidden.

Mean Dean sighed theatrically and turned to Peter. "Hey, Duke of Wellie, toss me an orange, will you?"

Peter walked uncertainly over to the bowl. Angel showed with her eyes that it would be all right, so he picked out an orange and threw it a little too firmly across the kitchen.

Mean Dean, with one hand still on the egg whisk, caught the orange deftly with his other. "Looks like you've got a good cricketer's arm," he remarked.

Peter couldn't stop himself from beaming with pleasure.

"Now," Mean Dean said, again in a low voice, "just a few squeezes of this little beauty into your egg mixture is going to make all the difference."

He began easing slice after slice of the egg-soaked bread into the frying pans, flipping and dipping with intense concentration.

In no time at all, one of Gum Tree's largest serving platters was piled high with layers of the crisp, yellowy toast.

Peter slid hopefully into an empty space at the table, then watched, fascinated, as Mean Dean rudely served himself and started eating. It was as if he were alone at a restaurant table.

"*Mm* … delicious!" he crowed in self-congratulation.

Everyone else, including Peter, agreed – once they finally got some.

"Mr Dean, I thought you were a businessman, not a chef," Peter said shyly.

"Well, businessmen have to eat too."

"Yes, but don't millionaires have servants to cook for them?" interrupted Mrs Millet.

"He's not a millionaire anymore," Angel corrected.

Mr Dean's eyes snapped up from his plate. But before the conversation could continue, Matron put her head round the door.

"There you are now Mr Dean – paperwork immediately!" she told him in a no-nonsense voice. "You need to get your admission forms into the post on time."

Matron was always on time; she had a little watch pinned to the chest of her nursing uniform to prove it. She was glancing at it now.

"I won't need to fill out the papers," Mr Dean told her calmly, "because I won't stay another night here."

Peter wasn't sure why, but he felt a pang of disappointment.

Matron just looked relieved. "Very well, then. Come to my office in the entrance hall, and sign out as soon as you're ready."

Everyone got up to leave.

"What time's Peter's birthday tea, then?" Mr Biggs asked Nonna.

"Shall we say, two o'clock in the Gum Tree dining room?" she suggested, smiling at Peter.

"I'll be there," interrupted Mean Dean.

And for some reason, Peter's heart skipped.

BOOK II

The Cloak of Protection

6

The Treasure Hunt

After breakfast, Peter was just preparing to lie down for a nap on his foldaway bed in Nonna's room, when a thin strip of paper on the pillow caught his eye.

Welcome, welcome, Peter Blue, to a birthday treat made just for you!

It was his annual birthday treasure hunt. He turned the paper over to find the first clue.

Clue 1:

I shine like night in black on white when Peter goes to get a bite;

Morning, lunchtime, evening, night – I am, of course, the _____.

So easy! Peter set off at a fast walk to the kitchen and found the big black jar right on the bottom-most white shelf of Angel's pantry. It was, of course, the Vegemite! Underneath the Vegemite jar, Peter found the next clue.

Clue 2:

In a room filled with words from the ceiling to the ground;

We're always telling stories, though we never make a sound.

So easy again! Nonna must have really lost touch with the abilities of eleven-year-olds. Peter paused to spread some butter and a thick smear of Vegemite onto a slice of bread before setting off to the Gum Tree library.

After only a brief scan of the tightly packed shelves, Peter found the third clue. It had been left sticking up between the spines of two books right next to where he usually sat for homeschooling with the Moth. So easy!

Clue 3:

With so many syllables, you'll never make me rhyme;

I'm the flower of LaRosa, but not the rose this time.

LaRosa was Nonna's family name, but her favourite flower was nasturtium.

Nonna and Mr Biggs waved out to him from the veranda, then clapped when Peter reached the window box crowded with yellow and orange nasturtiums. He dug out a rather grimy-looking clue from the dry earth and blew away the dirt.

Clue 4:

A fallen Turkish empire with treasures buried deep;

Look below the place where Peter likes to sleep.

It's so obvious, thought Peter, trying not to smile too smugly before setting off at a run to the Gum Tree day room. Scrabbling below the base of the ottoman footstool, he felt around for the clue but found nothing above or below it. He reread the clue: *treasures buried deep.* Maybe it was inside. He jiggled the edges of the long rectangular cushion and was surprised when it came up, rather like the top of a treasure chest. What a secret! How had he not known this could open? There was a package in there. Peter pulled it out and could tell by the soft feel of it what to expect: socks and underwear, like last year. He ripped it open, confirming his deduction. There were also some shirts. He put on a blue cotton one, over his T-shirt, then pushed the ottoman lid closed. The force of the jolt dislodged a slip of paper from the cushion frame. Was this an extra clue? The paper looked more yellowy than the others, and it was folded in thirds. Peter opened it and read it slowly:

This message shall invoke from ages past bespoke,

Protection of the cloak from within the mighty oak.

Seek beyond the guard robes of the hollow splintered tree,

With well-timed knocks, thrice knotted, at twelve then nine then three.

Wha-a-a-at? Had Nonna got him some kind of coat or jacket for his birthday as well? This treasure hunt was suddenly getting hard. Peter squinted hopelessly at the clue and read it slowly through again. He still didn't know where to start. Could any of the trees outside beyond the moat be oaks? As far as he knew, they were all natives – eucalyptus, bottlebrush, and wattles – and, after all the bush fires, none of the trees looked very mighty.

Maybe he could find a picture of an oak tree somewhere inside the residence. A quick glance round the day room showed mostly portraits of stern people in old-fashioned clothes, but no trees. Peter set off to survey the rest of the old Victorian house, but, finding nothing, he decided instead to start looking for cloaks. Even though he was in no hurry to revisit the ghost of the dead men's coats, he was also too curious to stay away.

Back inside the cloakroom now patchily lit by slanting rays of morning sun, Peter's heart pounded as he approached the wardrobe door. It was still open from last night, and, thankfully, there were no ghostly breezes rushing out at him.

Peter rechecked the clue: *Protection of the cloak from within the mighty oak.*

Maybe these wardrobe walls are made of oak wood! he thought, suddenly inspired.

He looked at the clue once again: *Seek beyond the guard robes of the hollow splintered tree.*

The splintered tree could mean an oak that was chopped down for wood.

Cautiously, Peter stepped inside the wardrobe and began sorting through the musty line of coats and jackets. Their shoulders sagged on the hangers, and none of them looked very protective. Also, what about the well-timed knocks? Where was he supposed to start knocking?

Trying not to think about the ghost, Peter squeezed through the coats to the back wall of the wardrobe and tried knocking on one of the wood panels. It felt strong enough to be a mighty oak, but it didn't sound hollow.

He squeezed himself further along the wall to try the next panel.

Knock, knock, knock.

That part sounded solid too. A few steps further along, Peter tried again.

Knock, knock, knock.

That also sounded very solid.

Coat hangers like bony fingers stabbed at his flesh as he shuffled two more steps sideways, almost to the wardrobe's end.

Knock, knock, knock.

Was it his imagination, or did this panel sound slightly hollow? Peter tried again.

Knock, knock, knock.

Yes, it sounded lighter and more rounded.

It might be a secret door, Peter thought, running his hands across the wood.

Peter knocked again. And then he froze at the sound of an answering knock coming from somewhere beyond the wall.

Knock, knock, knock.

Peter didn't dare move.

The knocking came again, louder and more impatient.

Knock, knock, knock, knock, knock!

The ghost?

It was only when Peter heard quick footsteps in the entranceway that he relaxed, feeling silly. Someone was knocking at the front door. There was no ghost. Gum Tree was getting another visitor, which was almost as rare as seeing a ghost.

CHAPTER

Cleo Choat

"Yes?" inquired Matron in a voice thick with suspicion.

A woman's voice, deep and glossy, asked, "Is this the Gum Tree Rest Home?"

"Yes. And you are …?"

"My name's Cleo Choat. I've come to see a boy I'm told is living here: Peter Blue."

Peter's heart quickened again. He'd never heard of anyone called Cleo Choat, and in five years at Gum Tree, he'd never had a visitor.

"You may speak to Peter Blue's grandmother," Matron replied stiffly.

But the voice at the door didn't like to be told no.

"Don't bother the grandmother; just bring me the boy," urged the voice.

Peter's heart almost stopped.

"I don't like your tone," Matron responded.

The voice softened. "I knew his mother you see … there are things I need to see him about – in private."

"I'll get his grandmother," Matron said sternly.

"Oh, very well," Cleo Choat agreed huffily. "Shall I come inside?"

"I don't see why," said Matron with equal huffiness.

As soon as Peter heard the front door click shut, he crept out of the wardrobe and over to the window to sneak a look at his visitor.

Click-clack, click-clack.

She was coming towards him. Just in time, Peter ducked below the ledge of the open window.

Cleo Choat's shadow seeped across it, eclipsing the morning sun.

Click-clack, click-clack.

Peter's nostrils were invaded by a thick and powerful smell. It was something he couldn't identify, but for some reason, the smell frightened him.

Psshht! Psshht!

Was she spraying perfume? The first smell was now overlaid with a perfume stench. Peter wanted to cough. The smell was closing in on him. He heard a snickering laugh. Was she leaning in the window? Could she see him?

Keeping his eyes squeezed shut, Peter kept as still as he could beneath the ledge until he heard, with great relief, the sound of Nonna pulling open the big front door.

"Hello. ..."

Psshht-psshht! Click-clack, click-clack.

Cleo Choat moved away, and the light returned to the room.

Peter straightened up just in time to see a woman with thick-rimmed square glasses, long, frizzy-looking hair and a tight-fitting black dress stepping up onto the veranda. She walked with a slight stoop, but, unlike the Gum Tree residents, who stooped at their backs, Cleo Choat stooped at her neck.

"Cleo who?" Nonna was asking.

"Choat." The voice was impatient again. "Your daughter Thelma and I studied science together."

"Thelma never mentioned you when she moved back here," Nonna said testily.

"Look, I'm actually interested in talking to her son. I've come all the way from Europe."

"Oh, I see." Nonna was sounding unsure. "Well, he's only eleven. As of today, actually."

Nonna paused and then laughed conversationally.

"I know," said Cleo Choat. "That's why I came. I wanted to wish him happy birthday."

"Well, isn't that nice. Look, maybe we got off on the wrong foot. Why don't we have some tea?"

Cleo Choat protested, "I really would like to see your grandson. ..."

"I understand!"

Their footsteps moved across the veranda.

"A rest home's no place for a young boy! Thelma wouldn't have wanted that. ..."

Cleo Choat's voice faded as they headed away to the north veranda. *The horsehair sofas there will prickle her legs,* thought Peter. *Good.*

A few moments later, Peter heard hurried footsteps in the hall, followed by a light rustle of papers. Matron was returning to her office, followed by someone with a much heavier tread.

As a precaution, Peter stepped back into the wardrobe and closed the door.

"Ah, Mr Dean, sign out here please," Matron instructed.

"Never had such an uncomfortable night!" snapped the voice of Mean Dean. "Honestly, do you *really* call that the new wing?"

"Well, it's newer than the old wing."

"Lousy old dump!"

"I'm sorry you weren't comfortable," Matron said, not sounding at all sorry.

"Well, that's not the half of it," Mean Dean said, adjusting his tone slightly. "Now the whole town's shut down with these fire alerts."

When Matron didn't respond, he sighed loudly. "And the banks have cancelled all my credit, and my broker's not picking up the phone, probably hiding under the bed in his fancy Manhattan apartment."

Mean Dean gave another sigh.

"Mr Dean, I fail to see what any of this might have to do with me."

"Well, it's like this, Mrs Matron." He paused, sighing some more. "I'm afraid that, with the greatest of regret, I am faced with the daunting realisation that I must necessarily spend one more uncomfortable night on these less-than-fine premises."

Mr Dean was staying one more night? Peter felt his heart skip. And then it jumped at the rattle of Angel's tea trolley.

"What's this?" Mr Dean asked.

"Homemade oatmeal biscuits, to serve the guest who wants to adopt Peter Blue."

Peter felt his throat tighten. Maybe there wasn't enough air in the wardrobe.

"And to make things worse, Nonna LaRosa has health issues, so she might just agree to it."

"Do you mean adopt the Duke of Wellie? But she can't just come in and adopt him. She needs papers!" Mr Dean protested.

"Speaking of papers," said Matron, "Here are yours, Mr Dean. If you're staying tonight, they need to get to the state government today. Put them in this afternoon's two o'clock post."

There was a shuffling of papers.

Angel's voice spoke again. "Very strange-looking woman too; hair much too long for a woman her age, and a very large pointy nose and chin."

Peter pressed his ear to the wall.

"I hope the tea's not getting cold," said Matron.

Peter heard a loud cracking sound.

"Ow … blimey! Well, these biscuits of yours should get rid of her quick enough," Mr Dean said. "Break her pointed jaw at least."

Angel wordlessly rattled the tea trolley off down the north corridor.

Peter waited quietly in the wardrobe, worrying about Nonna's health problems. Was she going to die and leave him to people who didn't want him – or, worse still, that smelly woman who did want him? Even after he heard both Matron and Mr Dean leaving, Peter decided it would be best to stay hidden as long as Cleo Choat was still on the premises.

He stared down at the clue in his hand: *With well-timed knocks, thrice knotted, at twelve then nine then three.*

A fragment of memory began to free itself from a larger mosaic somewhere in his mind. Peter fingered the folds of the yellowy paper: "once, twice, thrice." *Thrice* meant three, but that still didn't explain how he was supposed to knot a knock.

Of course, it could mean a knot of wood. Peter slid back along the wardrobe wall to the panel that had sounded hollow before. There were a few rough spots where the wood spiralled away like knots in a tree trunk. He found four of them in a rough circle. But he needed three knots, not four.

Think, Peter, think.

Or was it three knocks or both … but then, what about the twelve, nine, and three? That would be a lot of knocks.

He pushed impatiently on one of the raised knots of wood, but nothing happened.

Then, his thoughts were interrupted by the sound of footsteps in the entranceway.

He heard Cleo Choat's disapproving voice. "Does he often hide like this?"

They were looking for him. In desperation, Peter started pushing randomly on the knots of wood.

He heard Nonna say, "Let's try outside."

Footsteps crunched in the car park outside the cloakroom window. A kookaburra laughed overhead.

Think, Peter, think.

If thrice was for the number of knocks, how was he supposed to make them well timed?

Or was time a clue? He studied the circle of knots.

You're getting warm, the wood seemed to say.

A circle and time. A clock face? Of course! The clue was "at twelve then nine then three."

There were voices outside the cloakroom. They were coming in! Peter could hear the door opening. He stared at the circle of wood knots. Time? He could see the knots rounded like a clock face: twelve o'clock, then nine o'clock, then three o'clock. …

Footsteps crossed the room. They were at the wardrobe door. He could already smell her perfume. He needed to act fast. Behind the coats and barely breathing, Peter knocked firmly on the top knot, at twelve o'clock, *once.* The wardrobe door was opening. He knocked on the knot on the left side, at nine o'clock, *twice.*

Cleo Choat was getting into the wardrobe.

Peter gave a third knock on the right-hand knot, at three o'clock, *thrice.*

His breath caught as the panel swung away soundlessly, then closed again like a revolving door, taking Peter with it.

He found himself standing at the end of a narrow corridor lit by a silvery glow. It was another wardrobe, he realised, but with only one coat hanger, a few steps away and against the far wall. On the hanger was a large, man-sized jacket. It took a moment for him to realise that the silvery light was coming from the jacket, which was bluish in colour.

Protection of the cloak from within the mighty oak? he wondered.

He stepped up close to the jacket and pulled one of the sleeves towards him. Unlike the jackets on the other side of the wall, this one didn't smell musty at all. It smelt like the bush, and it smelt like something else, something familiar – the jacket smelt like Dad.

Peter's fingers shook as he pulled the jacket down from the hanger and checked for the familiar ID plate behind the collar: Agent Byron Blue, Global Advanced Intelligence Agency (GAIA).

He carefully patted down the fabric of the big sleeves, as if searching for his father's arms. Then, he turned the jacket over and slowly traced his finger around the large GAIA spiral on the back. Turning the jacket over again, Peter concentrated on the front, studying the silver dome buttons one by one. Each button had its own etched image: the falcon on the top front button, below that the dolphin, followed by the traveller with the long stick, the pelican, the frog, the compass – all so familiar to him.

Suddenly, Peter couldn't wait to feed both arms into the sleeves and try on the jacket. Even though it was much too big, it made him feel safe, as if it were a disguise. The silver-white glow was coming from little pinpoints of light that circled the waist. He could turn them on and off by using a button at the wrist. He remembered Dad doing that.

The jacket seemed to have an energy of its own that was mixing with Peter's breathing and making him sleepy, as if he were floating in waves on a restful sea. There was enough room to take a nap, but, surprisingly, Peter didn't want to. Instead, he wanted to think. The Moth would have been proud.

The big question was, how did Dad's jacket come to be here at Gum Tree after so many years? Why would Dad have taken it off? The GAIA jacket was his protection against fire. And who put it into the guard robe of the hollow splintered oak? One thing was sure: this treasure hunt no longer had anything to do with Nonna.

CHAPTER

Nonna Remembers

In the kitchen, Nonna was smoothing down the icing of a triple-layer cake.

"I've got good news," she said.

"Has she gone?" asked Peter.

"Who?"

Cleo Choat."

"Yes … so you know about her? That's my good news."

"Good news that she's gone?" asked Peter, hoping for confirmation.
Angel laughed supportively.

"No!" Nonna flicked a strand of straight bobbed hair from her face and looked sternly at Peter. "The good news is that you had a nice visitor, a friend of your mum's. Were you hiding, Peter Blue?"

Peter shrugged dismissively.

"She didn't want to give up the search!"

"Are you sure she wasn't a burglar or something?"

"No, silly! She even left you a birthday gift." Nonna indicated a small rectangular package on the kitchen table.

Peter glanced over at the gift. "But what makes you say she was nice?"

"Peter, what's got into you?" Nonna said warningly. "She was a lovely woman. She's coming back."

"When?"

"Very soon. She didn't say specifically. She had to leave suddenly, after we'd been in the wardrobe looking for you. Very odd – she suddenly got sick. Anyway, she wants you to come live with her one day."

"Well, she can't just adopt me; you need papers for that," said Peter, parroting Mr Dean.

"She did bring papers, from the time of your birth, and they were signed by your mum and dad. It was definitely Thelma's signature; I'd know it anywhere. In fact, that's my good news, Peter."

"What?"

"Cleo Choat's your godmother!"

Peter stared hard at Nonna. This was bad.

"But, didn't you think she kind of smelt odd?"

"She was wearing rather a lot of perfume," Nonna admitted. "But we do need to start planning, Peter."

"There's nothing to plan." Peter drew the jacket in closer to his chest.

"Well, Hester Moth's a primary-school teacher, but she can't homeschool you forever."

"Nonna, are you going to die?" blurted Peter.

Nonna picked up the spatula and busied herself with the cake.

"I'm not as well as I could be, Peter," she said finally.

Angel bustled around the kitchen sink, pretending to give them space.

"Well, maybe I could change my mind, then, and go to Aunty Surla and Uncle Gorrman in London," Peter said reluctantly. "Surla's Mum's sister, so she can't be that bad."

"Well, there's a problem with that too." Nonna focused her gaze on the cake. "I'm afraid now that they have a son of their own, they've said they don't want you."

Peter swallowed. So, it was true.

"And Cleo Choat *does* want you," Nonna said encouragingly.

Suddenly, Nonna seemed to see Peter more closely. "What's that you're wearing? Are you playing dress-ups?"

"Of course not!" Peter scowled. "I'm eleven! Remember?"

Nonna laughed. "Is it Mr Biggs's jacket?"

"No."

"Where did you get it from then?"

"It's my birthday present ... from Dad."

Nonna jumped, leaving a splodge of blue icing on the sleeve of the jacket.

"Don't worry; it's waterproof." Peter licked the icing away. "It's some kind of special GAIA material."

"That does look like Byron's GAIA jacket!" Nonna tugged at the excess material on the sleeves. "Well, I'm glad it's waterproof because you're swimming in it."

"Ha ha!"

Nonna stared at the jacket. "Come to think of it, that old man said it was fireproof too."

"What old man?"

"The one who came here after the fire. Said he'd put the jacket safely in the cloakroom for when you were older. I thought he was a swagman at first, on his walkabout, sheltering from the bush fire, but his accent was very British."

"What else?"

"Well, he was a very strange and memorable sort."

"Which is why, for five years, you forgot completely to tell me anything about him," Peter said accusingly.

"And the bush fire stopped quite suddenly, just after he got here," Angel reminded Nonna.

"Did he have a very long beard?" Peter asked thoughtfully.

"Yes, come to think of it."

"Then, I think I remember him too."

"Well, I very much doubt it. You were sick and dehydrated after three days lost in the bush. To this day, nobody knows where you were – missing for three whole days," said Nonna.

It was true; Peter had never been able to remember where he'd been. But he didn't want to think about that now.

"So, what happened to the old man?"

"Oh, he stayed for the building of the moat, and then he just wandered off. Said something about feeding some frogs. Isn't that right, Angel?"

Both women cackled with amusement, and then Nonna passed Peter the package from Cleo Choat. "Here, don't forget this."

"Although I don't know who this Cleo Choat woman thinks she is!" interrupted Angel. "Arriving here with no warning."

"She's a successful scientist – that's who she is. ... She said she could teach Peter to be a scientist too, just like his mum."

"I don't want to be a scientist!" interrupted Peter.

"Well, she said she wanted to show you the world."

"Well, the world's going to end soon," Peter said sullenly. "Mr Biggs said you only have to read between the lines of the newspapers nowadays to see that we're clearly doomed."

Tugging off the last of the wrapping on Cleo Choat's package, Peter found a tiny silver frame.

"It's a photo … of Mum!"

"Oh, look at Thelma – what a beauty!" Angel cooed.

Thelma LaRosa stood in a white dress, smiling from a podium and holding a silver plaque high over her head.

"That must have been when she got the award." Nonna was becoming tearful. "The Pelican Spirit Award. It's GAIA President Buchanan's highest award."

"And he gave it to Mum?" Peter gasped.

"It was for her service to the world." Nonna lowered her voice. "Your mother invented some kind of formula called Chrysalite. To this day, I don't know what it was; it had something to do with fire, and it was all very secretive. I was told never to talk about it, but I suppose now, after all these years, there's no harm."

Peter turned the picture frame over and saw a message scribbled on the cardboard support:

So glad we're back in touch!

Thelma x

"See, this further proves that Thelma and Cleo Choat really did know each other," Nonna said with satisfaction. "I suppose they lost touch after Thelma and Byron moved down here to Australia."

Peter shrugged. He didn't care about Cleo Choat; he just wanted to look at Mum, smiling out at him. A half circle of people stood with her on the stage, but it was his mother's smile that filled the frame.

"Which one's President Buchanan?" asked Angel.

"Oh, you won't see President Buchanan there," Nonna explained. "Thelma didn't ever get to meet him face-to-face."

"How come?" said Peter.

"Well, I suppose he was busy somewhere in the field. But Thelma once told me he was always available to talk. 'Just a heartbeat away,' she used to say."

"So, she never laid eyes on him?" Angel mused.

"Well, none of them did. Thelma and Byron used to call him Invisible Bu-h, or just Bu-h."

"Invisible Bu-h." Peter repeated.

Nonna covered her mouth suddenly. "Actually, I think that was some kind of code name."

"Bu-h! Are you there?" Peter spoke into the corner of his collar, the way he'd seen Dad do. "Hello Bu-h!"

A sudden loud crackling sound emitted from the jacket collar, startling Peter and sending the two women scuttling across the kitchen.

"Well," said Nonna, recovering, "if you don't want to be a scientist, maybe you'll become a great adventurer like your father."

"No," Peter told her. "I'm more of a philosopher type."

"Oh, very nice. Where did that come from?" said Nonna.

Peter shrugged; he wasn't sure himself.

9

Cabbage Soup and Brown Envelopes

O n the way to the day room, Peter heard the unmistakable wail of Mrs Weakes, whom he found parked up in her wheelchair outside, way down next to the moat.

"Peter Blue, thank goodness!" she shrieked. "I just woke up and found myself here!"

"What's going on?" asked Nonna, limping towards them and clutching her bad hip.

"Not *what* but *who!*" snapped Mrs Weakes.

When they entered the day room, Peter saw immediately that things were not right. In the centre of the room, sitting on the two-seater chair always used by the Trelawney sisters, Mr Dean sat talking loudly into the old red phone.

He grimaced at the sight of Mrs Weakes returning.

"Keep it down this time, will you!" he warned.

"See? That's what he's like," complained Mrs Weakes to Peter. "Imagine! I was just having a peaceful nap, minding my own business when—"

Mr Dean slammed down the phone receiver. "Peaceful nap? The old wombat was snoring so loudly, I had to put her out for air."

"So, it *was* you!" Mrs Weakes gave him one of her evil squints. "You just wheeled me out and left me alone in the wild. I could have been eaten alive."

"Your snoring would have scared off any wild beasts," Mean Dean muttered. "You sounded like a sack of broken bagpipes in a gale-force wind."

Mrs Weakes turned to Nonna. "That man frog marched the Trelawney sisters from their regular spot. Pretended to offer them tea, then set them adrift in the corner, so he could steal their seat next to the phone."

"Well, no harm done," called one of the Trelawney sisters nobly from their new place next to the fire escape. "We rather fancy these old wooden chairs."

"Yes," added the other sister good-naturedly, "they keep our backs straight. They're a little hard, of course, but no harm done."

The phone rang, and Peter and the rest of the residents stopped their own conversations to listen to Mr Dean's.

"Any progress?" he asked the caller. "Oh, dang it! I kept telling you we were in too deep. ... Well, it was your job to watch the fluctuations – you're the stockbroker. And now I'm stuck here in la-la land with a bunch of octogenarians!"

There was a pause.

"What? Don't you start bringing my age into this!" Mr Dean slammed the phone down childishly.

Peter knew that octogenarians were people in their eighties and guessed that Mr Dean could easily be in that group himself.

Mrs Weakes wheeled her chair over to a spot just in front of Mr Dean and said, "This man wants keeping an eye on."

Mrs Millet, who already had her eye on Mr Dean, was sitting comfortably on Peter's ottoman, just across from the telephone table.

"He's been talking on the phone to someone else who's broke," she whispered to Peter.

"I think you mean his broker," Peter replied knowledgeably, though he wasn't sure what one was. He wished Mrs Millet would get out of his place and go back to her powder-pink wing chair, where she usually sat, next to Nonna.

Mrs Worthington Smith-Jones floated past and began using her lace handkerchief to polish the telephone table next to Mr Dean.

Peter hoped she wouldn't ask Mr Dean if he'd been home lately. He might take it the wrong way, since he'd been locked out of his house by the bank.

Instead, the phone rang again, and the sound of Mr Dean's barking voice quickly filled the room.

"There's no bull market, you idiot! The bull has long bolted! We're in a bear market, I'm telling you, and now, thanks to you, I've got the wolf at my door!" He laughed ruefully.

Peter wished he could understand what Mr Dean was talking about.

"Now listen to me." Mr Dean was staring darkly at the laptop balanced on his knees. "Just a sec ... just a sec."

He was trying to hold the old red phone and scroll an image on his screen at the same time. "I'll put you on speaker."

Peter watched Mean Dean fiddling around with the old red phone.

"What? There's no speaker phone on this old piece of junk?" He banged it angrily on the table before continuing his conversation.

"Now listen carefully." Mr Dean lowered his voice. "Here's the plan."

It seemed to Peter that everyone in the day room was waiting to hear the plan, even Mr Witherspoon, who was hovering nearby in the shadow of the Indian rubber plant. Peter saw that he was clutching a brown envelope.

Mr Dean must have spotted him too, because he put his caller on hold and turned to Mr Witherspoon irritably.

"Hey! I thought I asked you to take that envelope to the mailbox for the afternoon post! They're Matron's papers for the government." Mean Dean pronounced the words *Matron* and *government* extra loudly, glancing impatiently at his watch. "Do you understand me?"

"Something to eat?" asked Mr Witherspoon raspily.

"No! You dumb idiot, it most assuredly is not something to eat! It's an important envelope. Now take it to the postbox at the end of the drive."

Mr Witherspoon stood still for a moment.

"The pickup's in ten minutes. Go – now!" Mr Dean waved him away irritably and went back to his phone call.

Peter was doubtful that the message had got through. But he had other things to worry about, such as how to get his ottoman back from Mrs Millet.

"That won't be very comfortable for you, Mrs Millet," Peter said politely. "It's got a broken spring."

"I'm perfectly fine, thank you." Mrs Millet patted her hair. "The views here are excellent."

Peter sighed and went to join Nonna on her paisley sofa, opposite Mr Biggs by the window.

"So, here's the plan," repeated Mr Dean, still talking as if he were the only person in the room. "We're going to find one itty-bitty little asset that hasn't been taken by the banks, and then we're going to leverage it for some start-up money. We just need enough to get back in the game."

He paused to listen.

"What? Well, look again!" Mean Dean slammed down the phone, frowning deeply.

Peter whispered to Mr Biggs, "Why was he talking about buying bulls before?"

Mr Biggs let out a chuckle, which turned into a cough. "A bull market is actually just a way of talking about any market where prices are going up. It could be a market for anything – stocks, bonds, gold, other assets."

"Not for bears, though?"

Mr Biggs laughed his own bear laugh. "No, a bear market is a way of describing the opposite effect, when the market's going down, over time."

"Oh, nothing to do with real bears and bulls, then." Peter frowned. "And what's an asset?"

"An asset is just something someone owns; it could be anything." Mr Biggs studied Peter in his oversized jacket. "In the case of Devlin Dean, he's looking for an asset that he could leverage to borrow some money so he can invest in the stock market. Do you understand leverage?"

"Maybe," Peter said doubtfully.

Mr Biggs put down his newspaper. "Let's say you wanted to borrow one hundred dollars from me, and I wasn't quite sure you'd be able to pay it back. You might offer me some leverage – maybe that big jacket you're wearing – kind of like a guarantee. ...”

"I get it," said Peter. "But you can't have the jacket; it's mine."

"What?" barked Devlin Dean. "Not one single asset? There's got to be something."

His eyes swept the floor space around them, as if he might be half expecting to find an asset lying about the Gum Tree day room.

"Don't tell me the banks have taken the yacht … and the penthouse apartment in Manhattan? What about the villa in St John? They won't have got their hands on that yet." Mr Dean groaned. "Okay, what about the Yugen house in Budapest?" More groaning. "The beach apartments in Riga? No, don't tell me – all of them? Well, what about the other properties here in Australia? What about the offshore accounts? My Swiss bank accounts? They must have busted into our computer records! Who do they think they are?"

Mr Dean looked round the room, dismayed.

"Nah, I won't be staying in this dump for long," he muttered loudly enough for even the very hard-of-hearing to take offence.

"I can't do anything sitting here in the dark with a bunch of wrinklies eating cabbage soup."

"Oh goody! Is it cabbage soup today, Angel?" called one of the Trelawney sisters, who'd been listening to Mr Dean's conversation.

"I think I do have some cabbage!" said Angel, winking at Peter.

"Oh Geez." Mean Dean slapped his forehead. "What have I done?"

Peter moved back to the ottoman and cleared his throat purposefully, but Mrs Millet ignored the hint.

Behind them, Mrs Weakes moaned loudly to Pop Olsen, who was sitting motionless in his usual place on the three-seater sofa with the stick insects.

"None of us has managed to get a good sleep this morning, thanks to him!"

Pop Olsen didn't reply, but Mr Dean's eyes bolted up from his laptop.

"What's wrong with you all? You bunch of old loafers! You're supposed to sleep during the night!" Mr Dean pointed at Pop Olsen and the stick insects. "Look at those three men! Are they dead already or just sitting in the departure lounge?"

"They're alive," said Peter helpfully. "I just saw Pop Olsen move."

Pop Olsen, at the sound of his name, boldly adjusted his position again, while the other two men stayed still.

"Hey, you guys – Snap, Crackle, and Pop – why don't you get up and do something?" called Mr Dean.

"Maybe they're tired after a long life," Peter suggested.

"Well, then, what's your excuse?" Mr Dean snapped back.

Peter felt stung.

"Hey, Pop!" Mr Dean shouted. "What's the wireless code here?"

"The wireless is over there," interrupted Mrs Millet. "It doesn't need a code; you just switch it on. Switch it on for us, Peter."

Dutifully, Peter turned the dial of the old wooden radio.

"*Ooh,* swing music." Mrs Millet smiled over at Mr Dean. "One could almost feel like dancing."

"Get with the program, will you!" Mr Dean growled at her. "I want a wireless connection for my laptop, Wi-Fi to get online. I need real-time information."

Mr Dean sighed extra loudly. "And I can't see myself think in this darkness. You're all like the prisoners in Plato's cave."

Suddenly, he was up and striding towards the windows, tugging roughly at the first of the long blinds. It released with a high-speed snap, like a lizard's tongue would do.

Pop Olsen and the stick insects flinched in fright.

Mr Dean whipped up the next blind.

Snap! Flinch!

And the next.

Snap! Flinch!

Even Peter shrank back from the steely brightness of the outside light.

Mr Dean then strode purposefully back to his laptop and continued swiping his index finger across the screen.

"Wait! There is a wireless provider here! It's called Gala. No – GAIA. ..."

"GAIA?" Peter took a few anxious steps towards Mr Dean.

"The signal's gaining strength."

"Oh, that might be mine then," Peter told Mr Dean uncertainly.

"Okay, goody!" Mr Dean rubbed his hands together. "What's the password?"

"Um … I don't know." Peter fumbled uselessly at his jacket seams. "I just got the jacket this morning."

Mr Dean looked momentarily impressed. "So, it's a wearable device? Well, what's the password?"

Peter looked at the floor without replying.

Mr Dean slammed his fist on the table and said to the room, "How can I get any news about myself without a wireless connection?"

Mr Biggs raised himself up from his chair with a protracted sigh and walked slowly over. "Here, try these," he told Mr Dean. "Traditional print media; they're called newspapers."

Mr Biggs dropped a copy of the *Jarra Jarra Enquirer* onto the telephone table. "This one's carrying a full-page article on you, quoting from a source at the New York Stock Exchange. Look, there you are on the front page of this one too."

Mr Biggs dropped one newspaper after another onto Mr Dean's lap. "Oh, and here you are on the front page again. The financial papers are full of you too."

Mr Dean, speechless for once, opened out the front page of the *Enquirer* to expose a giant head-and-shoulders photo of himself. His eyes were two angry circles, and his mouth was wide open, as if he'd been caught shouting an instruction.

Peter read the headline: "Local Multimillionaire Mean Dean Missing in Action!"

The smaller headline underneath read: "Australian Devlin Dean goes 'down under' in Friday market crash."

Peter scanned the story.

"Police fear that failed financier Devlin Dean may have topped himself while markets bottomed."

"They think I might have killed myself." Mr Dean laughed.

"Now there's an idea," muttered Mrs Weakes.

Matron chose that moment to pop her head round the door.

A faint smell of watery cabbage entered the room.

"Any sign of the bush fire, Mr Biggs?" Matron asked, as if enquiring after a late guest.

"No, nothing so far." Mr Biggs used his large hand to tent his eyes from the glare as he peered out of the day-room window. "But it's as dry as tinder out there."

"Though there's not much out there left to burn," Nonna told Matron.

Except lunch, thought Peter grimly. He wondered if you could burn soup.

"Well, the fire warnings are still in place, so, everyone, please keep alert."

"I don't think these people do 'alert'," Mr Dean said sarcastically.

"Ah, Mr Dean. Settling in comfortably, I hope," Matron said with equal sarcasm. "Did those government forms get into the noon post?"

"Yes, Mrs Matron. All signed and sealed." Mr Dean looked round nervously, probably for Mr Witherspoon, who'd not yet returned.

Matron nodded, then closed the door.

When the phone rang again, Mr Dean snatched it up without even saying hello. "Did you find anything …? Not one single asset …? What about the sheep farm in New Zealand?" He groaned. "What about the hardwood forest in Argentina? Look again!"

This time, he slammed down the phone so hard that a piece of the handle flew across the room and landed at Pop Olsen's feet.

The phone rang again straight away. "Did you read the papers? It looks like everyone and his dog's looking for me to pay up. Luckily, some of the creditors think I've killed myself. But what they don't know is, the place I've come to is actually a fate worse than death. … What? Oh Geez, not the Belargo brothers. They're after me too? Find me an asset, quick!"

Angel came in, bringing another wave of the flavourless cabbage smell from the kitchen.

"So, it is cabbage soup for lunch, Angel?" asked Mrs Worthington Smith-Jones, seeking confirmation.

"Yes, it's on its way. I've left it simmering."

"But don't leave it simmering too long," Nonna cautioned Angel. "You know what can happen."

Mr Dean was on the phone again.

"Geez," he told his broker loudly, "these folks here need something to do … to not to be so irrelevant."

Mr Biggs coughed irritably and rattled his newspaper.

"Who are you calling irrelevant?" protested Mrs Weakes sullenly.

Ignoring her, Mr Dean put his hand over the receiver and beckoned to Peter.

"Hey, you – Duke of Wellington – come here and make yourself relevant!"

Peter stepped forward.

"Why aren't you in school, by the way?"

"Um … I'm having a day off from homeschool for my birthday."

"Homeschool? Who's your teacher? Not one of these useless layabouts?"

"No, she's not here; she might be marking my homework," he said, hoping to make the Moth sound relevant. He noticed that the sofa bed by the potted plants, where the Moth regularly sat, had for some reason been moved right out of the day room.

"Well, how about I teach you how to use a computer? You can start by just holding it." Mr Dean handed Peter the laptop, adding irritably, "But hold it still. Now I'm going to scroll through my list of assets and mark them off on the hard copy."

Watching the long list of assets scrolling out across the floor like lunch paper, Peter began to feel the familiar empty space in his stomach, one that he didn't want to fill with cabbage. Sleep would help take away the emptiness, but he would need the ottoman for that, and Mrs Millet didn't look like she'd be budging from it anytime soon.

Peter wondered where the Moth had gone. Maybe she was in the library, surrounded by books. If the Moth ever felt an empty space inside her, she would fill it with books. Mr Biggs filled his empty space with newspapers and his pipe, and Mr Dean, of course, filled his with money. Or at least he used to before he lost it all.

It's so obvious, Peter thought. *Maybe I am a philosopher.*

A wind blew up outside the window, making a strange sound: *Shoooo-ster!*

The giant gum tree stirred in the distance, and Peter felt the jacket energy wash about him.

Sitting and holding Mr Dean's laptop, it was hard for Peter to believe he was still in the same life. So much had happened since yesterday.

"Concentrate!" snapped Mr Dean. "You almost dropped it again."

The double doors opened, bringing in Mr Witherspoon, along with a new smell of burning cabbage.

"Oh dear!" Angel flew, gasping, into the corridor.

Mr Witherspoon seemed to be chewing on something floppy and flat. It could've been a cabbage leaf, except it was brownish. Burnt cabbage, maybe?

Mrs Millet straightened up. "Are they wafers, Mr Witherspoon?"

"Something to eat," he replied, shuffling towards Peter.

Suddenly, Peter put down the laptop. "Stop, Mr Witherspoon! Don't eat that!"

Mean Dean's eyes bolted up from his asset paper. "What is it? What's he's eating?"

No one spoke.

"Dang the lot of you!" The floorboards shuddered under Mean Dean's stamping feet as he advanced on Mr Witherspoon. "You ate my paperwork for the government, you flaming idiot!"

"Wait!" cried Peter, suddenly hit with an idea to get Mr Witherspoon out of trouble. "That was actually good thinking by Mr Witherspoon! Now those Belargo brothers and the bankers and every man and his dog, who are looking for you, will never find you. Not even the Australian government will know you're here."

Mr Dean muttered something, then a slow smile spread across his face.

"Witherspoon!" he eventually said. "You flaming genius!"

CHAPTER

10

The Fire

With an ear-splitting whistle, Mr Biggs silenced the guests. They were in the Gum Tree dining room, and Peter was getting ready to blow out his birthday candles.

"All right everybody!" Mr Biggs called. "I want to hear eleven big claps for the birthday boy. One, two, three. ..."

Peter quickly lost count of the uneven slapping hands, but there were way more than eleven claps.

Over the din of clapping, Mr Biggs explained, "We're so old ourselves that we're not used to clapping so few."

Peter giggled politely while taking fretful glances at the cake candles that were burning very low.

"Quick! Blow out the candles before they melt the cake!" wailed Nonna.

At the sound of the word *cake,* the clapping ceased.

"Thelma would have been so proud of you," whispered Nonna, just as Peter was taking a big breath in.

At the mention of Mum, the air somehow caught in his throat, and when he blew on the candles, the flames barely quivered.

The crowd staged a friendly groan.

"Come on, lad, you're 11, not 111," said Mr Biggs. "Let's have one more go together."

Mr Biggs took a large breath in, which, unfortunately, led him directly into a fit of coughing.

"*Aargh!* He's spitting all over the cake," complained Mean Dean.

"A little less pipe smoking might be in order, Mr Biggs," offered Matron primly.

The candles kept weeping their wax, so while Nonna was patting Mr Biggs on the back, Peter took another shot at them. This time, he succeeded in blowing out ten of the eleven candles.

"One wish." Nonna pointed at the remaining candle.

The crowd clapped.

"Tell us what you're wishing!" they begged.

Peter stared dolefully at the flaming yellow stub, his head empty of wishes. There was nothing to want and nothing to wish for. Mum and Dad were dead, and now Nonna was sick. He had no friends except the residents, and he would probably have to leave them soon too.

He closed his eyes. The residents waited in respectful silence. It would not be the first time a guest of honour at Gum Tree had fallen asleep during an event. Peter, in the meantime, felt the sadness working upwards from his throat into his eyes. He squeezed his lids hard, trying to send back the tears.

"Come on, tell us your wish," urged the cheerful crowd.

But Peter didn't have one.

"*Shush,* you fools! He's crying!" Mrs Weakes admonished them.

A bush telegraph of gasps relayed around the room.

"One should never tell one's wishes," said Mrs Worthington Smith-Jones with a sniff.

"Of course," agreed one of the Trelawney sisters defensively.

"Far be it for us to pry," added the other sister.

For a moment, no one knew what to say.

Mr Witherspoon broke the silence by saying, "Something to eat?"

"Yes, something to eat – a perfect wish," they all agreed.

Nonna pressed a bouquet of tissues into Peter's hand, and he blew his nose with his head down. It was only after he finished that he realised he'd been leaning right over the cake. Peter peeped out from under the tissue mound. Of course, Mr Dean had noticed.

"Oh Geez, now you're blowing snot over it."

"Tea!" called one of the Trelawney sisters. "Anyone for a hot cuppa?"

While Angel poured tea, Nonna skilfully cut slices from all three layers of strawberry lamington, chocolate fudge, and cream sponge.

"I'll just have a small piece," droned Mr Dean. "It must be riddled with germs."

"Oh, shut your cakehole," said Mr Biggs good-humouredly, handing Mr Dean a party hat.

Grudgingly, Mr Dean put it on, then rolled his eyes at Peter, who giggled and suddenly began to feel more festive.

Cake forks flashed through the air, conducting mini conversations.

"This one's your best ever," enthused Mrs Millet.

"Lovely decorations too," murmured one of the Trelawney sisters, pointing at the bright-yellow tablecloth and the lawn-green napkins.

"Primary colours, for a new start," remarked the other sister, looking at Peter.

Mean Dean held up one of the napkins.

"I don't know why you want spring colours at the beginning of autumn," he grumbled.

Peter looked around at his guests. He was sorry that the Moth hadn't shown up. She'd been acting strangely since yesterday. She'd sent over a birthday gift, a book about ancient Greece, and Peter had been pleased to get it, until he read in the card that Chapter 1 was required reading for tomorrow. Still, he mostly liked his lessons with the Moth – at least the ones they were able to stay awake for.

Peter took an empty seat across from Pop and the stick insects.

"Fire!" said Pop suddenly in a hollow and raspy voice. He was pointing at Peter's red hair.

"It's just hair … you flaming idiot!" interjected Mr Dean.

"Fire!" Pop repeated obstinately. Sniffing at the air.

"Cuckoo," said Mr Dean, childishly dialling the air round his ear, then pointing his finger at Pop.

"Fire!" Pop wheezed. He wasn't pointing at Peter now but out the window at the bush beyond.

There was actually a hint of smoke about. Matron gave a sharp call for quiet and sniffed the air – the others began sniffing too. Then, a very distant wail of fire sirens was heard.

"Prepare for evacuation to the south lawn," Matron ordered, in a tone of false calm. "Angel, sound the alarms. Mr Biggs, help with the lawn chairs. Everyone else, evacuate – wheelchair-assisted first! And be quick about it!"

Matron hollered the last part, the false calm having disappeared from her voice.

Peter tore out across the lawn to the north side of the moat to get a glimpse of the convoy of red engines skidding one by one off the main road and down a narrow side road. When the last one had disappeared into the bush, the evacuees on the lawn were left with billows of churned-up dust and a heavy silence.

For a long time, everyone waited. Even nature seemed to be holding its breath.

Is the air getting hotter? Peter wondered. *Is the fire creeping closer?*

An hour must have passed then, another.

Peter read the first page of his birthday book, while Mr Dean paced around, complaining to Matron that he needed to get back to the telephone.

Finally, Matron allowed Angel to go inside because she needed to start dinner.

"I would've thought that cook more of a fire risk than the whole forest put together," Mr Dean whispered to Peter, who giggled, then felt guilty because Angel was so dear to him.

The evening air was suffocating and still.

"We're lucky there's no wind," said Mr Biggs, sucking nervously on his pipe. "That helps stop the fire from spreading."

"Still, it's difficult to breathe," Nonna LaRosa complained, fanning herself with both hands.

Watching the distant pillar of billowing smoke, Peter heard whispers behind him.

"Another bush fire. So upsetting for the poor boy."

"And on his birthday too. ..."

"This is ridiculous!" Mr Dean said again. "I've got phone calls to make."

But Matron refused to call off the evacuation till the fire warden came to give the all-clear.

Smuts of ash floated through the air, leaving black smudges here and there on people's skin; some of then landed on Mr Dean's white shirt.

Peter hoped the fire wasn't getting closer. He looked over at the Great Gum.

"See that tree?" he told Mr Dean. "It's a magic tree."

Mr Dean grunted.

"It's an ancient jarrah," put in Nonna. "There used to be a lot around these parts, but they're all gone now."

Nonna looked meaningfully at Mr Dean.

"Yes, Devlin's family did well on them," noted Mr Biggs sombrely.

"Oh, those jarrah trees – you're telling me!" said Mr Dean. "They don't call this the lucky country for nothing. Imagine when my dad and my grandad discovered that not only would the jarrahs bring a fortune in logging, but the soil they grew in was also teeming with goodies that could be mined for big profits. Laughing all the way to the bank they were."

"While leaving great gashes of dry dead land across the horizon," muttered Mr Biggs.

"But how could they just kill the trees?" Peter asked accusingly.

"Hey, come on! Keep your hair on!" warned Mr Dean. "If my family hadn't taken them, someone else's would've."

"But is that a good enough reason?" Nonna persisted.

"Well, there was nothing wrong with it! Just business; huge demand round the world for the wood. Would you rather see a family go without a home?" Mr Dean turned to Peter. "Or is it better for a few trees to be cut down? They can grow back anyway."

Peter wasn't sure what to say to this. Of course he wanted people to have homes.

"Except it takes more than five hundred years for a jarrah like that to grow back," said Mr Biggs sadly.

"So, why were humans made smarter than trees?" argued Mr Dean. "I mean, if we're not supposed to chop them down."

"Trees are smart too!" interrupted Peter, then worried that he was getting into an argument he couldn't win.

"Oh, you philosopher types are all the same!" Mean Dean's face was getting red. "Lose touch with the real world. My dad was the smart one. ... And as for the trees, haven't you ever heard the phrases 'thick as two planks' or 'blockhead'?"

"Or 'chip off the old block'," added Mr Biggs, disapprovingly.

"What exactly do you and your broker do?" Peter asked, anxious to change the subject. "I mean, what's your job?"

"Just work with money, mostly. Day trading and property investment," mumbled Mr Dean. "But the game's changed since I got in."

Mr Dean looked round the circle of blank faces.

"What I mean is, I miss the good old days when I could buy a property in the morning, then sell it in the afternoon for a few million dollars' profit."

"Well," said Mr Biggs sadly, "I miss the good old days when the jarrah trees grew higher than the sky, and people walked among them, looking like children weaving through the legs of giants."

Mr Dean gaped at him and, for once, seemed unable to come up with a reply.

"You won't chop the Great Gum down, will you?" said Peter.

"Don't be ridiculous!" Mr Dean told him gruffly.

Finally, the sound of an approaching siren heralded the arrival of a small fire-service van. The fire warden driving skidded much too quickly across the lawn, halting dangerously close to the nervous residents in their lawn chairs.

"Takes himself a bit too seriously," muttered Mr Biggs as the warden leapt importantly from his vehicle.

"The bush fire's under control!" The warden shouted each word out extra loudly with his hands cupped round his mouth. "I repeat: the bush fire's under control. We have containment. You can all go back to your rooms."

"Thank you," said Matron in a clipped tone. "For your reference, some of us are slightly hard of hearing, but none of us is stone deaf."

"We soon will be, though," muttered Mean Dean, rubbing his ears irritably.

While most of the residents began meandering back towards the residence, Peter followed Mr Biggs and the warden over to inspect the firestop.

"There's still burning inside the containment line, just over there in the south-east," the warden told Mr Biggs in a self-important voice. "But nothing that a good dose of water from the helicopter tankers won't fix."

"Helicopters?" Peter began searching the sky.

"Yeah. ... They'll be over in a minute." The warden seemed surprised to see a child in amongst the old people. He added boastfully, "Do you want to see my flashing orange light?"

"Ah ... no thanks," said Peter politely.

Nonna LaRosa came up behind him.

"Dinner, bath, and bed for the birthday boy?"

"Not yet ... I'd better stay out and keep an eye on the fire," Peter told her, pointing glumly towards the smoke.

Nonna hesitated.

"I'll be okay. I'm eleven, remember?" said Peter. He could hear the distant sound of helicopters trundling through the sky.

"I suppose it's all right," said Nonna. "It's only that I have this funny feeling as if ... as if—"

"What? Is the fire going to get us?"

"No. Not that. More a feeling that there's something out there." Nonna squinted into the fading light of the bush, then shrugged.

"But, you know, I can't trust the sight anymore."

"So, can I stay out, then?"

Mr Dean's voice suddenly rose up from across the courtyard. He was talking into a mobile phone. "Have you found anything or not? What ... still nothing? I'm out here in the middle of a bush fire while you're sipping cappuccinos in Manhattan!"

"Is he barking on his phone at that poor broker again?" muttered Mr Biggs.

"Except it's not his phone," Peter observed. "It's the same yellow colour as the volunteer fire van."

Peter followed behind the warden, who was already hurrying over.

"Hey, you! Put that phone down. It's a mission-critical device!"

Mr Dean tilted the big yellow phone away from his mouth, "Keep it down, will you!"

"Disconnect!" the warden shouted. "That's for emergency use only!"

"This is an emergency!" Mr Dean shouted back irritably.

The warden looked temporarily thrown.

"It's all your fault!" Mean Dean snarled into the receiver. "I told you that bear wouldn't be going anywhere!"

"Bear?" repeated the warden doubtfully, trying to wrench back his phone.

"The only way out now is to squeeze it for all it's worth."

The warden snatched back the device.

"Hello, are you in trouble?" He frowned over at Peter. "No one there. ..."

"He's probably hiding under the bed of his fancy apartment," Peter told the warden, but he felt guilty when Mr Dean laughed and the warden looked confused.

In an attempt to mend the situation, Peter said, "I could have a look at your flashing light now."

"No chance," replied the warden huffily.

CHAPTER

11

Meeting of the GAIA Secretariat

hooooooooooooooo-ster!

"Right on time!" Principal Erthia Halowell said approvingly as Agent Etheron shot through the tubular entrance made just for him and began a high-speed spin round the circular ceiling.

Agent Artiss Fleur's cowboy hat got caught in the cross draught, and he sprang athletically from his chair to catch it.

Shoo-ster! Shoo-ster!

"It takes him a few moments to wind down," explained Professor Theodorus Meriwether as he tried to protect his perfectly combed silver-grey hair.

Suddenly, the booming voice of GAIA President Jove Buchanan filled the meeting room space from the surround-sound system.

"Sounds like we're all here."

"Yes, all present and accounted for. Even the Shooster's just blown in from Australia," Artiss Fleur affirmed.

Professor Meriwether's meeting papers spiralled upwards from the table.

"The Shooster's had a long reconnaissance Down Under," Professor Meriwether confirmed as he snatched up at the flying papers.

"Although he really is a most undisciplined agent," remarked Principal Halowell, barricading the sides of her high purple bun with her long arms.

The voice of President Buchanan chuckled. "Well, what he lacks in good behaviour we know he makes up for in superior intelligence."

The three at the table laughed.

President Buchanan cleared his throat meaningfully, then said, "Agent Etheron! At ease, please!"

The Shooster began adjusting down the strength of his spin.

President Buchanan added, "Please take your place in the Hovva."

Slowly, the unruly Shooster began to syphon himself into the see-through spiral tube, which sat suspended above the heads of the three at the table. The Hovva was GAIA's high-tech answer to a comfortable meeting room seat for a quantum of wind.

"Now," continued the president, "I'm going to ask the professor, who's called us together today, to come straight to the point."

"Ah, thank you, Bu-h," Professor Meriwether said, using the GAIA president's code name.

The professor stood up and looked nervously round the table. Then, instead of coming to the point, he sneezed loudly.

Aa-a-a-a-ah-choo!

The others waited politely while Professor Meriwether fumbled for his handkerchief, which he usually kept starched and folded in a neat triangle in his top cardigan pocket. But, today, he pulled it limp and crumpled from the pocket of his equally crumpled trousers.

"I'm afraid the Shooster and I have some rather unpleasant news." Professor Meriwether sighed and adjusted his bow tie in a way that made it hang more crookedly. "And following that, we have some even more unpleasant news to report."

"Oh, come now!" interrupted Principal Halowell, raising her long slender neck and smiling brightly at him. "Nothing's ever as bad as it might seem."

"Well, I'll let you be the judge of that."

Professor Meriwether took a deep breath. "Our cover's blown on the Sleeping King; the Anthrogs now know for sure that the boy lives."

There were gasps around the table.

"So, what could be worse than that?" Artiss Fleur exclaimed.

The professor sighed again and mopped his forehead. "The Shooster has brought back direct evidence that the Anthrogs have breached the boy's hideaway with some form of first-level contact."

"What kind of evidence?" Agent Fleur leant forward, frowning.

Professor Meriwether glanced up at the Hovva and said grimly, "Olfactory evidence! I've never smelt anything like it."

Instinctively, Agent Fleur and Principal Halowell brought out their handkerchiefs, holding them at the ready, next to their noses.

"Well, I did warn you that the news would be unpleasant," the professor continued lamely.

"All right, Shooster." President Buchanan's voice came through. "Present your evidence!"

On command, the Shooster spun out from the Hovva, increasing speed as he began a download of stored smells from his mission Down Under.

"*Mm!* Eucalyptus leaves, native grasses," Principal Halowell remarked approvingly, "*Oooh,* wattle flowers! Lovely!"

"Wait, what was that?" Artiss Fleur choked, plunging his whole face forward into his waiting handkerchief.

Professor Meriwether sniffed the air and wrinkled his nose. "Boiled cabbage."

"Well, it is an old folk's home!" The principal laughed, dabbing at her nostrils.

The Shooster calibrated his spin above the table, level with their noses.

"*Ooh!* I think I just got a whiff of the boy king's socks." Artiss Fleur gave a strangled laugh that turned into a cough.

Professor Meriwether wrinkled his sweaty brow. "Come on, Shooster, get to the point!"

The Shooster whirred around some more.

"He doesn't like the smell any more than we do," said the professor from the corner of his mouth.

Artiss Fleur nodded sympathetically, then choked. "What was tha-a-a-at?" He shoved his handkerchief roughly back into his nostrils.

"Vegemite." Professor Meriwether smiled up at the Shooster spin. "They love the stuff down there!"

The voice of President Buchanan conferenced back into the room. "Okay, Shooster, I know it's hard for you, but we're waiting for the Anthrog fetor sample. I've got a remote team here ready to take a copy of it, so give us your worst!"

The Shooster seemed to waver.

Professor Meriwether smiled up at him encouragingly.

"The sooner you present the fetor, the sooner you can delete it from your memory."

The Shooster held himself quivering in a holding pattern, in preparation for a high-speed release. When it came, papers flew, light bulbs flickered, and even the old stone walls seemed to shudder as the fetor spiralled out, cloying the air with its vile, indescribable stink.

Artiss Fleur buried his face in his cowboy hat. "That's the Anthrog fetor, all right!"

"Unmistakable!" The principal choked.

Even the voice of President Buchanan began to sputter.

"Thank you, Shooster … we have a copy on that. Halt! And to your Hovva, quick smart!"

It took some minutes before the conversation could resume, then President Buchanan's voice came back through, his tone grim.

"We've got a confirmed match. An Anthrog Drone, and you're right, Meriwether, she's been in very close proximity to the boy."

Artiss Fleur's eyes narrowed. "So, the Chrysalite has been breached, and we've lost what little advantage we had against the Anthrog offensive."

"Well, it's not in my nature to ever lose hope," Professor Meriwether replied. "But it doesn't look good."

The professor's expression was dismal, and the pockets of his long cardigan sagged towards his kneecaps.

"Cheer up, everyone!" insisted Principal Halowell. "One might still pin a modicum of hope on our so-called Sleeping King."

The others nodded.

"But then, there's the problem of our insisting on being so deeply steeped in secrecy. How is the poor boy king ever going to find his way to GAIA?" continued the principal.

"She's right," said Artiss Fleur. "We need to get out and face the enemy."

"Well, this island – the GAIA field – is still the one place on earth that the dark ones haven't breached," said President Buchanan in a measured tone. "And I'm not prepared to gamble with the planet just because my top people have a problem with patience!"

Professor Meriwether sniffed and wiped at his face again before adjusting his bow tie to an even more crooked angle.

"What on earth's wrong with you today?" asked the principal, suddenly losing patience with her soggy colleague.

"Another superstorm coming. It brings up my fever."

"Well, before you confine yourself to your weather tower," urged President Buchanan, "tell us your thoughts on this boy king."

"Well. ..." The professor looked thoughtful. "If you look at the DNA samples on record for him and review his soul heritage, the boy's carrying enough light inside himself to save a hundred worlds."

"If he can just figure out how to switch it on." Principal Halowell laughed a high, clanging laugh.

"But even then, will he be assured a place at your once and secret school?" asked Agent Fleur.

"Ha! You know we have our standards – king or no king. That is to say, he'll have to prove himself along the way, just like the other initiates at Spiral Hall."

"But why must he be so alone?" asked Artiss Fleur.

"Well," said President Buchanan, "he who walks his path alone can be sure the quest is truly his."

"But what is this boy's quest, really?" Artiss Fleur demanded. "I mean, apart from escaping almost certain death at the hands of the Anthrogs."

"Peter Blue's quest is the most difficult of any initiate destined for greatness." President Buchanan's voice grew husky. "It's the quest to become what he already is."

For a while, the room was silent, then Artiss Fleur said, "Well, if he's his father's son, he'll prove himself, all right; Byron Blue was the bravest agent GAIA's ever had."

"Even braver than you, Agent Fleur?" the principal smiled teasingly.

"Well, Byron did take on the Anthrogs single-handedly."

"At the time, I called that insubordinate," grumbled President Buchanan. "But. since his intentions were of the highest order, nothing has been held against his memory."

"It's true his actions did put us in the mess we're in now," Artiss Fleur replied.

"Forced us underground, at least after Byron failed," said Professor Meriwether.

Artiss Fleur's eyes narrowed again. "Well, Byron didn't fail, in the sense that he succeeded in saving his son."

"Well let's focus on the son, then," President Buchanan advised. "Tell us, Meriwether, what have you learnt about this boy?"

"Yes, tell!" Principal Halowell exclaimed brightly. "If Peter Blue's to be a student at Spiral Hall, then we'll need to know more. Is he a scientist like his mother or an adventurer like his father?"

"Good question," agreed Artiss. "What's this Sleeping King's power?"

"Well, we're not quite sure actually." Professor Meriwether laughed a little too loudly. "We know from the Shooster's visit that he's perfected the sleeping part of his title, but he might still need to work a bit on the kingly stuff."

President Buchanan chuckled benignly. "Tell us, Halowell, what does the Force say about the boy?"

Principal Halowell nodded, closed her eyes, and held her long slender fingers to her temples.

"The Force continues to favour the boy king; Nature has always been on his side." She concentrated some more. "Oh yes, very nice."

"What?"

"The Force has sent the boy king a gift." She opened her eyes and smiled brightly around the table. "They're calling it the Awakener."

The Arrival of the Friendly Beast

CHAPTER

12

The Rescue

A bush wallaby separated from its mob is chased by fire.

Forward, faster it bounds, but the wallaby can't outpace the hot breath at its back.

The flames overtake it, leaping recklessly into the rising winds, scattering upwards to the canopy, and then rushing ahead across the bush, only to circle back and surround their prey.

Trapped within the fiery ring, the wallaby sniffs the air and smells only death – its own. Still, it continues, bounding uselessly round and round, desperately seeking some safe passage out from the flames. Finally, with one powerful upsurge, the wallaby leaps into the wall of fire.

Now the flames move with it, biting and clawing at the hind flesh. Fright-filled shrieks rip through the heavy air, unfamiliar sounds coming from the wallaby's own throat. On and on, it charges, the soul loosening free from its body.

At the wallaby's shoulder, the quiet breath of the eternal mother waits. But the wallaby resists, needing to go on.

There's still one thing left to do. ...

Peter stared out into the gathering darkness at the stunted line of trees beyond the firepit. Their crowns had all toppled in the last fire, leaving only severed arms raised towards the sky. *Trees are brave,* Peter thought. *Trees die standing up.*

In his dreams, Peter sometimes heard the souls of the trees howl. Suddenly, his senses were alert. He could hear howling now, coming from the bush.

"Did you hear that, Mr Biggs?" Peter called behind him. "Nonna was right. There is something out there!"

Mr Biggs, seated under the porch light, hurriedly folded his newspaper. He set out across the now-darkened lawn, calling back, "Be right there, Peter!"

"Something's coming!" Peter shouted.

A flaming shape lit up the darkness, careering down into the firepit, then up and out again.

"It's an animal! On fire!"

It was bounding in a direct line towards Peter.

Instead of running clear, Peter surprised himself by wrenching off the GAIA jacket and swinging it like a bullfighter's cloak in front of the flaming animal.

"Peter, no!" Mr Biggs called, too late.

Peter dragged the animal to the ground, smothering and staunching the patches of flames that leapt about its fur and skin.

By the time Mr Biggs had puffed to the scene, Peter was already gingerly pulling up the jacket to show an injured wallaby collapsed on its side. The whites of its eyes glowed. It was only when the thick smell of roasting flesh caught at Peter's nostrils that he gave up being brave.

"Help! Help! *Aa-a-a-a-a-a-a-ah!*"

"*Shh!*" Mr Biggs locked his big-bear arm round Peter's shoulders. "You did well. It's all right now."

Peter was gulping for air, but the choking smell of smouldering flesh hung thickly around them.

Mr Dean pulled up behind them and sputtered, "What is it? A kangaroo?"

"No, a wallaby!" Peter could tell by the smaller size. It was about four feet long.

"Peter's right," confirmed Mr Biggs, kneeling unsteadily on the hard ground. "The poor fellow's passed out; from the pain, probably. What shall we do?"

"We have to save him!" wailed Peter.

"Oh Geez, what a stench," complained Mr Dean.

"Shut up!" said Peter surprising himself again. "Either help, or go away!"

"All right, all right. Don't go bush on me; I'll help. For starters, go and get that so-called cook of yours. She's supposed to be a nurse, isn't she?"

"Good thinking," agreed Mr Biggs, adding, "And don't let Matron see you."

But Peter, already sprinting to the house, didn't hear.

Angel, led by Peter, arrived quickly. She was carrying a medical kit. Nonna LaRosa and Mrs Millet followed close behind Angel.

"What is it?" squealed Mrs Millet.

Mr Biggs replied, "*Shh.* It's a wallaby. ... The poor thing was actually on fire ... arrived right at Peter's feet."

"Is it still alive?" Angel asked doubtfully.

"Of course it's alive!" sobbed Peter, falling to his knees next to the wallaby's slender head. "Just a moment ago it was bouncing across the firepit."

Peter stared hopelessly at the raw gashes that cut deeply into the animal's blue-grey fur.

The wallaby's throat began to contract, emitting a strange sound like the *boing-boing* of an uncurling spring.

"Oh Geez," said Mr Dean, recognising the sound of death.

"We have to save him!" wailed Peter. "We have to!"

"Well, I'm not a vet," said Angel. "But I can try!"

She produced a syringe from her kit. "Attention, everyone, and hold."

Instinctively Peter, Mr Biggs and Mr Dean clamped their hands gently onto the wallaby's hindlegs, while Angel, dodging the most-wounded areas, deftly released a series of painkillers into the animal's rump.

Next, she began swabbing antiseptic from a bottle all over the wallaby's open wounds.

"He *is* going to make it, isn't he?" Peter asked.

Angel, feeling for the pulse on the wallaby's neck, didn't reply, which Peter took to be a bad sign.

"What do you think?" Mr Dean asked her grimly.

"I ... I'm afraid it isn't good." Angel looked up sadly. "I'm not a vet, but the wounds are pretty advanced. It's hard to be hopeful."

"Please don't let the wallaby die!" Peter begged.

Nonna exchanged a look with Angel, but neither of them spoke.

"Well, there's barely a pulse," Angel said with a sigh, her hand searching for vital signs around the neck artery.

Angel bent her head, putting her mouth close to the animal's head, then set off into a high-speed whispering prayer, her face rising and falling against the prostrate wallaby's ear.

Peter guessed she was using the ancient language of her people, the Aborigines.

Everyone waited in silence.

Peter reached forward to stroke the blue-grey fur. He could feel the life force seeping from the wallaby's soft body, almost like water emptying from a tub.

"I'm sorry. It's time to let its spirit free." Angel patted Peter's shoulder.

Peter began to cry. "It's not fair! It's not fair! I hate fire! I hate nature! Why does everyone have to die?"

Then, as if in response, an unexpected thing happened. The wallaby's belly began to twitch.

Peter's breath caught noisily. "What's he doing?"

They peered through the semi-darkness.

"Are they death convulsions?" asked Nonna.

The wallaby was suddenly all arms and legs, twitching and flailing.

Mr Dean let out an odd laugh.

"How can you laugh at him?" Peter bristled.

"First of all, because it's not a *him!*" Mr Dean was suddenly all smiles. "Look!"

"Oh, I see what you're saying," Angel said.

Angel and Nonna were laughing softly now too.

"Peter, look who's coming out to say hello."

Two paws became three paws, then four paws, followed by two little legs, then a tail.

"Look!"

A joey popped out of its mother's pouch. Then, seeing the circle of watchers, quickly turned, head first, to scramble back in.

Instinctively, Peter leant over to scoop it up with his bare hands. The fur was soft, but its tiny claws were sharp.

"Watch out!" warned Mr Biggs. "That's still a wild animal you're dealing with."

"Don't let it escape," warned Angel. "It won't survive alone out there in the dark."

"Here, let me try something." Mr Biggs snatched up the jacket Mr Dean had draped over his arm.

"Hey, no way! That's my best jacket!"

"Shush," Nonna told Mr Dean as Mr Biggs deftly flicked the jacket over the surprised creature and scooped it up.

"The little blighter's heavier than I thought," Mr Biggs said, struggling desperately to keep hold of the twitching, biting bundle.

"Hand-stitched that jacket was, with a 300-thread count," Mr Dean groaned.

"Can I hold it?" Peter begged.

"Well, start by taking the legs," instructed Mr Biggs, huffing with exertion.

"What a fighter!" Peter gushed.

The little joey began pedalling its strong back legs through the silk lining of Mr Dean's jacket. There was a ripping sound as Peter fought to retain his grip on the joey's legs.

"I got that jacket from the millionaires' club of Madrid."

Ignoring Mr Dean, Angel hurriedly fixed another smaller injection, a sedative for the joey, who yelped with indignation at the jab in its rump, then launched into a fierce struggle to free itself.

Mr Dean stepped in to help and was rewarded by a nip on the arm.

"Ouch! Little beggar's got sharp teeth." Blood poured. "There goes another white shirt!"

Then, finally, legs still pedalling, the joey surrendered and fell asleep.

"That'll buy you some time," said Angel, glancing back down at the fading mother. Turning to Mr Biggs, she added jokingly, "Oh, and congratulations! It's a girl."

Angel pulled a thermometer out of her bag and clicked it inside the joey's ear. "Nice and warm for now, but these little ones have to be kept at a constant temperature."

Angel glanced round the circle of helpers, her eyes settling on Peter. "Why don't you unbutton that enormous new adventure jacket of yours? Let's try something."

She bundled the sleeping joey inside the folds of Peter's jacket.

"The sound of your heartbeat will help calm it," said Nonna.

"This is a special temperature-controlled material – for GAIA agents," Peter whispered proudly.

Angel turned her attention back to the mother, feeling for her pulse. "She's gone."

"Look's like the bush fire's gone out too," said Nonna.

For a moment, they all stared out towards the now-darkened horizon.

Peter leant his face close to the sleeping joey, whispering, "You're safe now, "but you'll miss your mother a lot – I know."

13

Operation Stealth Wallaby

Peter stood holding the sleeping joey, hardly daring to move. Only this morning, he'd put on Dad's GAIA jacket – now he'd already used it to save a baby wallaby!

Mr Dean, on the other hand, would probably never wear his special hand-stitched jacket again. The lining was ripped, and it now lay across the mother's body, soaked with large blooms of blood from her open wounds.

Mr Biggs and Mr Dean, under Peter's instruction, were digging a grave for her.

"Geez, this ground's hard as concrete!" Mr Dean complained.

"Thanks to the drought," said Mr Biggs. "The droughts get longer and longer every year. They also bring the fires."

Peter rubbed his fingers across the pads of the joey's feet. "She's been out of the pouch quite a lot, hopping around. I can tell by the roughness."

Angel used her torch for illumination as she peered into the sleeping joey's mouth. "But judging by its pure white chompers, I'd say it's only ever had mother's milk. So, someone needs to get to Jarra Jarra for baby formula before this joey wakes up."

The light in Matron's office snapped on.

"We'd better hurry," Angel urged them.

"You're right." Mr Biggs put down his spade. "Or, before you know it, Matron'll be out here doing cartwheels on the lawn."

"Some of the other residents might be along too," Nonna said worriedly.

"Although probably not doing cartwheels," muttered Mr Dean in a way that made Peter giggle.

Angel ushered them all through the screen door and into her kitchen. Every bench top was cluttered with pickling jars, and a powerful vinegar smell filled the air.

"Better close the door to the corridor, just in case," said Angel.

"Well, whatever you do, don't close the windows!" Mean Dean coughed, holding a handkerchief to his mouth and nose, and breathing dramatically.

Angel scowled defensively. "I was right in the middle of pickling when Peter called me."

"Pickles – very fitting," said Mr Biggs with a conciliatory cough. "I mean, since we do find ourselves in somewhat of a one ourselves."

"He's right," agreed Nonna. "What on earth will we do now?"

"All right, all right, Wallaby Insiders," said Mr Dean, stepping into the leadership vacuum. "Operation Stealth Wallaby begins now."

Peter felt a thrill of excitement zap through him.

"We need to identify our top five priority action points and get cracking on them before the little wriggler wakes up. Biggsie, you're an old journalist; you can write the list."

Mr Biggs took a spiral pad and a pencil from his pocket. "Righto. First priority, then …?"

Mr Biggs tapped his pencil on the pad with mock efficiency and then looked at Peter.

"Priority number one." Mr Dean sucked in his breath. "We need a car. Which one of you old wrinklies has a car?"

Everyone was silent.

"Oh Geez!" Mr Dean gazed up in the direction of his former hillside manor house. "I used to have two Bentleys and a driver."

"Well, I have a car," Mrs Millet said finally. "But I don't use it in the dark. It's only for the hair salon … in the daytime."

Mr Dean rolled his eyes at her.

"Right – we have a car!" Mr Dean clapped his hands.

"Priority two, then?" said Mr Biggs.

"I'm guessing that no one here actually knows more than a wombat's bottom about keeping a baby marsupial alive, so we need to call the wildlife centre and get a vet over here!"

"Roger that!" said Mr Biggs in a way that made Peter giggle.

"You can take that action point, Biggsie."

Mr Biggs fumbled for his mobile phone.

"Not now; after we finish the list."

"Got it – right. … So, what's the third priority, then?"

Mrs Millet waved her hand. "Priority three: we have to reverse my car out of the garden storage shed in the dark."

"That's not a priority," scoffed Mr Dean. "That's a means to achieving a priority."

"Oh, all right. It's just that I'm not that used to driving backwards."

Everybody looked at Mrs Millet, unsure, until Angel raised her wooden spoon at them.

"Why are you all still here? What if the joey suddenly wakes up? What are we going to feed it? Pickles?" She ran a vinegary finger across the priority list and then ordered, "Change priority one to milk, and come straight back with it before you do anything else. Lactose-free is best. I think marsupials are lactose intolerant."

Angel turned to Nonna. "Make sure you get powder formulas, so we can adjust the strength. Oh, plus some different-shaped bottles, and I'm guessing a long teat will be best for a wallaby's lips."

Mr Biggs was scribbling in his book, trying to keep up.

Mr Dean said, "All right, Nonna, you take the lead on baby formula."

"No problem," Nonna told him. "It wasn't that long ago that Peter was still having night milk of his own."

Peter rolled his eyes at her.

"Which reminds me," added Nonna. "What about nappies?"

"Good idea!" Peter grinned up at the grown-ups. "For number one!"

Mr Biggs raised his pencil. "No, priority number four. We just agreed that the milk should be number one."

"No, nappies for doing number one," corrected Peter, who suddenly had an attack of the giggles.

The grown-ups stared open-mouthed, waiting for Peter to take a breath.

"Number two will be easy to pick up without nappies," Peter explained. "I've seen wallaby scat before; it's like dry pellets."

Mr Biggs wrinkled his nose and wrote "nappies," Commenting, "That's number four, for going number one but not number two."

"I'd like to move to priority number five now." Mr Dean wiped his forehead with his handkerchief and made a show of distancing himself from the open pickle jars.

"Well? What'll it be?" Mr Biggs looked up from his notebook.

"If you must have a priority five, let's agree that we need boiling water, and I'll take care of it."

"Perfect," agreed Mr Biggs. "We'll be needing a good cup of tea by then."

"No, silly! Boiled water to make the milk formula. Everything has to be sterile."

"Oh." Mr Biggs looked a little sheepish.

"Don't worry, Biggsie," Mr Dean clapped his shoulder. "We'll be asking Angel here for something stronger than tea by then, and I'm not talking about pickle vinegar."

The Wallaby Insiders were back from their mission surprisingly quickly.

"Is she still out cold?" they asked.

"Unconscious, yes, but not cold," Peter told them. "Thanks to my special temperature-controlled jacket."

Nonna sat down at the wooden table and began measuring different brands of baby-formula powder into bottles and handing them off to the others to shake. "So, what's our plan when the joey wakes up?"

"I'll just keep holding her," Peter told them confidently. "And we'll feed her the milk."

He was surprised and a little hurt when the grown-ups laughed at him.

"That's what you think! Ha ha!"

"It'll be game on, that's for sure," said Mr Dean in a voice that signalled he was looking forward to it.

Angel cast a nervous glance at the door.

The joey shifted position.

"Won't be long now before she wakes up."

Everyone glanced nervously at each other.

While they were waiting, Angel took the joey's pulse with her stethoscope.

"Aha." She moved the circular piece around the joey's chest inside Peter's jacket. "Good … good."

Angel slid the dome onto Peter's chest. Her face suddenly registered concern.

"What?" Peter demanded.

"The wallaby's heartbeat is steady, but yours is racing dangerously."

They both giggled, and Peter sensed a new feeling growing up inside him – a feeling that wasn't quite joy but wasn't misery either.

Then, suddenly, with no warning, the joey was awake and pedalling her paws and feet in panic as she took in the unfamiliar surroundings.

Chrrkkk! Chrrkkk!

She dropped neatly to the floor and began a desperate hopping spree around Angel's cluttered kitchen. Pickle jars began dropping and smashing onto the hard flagstone floor in the wake of the wallaby's heavy tail.

Chrrkkk! Chrrkkk!

Soon everyone had joined the chase, with no plan and no teamwork.

Nonna and Mrs Millet dabbed different brands of warm milk on their wrists, but they couldn't get close enough to the wallaby to have her taste them. At the same time, Mr Dean and Mr Biggs, paddling through glass and pickle juice, kept making uncoordinated attempts to close in on the frightened joey.

Eventually, she was cornered on a high shelf, behind the cereal jars.

"Try catching it with your famous jacket," Mr Biggs urged Peter.

Holding the jacket, Peter edged towards the creature, but just as he got close enough for contact, the joey nudged the cornflakes jar from the shelf.

The jar landed with a heavy thud on Mr Biggs's foot, bringing tears to his eyes. The Weetabix jar came next, and without the benefit of Mr

Biggs's foot, the big jar shattered into fragments on the flagstone floor. The flour jar followed, then pasta, followed by rice.

Angel started sweeping.

Tut, tut.

"Tut, tut yourself …!" Peter replied, advancing again.

But the joey was in no mood for conversation. Awash in pickle juice and spilled formula, her little body had begun to shiver rhythmically.

Peter remembered fretfully what Angel had said about the danger of her getting a chill.

"Where's the vet?" Mr Biggs said impatiently. "He should be here by now. He'd know how to catch the little scamp."

Peter surprised them all by saying, "We can do it. We just need teamwork."

"Smart boy," said Mr Dean. "Everyone, form a tight line of defence, and we'll drive the little blighter towards that fruit crate. Then, we can trap her inside it."

The joey paused, bright eyes staring back at them.

Tsk-tsk!

"Right," said Peter. "Everyone, go!"

The joey played along with them right until they reached the crate. Then, she hopped cleanly over it and disappeared into the broom cupboard.

Matron, on her soundless white pumps, chose that very moment to step into the kitchen.

"Everything all right in here?" she asked, her voice suggesting clearly that things were not.

Matron sniffed the air suspiciously while prodding a piece of glass with the toe of her clean white shoe.

"I was just doing some pickling, Matron," Angel said as she rattled a pot busily into the sink.

"Goodness, you've a lot of helpers. Mr Dean you've got blood on your shirt. Have you had a fall?"

For a moment, nobody answered, then Mr Biggs hobbled across the kitchen on his injured foot. "I'm afraid I finally had to teach Devlin Dean a lesson. His behaviour had become pretty intolerable. You see?"

"Yes, I see," said Matron absently, then added, "I mean, no, of course I *don't* see. Mr Biggs, what on earth were you thinking?"

Mr Dean stepped forward. "It's true, Mrs Matron, I did have it coming."

"But in front of the boy!"

Peter, who'd positioned himself beside the broom-cupboard door, smiled lamely at her. "It's all right, Matron, they're all friends again now."

As Matron turned to go, a floorboard creaked heavily in the broom cupboard.

"What's that I hear in the broom cranny?" she asked.

"Rats?" offered Mr Biggs.

Matron moved stealthily across the vinegar-soaked floor to the cupboard and jerked open the door. The insiders waited for her reaction, but none came.

Then, they watched her peer around inside behind the mops and brooms; still nothing.

Finally, Matron lifted the watch pinned to her grey nurse's blouse. "Well, I'm off to bed."

"Goodnight," they responded, a little too enthusiastically.

Angel closed the door behind Matron.

"She's gone!" Peter said.

"Yes, thankfully."

"No, I mean the joey's gone!" he said.

"Can't have! She's just camouflaged behind the brooms." Mr Dean stepped into the narrow space, looking up and down the whitewashed walls. "Strange."

Everyone took turns peering in. The joey was gone.

"Has anyone got a torch?" Nonna asked anxiously.

"I have," said Peter, surprising everyone by powering on the light on Dad's jacket sleeve. He began directing the strong needles of light carefully into the back corners of the cupboard. But there was no joey.

It was only when Peter wedged himself right up against the back wall that he noticed the broom cupboard actually turned a corner.

"There's a kind of cubby here." Peter quickly spotted the joey cowering on the narrow built-in bed in the corner of the tiny room.

"Where are you?" Angel's voice through the wall was muffled.

"In the secret cubby," Peter called, his face lighting into a wide smile.

"This is where we'll live," Peter whispered to the quivering joey.

Angel popped her head round the corner.

"The snuggery. I forgot this was here. At the back wall of the fireplace, it's the warmest place in the house."

Mr Dean squeezed in after her. But Nonna, Mrs Millet, and Mr Biggs were too big to get through the narrow cavity, and could only take turns peeping in.

"In Victorian times, the kitchen hand or the stable boy would've slept here," Mr Dean told them.

The joey was watching them.

"Who's a clever cookie? Hiding from Matron!" Mrs Millet praised her from the doorway.

But the clever cookie responded by making a new sound: *nyitch-nyitch-nyitch!*

Peter crept towards her. "She doesn't know where she is or why her mother doesn't come."

Nyitch-nyitch-nyitch!

"She must be really hungry."

Nyitch!

The Wallaby Insiders all gazed uneasily now at the large, moist eyes staring back at them. Everyone sensed this was no longer a game.

"I bet she's never spent a night out of the pouch," Peter said worriedly. "And she's all wet and cold.

"We need to take her temperature," said Angel.

They all nodded silently.

Even Mr Dean began to look concerned.

"She doesn't trust us," mumbled Mr Biggs.

Peter was becoming tearful. "What if she never learns to take food from us? Will she just starve?"

"All right, calm down." Mr Dean told them gruffly.

He walked over to Angel and muttered something that Peter couldn't hear.

Angel looked shocked, then nodded.

"Right! Peter, go and get your backpack! I've got an idea. It's a good idea," Mr Dean said, adding grimly, "but you're not going to like it."

CHAPTER

14

The Good Idea

When Peter re-entered, carrying his backpack, Mean Dean was standing with Angel at the kitchen table, holding a large blood-stained carving knife and something furry and grey that looked like the joey but wasn't moving. Mr Dean had blood on his white shirt.

Peter's breath caught. "What's that?"

Mr Dean didn't answer, but he didn't try to stop Peter from looking. Nonna lowered the lights so the kitchen glowed as if lit by candles. "The mother's pouch?"

"That's right. Give us your backpack," Mr Dean said in a quiet, growly voice.

Peter passed it, then stood, trying to be brave, as he watched Angel and Mr Dean lining the backpack with wax paper and easing the pouch fur inside it.

The pouch smelt of soot, oil, and burnt flesh, but, inside, Peter knew the joey would find the scent of his dead mother.

They were interrupted by the return of Mr Biggs and the smell of pipe smoke. He muttered, "Still no word from the vet. Hopefully, he's on the road already."

Peter didn't want the vet to come and take the joey away. He tiptoed over to the broom cupboard where the joey crouched, whimpering and quaking.

Mr Dean handed Peter the pouch. "Now, how are we going to do this?"

Using the light of Dad's GAIA jacket to guide him, Peter carried the backpack into the cupboard.

"*Tsk-tsk!*" Peter tried as he held out the pouch.

Nyitch-nyitch, replied the joey woefully.

Peter edged closer.

The joey's big watery brown eyes looked sad, but her nose was raised and twitching.

But as soon as Peter got too close to her, she began making loud *chrrkkk-chrrkkk* noises and hopping backwards.

What now? He'd seen joeys climbing into their mother's pouches. The mother would stand patiently while the joey clumsily crammed itself in – usually, head first, with long jumpers and tail following.

Suddenly, Peter had an idea. Using the door handle as a guide, he adjusted the backpack to what he thought would be the right height for a mother's pouch. Then, ignoring the panicked *chrrkkk-chrrkkk,* Peter closed the door, leaving the joey alone with the pouch hanging open on the door handle.

It was only a few minutes before the insiders heard a bumping and scuffling sound behind the door, signalling that the little wallaby was home.

"And now, dinner time for joeys," Peter said with relief.

Angel plucked a fresh baby bottle from the warm water. "This one's ready to go."

Peter opened the door and knelt down in front of the pouch.

"*Tsk-tsk, tsk-tsk,*" he sounded, leaning the bottle teat into the opening and feeling around.

Tsk-tsk! She was answering him.

"Rub some drops round its mouth and nose if you can," whispered Nonna.

"Yes, give her a taste of it," whispered Mrs Millet, from her seat at the table next to Nonna.

Digging his hand into the warm pouch, Peter managed to wipe milk all around the joey's flinching snout. He smiled when she started pushing the drops around with her tongue.

"She's tasting it!"

"You're almost there!" Mr Dean crouched down inside the cupboard next to him.

Peter felt the wallaby's strong lips pulling at the bottle so forcefully that, kneeling before the pouch, he could barely keep hold.

"She's trying it!" Peter told the others.

The joey sucked down the whole bottle before starting up on a new round of *nyitch-nyitch*.

"She wants more!" Peter's knees ached from holding the same position, but he didn't care.

Angel giggled and passed in another bottle.

When the second bottle was passed back empty, Mr Biggs remarked nervously, "That's a lot of milk going in. What about the number one?"

Angel brought him a third bottle, plus a disposable diaper, which she handed to Mr Dean. He did his best to line the pouch with it while the joey was sucking.

"She trusts us!" Peter told Mr Dean, smiling.

The joey paused in mid gulp, looked up at him, then, without warning, vomited up on Mr Dean's white shirt.

"Trust and vomit," Peter said ruefully.

"Joey spew!" Mr Dean gave a gagged response.

"Peter was just the same as a baby," Nonna said unworriedly.

Peter pulled the joey out of the pouch and hugged her close while Angel mopped the milky sick with a towel.

"That reminds me – there's something else we have to do," Angel whispered. "The little ones need help to go."

"To go where?"

"To go pee-pee. The mother usually licks the stomach to help the joey get it out. Here, I'll show you." Angel took the joey from Peter's arms and handed her and the bottle to Mr Dean.

"Don't drop her," Peter warned.

Mr Dean, speechless with shock, stared down at the little joey now snuggled into his armpit and gulping her milk.

Angel showed Peter how to massage the joey's little stomach with one finger, using downward strokes. "Pretend it's the mother's tongue."

It took only a few seconds for warm pee to flow out of the joey and onto Mr Dean's white shirt.

"*Aaaargh!* Thank you very much!" Mr Dean didn't even seem that mad as he placed the joey into the pouch and got up. He just pulled off the shirt, threw it into the fire, and then sat down wordlessly at the table in his singlet.

Peter noticed that Nonna had laid out plates and glasses. He hadn't realised how hungry he was. As soon as the joey had fallen back to sleep, Peter tiptoed over to join the grown-ups.

"She's fast asleep," he told them.

"Good," said Mrs Millet, "because it's nearly midnight; must be way past that little joey's bedtime."

"She's nocturnal," corrected Nonna.

"Well, she's safe and happy. That's what counts," said Mr Biggs.

"Yes, that's something worth celebrating," said Angel, handing Peter a large glass of milk.

Angel handed out smaller glasses to the others. "Cooking sherry's all I've got."

Angel raised her glass in a toast.

"Cheers," responded the grown-ups, their voices muted with tiredness.

"Well done, Peter; and good courage, Devlin!" added Nonna.

Mr Dean smiled as he raised the glass to his lips, but his smile turned to a grimace as the sherry reached his mouth.

"*Aaaaghh!*" His head lurched forward with disgust. "My palate will never survive!"

"Better just drink it down in one, then." Mr Biggs chuckled.

"Right! For a little more courage." Mr Dean glanced at Nonna and saluted her with his glass before knocking it back in a single swig.

Nonna clinked glasses with Peter.

"Cheers to the brave joey!" Peter said and, not wishing to be outdone by Mr Dean, drank his whole glass of milk down without stopping.

"You're almost as fast as joey over there," joked Mr Biggs.

"But no vomiting, all right?" Mr Dean leant back in an exaggerated way, and Peter couldn't stop himself from giggling.

Angel passed out plates. "Not a very balanced meal, I'm afraid."

"What is it?"

"Birthday cake: lamington, chocolate fudge, and cream sponge."

Mr Dean wolfed down three pieces of cake, one from each layer. He seemed to have forgotten about the germs.

For a while, there was no sound except the cicadas outside chirping through the stillness.

Mr Biggs looked at his watch.

"Ten minutes to twelve, so it's still your birthday! Don't know what happened to the vet, though." Mr Biggs looked across at Peter. "You know, he's probably expecting to take that little one with him."

Peter stopped in mid chew, nearly choking. "No! I'm keeping her."

"Well, we can all visit her at the wildlife centre."

"No, she needs me!" Peter insisted.

"*Ughhh!* What's this?" Mr Dean spat something onto the plate. It was a candle stub.

"My wishing candle!" Peter said triumphantly. "And now I've finally got something to wish for."

For a few moments, nobody spoke.

Then, Angel said, "What about Matron and the no-pets rule?"

"We'll move into the secret cubby together."

"What about toilet training and night feeding?" added Mr Biggs.

Peter tried to think like a grown-up. "What about learning to take responsibility? I saved her life; now I have the responsibility to take care of her."

"But, perhaps, the wildlife centre will be better equipped to take care of her," offered Mr Biggs, glancing at Nonna, then looking at his watch again.

Peter could feel his bottom lip begin to quiver. He turned to Mr Dean for support.

"What? Don't look at me," said Mr Dean. "I'm a failed parent – my own kids and my ex-wife don't even speak to me."

"But you think I could do it, don't you?" Peter persisted.

"Yeah … of course you could. If you can catch her." He chuckled.

"Be serious!"

Mr Dean sighed loudly. "Of course you could. You're a brilliant kid. Best I've ever met."

Peter looked triumphantly over at Nonna.

"Of course, I haven't met that many kids," Mr Dean added devilishly.

"Well, let's see what the vet says about it, then." Nonna refilled the sherry glasses and raised her own high. "Cheers to all of us!"

Mr Biggs took a large gulp, then pulled out his notebook to survey the list. "We've managed everything on the priority action list, except the vet, who's supposed to be on his way."

Mr Dean, who was helping himself to a third glass of sherry, said, "Well done, Biggsie. You're a wasted resource!"

Peter looked to see if Mr Biggs was offended by being called a wasted resource, but he seemed quite pleased.

The grown-ups swallowed down another round of the sherry in little glasses, and Peter thought they seemed to like it better now.

Then, a tapping at the screen door made them all jump.

"Anyone in?"

Angel pulled open the screen door.

"Hi. I'm Andy the vet."

"Hi," said everyone, except Peter, who couldn't bear to think of the joey being taken away.

Mr Biggs got up to shake the vet's hand. "Thanks for coming at such a late hour."

"Sorry I took a bit longer than I promised." The vet looked very young, but he had big intelligent eyes and a dimply smile like Angel's. "Actually, I couldn't get away. The wildlife shelter's full of new arrivals from the bush fire."

"Well, come in and sit down," Angel whispered. "Your Flora's boy, aren't you? I used to know you when you were in rompers."

"You still are in rompers, aren't you?" put in Mr Dean.

"You do look young," observed Mrs Millet. "Are you sure you're a vet?"

For a moment, Andy seemed to study the lines of sealed pickle jars along the bench. "Actually, no – not quite. I just passed my first-year study and came back to start some practical training. They're so short staffed here. So, where is the little fella?"

Peter pointed towards the broom cranny, and the wallaby chose exactly that moment to poke out her slender snout.

Andy crept over closer to the joey. He was wearing a green hoody that said "Lend a Paw", and Peter noticed that his jacket was a little big for him too.

"How did you catch it and get it so calm?" Andy asked.

"Oh, it was nothing," Peter said proudly, while Mr Dean pretended to choke on a mouthful of sherry.

From his hoody pocket, Andy pulled a small harness attached to a lead and deftly attached it to the joey's torso.

"This'll help for now."

Andy sat next to Peter and opposite Mrs Millet. "You are now a new member of the Joey Insiders Club," said Mrs Millet, sipping her drink and cackling like a kookaburra.

Andy looked confused, and Peter saw him cast one eye towards the exit.

"The Matron here at Gum Tree has a no-animals rule, so we're the only ones who know about. ..." Mr Biggs explained, pointing theatrically with his cake fork towards the joey.

"Oh, I see." Andy sighed. "Actually, we have more than twenty motherless marsupials at the centre – echidnas, possums, kangaroos, wallaroos, wombats – most of them joeys, some of them premature and needing three and four hourly feeds."

"So, who feeds them?" Angel asked, shocked.

"Volunteers mostly, and a few full-time park staff."

"What will happen to them?"

"Some of them don't make it, some go back to the wild, but many end up living at the centre." He scratched through his frizzy mop of hair. "Your little fella's already quite big, so he could wean in a month or two, and then go straight back to the bush, join a small mob. ... Shouldn't be too difficult to find a group that'll take him in."

"But until then *she's* mine," interrupted Peter. "Right, Nonna?"

Nonna looked nervously round the table.

"You can't own an animal," Mr Biggs told Peter kindly. "She's part of nature."

"Well, she can own me, then," said Peter, satisfied. "I'll be her human."

"Well, if the centre's as full as you say it is. ..." Nonna was wavering.

Then, Mr Dean clinched it by clapping her firmly on the shoulder. "Good on you, Nonna! So, Operation Stealth Wallaby continues."

"Oh hooray," said Mrs Millet, and Peter decided she was quite a good sort after all.

"Wait!" Nonna cautioned. "Just until she weans onto solid food and gets back to the bush, then."

Andy nodded. "I've got some horse pellets in the van. Keep her on milk every four or five hours, for a month or so, then see if she'll start nibbling on the solids. What are you like at three in the morning?" he asked Peter.

"Well ... I've been sleeping quite a lot lately. ... So, maybe it's about time I woke up a bit."

Mr Dean stayed to help Nonna put Peter and the joey to bed in the secret cubby.

"You could hide in here too, Mr Dean," offered Peter. "I mean, from the police and the Belargo brothers – you know, while you're still looking for your asset."

"Thanks, mate, I'll keep it in mind," said Mr Dean. "My living standards are in free fall, but I'm still not quite ready to move into the back of a chimney."

When he was alone, Peter lay in the dark, thinking about how much his life had changed since yesterday. He'd made his first best friend, the joey, and his first enemy, Cleo Choat. Then, there was Mean Dean; he wasn't sure about him, somewhere in between – perhaps his first frenemy.

Out in the kitchen, Nonna sat far into the night, searching through her inner eye for the thing that was troubling her. Even with the arrival of the wallaby, there was still something else out there beyond the moat. Something she didn't like.

Clutching in pain at her hip, Nonna knew she didn't have long. If she couldn't be with Peter, she would wish at least for a better view of his journey ahead. The sight showed only a blurred image that shifted in and out of her inner view like a distant figure moving through rain. But it was rain that never came and a face that refused to let itself be recognised.

CHAPTER

15

Beyond the Moat

Peter woke to inky blackness and the sound of shuffling somewhere close. Was it the joey? He reached into the pouch, but the little body lay calm and still.

Peter's skin prickled with fear.

Through the darkness, he heard the sound of labouring breath. Could it be Mr Dean escaping the Belargo brothers? Or Cleo Choat come back to take him away? He felt around for the jacket light on his wrist. Dare he switch it on? Or, should he scream? But then, Matron might come and find the joey.

He snapped on the light.

It was the old man Tollen, with the long beard, standing above him and shielding his eyes from the glare.

"What are you doing?" Tollen asked accusingly.

"Well, what are *you* doing?" countered Peter.

"I forgot my candles," said the old man as his only offer of explanation.

Tollen planted himself on the edge of the narrow built-in bed.

"Are you in my dream again?" Peter asked.

"No," Tollen said testily. "This time, you're in my dream. It's easier that way."

Tollen looked around the narrow cubby, asking in disbelief, "Is this where they put you?"

"It's only temporary," Peter replied.

Tollen sniffed the air. "I smell vinegar mixed with wild beast."

"Pickles," explained Peter, shining the light on the joey.

Tollen reached in to pat the soft fur behind her ears.

"Pickles? That's a good name; did you choose it?"

"Um ... no. Well, actually, yes, that is a good name," Peter agreed, then added conversationally, "Is Rani here?"

"No! Rani knows my dreams are off limits. All the frogs know that."

Even so, the old man checked both his pockets, then looked up expectantly.

"But remind me, Peter, why I came."

"Um. ... Could it be about my protection?" Peter shrugged, then indicated the jacket. "I found it. Now I'll never take it off, even when I sleep."

"Good boy." Tollen nodded, satisfied. "But that's not why I came. It's to do with your quest."

"Well, I haven't found that yet," Peter said apologetically.

Tollen pointed his long bony finger at the GAIA spiral on Peter's top-left jacket pocket. "You'll find your quest in here."

"In my heart?"

"No ... well, yes, but also in your pocket."

"The jacket pockets are empty," Peter told him. "I checked all twelve of them."

"Check again," the old man said patiently.

Peter began fumbling in the top pocket. "There is something here."

Feeling a thin card wedged against the inside lining, Peter used his first two fingers to work it up and out into his hand, which he noticed had begun to shake. Maybe the card would hold an important message left there by Dad, just for him.

Peter was immediately disappointed to see that it was just a regular GAIA business card, printed on pulpy recycled paper – just like the ones his mother and father used to leave about the research cabin. Peter turned it over and read it aloud:

Spiral Hall
School for the Ecodemically Gifted

Agent Artiss Fleur
Adventure Mentor

Mailing Address: 5 Singlewood Lane, Central London, UK

"Spiral Hall," Peter said. "Do you think I could go there?"

When Tollen didn't reply, Peter glanced up, only to find the old man gone.

Peter frowned at the card, feeling a momentary glow of possibility. But then, he thought glumly, *I could never get into a school like that.*

When Peter opened his eyes again, he felt something wet and strong latched onto his finger.

"*Aaarrgghh!*" Jerking his finger free, he bolted up into a sitting position.

Nyitch-nyitch!

That was the joey's hunger cry. He remembered it from last night. Quick, milk!

The luminous hands of Peter's watch read: 3.15 a.m.

"Don't cry!" he told the joey. "I'm going to feed you."

Peter paused, trying to adjust his eyes to the darkness. "I just need to figure out where the exit is."

Peter directed the light expertly from his jacket cuff and then stumbled out to kitchen. The flagstone floor was cold beneath his bare feet. On the kitchen bench, Angel had left him two sterilised bottles. While Peter was waiting for the kettle to boil, he remembered another strange dream, something he should do, but his tired mind was blank.

He had an urge to check his jacket pockets again. He pulled out the business card of Agent Artiss Fleur. How had he missed this yesterday? Artiss Fleur must have been a friend of Dad's. Peter's gaze fell on the mailing address at the base of the card: 5 Singlewood Lane, Central London.

Peter wondered how Spiral Hall selected students. If he knew that Peter was up before sunrise, saving a baby wallaby, Agent Artiss Fleur would probably want him to start there straight away. But how would the school ever find him? Peter stared out across the empty lawn. Even Mr Dean, a world celebrity, had successfully managed to get lost here at Gum Tree.

A small wind blew up outside the window, unsettling a scattering of leaves.

Shoo-ster! Shoo-ster! it seemed to say.

The jacket hummed.

Then, the hunger cry came again: *nyitch-nyitch-nyi-i-i-i-i-i-itch!*

Back in the cubby, Peter angled the top of the baby-milk bottle straight into the joey's strong lips.

She spat it out.

Oh no, not this again! Peter kept pushing. This was a struggle he had to win, for the joey's sake.

Then, suddenly, she was pulling down the milk.

"You're a quick learner, Pickles," Peter said, praising her.

He then added, "By the way, Pickles is your new name."

Squirk, squirk! The joey seemed to like it too.

Peter flicked off the jacket light and lay back in the dark. Sometime towards the end of the second bottle, he and Pickles both released their hold, and for some hours, the cubby was quiet again.

Shuffle-shuffle! Mew-mew!

When Peter woke up the next time, the light of morning was leaking through the wall vents at floor level, and the birds were up and singing. His watch said 6.25 a.m.

Peter crept back to the kitchen to fix two more jumbo bottles of formula, plus a glass of milk for himself. After they'd both drunk everything, Peter had an idea.

"Come on, Pickles, I want to introduce you to a tree I know."

He clipped the lead that Andy had brought onto the joey's harness, then pulled the cord loosely at the top of his backpack and slung it over his shoulder, with Pickles inside the pouch.

"You're a heavy one," Peter whispered as he dragged open the door from the broom cupboard and stepped into the kitchen.

The joey didn't reply, but she didn't squirm either.

This is what you're used to: motion, thought Peter.

"If I started hopping, that'd be perfect for you," he said aloud.

Outside, the sky sat low and heavy. Peter wondered if it might finally rain.

"You would've never seen rain in your whole life," he told the joey.

When they got to the Great Gum, ash and soot still floated here and there through the air. Peter stared sadly down at the fresh grave.

"This is a magic tree," Peter whispered. "It'll watch over your mum."

They moved off towards the moat. Peter said, "I'm not allowed cross here, but we can walk around a bit on this side, if you like."

Tsk-tsk! Pickles seemed to agree.

Keeping Pickles on the lead, Peter helped her out of the pouch and onto the dry ground. The joey stood for a moment, sniffing the air, and then, with one sound tug, the lead slipped through Peter's hand. Peter reached for it, but it was too late; the joey was already bounding through the firepit and into the bush, without a backwards glance, leaving Peter to chase behind her.

The joey eventually stopped at a nearby clearing. Peter saw with relief that she even seemed to be waiting for him. Puffing and snatching up the lead, he was about to reprimand her when he saw that they'd arrived at the place where Mum's research cabin had been – before it burnt down.

"This is where I used to live," Peter said sadly.

The joey hopped towards some stone steps which led underground to the room Mum had once used as a science lab.

Peter found himself being pulled down inside by the curious joey.

Above them, a light breeze had broken up the cloud cover, and the morning sun now shone enough light into the underground space for them to see by. Not that there was much to see. The ceramic floors were crowded with autumn leaves, and the air smelt of dirt and stale smoke. Peter pulled open a soot-stained cupboard door that hung only by a hinge. In the cupboard, he found a broken glass beaker.

"When Mum worked here, all these shelves were full of science equipment and stuff," he told the joey.

On the orange brick wall closest to the stairs, there was faded gold writing. Peter remembered it: the periodic table of chemical elements. Ms Moth had been teaching it to him in science – metals on the left, and non-metals on the right.

Mum's table had been painted in gold, now blackened from the fire. Hydrogen, helium, lithium. ... He looked for the one element at the bottom middle of Mum's table, which was not on Ms Moth's table of elements. *C-h-r* was all that was visible; it was smudged with soot. He rubbed at the charred brick, revealing the rest of it: *Chrysalite.*

"That was Mum's own invention. It didn't belong on either of the sides of the table; it was something different, she told me," Peter said aloud, explaining it all to Pickles.

Without thinking, Peter crouched down to check the cavity behind the brick, where Mum had sometimes left playthings for him to use when she was working. He scraped away at the dust and soot at the edges of the brick, then pushed it firmly. The brick sprang out into his hands, just as he'd expected it would.

Keeping the joey's lead looped over the wrist of one arm, Peter used his other hand to feel around inside the open cavity, which would of course be empty, unless Mum had put something inside for him on the day of the fire. He groped around the space, finding nothing.

Then, suddenly, his heart beat faster as his fingers settled on something small, with sharp corners. He pulled the object carefully out into the light.

It was a tiny glass pyramid, the base of which fit neatly onto the palm of Peter's hand.

When he held it up to the light above the cellar steps, he saw a thin silver coil, like a GAIA spiral, bobbing and floating around inside the pyramid.

The silver coil seemed to pick up the light, and for a few moments, spiral reflections glistened around the cellar walls. Peter and Pickles both stood mesmerised, staring at the tiny silvery coil. Then, a shadow passed across the light. The wall images faded, and the coil straightened and sank lifelessly to the bottom of the pyramid, lying there like a dead worm.

Staring at it, Peter willed the coil to bounce up and start spinning again. But it didn't move. Suddenly, Peter had a feeling he was being watched. He raised his eyes to the top of the stairs, and in the same instant, the shadow passed. Had he seen someone there? He couldn't be sure. He heard a faint sound.

Click-clack, click-clack.

The joey stood frozen, staring up through moist brown eyes at the now-empty opening. She sniffed the air.

Peter sniffed too. Maybe he smelt perfume; he couldn't be sure.

The sun came out again. Peter pocketed the glass pyramid, but not before he saw that the silver spiral was up again and spinning fast now. *Run!* it seemed to be saying. Peter scooped the joey into the pouch. He knew another way out of here – through the back tunnel, to the stream.

Once they were in the open air, he ran as fast as he could through the bush, with the joey bouncing against his back. He didn't stop till he was back inside the moat.

Then, puffing for breath, he told Pickles, "That was close. From now on, I'm going to take really good care of you."

It was only then that he realised he had no real clue how to take care of an animal. He needed knowledge.

CHAPTER

16

The Prisoner

By the time Peter reached the big square library room, he felt recovered and full of purpose.

Over in the nature section, he found a whole shelf of books dedicated to the kangaroo family, including wallaroos and wallabies. Scanning across the titles, he found three books on wallabies. Two looked thick and serious, but Peter liked the third, which was thin, and had lots of pictures and hardly any writing. He liked the title too: *Whoa! We've Got a Wallaby.* The book was written by Teddy and Elma Sedgewick.

On the back cover, Peter read that the Sedgewicks were American, from Texas, but even so, they seemed to be quite experienced with wallabies. On the front cover picture, he counted seventeen wallabies sitting with the Sedgewicks on a big outdoor sofa.

Since Pickles was asleep, Peter pushed the pouch under the table and sat down to read. The book was easy to follow because the Sedgewicks had written it like one big conversation:

Ted Sedgewick: To clean your wallabies' ears, you can use a little disinfectant on cotton wool. Just ball it around gently with your finger. You don't need expensive pet grooming products for your wallabies – although Elma can't resist loading up with all kinds of shampoos and what have you from the pet store.

Elma Sedgewick: Well Ted is certainly one to talk after he bought those expensive squeaky toys that none of our wallabies ever took to. Wallabies like action games hide and seek and tag but they also like to be free within an open space.

Peter stared out the window, past the spinifex grass and across the fire moat, and shivered with fear at the thought of the big open space.

Ted Sedgewick: It's true wallabies need lots of open spaces to exercise in. Yo'all going to need to keep them out of your living rooms, off those sofas, and away from your breakables because they can be wreckers.

Elma Sedgewick: We repeat they can be wreckers!

Peter looked round the library now at the varnished Victorian chairs, with their curved polished wood and shiny cushions, and then he noticed all the glass objects and paintings.

"We'll have to get out of here before you wake up," he said to the backpack with the joey sleeping side.

Peter then quickly skimmed through the section on diet:

Ted Sedgewick: Yo'all don't want to be feeding your wallabies only pellets; give them fresh leafy greens to chew such as grape vines and romaine lettuce. You can also give raw sweet potato, carrots, grapes, apples and apple twigs to your wallaby.

Elma Sedgewick: But in general, go easy on sweet food items to prevent obesity. Ted needs to watch his sugar intake too. He's getting very soft around the middle. All that pouching flesh might work on a mother wallaby but we don't want to start looking too much like our pets now, do we?

Ted: Which is why every now and then I have to trim Elma's whiskers.

Elma: Oh Ted you're such a kidder! Thwack!

Peter giggled. He liked the Sedgewicks, but the food pictures were making him hungry enough to eat horse pellets. Time for breakfast. He stood up from the reading table and was just picking up the backpack when he heard the delighted cry of Ms Moth from the doorway.

"Peter! You're early!"

Peter tried to stop his face from falling.

"What commitment!" the Moth beamed at him. "First day back after the break, and here you are, looking fresh, sitting with your backpack and waiting for me. I was expecting you to be late and to have forgotten your books, etc. ..."

She waved the fingers on her small hand.

"Well, now that you mention it, I have forgotten my books," Peter managed to say. "I'd better go back and get them."

"Oh, no need, no need. I've prepared a lesson for you in advance."

Ms Moth sat down opposite him at the table. He was locked in. Reluctantly, Peter slid the bag back under his chair and pulled the cord tight. The Moth's eyes darted towards the wallaby book as Peter tried to slide it from view.

"Peter, wild animals do not belong in the home!" She arched her eyebrows sharply.

Please don't wake up! Peter silently willed the wild animal at his feet to stay asleep.

"Now, what I had in mind for today is the Greek classics." Ms Moth swept her pale arm around, indicating the floor-to-ceiling books. "I propose that we read as many as possible from this vast library before you leave."

Peter looked at his watch.

"Not today, silly! Before you go to London."

"But I'm not going to London," Peter said, correcting her.

"That's as it may be," she said in that annoying way grown-ups did when they thought they knew better.

"Now, have you heard of Plato?"

"Um … is it the same Plato who had prisoners in a cave?"

The Moth looked pleasantly surprised. "Ah, you mean Plato's cave allegory! Yes, very good. How did you hear of that?"

"The new resident, Mr Dean, told us yesterday that we were like those prisoners."

At the mention of Mr Dean, Ms Moth's face clouded into such a range of emotions that even Peter, who, like most eleven-year-old boys, was not attuned to the feelings of grown-ups, felt curiously shocked.

She quickly recovered herself. "Did you know that Plato wrote down a lot of clever conversations conducted by another ancient Greek man, called Socrates? Socrates was a very humble man; he considered himself to be very wise."

"Doesn't sound very humble," mumbled Peter.

"Ah, but let me finish. Do you know why he considered himself to be so wise?"

"No."

"Because he was able to admit that he knew nothing."

Peter gulped. He could sympathise. How could he have got himself caught with a stowaway joey and the one Gum Tree resident who was strictly against animals?

"Plato wrote down the conversations of Socrates, and people read them and learnt from them. They're called Socratic Dialogues."

"Well, it sounds a bit like Ted and Elma Sedgewick. They write about their wallabies in a dialogue."

"Well, yes," the Moth said grudgingly. "But perhaps not with quite the same literary prowess."

The Moth wrinkled her small nose at the wallaby book, then cast the Sedgewicks at arm's length across the table.

"Now, I hadn't been planning to take you through Plato's cave, but why not, since it's about fire."

"I don't like fire," said Peter sulkily.

"Well, not bush fires, symbolic fires. Fire as a source of wisdom, to be precise."

Peter yawned.

"I see that philosophy doesn't interest you."

"Philosophy? I do like philosophy. Is that what this is?

"Of course. *Philo,* 'lover of' *sophy.*"

"And who was Sophie?"

Ms Moth smiled patiently. "It's the Greek word for *wisdom.* A philosopher is a lover of wisdom."

"Now, the story begins in a cave where a group of prisoners have been chained up since birth, facing in only one direction and unable to move. Can you picture it?"

"A bit like the day room, I guess," said Peter, giggling.

The Moth sighed and pulled down a book called *Plato's Republic* from the shelf behind her.

"Now, behind the prisoners was a line of statues and objects."

"What kind?"

"Well, you know, human figurines – athletes and wise men in togas – a few Greek chariots, and the like. ..."

"What about trees?"

"All right. A nice olive tree, shall we say?"

"What about some animals?"

"All right, yes. A horse and a charioteer."

"And a wallaby."

"Yes, well, not very Greek." Ms Moth regarded him strangely. "But why not? Now, listen carefully, because here's where the fire comes into it. The fire's burning behind the line of statues, and its light is capturing shadow pictures of the objects, which the prisoners are able to look at on the wall in front of them."

"How?"

"Like a movie projector. Oh, and I forgot to say that there are also the jailers who sit behind the prisoners, moving the objects around and making little shows to amuse them. You know, so the prisoners won't complain too much."

Peter didn't say anything. His stomach whined with hunger. "When do they eat?"

"Well, it's not important to the philosophy lesson. But let's say they get three meals a day."

"Do they get fish and chips?"

"Let's say, on Fridays, they get a little fish, shall we?"

Peter nodded soberly.

"Now, these prisoners have never been able to turn around and have never been outside, so, of course, what do they think about these shadow images?"

Peter looked at her. "What?"

"You tell me," she said. "Think, Peter, think!"

"I suppose they think they're quite interesting," mumbled Peter.

"Ye-e-e-es." Ms Moth wanted more from him. "Those shadow reflections on the wall were all they'd ever seen in their whole lives, so what would they believe about them?"

"Um. ..." Peter swallowed a yawn and waited for the Moth to supply the answer.

"The prisoners thought the shadows were real, Peter. That was their only view of reality."

Tsk-tsk.

"What was that?"

Peter clutched his stomach.

"I forgot to have breakfast," said Peter, trying to keep the panic out of his voice.

The joey was awake and scrabbling about in her pouch.

"Maybe there's a snack in my backpack."

The joey was pushing at the drawstring. Peter leant down quickly to pull it tighter.

"Nope. No snacks here. ..."

The Moth sighed. "Let's finish the story."

Peter nodded. He needed a plan. *Think, Peter, think.*

"Now, one day, one of the prisoners figured out how to loosen his chains. Imagine, Peter! For the first time in his life, he is able to turn around. For the first time, he saw the actual statues: the tree, the person, the horse. ..."

"The wallaby."

"That's right, the wallaby!"

115

Tsk-tsk! added the joey.

"What was that?"

"Just trying to make a wallaby sound," Peter said. "You know, to make the story more authentic."

"*Tsk-tsk!*" Peter said. "*Nyi-i-i-i-itch! Chrrrkkkk!*"

"All right, well done. That's enough now. So, what does the man think?"

"He sees that the shadows are fake, and he thinks the statues are real. I get it. Wow, that was interesting," said Peter, rising to leave.

"Wait. Yes, you're right, but sit down. There's more."

Peter sank back into his seat.

"The prisoner without chains still has no idea that there's a world beyond the cave, with real people moving around."

And animals, thought, Peter swallowing nervously. He felt a brush of fur against his leg; the joey was also free.

"Then, the prisoner's eyes are drawn to a distant light, and even though it's harsh and bright and he is fearful of moving towards it, he feels he must."

"Before the guards come back and tie him up again," said Peter.

"Yes, quite right," agreed the Moth. "So, the prisoner staggers up the narrow tunnel, legs like jelly. He's almost blinded by his first glimpse of the light of the sun, and dazzled by the sight of real people."

Peter felt the warm breath of a real wallaby on his toes. He wondered if the Moth was wearing open sandals.

"In time, the prisoner learns to look up towards the sun, and to understand that the sun is the cause of everything that he sees around him. Do you understand any of this, Peter?"

"Yes, I think so."

Ms Moth continued, "How does the prisoner feel when he can finally walk around without chains?"

"Um … free?"

"Excellent!" The Moth slapped the polished wooden table with her small hand. "He feels free!"

The joey was also free, while Peter, unfortunately, remained a prisoner.

"So, what must the prisoner do now, with his freedom?"

"Um … go around and enjoy the nature?"

"Well … yes, but what must he also do?"

"I don't know."

"Peter, think of the others. He must also return to the cave. He must go back and teach the others. Many of them won't believe him. They'll call him a liar. They'll want to stay safe, with their own version of reality."

Peter looked at her with blank panic, silently willing the Moth not to turn round.

"Time for a break," she said. "Go on. When you get back, I would like your thoughts on fire as a metaphor for wisdom in your own journey into ed-ew-cation."

Peter realised he couldn't possibly leave with the wallaby roaming. He would have to find a way to distract the Moth, and quickly. He was surprised when an idea hit him immediately.

"Actually, I'm feeling a bit nervous about the fire. Could you read to me a little first?" he asked.

The Moth smiled and opened the book. "Here it is. Book VII, the Cave Allegory."

"Perfect," said Peter. Now, the Moth would have her eyes on the book, and he could have his eyes on the joey. And with any luck. …

The library faced east, and the morning light was flooding in. Even with the old-fashioned ceiling fans turning the air, it was getting warm.

The Moth began to read in an animated voice.

Peter leant over the table, pointing to the book. "Sorry, not that bit, this bit."

"The appendix?"

"Yes, and then maybe this bit."

"The acknowledgements? Are you sure?"

"Yes, they'll make me calm," Peter assured her, settling back.

The Moth shrugged, then, squinting at the smaller text, began to read slowly and carefully through the notes. "The cave allegory is Plato's most profound message to the student of philosophy who yearns to break free of the bonds of traditional education and surrender himself to true nature."

She paused. "Note 2."

Her words were coming out like small sighs now.

It won't be long now, Peter thought.

Halfway through Note 5, the Moth's speech began to slur. Her head nodded, then slumped forward.

Peter snatched up the joey and made his escape.

CHAPTER

17

Insomnia and Sightings

For a few weeks, life went on at Gum Tree, with no more unexpected arrivals. Cleo Choat didn't return, and Mr Dean continued his search for an asset. Pickles the wallaby also learnt to use a litter toilet, and Peter got better at the three o'clock wake-ups.

He would give Pickles some milk, then watch her hop around a little till she fell back to sleep. But the late-night play times gradually got longer and longer, and Peter got more and more tired. Then, one night, Pickles just refused to go back to sleep at all.

"It's not fair," Peter whined. "I gave you all those games of tag and let you jump on my tummy, and now you still won't go to sleep!"

The joey twitched her ears, with no sign of remorse, and although she allowed Peter to push her, snout first, back into her pouch, as soon as Peter flicked off the light, she was out again, making *bumpity-bump* sounds around the cubby.

"Quiet! Stop it!" Peter sat up, mad. "I have to go to school tomorrow. All you have to do is lounge around in your pouch, with the Wallaby Insiders."

Pickles turned and looked at him with her moist brown eyes.

"Sorry, that was mean. It's not your fault."

Of course she wanted to get out of the narrow room and explore more widely. Still, Peter knew he had to be firm.

"No!"

Tut-tut insisted the joey, and kept scratching.

Peter turned the light back on and checked his watch. It was nearly four in the morning. This must be how parents felt when naughty kids wouldn't go to bed.

"Right. I'm going to sleep, and you can make your own arrangements!"

Peter made a show of sighing and turning his back on the wallaby, to show disapproval. He even put an extra pillow over his exposed ear. Then, he was almost asleep again when the *thump-thump* started up. It sounded like Pickles was body slamming the cupboard door, but Peter couldn't pull himself awake.

Then, there was silence – the wrong kind of silence.

Peter was suddenly wide awake and bolting out of the narrow bed.

Don't panic, Peter told himself as he hurried off along the south corridor.

Halfway down, he caught sight of the joey plodding along like an old resident on crutches, leaning over on her small paws, then pulling her body forward in her wallaby way.

Peter was relieved to see her and didn't want to make any sudden moves.

Pickles paused and sniffed at each doorway until she got to the room belonging to the Trelawney sisters. She raised her front paws up towards the door handle.

"Oh no, you don't." Peter crept on tiptoes towards her.

But before he reached her, the door opened.

"What's this, Cora, a visitor?" Pickles hopped right into the room, and the door closed.

Peter stepped up to listen at the door, wondering what to do next. He was alarmed by the sound of fracturing glass.

"Oh, the photos!" wailed one of the sisters.

"There goes Harold."

"And your Elwood. ..."

"Oh dear, watch the tail! There goes Cyril on our wedding day!"

Peter knew he had to knock on the door and take responsibility. But, for now, he stood frozen, imagining all those frames containing the Trelawney sisters' dead husbands smashed to the floor. He thought of Elma Sedgewick's words in the book: "they can be wreckers."

When the room was finally silent, Peter arranged his face into a picture of utmost regret, and knocked.

Edna Trelawney, in a cotton nightdress, opened the door.

"Peter Blue?"

"I'm sorry about the wreckage." Peter tried not to look at her purplish scaly legs.

"That's all right, Peter. We've decided we're going to be pleased about it. You can choose your reactions to things, you know."

Peter gaped at her. "Oh, okay. Well, I'm sorry we woke you up."

"You didn't. We're always awake at this time. Cora's an insomniac."

Edna opened the door wider, and Peter saw Pickles up on the bed. She had tucked herself into Cora's cotton robe, as if it were a guest tent.

"Oh look, Cora's asleep," said Edna.

"Well done," she told Pickles. "Shall we see you back here tomorrow at about the same time?"

After that, every night at three o'clock, Peter and Pickles called on the Trelawneys, who would wait with milk and biscuits.

"We've been holding on to the past," Edna explained to Peter.

It was one night after Cora had fallen asleep with Pickles in her lap. Peter wondered if he'd been doing the same with his past.

Then, the night came when Edna opened the door only a crack to them, holding a finger to her lips.

"Cora hasn't woken; she's still asleep. It's a miracle, Peter! The joey's cured her."

Peter nodded, wondering if they'd still be invited in for milk and biscuits. He took a hopeful step towards the door.

But Edna only smiled brightly at him and said, "It's time to move on, Peter."

Walking back down the corridor, Peter wasn't sure what to do next. Cora Trelawney was cured of her insomnia, but Pickles was not. As they passed Ms Moth's door, Peter heard a strange sound from within. Was the Moth crying?

The joey pricked her ears like a night nurse listening for symptoms.

121

"Oh no, you don't!" Peter gave her harness a swift tug.

Out in the courtyard, Peter saw the red glow of Mr Biggs's pipe and heard the familiar coughing noises.

"You're up late, Mr Biggs."

"Good chance to smoke in peace without Matron reminding me about the health risks."

Peter nodded and yawned. "The joey can't sleep."

"Oh dear. I think we warned you she was nocturnal."

"The Sedgewicks say you can train a wallaby to observe more-sociable hours."

Mr Biggs affected a small cough to remind Peter that Americans couldn't be expected to know anything about marsupials.

"The Trelawneys are calling Pickles a miracle worker," Peter said conversationally. "They say she's cured Cora's insomnia."

"Is that right? Well, that reminds me, the wallaby's also cured Mrs Worthington Smith-Jones. She became an insider today while you were at school."

"Wow! Wasn't she shocked?"

"When she first saw Pickles, yes; she almost fainted. But by the end of the day, we couldn't keep her away. She says the joey's cured her longing for England."

"Oh," said Peter, who'd personally never felt any such longing.

Mr Biggs put down his newspaper and glanced around. "Where is Pickles, by the way?"

Peter, in his tiredness, had let the lead slip from his fingers, allowing the joey to wander off. He hurried off to scour the courtyard, while Mr Biggs went off in the opposite direction.

Squinting through the darkness, Peter thought he heard a faint sound coming from the shadows.

Click-clack, click-clack.

The sound reminded him of something he didn't like.

Cleo Choat? But then he decided she wouldn't come back in the middle of the night.

Peter sniffed the air. Was that a slight smell of perfume or just the memory of it?

Click-clack, click-clack.

"Mr Biggs …!" Peter called in a quivering voice.

"What's up, Peter?"

"Do you hear something or smell something?"

The wind blew up. *Shooster-shooster!*

Then, Pickles was beside him, and the dark shadowy feeling seemed to pass.

"It was nothing, Mr Biggs!" Peter called out again. "I found Pickles."

At three o'clock the next night, Peter found Mr Biggs back at the same table, this time, without his pipe.

"Mrs Weakes became an insider today," Mr Biggs told Peter. "The Trelawneys told her Pickles would cure her many illnesses."

"But Nonna says Mrs Weakes makes up her illnesses, then writes them in her blue book to make them real. So how can Pickles cure made-up illnesses?"

Mr Biggs rattled his newspaper and chuckled. For once, he didn't cough.

"Why aren't you smoking?"

"All my pipes are missing. I can't understand it."

They sat in a friendly silence, Mr Biggs reading, and the joey watchful.

The wind blew up around them, rattling the newspaper.

Shooster-shooster!

Peter's eye caught some words on the back page of the newspaper. It looked like "Blue Vitamin Cordial". He leant in closer, not because he was interested in vitamins but because the letters seemed to have started reshuffling themselves across the page.

Leaning his nose in until it almost touched the page, Peter squinted at the headline as it dissolved into new words: "Dear Peter Blue, you are cordially invited to Spiral Hall."

That was the school on Artiss Fleur's business card. Peter rubbed at his eyes. The gentle breeze was circling the table now.

I'm seeing things, thought Peter. *My name can't be in the paper.*

But, still, he strained to keep reading as more words tumbled into new sequences across the page: "the autumn intake". More words started reforming themselves: "School for the ecodemically gifted".

123

His invitation!

"Mr Biggs!" Peter gasped. "Either I'm very tired, or I think I'm finally figuring out how to read between the lines."

Mr Biggs chuckled absently. "Wind's picking up, isn't it?"

The wind rippled the paper gently, almost as if guiding the text across the back page: "Initiates must assemble at the GAIA Hub by five o'clock in the afternoon on the day of the autumn equinox. Latecomers not accepted. Please find—"

The invitation text suddenly stopped.

"Please find what?" Peter whispered aloud.

The paper drew itself inwards like a sharp intake of breath that sucked the invitation text into one inky puddle of typeset mess at the centre of the page.

Then, with a sudden show of force, the paper spat the inky mess back across the page to form just one large and boldly printed word. It was a word Peter didn't know; but, for some reason, it terrified him. The word was *Anthrogs*.

When Peter came around, he was lying on the kitchen table, with Mr Biggs and Pickles peering over him.

"You must have fainted," said Mr Biggs.

Mr Witherspoon was at the other end of the table, sitting in front of a large pickle jar.

"Something to eat?" he asked them.

"Not now!" Mr Biggs replied gruffly.

"I saw something on your newspaper!" Peter gasped, holding his head in his hands. "It was so ugly!"

"*Shh, shh.*" Mr Biggs put his big arm round Peter's shoulders. "You've been hallucinating. Do you know what that means?"

"Um ... that I've gone crazy?"

"No!" Mr Biggs laughed. "It means that you need to change your sleep schedule. The milk's not enough for the joey anymore. She needs to get onto solids, and you need to get some sleep."

Pickles hopped up onto the table as Mr Witherspoon cracked open one of Angel's big jars of pickles.

"But feeding her solids means sending her back to the bush."

Mr Biggs didn't reply.

Peter knew he was being selfish.

"Okay," Peter said with a sigh. "I'll start the weaning tomorrow, but the Sedgewicks say in their book that it could take some time."

"Oh, I don't know," said Mr Biggs, pointing towards the end of the table.

The wallaby was crouched next to Mr Witherspoon, crunching down a pickled cucumber chunk. Pickles was eating pickles!

"Something to eat?" Mr Witherspoon said joyfully.

18

The Gum Tree Remembers

Peter found Mr Dean on the south veranda, scrolling through his lists of assets.

"Have you found anything?"

"No, and I'd settle for someone's old kitchen sink at this stage – just need enough capital to sink my teeth back into the market for a day or two."

"Pickles started on solids last night," Peter told him. "She ate pickles."

Mr Dean didn't look up.

"You're not even listening," Peter said sulkily.

"I heard you!" grumbled Mr Dean, still not looking up. "The little wriggler ate those appetite-killing cucumbers. I'd have thought just the smell of them would be enough to send her hopping back into the wild."

"Don't joke about that," Peter said glumly. "Mr Biggs said the vet's already been going around with the rangers, looking for a wallaby pod. But they haven't found one yet."

"Well that's good, right?"

"Ye-e-e-es ... except Mr Biggs said that the Jarra Jarra bush without wallabies is unthinkable and we have to save the forest."

"Well, I have to focus on saving myself right now," said Mr Dean dismissively. "The Belargo brothers gave my broker a visit, and they're on their way to Australia."

Peter didn't know what to say.

"We could fit a foldaway bed into the secret cubby with me," he said eventually.

"Thanks. I'll keep that in mind."

Mr Dean went back to scrolling impatiently down the lists of assets on his screen.

"What makes you so sure you even have an asset?"

"Gut feeling," Mr Dean mumbled.

Peter glanced down at Mr Dean's stomach, now covered with a red-striped business shirt.

"Can you trust that gut?"

"Always worked in the old days when I made my first big investments."

"Well, can I help?"

"Yes," he said, handing the laptop to Peter. "Put these assets in order for me: alphabetically, by country."

Peter settled into the task.

Tsk-tsk! The joey was in the backpack, getting impatient for her walk.

When Peter was done with his task, he said, "Wanna come for a walk with us, Mr Dean?"

"Nah, thanks. I don't do walks."

"Go on! Just to the Great Gum Tree and back."

"Oh Geez, Peter, don't make me!"

"It's not me; it's the tree," Peter was surprised to hear himself say. "It's the Great Gum that wants you to come."

Somehow the look on Peter's face must have had an effect on Mr Dean, who slid his device into its case and stood up reluctantly.

"All right, all right. Just to the jarrah tree and back."

As they made their way to the foot of the Great Gum, Mr Dean took frequent stops to stare back at the house, then off towards the tree again. He seemed confused by what he was seeing.

At the tree, Peter showed Mr Dean the space where the great scoop of tree was missing from the trunk.

"See this big hollow?"

"Yeah." Mr Dean ran his hand inside it.

"It used to be lower down, and I could climb right in it. Now it's too high. Could you lift me up?"

Mr Dean gave him a leg up.

"Pickles wants to get in too."

Tsk-tsk!

Mr Dean gave a fake sigh of exasperation as he picked up the joey and placed her into the hollow, next to Peter.

"See that branch, the really strong one up there?" said Mr Dean.

Peter craned his neck upwards. "Yeah."

"When I was a boy, I used to swing on a branch just like that on a tree just like this."

"Well," said Peter, "if it was a tree like this, then it must have been this one, because Mr Biggs said there haven't been any other jarrah gums around these parts for at least a hundred years."

Mr Dean considered this. "Come to think of it … you know, it could've been this one."

"The Gum Tree Rest Home was named after this tree," said Peter.

Mr Dean turned to stare back at the distant building.

"Gum Tree Manor," he said, interrupting his own reverie. "How could I have forgotten? I haven't actually stood back and looked at the property from this angle since I came here. I can see it clearly now."

"What?"

"Gum Tree Manor, home of my Great-Aunt Letty." He turned to the Great Gum, running his hands across the smooth broad trunk. "I know this tree. My sisters and I used to come here as kids. But it was all bush back then."

Mr Dean stared back across at the residence. "It's those ugly additions on both sides that make the house so unrecognisable. The old wing, there, was once just a line of stables. I'm talking about seventy years ago, mate. I would've been about your age or thereabouts. … We used to visit Great-Aunty Letty quite often. Then, one day, we had to stop coming."

"Why?"

"Oh Geez! It's all coming back to me now; it was those dang Devonshire scones."

Peter had been trying to imagine Mean Dean as a boy with sisters, swinging under the Great Gum, but it was too much of a stretch.

"So, what was wrong with the scones?"

"Nothing wrong with the scones; I always enjoy a good Devonshire scone. Problem was, my mother and my aunt had a falling out over them."

"Wait. What's a Devonshire scone?"

"You've never had a Devonshire scone?"

Peter shrugged.

"Clotted cream with berry jam on an airy light scone, best served with creamy tea." Mr Dean, who was still staring fixedly at the house, licked his lips.

"But how can anyone argue about a scone?"

"Easy! Aunt Letty was originally from Cornwall."

"So?"

"So, Cornish people always put their clotted cream on first, followed by the jam. In Devonshire, they do it the other way."

"So?"

"Well, Mum's family was originally from Devonshire, so, of course, she insisted on jam first. One day, Great-Aunt Letty must have asserted her heritage by putting a bit of cream on first. I just remember they argued about it so much that Mum didn't ever speak to her again."

Peter could see where Mr Dean must have got his bad temper from.

"I remember I wasn't happy about it either."

"Why, because you didn't like your cream on first?"

"No, because I didn't get to go on her swing anymore!" Mr Dean patted the smooth flank of the Great Gum. "Look at you! You've grown, haven't you?"

Peter was astounded to see Mean Dean suddenly talking to a tree.

"Then, Great-Aunt Letty died," he continued.

"So, after she died, did you come back and play on the swing?" asked Peter.

"Nah. Well, I didn't care about swings by then. I was grown up and living in Hong Kong. ... Then, this place became a government residence."

"The Gum Tree Rest Home for the Old and Infirm," said Peter.

"Speak for yourself!" Mr Dean told him.

They both laughed.

Tsk-tsk!

Then, Mr Dean looked thoughtful. "Wonder how the house did end up in government hands? Come to think of it, my mum should've inherited it."

"Ask the tree!" Peter found himself saying.

"The tree doesn't know. It's not a property barrister."

Immediately, Peter's vision began to swim. The trunk was becoming soapy and wavy.

"Quiet! I think the tree's showing me something from its memory."

"What? Oh, don't go bush on me, Peter!"

"*Shh!* I see a very old lady writing something at a desk. She's got this type of old-fashioned ink pen."

Peter watched the pen sliding across the paper. He could see her clearly as she paused and took a sip from her teacup. It was as if Peter were in the room with her.

"You're barking mad like everyone else in this place," said Mr Dean.

"*Shh!*"

"Well, who is she then? Is it Mum? Is it Great-Aunt Letty?"

"How would I know? I've never taken a message from a tree before."

"Well, what's she writing?" Mr Dean asked impatiently.

Peter sensed the tree must be showing this for a reason. He strained to look at the letters on the page, but from where he stood, they just blurred across it.

The old lady paused to take a bite from a scone.

"Actually," said Peter, "I think it is Great-Aunt Letty."

"Just tell me what she's writing."

Peter trained his sight over the old lady's shoulder and watched the ink sliding across the top of the page.

"Gum Tree Manor."

"I just told you that's what it was called. You're making this up."

"*Shh!* I'm just telling you what I'm seeing."

"Who's she writing to, then?"

"Dear. ..." Peter squinted into the space between his eyes where the vision was coming from. "Premier ... something ... in fifty years. ..."

"She's writing to the government about the house?" Mr Dean was now giving Peter his full attention. "Fifty years? Interesting ... what else?"

"Wait."

The old lady was taking another bite of her scone.

Peter laughed, then felt his vision being pulled away.

"It was Great-Aunt Letty," said Peter.

"How do you know?"

"Cream on her chin and jam on her nose. Cornish, right?"

Mr Dean laughed out loud. "Well, say hello to the old dingbat from me, then."

"She's gone," said Peter. "Oh, wait ... no, she's still here, in this tree. She wants to say something to you!"

"What?" Mr Dean asked nervously.

"I'm not sure. I've never done voices." Peter strained, then giggled. "I think she's saying ... you're an ass."

Mr Dean's jaw dropped. "The cheeky old so-and-so. ..."

Then, something seemed to hit Mean Dean, and his eyes widened.

"What is it, Mr Dean?"

"Not *ass,* although I am one, *asset!* My asset! You and this goddamned tree have found me my asset!"

"You mean Gum Tree Manor?! But it belongs to the government."

"I just bet that Great-Aunt Letty leased the house to the government for fifty years, just to make sure my mum couldn't inherit it. Extraordinary!" he said. "I was about thirty when Letty died, and I'm eighty now so. ... Sorry, mate, I gotta go."

A smile filled Mr Dean's face, and then, suddenly he was running towards the house.

"Hey, wait! Get us down from here!" Peter called, but Mr Dean was already out of hearing, his red-striped shirt flapping out behind him as he jogged like a schoolboy back through the spinifex grass.

Watching him go, Peter felt suddenly empty. He was hungry too and wished he could eat some cream-and-jam scones.

That night, Peter couldn't sleep. Mr Dean had left with the taxi driver who'd become a shareholder in his company. The residence felt empty. Soon Pickles would be gone too. It was only a matter of days before one of the wildlife rangers would find her a pod. He thought of Spiral Hall and the strange invitation, then he thought of Cleo Choat.

Click-clack, click-clack.

Would he be gone soon too?

CHAPTER

19

The New Dusk

The Anthrog Overlord stared out at the London skyline. A dark storm was blowing and battering at the glass of his floor-to-ceiling windows.

He turned to the sharp-featured Drone, dressed in black, who stood a few steps behind him.

"Well?" he said with a calmness that belied his impatience.

The Drone looked up sharply from her triangular handheld device.

"It's happening!"

"Tell me more."

The Drone twisted her lips into a half-smile.

"The human separation index is finally tipping in our favour."

"Meaning?"

"Meaning ... that I've done it!" She clenched her pale fist. "Meaning that I've cracked the Chrysalite!"

The Overlord took a few steps towards her.

"You've done it, then, where all others failed?" He was shorter than she, and his slate-grey eyes stood level with her neck. "But how?"

"Well, I can hardly believe it myself!" The Drone, who rarely expressed any emotion resembling human joy, smiled again in a way that accentuated her sharp jaw.

"The Chrysalite beings have been so impossible to detect because they're so sickeningly goody-goody. For example, they've never once attacked our Anthrog greed seekers in the field; they just work away undercover, healing the world just as quickly as our forces work to tear it apart."

The Overlord's eyes narrowed. "So, how did you finally get to them?"

"Well, it was ingenious really. If I didn't hate GAIA so much, I'd congratulate them." She adjusted her thick-rimmed square glasses on her jutting nose. "The Anthrog foragers uncovered a circular pit of Chrysalite activity that had been put there as a location-based protection." She hesitated, then continued. "It was for someone very important to GAIA. He breached his own protection, and it was luck really. I was right there, and the Chrysalite sample that was I was able to catch was so concentrated and so rich that I was finally able to breach its intelligences."

Her sharp smile morphed into a smirk.

The Overlord clapped his small pudgy hands.

"Then let the Chrysalite annihilation begin."

"I'm going to begin incubating a new hybrid crop of killer warriors today, but it will take some weeks before they will be born."

The Overlord could feel saliva gathering at the corners of his plump lips.

"Then our siege on the human race will finally start to gain strength!" He raised a defiant arm, straining the seams of his custom-made suit. "And this once-great Earth star will become just another Anthrog colony, sunk into its final days of dusk!"

The Overlord moved his tongue over his plump lips. "And all that power sucked out of it, all for me!"

"Don't you mean all for us?" The sharp-featured Drone gripped a warning hand in the bend of the Overlord's elbow.

"That's right," he whispered. "Power, all for us."

The Drone's slanting white cheek felt cold when the Overlord reached up to kiss it, but he knew the back of her neck would be warm.

"And now, my clever one, we can begin preparations for the final vanquish; prepare to let the Anthrog dusk fall."

"With me as your new leading Drone," she added testily.

"Your good work will not go unrewarded." He touched a stubby finger to her long crimped black hair. "Now, thanks to you, nothing and no one stands in my way!"

The Overlord leant his face up to the back of the Drone's neck, but she angled herself deftly from his reach.

"And yet, there is still one possible—"

His slanting eyes flashed warningly. "Tell me!"

"This so-called Sleeping King may yet bring us trouble."

"But ...?"

She glanced sideways to avoid his look. "It was not as we thought. ... The boy still lives. The circle of Chrysalite protection I spoke of ... was for him."

"And ...?"

The Drone snickered meanly. "Trust me when I tell you he's no threat to us yet. Or, at least, the legacy of light GAIA spoke of so highly at his birth must be buried deep."

"How so?"

"The boy I saw was stamped with the same hopeless, sleepy indifference that marks most of humankind."

The Overlord laughed greedily. His appetite was impairing his ability to think.

"Still, we must eliminate all possible risk. You must bring him in ... but without inviting the scrutiny of GAIA. We don't want them all over us yet." He rubbed his chubby hands together. "I'm saving GAIA for last."

The Drone nodded.

"Now, enough talking," the Overlord ordered. "Stand still, and show me your neck."

BOOK IV

The Metamorphosis

The Spirit of Earth

Peter staggered into the pantry and stood there, shovelling handfuls of dry cornflakes into his mouth.

Mum must have felt like this when I was a baby, he thought. *Although she might have eaten more politely.*

"You're looking very thin," Nonna said worriedly when she saw him. "Take off that big jacket so that I can see you properly."

"No! Why?" The jacket had become such a part of him that Peter never really took it off.

Nonna tugged open the flaps. "Peter, your ribs! We're going over to Angel's cottage right now to get her sewing machine, so we can resize this jacket."

When they got there, Nonna said, "Look! He's all skin and bones."

Angel gasped and held out a basket of scones. "Here, eat one quickly."

"Ah … no thanks." Peter was too tired to chew through one of Angel's hard scones.

But Angel held fast with the scones until Peter was forced to bite into one. Surprisingly, his teeth sliced into it easily.

"Delicious!" Peter gasped. "But how …?"

Angel gave a half-smile, with just one dimple showing. "Mr Dean baked them. Came in late last night, with some story about his boyhood."

"Do you have cream and jam?" Peter asked while he loaded up his plate with Mr Dean's light-as-air scones.

He ate standing up, while Nonna cut from the middle of the jacket, using some big sewing scissors.

"I going to leave enough material for you to grow into, but the rest has to go."

Pickles stood underfoot, letting the strips of excess material land on her back.

"Looks like she wants her own jacket," said Angel, stooping to pick up the scraps of fabric.

"What's this?" interrupted Nonna. "I hope I haven't cut into something I shouldn't have."

"It's another pocket," Peter observed. "So that makes thirteen pockets, not twelve."

"There's a piece of paper inside. It looks like Thelma's writing."

"A letter from Mum!" Peter's eyes widened. "Let me see!"

He was immediately disappointed to see that it was just an old shopping list, made out for lollies:

> chocolate
> licorice straps
> jelly beans
> salted peanuts
> cream do-nuts

"Yum!" If Peter hadn't been so full of scones, the list would've made him hungry.

"It's funny, though." Nonna stared at the list. "Your mum didn't buy sweets very often."

"Maybe she was planning a party for me," suggested Peter.

Nonna shrugged and slid the list back into the hidden pocket. Peter just felt glad to have something else of Mum's to keep with the photo frame and the funny glass pyramid with the floating spiral. Everything else had been lost in the fire.

While Nonna was fixing the jacket, Angel made Peter take a long bath, then she put him to bed in her spare room. On the wall at the head of the bed, Peter noticed a painting made of dot art that looked just like the GAIA spiral.

"It's a water hole," Angel explained. "For my people, the spiral means water."

Suddenly, Peter felt thirsty. Angel held a glass of cool water to his lips. He could feel his eyes closing. Then, Angel was creeping from the room.

Outside, a flock of cockatoo passed overhead in a confusion of wing flapping. Peter felt safe in Angel's bed, but he missed the jacket. For a while, he was aware of himself falling in and out of shallow sleeps. It was as if he'd forgotten how to nap. But then, he must have slept for many hours, because when he woke again, the room was filled with the slanting light of late afternoon.

Angel's house was silent, but Peter felt he wasn't alone. A little way from the bed, hanging neatly over a wooden chair, he saw the altered jacket. It did look smaller, but there was something strange about the chair, which was becoming stretched and deformed. Peter sat up in alarm. The back of the chair was morphing upwards through the jacket neck and outwards through the sleeves, and the legs were lengthening, as if the chair itself was trying to stand up.

Peter rubbed his eyes, and when he looked again, a wispy human form with skin the colour of pale varnished wood stood in front of him. The figure was a man dressed in a jacket that was much too small for him. He looked familiar. Peter suddenly was staring into the eyes of his father.

He was so shocked that, instead of saying the word *Dad,* he whispered, "Byron? Byron Blue?"

Dad was smiling and looking pointedly at the sleeves of the GAIA jacket, which stopped at his elbows, while the hem rose high above his waist.

"Sorry about the jacket," Peter told him. "Nonna and Angel wanted to be able to see my ribs."

Dad's own ribs began to shake soundlessly. For a minute, they were both laughing.

Then, Dad seemed to find his voice.

"I thought you were never going to take it off. I've been trying to get through." He wheezed thinly.

Before Peter could answer, Dad was pointing at the open window. Peter looked out and was surprised to see Dad now standing below him on the lawn.

Without hesitating, Peter jumped out onto the yellow springy grass. It should have been an easy jump, but he landed clumsily and felt his teeth jar against his jaw. *It's a sign that this is not a dream,* he told himself.

Peter chased behind Dad across the fire moat and all the way to the clearing near where they used to live. Peter ran to hug him. He wanted to squeeze him tightly, but Dad's body was all wispy and see-through.

"Where are you, Dad?"

Dad was wriggling out of the jacket and helping Peter into it.

"A perfect fit." Dad wheezed and started fiddling with the dome fastener at the back of the collar.

It made Peter's neck feel warm and his scalp prickle.

"What are you doing?"

"I'm calibrating," Dad told him. "Think of a password; any word with a special meaning for you, and only you."

Peter said, "That's easy—"

"*Shh!* Don't say it out loud." Dad looked about, as if to check that they were really alone. Then, he whispered "All right, let's try it. First, clear your thoughts; then, slowly float your word across your mind."

Peter shut his eyes tightly and did as he was told.

"Good. Now, hold the word there strongly for at least three seconds – longer if you can."

Peter did as he was told.

"I didn't think you liked them." Dad chuckled.

"Not the cucumbers," said Peter. "My new best friend."

Dad smiled a twinkly smile.

Peter could see the black of his hair now and the dark brown of his eyes.

Dad pointed to the button in the centre front, with the pelican etched on it.

"That's the power centre of the jacket," he explained. "You could even call it the soul."

Peter nodded.

"Okay, ready?"

"For what?"

"Fuse!" Dad commanded.

Peter yelped in surprise as a whoosh of air sucked the jacket in hard against his skin, then released.

"You're connected now." Dad sounded pleased. "Come on, let's practise. Try to power off using the password!"

"Pickles?"

"Not out loud, in your head. Using your intent, think the password, then say the word *release*."

Keeping his finger on the pelican dome, Peter let the word *pickles* float through his head, and then he said, "Release."

But nothing happened.

"Keep still," said Dad, "and give the command decisively."

Peter tried again, letting the word explode from his throat.

"Release!"

It worked! Peter felt the jacket around him letting go like the last air coming from a balloon.

"Good! You've mastered it," Dad praised him. "This is your working jacket now."

"But it's your jacket. How can it work for me?" asked Peter.

"Because we've got similar DNA," Dad explained.

"I don't get it."

"Because you're my son, we can share the same gene jacket. Get it?"

"Oh. ..." Peter smiled. "I didn't know ghosts could make such good jokes."

Dad's face clouded. "Except this is not a joke; this is your jacket now, and your journey. It may be that, one day, many will depend on you."

Peter wanted to protest, but Dad was pointing his semi-transparent finger at the GAIA spiral on Peter's top left pocket.

"No matter what anyone else tries to tell you, Artiss Fleur is someone you can trust with your life."

Peter nodded.

"Now, I need you to find Artiss Fleur and deliver him a message from me."

"Dad I'm only eleven," Peter whined. "I can't just go off and find Artiss Fleur! I'm not a big adventurer like you."

"I'm afraid it's mission critical."

"Da-a-a-a-ad!" Peter whined again.

"I'm sorry, son, you're my last hope."

"Okay." Peter sighed worriedly. "Tell me, then."

"The message is: 'Never capitulate!' Repeat it back to me."

"Never capitulate?" Peter repeated uncertainly.

"Artiss Fleur will know what it means. Be sure you're alone when you give the message to him, and only him. No one else at GAIA will do."

Peter nodded solemnly.

Dad laid a wispy hand on Peter's shoulder. "But I must warn you that there are dangers. This jacket is a powerful tool for good, but where power resides, evil must inevitably be drawn."

"What kind of evil?"

Dad hesitated, glancing one more time around the bush clearing.

"You'll know this evil by its stench. Once you smell it, you'll never get it from your memory." Dad groaned. "Just talking about it brings an etheric infusion of it into my field."

Peter thought of Cleo Choat. "I think I know that smell. But what is it?"

"It's something not of this world but strong enough to bring it down."

Byron Blue's image was starting to fade.

"Wait, Dad, don't go!"

"I'm still here," he said, "but it feels like I can't stay much longer."

"Where will you go? I mean, where is death?"

Dad stared hard at Peter.

"I really don't know," he said finally. "I've been spending a lot of time underground."

Peter winced and hung his head.

"But the spirits of earth have been good to me," he added. "Come on, they want to show you something."

Dad picked up a stick and drew a large spiral in the sand.

"Now that you're a ghost, you can draw perfect circles," Peter told him encouragingly.

Dad smiled and pointed at the circle. "See!"

Peter knelt down to look into the spiral but could only see dry yellow dust. "See what?"

Almost imperceptibly, the dust began a slow circular shift, gathering speed, spiralling, until the ground had taken on a watery blue colour.

Peter dipped his hand in it. "How did you do that?"

"See!" Dad's own image was wilting now.

Staring back down into the spiralling water, Peter didn't know what he was supposed to be seeing.

"See what?" he whined again.

"See! See!" Dad repeated.

"I can't see anything!" Peter snapped defiantly. "I can't see weird stuff like you can!"

He waited for a reaction, but any whining just seemed to wash right over Dad now that he was dead.

"Look from a place just behind your eyes," Dad told him.

Peter tried again. The spiralling water began to harden into a new form that looked like a big spiral of wood. It was a table that filled a big circle-shaped hall. Floating above it, Peter saw children sitting at the table in a spiral formation. They were having some kind of meeting. Every seat in the spiral was taken except the one in the very centre.

A girl looked up and saw Peter. Then, all the children were pointing and looking up at him.

"See! See!" they shouted.

Why did he have to keep seeing?

Peter floated up beyond the dome ceiling.

Not see, but *sea!*

The hall with the spiral table was on an island surrounded by sea. The sea was rising into a giant wave that was about to engulf the island. Peter hovered over the sand, wondering what to do. He hovered too close and was pulled from the sky by the rising wave, then carried forward. The wave was crashing. ...

"Wake up!"

With a thud, Peter hit the sand.

Mr Biggs was standing over him. "What are you doing all the way out here, Peter?"

Peter sat up and looked around the empty clearing. He saw the etched spiral in the sand; it wasn't a dream. Something landed on his chest. It was Pickles, wearing a new blue vest.

"Look at you!"

Tsk-tsk!

The vest was fastened at the waist with one silver dome, the traveller. Peter squeezed her into such a tight hug that the wallaby began to make *chrrkkk-chrrkkk* noises.

Then, Mr Biggs gave him some bad news.

"Nonna took a turn while you were sleeping," he said grimly. "According to Matron, it's only for tests, but I'm afraid an ambulance came, and Nonna's been taken to hospital."

CHAPTER

21

The Return of Mr Dean

eter found Mr Dean in the parking lot, getting out of a taxi.

"Thanks, partner," he told the driver who had a share in his company.

"What happened to you?" Mr Dean asked Peter. "Been taking a dust bath?"

Matron stepped sharply from the shadows.

"What's this I hear about you owning Gum Tree?" she asked

"It's true," said Mr Dean. "All thanks to Peter the Great here."

Matron's mouth was set in a disapproving line.

"Please see me in my office tomorrow." She turned on her heel and was gone.

Mr Dean sighed. "Now that I've finally got my asset, looks like I've got a long night ahead in the markets."

Peter suddenly brightened. "I've finally reset the password on my jacket, so the GAIA Wi-Fi should work now."

"Oh, you beauty!" Mr Dean began pulling off Peter's GAIA jacket before the boy could change his mind. "So, what's the password?"

"Um. ..." Peter looked around the car park.

"Something to do with vinegar-soaked snacks?" Mr Dean whispered.

Peter nodded.

"Okay, mate, you'll get the jacket straight back in the morning."

The next morning, Peter was up early, pouring horse pellets into a bowl for Pickles, when Matron intercepted him.

"You're looking a bit pale and peaky this morning, aren't you?"

Peter swung round in surprise.

"I don't know. I haven't had time to look in the mirror yet."

Matron's eyes, keen and alert, held Peter's tired ones in their grip. "You also didn't have a chance to read the label on that bag, because they're definitely not cornflakes."

"Horse pellets. Oh!" Peter laughed unnaturally loudly. "Well, I'm hungry as a horse!"

Matron looked at him suspiciously. Peter wondered if she knew something. There were a lot more Wallaby Insiders now.

"Strange," continued Matron, "horses haven't been kept at Gum Tree for some years now."

There was a scratching noise nearby, Pickles in the cupboard, impatient for her breakfast. Peter wondered if Matron could hear it too. Using his shoes against the flagstone floor, he began making shuffling and scraping noises of his own, in a way that he knew Matron found disturbing.

"Now, I wasn't born yesterday, Peter Blue—" She pulled open the door to the pantry and began looking up and down.

Peter's heart almost stopped. Next, she would look in the broom cupboard.

"But I know this," Matron said.

Here it comes. Peter braced himself, heart racing.

"I know," she repeated sternly, "that you ... have not been eating enough."

She paused to look back into the pantry.

Peter gasped.

She bent down, her sharp eyes searching the pantry corners. "I also know that Angel's cuisine is not always to your taste. But you're a growing boy, and you need your strength."

Peter was shaking with relief.

"Ah, here it is!" Matron pulled out a large black jar, and then she got to work at the bench, with some butter and a loaf of bread.

Behind her, Peter sank down at the table, feeling droopy with exhaustion.

"What's the matter?" Matron handed him a brown paper bag. "Don't you like Vegemite sandwiches?"

"Yes, yes. I love them! Thank you, Matron."

"Good! Now follow me!"

Matron clamped a guiding arm on one of Peter's shoulders and led him at a brisk walk towards the front door.

"I'm taking you to the hospital for a visit; the taxi's waiting."

"But I. ..." Peter paused in mid breath.

"What? Speak, child."

"I'm not allowed to cross the moat."

"Well, there's a first time for everything," said Matron.

Peter felt his face redden at the memory of the trip to the research cabin, all those weeks ago. His first breakout.

"Besides," added Matron, "Nonna wants you to start venturing out a bit more. Just in case ... well, you know."

Peter did know, but he couldn't think about it now. He needed to find one of the Wallaby Insiders to go and feed Pickles, then take her out. But he didn't want to make Matron suspicious.

Think, Peter, think. Of course, he would need his jacket.

"I'll just quickly go and get my jacket from Mr Dean."

Peter found Mr Dean jogging in small circles round the bed, punching the air. He was wearing his necktie wrapped round his head and carrying a green bottle.

"Hey, Duke of Wellie! Guess what? I'm back! I'm back!"

"I know. I saw you last night."

"No, I mean I'm back from the abyss. ... I'm back in business, as in rich, rich, rich."

"So, you're a millionaire again? Already?"

"Yep, one asset; that was all it took. Been up all night. I couldn't have done it without this jacket – what a powerhouse of high-speed connections! How can I ever thank you?"

"You can thank me by taking care of Pickles until I get back. She needs her breakfast urgently."

"Sure, hand her over."

"I don't have her. She's in the cubby."

Peter saw that Mr Dean's attention was edging back to his laptop. "It's urgent! She's waiting for breakfast."

"What's in the bag?" Mr Dean asked hungrily.

"Vegemite sandwiches."

"Yuck! Better give me one anyway."

Peter handed over a sandwich, and Mr Dean bit into it hungrily. He then drank from the green bottle.

"Champagne toast!" he said to Peter. "The market's been a running bull all night; haven't been to bed yet. I'm buying up Wall Street and taking profits all over town."

"Mr Dean," Peter hissed. "Pickles needs you."

"Okay. I'm on it!" Mr Dean did one more dance around the bedroom.

"Thanks," said Peter. "Oh, and Mr Dean?"

"Yes, Peter."

"You might want to lose the tie when you go over to the main building."

Mr Dean yanked the tie off his head.

"Not that I really care what those geezers think of me," he said with a faint sneer, adding something that left Peter feeling surprisingly raw. "If all goes well, I'll be out of this place by tomorrow!"

22

The Moth's Transformation

Two hours later, Peter arrived back at Gum Tree to find Mr Dean's room empty. The secret cubby was empty too, but Peter was pleased to see that both the pouch and the joey were gone. Maybe Mr Dean had taken Pickles out walking.

Peter ducked his head into the day room. It was empty too. Strange, even Mrs Weakes and Pop Olsen and the stick insects were gone. Mr Biggs was not in his room, and the whole south corridor was eerily quiet. Where was everyone?

Well at least one person would be in: Ms Moth, who never went outside. Her door was slightly ajar, and Peter was about to knock when he saw through the crack that she was asleep in a half-sitting position on her reclining sofa.

There was something strange about her. Ms Moth's hair, which she usually pulled tightly back in a bun, was free and moving up and down like flowing water around her shoulders. Even more strangely, the Moth was smiling in her sleep.

Peter craned his neck round the doorjamb to try to see what was making her hair move. He was so shocked by what he saw that he almost stopped breathing.

There was the Moth, the only resident scared of animals, lying blissfully back on her recliner, and behind her, balancing her big bouncers on a tower of books, was Pickles. She was using her tiny paws to massage slow circles through Ms Moth's scalp.

Peter backed soundlessly away. He felt a flash of fear, followed by anger at Mr Dean. Where was that selfish man? Peter knew he'd have to find someone to help quickly, because neither gravity nor time was on his side.

Outside, beyond the lawn, one head, then another, bobbed up from the spinifex grass. There were people out there, pacing like ghosts, with their eyes to the ground. As he got closer, Peter heard little whispering voices around him, calling, "Pickles! Here, Pickles!"

It was a search party.

Even Mrs Weakes was walking among them.

"You can walk?" he asked her.

"Well, only in emergencies," she said shamefacedly.

Mr Dean was coming towards Peter now, with his shirt untucked and his red braces trailing at his knees.

"I lost my concentration, just for a moment. I'm so sorry," he mumbled, desperately gripping both of Peter's arms.

Peter wriggled free of Mr Dean's grip, even though part of him wanted to stay.

"But I'm going to put this right," continued Mr Dean. "I'm going to find her."

The crowd of insiders, who'd gathered to watch, all murmured their support.

Even the stick insects frozen in the grass were nodding their heads, and Peter felt some of his anger melting.

"It's all right," muttered Peter. "I know where she is."

After the sighs of relief subsided, Peter added, "But it's not good!"

"Where is she?" said Mr Dean.

"She's with my teacher, Ms Moth, who hates animals. She'll turn Pickles into Matron, for sure."

"Take me to her!" Mr Dean said bravely.

"She hates you even more," said Peter.

Mr Dean looked mildly shocked by this, then quickly shrugged it off. "Let's go!"

"But, why don't we hear her screaming?" asked Mrs Millet.

"Because she's asleep."

Mr Dean's eyes widened with hope. "Then, we're still in with a chance."

A wave of chatter broke out.

"That wallaby cured Cora's insomnia," said Edna Trelawny.

"Never slept better," said Cora.

"*Shh,* everyone," Mr Dean told the crowd. "Operation Stealth Wallaby has reached a critical and dangerous juncture. Peter and I are going in!"

Mr Dean then added unnecessarily, "Everything before this was just a rehearsal."

When they reached the Moth's door, Peter pulled Mr Dean back by the arm.

"I forgot to say, I think you're going to be very surprised by what you see in there."

Peter was right; Mr Dean was very taken aback by the scene of Pickles, the massage therapist with the twirling paws; and Ms Moth, with her blissful smile and long grey cascading hair.

"Well, well," whispered Mr Dean finally. "If it isn't the Sleeping Beauty."

Mr Dean stood motionless, gaping at her, until Peter was forced to tug on his sleeve.

"Quick!" Peter hissed. "It's all about to blow!"

"Oh right – too much champagne, Devlin."

Mr Dean looked at the name on her door, Hester Moth, then back at the woman on the bed. He then trained his bloodshot eyes on Peter.

"All right, here's the plan," Mr Dean whispered. "Now, as you can see, if anyone so much as breathes on that wallaby, all those books she's on are going to come crashing down. So, I'm just going to plunge right in."

"Good idea, and snatch her up."

"Who Hester Moth?"

"No, Pickles, you dingbat! Then, pass her out to me, and I'll make a run for it."

"Okay, got it. And you'll leave me to mop up?"

"Yes."

"She's got a lovely mop actually," said Mr Dean, staring wistfully at the Moth's long hair.

At first, everything went as planned. Just as the loud clapping sound of books cascading and hitting the floor began, Mr Dean was completing a well-executed wallaby pass into Peter's waiting arms at the door. This was all followed by high-octave squealing from the Moth.

With a surprised Pickles safely clenched to his chest, Peter couldn't resist staying on to listen from the hallway. The screaming within stopped unexpectedly quickly, and the room fell silent. Keeping a tight hold on the wallaby's harness, Peter peeped back through the crack in the door to see that Mr Dean was now massaging Hester Moth's head.

"It's all right. There, there." His voice was low and soft.

The Moth sounded confused but not angry.

"What are you ... doing in here?" she managed.

"Ah well. You were waving your arms, knocking over all these books. I thought you might've been having a bad dream."

"Oh no, it was a lovely dream." She sat up and looked around. "I dreamt ... oh my hair."

"Yes, beautiful, isn't it? I couldn't help noticing ... you should always wear it out."

Peter thought Mr Dean might be overdoing his promise to put everything right, but at least Pickles wasn't getting busted. Then, Peter nearly fell forward into the room when he heard the Moth say, "You don't even remember me do you ... Devlin?"

"Ah ...?" There was a note of alarm in Mr Dean's voice.

The Moth sighed. "You walked past me at school, year after year, and never looked at me or talked to me."

"At Jarra Jarra High?" His voice sounded croaky.

"Yes. Sixty-five years ago."

There was silence. Then, Peter was stunned by what Mr Dean said next.

"I bet you were a great beauty then too."

"Don't flatter me," she replied sternly. "It's much too late for that. You didn't notice me or talk to me ever at school, and then, all these years later, you arrive here and do the same."

"I can't understand why I didn't see you, Hester."

"Well it's too late now," Ms Moth told him firmly.

Peter peeped once more round the doorjamb and saw the Moth still in her sleeping beauty position, with Mr Dean down on one knee, moving his mouth like a prince who'd forgotten his lines.

Then, suddenly, he gave a loud laugh and found his voice. "Well, I've noticed you now, and I still don't want to talk to you."

Mr Dean plunged in for a kiss on Ms Moth's lips.

More books tumbled, and Peter and Pickles headed for the exits.

Ha ha ha!

Tchk-tchk-tchk!

Later that afternoon, Peter and Pickles were overtaken on the bush path by Mr Dean, who was hurrying in the direction of town. He looked like he still hadn't slept.

"Thanks for covering for Pickles. That was a close one," Peter said.

"The pleasure was all mine!" Mr Dean clapped Peter on the back, then scooped up Pickles, thrusting her against the clear blue of the sky.

"What a catch!" Mr Dean chuckled, and it occurred to Peter that he wasn't talking about Pickles.

"So, are you really leaving tomorrow?" Peter asked.

"Oh, that? Don't think you're going to get rid of me that easily. Anyway, I'm rolling in money again, and I've got some important shopping to do."

"Do you really love money, Mr Dean?"

He paused and looked at Peter.

"Do I love money? Do I love money?" Mr Dean shouted the question back to himself, then stared down at Peter, as if he were really seeing him for the first time. "You're a pretty unusual kid. Did you know that?"

"Um. ..." Peter didn't know what to say.

"I love what money can buy," Mr Dean said. "In this case, something very important."

"What's that?"

"An engagement ring, of course."

"Oh, that was quick."

"Well, when two people are eighty, there's no sense waiting around."

23

The Table Talks

eter found Angel and Mrs Millet at the kitchen table.

"Mr Dean's rich again, and he's had quite a bit of champagne," Peter told them. "And he was kissing with Ms Moth – on the lips."

Peter rolled his eyes in a grown-up way.

"Oh dear," said Angel. "I hope it wasn't the champagne talking."

"Not talking. I told you, they were kissing."

Mrs Millet sipped her tea silently. Peter guessed she was jealous.

"If only Nonna were here to read my tea leaves," Mrs Millet said ruefully.

"But Nonna lost the sight, five years ago, during the fire." Peter reminded her.

Mrs Millet leant her face close to Peter's.

"Maybe you could read them, Peter. You might have inherited the gift of sight from your nonna." She held out her empty teacup. "Have a look at the leaves. Do you see a man?"

Peter waited for Angel to protest, but, surprisingly, she said, "Go on, Peter, try."

Feeling a bit silly, Peter looked down at Mrs Millet's sludgy wet tea leaves. He tried to pick out some patterns but saw nothing except the dregs of a cup of tea.

"Don't look with your eyes," Angel told him gently.

Peter tried to find the place behind his eyes in the centre of his forehead that Dad had shown him. It was the same place that the Great Gum had reached into. Straight away, he felt his vision blur, then bore down through the bottom of the teacup and into the wood of the table. Then, he was inside the table. It was as if he were moving through the layers of wood, which vibrated and spun, opening up memory to him. A vision began to take shape. He was in a kitchen, it looked like this kitchen, and there was a man cooking at the stove. Peter could only see his back. He was a big man, but not Mr Biggs or Mr Dean; he had a tattoo on his upper arm. The tattoo flashed up and down as the man pumped a wooden spoon through a large mixing bowl. Mrs Millet was waiting behind him, in her pink dress, looking happier than Peter had ever seen her.

The image began to float and fade. Peter raised his head and was back in real time.

"That was weird," he told them.

"Did you see a man for me?" Mrs Millet pressed.

"Yes," said Peter.

She gasped and clapped her hands together joyfully. "Tell me everything, you brilliant, lovely boy!"

"Vera." Angel raised her hand gently. "Don't push him."

"Well," Peter hesitated, immediately beginning to doubt what had just happened. "Well, I was standing in this kitchen … and … the man I saw was cooking something."

Don't describe what you saw, the table seemed to say. *Just give your interpretation.*

Peter was about to tell the table that he had no interpretation to offer, when the words just came out of him, without him having to think: "Mrs Millet will one day eat many good meals at Gum Tree that she doesn't have to cook herself."

"Oh!" Mrs Millet clasped her hands together, unsure. "Mr Dean, then?"

It had not been Mr Dean, but Peter suddenly knew that he had said all he was supposed to say.

Mrs Millet's face wore a hopeful frown, while Angel's face had creased into a huffy one.

"My meals aren't so bad, are they?"

At that moment, Mr Biggs came in and saved them both from having to reply.

"I've just been to see the ranger, who tells me there are still no wallaby mobs to be found anywhere in the Jarra Jarra forest."

Mr Biggs looked glum, but Peter was glad.

"It's not that I'd like to see Pickles go, Peter," Mr Biggs added. "It's just the sorry state of the forests around here without wallabies that upsets me. And all my pipes are missing. I can't even smoke."

"Why don't we just plant more trees, then?" said Peter.

"Because tree planting on the scale we'd need costs millions of dollars!"

The kitchen door opened, and Pickles hopped in, followed by Mr Dean, who was looking even unhappier than Mr Biggs.

"Well, look who it is, the new owner of Gum Tree," said Angel sarcastically. "What are you planning to do with it?"

"Oh, it's all sorted. I'm going to arrange for another fifty-year lease to the government."

"Well," Mr Biggs said moodily, "it's the least you can do, after using our home as leverage to make your new fortune."

"Leverage?" Peter grimaced at Mr Dean. "I know what leverage is. We could have got locked out by the bank."

Tut-tut. Pickles clearly agreed.

"Oh, cut it out, will you! I knew I could pull it off. The market's my game."

"Our home is not a game," Mr Biggs said quietly.

"Whatever," Mean Dean mumbled. "Anyway, you win, because now all that money's going to ruin everything."

Mr Dean hung his head sadly.

"Why?"

"The problem, my dear Duke of Wellie, is that I've just been visiting my fiancée, and it seems there's been a misunderstanding."

"You mean, Hester Moth doesn't want to marry you after all?" Mrs Millet asked hopefully.

"Yes and no," he said in a brooding voice. "Hester wants to marry me, but she's under the misconception that I'm still bone poor."

"But won't she be happy when she hears you've got your millions back?" said Mrs Millet dreamily.

"Not a chance," growled Mr Dean.

Peter nodded understandingly; the Moth had always been an enemy of greed with a capital G.

"She told me this morning that she'd only been able to truly love me without the money." Mr Dean groaned and tugged at his hair. "She thinks we're going to live here in poverty together."

"You won't do that, of course," said Mrs Millet.

"Of course I will! I'll live under a cabbage leaf with her if she asks me."

For a while, nobody spoke.

Mr Dean looked pleadingly round the table.

"So, what am I going to do? I don't know what to do!" he groaned. "And I always know what to do."

Watching Mr Dean's hollow-eyed stare made Peter wish he could help.

Think, Peter, think! He was surprised when he was hit almost immediately by a big idea.

"I do have an idea, Mr Dean. It's a good idea," Peter added, "but you're not going to like it."

CHAPTER

24

The Scoop

"You must be joking! What planet are you on?" barked Mr Dean, once he and Peter were alone outside.

"What? It's a good idea," said Peter. "Planting trees costs millions, you know!"

"Yes, but to give away *all* my money!"

"That's right; I've even made a checklist of priorities on a piece of paper. I could only find four, even though I know you usually have five."

Priorities

1. Buy the whole Jarra Jarra forest, and protect it from fire.
2. Buy one million new trees, and start a replanting project.
3. Give your big house on the hill to the wildlife centre. The animals need space.
4. Start a homeless joey-sitting club for the residents, to keep them healthy.

"Look, Peter, these are all good ideas. In fact, I could even get the wrinklies out on fire watch, as well as planting duty," he added, "to save on costs."

161

"The trees agree," said Peter. "They say to make that priority number five."

Mr Dean rolled his eyes. "But good idea or not, it still won't help me with Hester!"

"Why not?" Peter tried not to show his disappointment.

"Because, even if I give all my money away today, I know I'll keep making more tomorrow. I've got some very big market positions out there now, made a few million bucks last night on the New York Stock Exchange while I was sleeping. It's in my nature. So, there'll always be more money coming in."

Peter frowned. "But Ms Moth doesn't have a problem with money; she has a problem with greed. If you get more money, you can save more forests, and more animals will get homes. That's not greed; that's helping!"

Tsk-tsk!

Pickles hopped behind Mr Dean, nuzzling her snout into the space behind his kneecaps.

"Oh, look at you two," joked Mr Dean. "You're nothing but a pair of hustlers."

His voice rose in disbelief, but Peter could tell he was coming around.

"Let's drive in your Bentley over to the wildlife centre, and tell Andy the good news," Peter said excitedly.

"Wait! I need to give this some more thought!" Mr Dean protested. But Pickles was already nudging him forward.

"When you're already eighty," said Peter, dragging him off by the sleeve, "there's no sense waiting around."

"Hey, don't steal my lines!"

"All right." Peter tried another approach, gushing, "Ms Moth will be so proud of you."

Mr Dean's eyes gleamed. "You really think so?"

"Of course," Peter told him, "because you'll be relevant."

Later, when Mr Biggs entered the day room, his bad mood had worsened. He slumped heavily into his armchair, next to Peter and Mr

Dean, sitting on Nonna's paisley sofa. Peter was still trying to persuade Mr Dean to donate his new fortune.

"I've just been down to the *Jarra Jarra Enquirer* to pitch my story idea," Mr Biggs told them, "but they said no."

"What story?" said Mr Dean.

"Is it a story about Pickles?" asked Peter.

"Yes, as a matter of fact. It's called 'The Last Wallaby of Jarra Jarra', but it's not going to happen," Mr Biggs continued grimly, "because they say nature news doesn't sell."

"We'll, they're right," interrupted Mr Dean. He held up a hand as if to shield himself from their irritated looks. "So, let's give 'em some news that'll really sell!"

Mr Dean winked at Mr Biggs, who raised his eyebrows questioningly. "How are we going to do that?"

Mr Dean clapped his hands, causing the stick insects on the sofa by the wall to flinch. "We'll give them a scoop. It'll be a scoop so big, they'll have the world's top media houses beating a path to their door. And that's saying a lot for a newspaper in a one-horse town like Jarra Jarra!"

Mr Dean looked around thoughtfully. "We could even do the press conference here – invite some business leaders, bankers, dignitaries, environmentalists – and fill the house."

"What's a scoop?" asked Peter, feeling left out.

"A scoop," explained Mr Dean, "is a piece of big exciting news, like a secret, that all the news groups want to get their hands on, but that you offer exclusively to just one. In this case, Biggsie will offer it to the *Enquirer,* in return for a big feature article."

Mr Biggs, shrugged his shoulders and looked helplessly at Peter.

"We don't have anything exciting here to report," said Peter.

"Ahem," said Mr Dean, smiling like the cat who just ate the ice cream. "Who among us is still missing in action, then? Police in some countries are still looking for my body. And who among us is preparing to donate all his money to help save the local forests and wildlife?"

Mr Biggs had water in his eyes. "Is that what we're going to be giving them?"

"You got it!" said Mr Dean, a little bit of water standing up in his eyes too. "Anything for Peter Blue."

"It'll be the biggest scoop they've ever had down there," confirmed Mr Biggs.

"*Ooh!* Are we having ice cream?" asked one of the Trelawney sisters from their two-seater by the phone, which they'd recently managed to reclaim.

"That's right," confirmed Mr Dean, "with chocolate sprinkles and cherries on top – the works."

"Thank you!" said Mr Biggs, really seeming to mean it.

"Wait!" Peter gasped. "What about the Belargo brothers?"

Mr Dean whipped his head round behind him fearfully, then folded his arms, pretending indifference. "I'll get my broker to invite them. He's on his way down here. We can settle our accounts."

"But … they want to kill you," whispered Peter.

"In that case, let's invite the mayor of Jarra Jarra, who's not very fond of me either, and the president of the Jarra Jarra Bank. They'd both have a go at me, given half a chance."

After that, everything began to happen quickly. It was agreed that the Enquirer would break the story in the early morning edition on the day of Mr. Dean's wedding party. And the press conference would be held the following day. Mr Biggs got to work planning an invitation list of newswires and the big newspapers, television companies, environmental columnists, and nature bloggers.

"I think, I'm even going to invite GOWD," he told Peter and Mr Dean.

"Invite God?" said Mean Dean. "This is going to be even bigger news than I thought."

"No, GOWD, the Global Organisation for Weather Disasters."

Mr Biggs was wearing a Lend-a-Paw hoody from the wildlife centre, and Peter noticed it was a good fit.

CHAPTER

25

Matron's Mystery

Peter knocked timidly on the door of Matron's office, noticing the sign on the entrance wall that he knew all too well:

By order:
Animals not permitted
on these premises.

The door opened.

"Did you want to see me?" Peter asked nervously.

Matron arched her eyebrows questioningly, but her mouth and jaw stayed set.

"Yes, Peter. It seems your secret's out."

Peter took a sharp breath in, but Matron seemed unworried.

"Take a seat."

She began consulting a blue folder on her desk, flicking through the pages until she found one page tightly packed with pencil-written notes.

"Now, tell me, Peter, do you remember on which date this wallaby rescue of yours took place?"

"Um. ..." Peter was shocked by the calmness of Matron's response. "Yes, it was on my birthday, actually."

Matron glanced at her wall calendar. "And since then, how many of the residents have become privy to the animal's presence here?"

"Um … all of them have met her, if that's what you mean."

"Hmm." Matron nodded and scribbled something in the blue folder. "Do you know what I have here in this book, Peter?"

"No." Peter shook his head.

"It's a full record of the state of health of all the residents of Gum Tree." Matron's mouth seemed to twitch at the corners, not into a full smile, just an upwards hitch of her lips that lasted for the same time it would take to blink. "Well, thank you, Peter."

Matron stood up, as if to signal that the consultation was over.

Peter stood up quickly as well.

"Um … thank you for what?" he asked her.

"Thank you for clearing up the mystery."

Peter wasn't sure what mystery she was talking about, but he had one of his own to clear up.

"Matron, aren't you mad at me?"

"Nonsense, Peter. I'm quite the opposite."

"But what about the strict no-animals rule? The wallaby – Pickles, that is – has been hiding away in a place not far from that sign outside your door."

"Oh that?" Matron said with a wave of her hand. "That sign was hung there some years ago by one of the residents, but I'm personally quite open-minded towards pets."

Peter didn't believe what he was hearing. "But Pickles is a wild animal!"

Now Matron's face broke into a real smile. One of the few Peter had ever seen her display. "Well, perhaps you'll need to be punished after all."

Peter's face fell.

"I was pulling your leg, Peter." She laughed in a way that was not at all matronly, and, for a moment, she looked like a young girl. "I want you to know that I thoroughly approve of this 'Pickles' of yours."

"But you haven't even met her," Peter said lamely.

"I don't have to. Look at these statistics." Matron ran her finger down some columns of numbers in her folder. "These indicate the medications dispensed to patients since the time of the rescue – record-low volumes and dosages. Vital signs in all patients have shown a marked improvement in recent months: high blood pressure is down, low blood pressure is up, breathing disorders normalised, heart conditions stabilised, and all indicators for wellness are beyond miraculous."

Peter nodded. "So, what was the mystery?"

"Well, you see, Peter," Matron said as she turned a page, "I plotted the information on this calendar chart, and the point of inflexion came right on the arrival day of that impossible Devlin Dean."

She cleared her throat. "I couldn't imagine such a correlation. If anything, my own blood pressure has gone up since Mr Dean's arrival."

Peter giggled.

Matron's hand was on the door handle now.

"Um … Matron?" Peter steeled himself to ask the next question. "Who did hang the sign up out there?"

Matron paused. "It belongs to your teacher, Ms Hester Moth, whose fear of animals is so pronounced that I have felt compelled to let it stay there."

"Well, I think you can take it down, then," said Peter, "because the joey's cured Ms Moth too!"

The Second Sight

N onna LaRosa wasn't expected home from hospital for two days, which was why, that evening, everyone was shocked to hear the sound of an ambulance siren making a high-speed approach to the Gum Tree front door.

Nonna threw open the ambulance back doors and stumbled over to Peter in the parking lot.

The ambulance driver made hurried apologies to Matron.

"Peter!" cried Nonna. "I'm so glad you're still safe. The sight's come back, and I know you're not safe here. You have to leave Gum Tree at once."

"What do you mean?"

"She's hysterical," the ambulance driver told Matron.

"Peter, she's coming!"

Peter's heart thudded with fear.

"Come now, what's all this?" said Matron soothingly. She led Nonna to the sofa on the north veranda, with Peter, Mr Biggs, and Pickles following close behind.

"The sight's come back! It happened this afternoon, in one of those scanner things. A beam of light hit me, and the visions opened up again." Nonna clutched the sides of her head. "Oh, but then, what I saw was terrible!"

"Keep a close eye on her," Matron whispered to Mr Biggs, "while I go and prepare a sedative."

Nonna turned to Peter. "I called Gorrman and Surla from the hospital, and they're ready to take you in. You'll have to start packing tonight."

"But … you said that they didn't want me. …"

"They want you, all right; can't wait for you to get there."

"How come?"

"Well, I had a secret that I knew would change their minds. It was too easy, really."

"What secret?"

"Never mind. You'll find out soon enough."

Nonna stood up shakily, then sat down again. "And to think I almost let you go with that woman! Thankfully, I got the sight back just in time."

"Not quite, Grandma," a sinister voice called from the shadows.

A bad smell seeped through the air around them.

Click-clack. Click-clack. Psshht! Psshht!

Peter grabbed Pickles and jumped behind the sofa. He knew that voice and that smell: Cleo Choat. From his hiding place, Peter studied the shadowed silhouette of her slanting forehead and large protruding nose. Even though he feared her, he couldn't help thinking what an unfortunately large nose she had for someone who smelt so badly.

Nonna called out into the darkness. "I know all about you now. You took my sight five years ago. You put a hex on me."

"It wasn't a hex!" Cleo Choat called back tauntingly. "It was pure science!"

"*Pah!*" Nonna spat. "There's nothing pure about your science."

Cleo Choat stepped out of the shadows and aimed a grey triangular device at Nonna.

"Well, here comes another blast now!"

A flash fired through the air. Nonna screamed. In that instant, the joey sprang up, airborne, flying in front of Nonna to intercept the hit.

"Pickles!"

The joey collapsed to the ground.

Peter pulled her back into hiding and felt her pulse. Thankfully, she was still breathing.

Tssshk! Tssshk!

"Leave here now!" Nonna screamed.

"That's right. Do as she says!" Mr Biggs hollered into the gathering dusk. "And don't ever come near this property again!"

"I'm not leaving without the boy!" Cleo screeched. "He's mine, and I've got the adoption papers to prove it!"

Peter crouched lower behind the sofa.

"Leave now!" Nonna repeated.

There was silence.

Then, Cleo Choat cackled. "If that's the way you want to play it, fine. Try this!"

Click-clack, click-clack!

A very bad smell began to spread like ether through the shrubbery and over the veranda. It got worse very quickly. It was an unimaginably powerful stench.

Mr Biggs and Nonna began coughing into the sofa cushions, while Peter, fighting for breath, pulled the GAIA jacket over his head to shield himself and Pickles from the worst of it. Just as his senses began to slip away, he heard howls of rage coming from Cleo Choat. The air immediately began to clear.

Peter peeped up over the sofa. By the light of the veranda, he saw Cleo Choat staggering fearfully towards Nonna's ambulance. Behind her, wearing a surgical mask and clutching the biggest hypodermic needle Peter had ever seen, stalked Matron.

Cleo Choat must be really frightened of shots, Peter thought. He noticed that Matron was keeping the giant needle level with the back of Cleo Choat's neck.

"No! No! Not the neck! I can't take anything sharp at the neck!"

Nonna and Mr Biggs were getting up shakily, and even Pickles was back on her feet.

Peter stood up to see Matron closing the back doors of the ambulance.

"Take her to hospital immediately," Matron instructed the ambulance driver. "I've given her a heavy sedative, but she'll need more. She's a very sick woman."

The doors slammed closed and the ambulance circled the driveway before disappearing into the night.

Peter ran over to Matron. He would've given her a high five if she hadn't been holding such a big needle.

170

27

The Crystal Ball

The next morning, after Peter had packed his bags, he went to find Nonna.

"Now that your sight's back, will you read my tea leaves?" he asked.

"Oh, forget about tea!" She laughed. "It's time to bring out the big bells and whistles!"

From the top of the wardrobe, Nonna pulled down a large box lined with red felt. "The crystal!"

Her eyes sparkled behind her thick glasses as she set the shimmering ball on the table and pulled up two chairs. "Your aunty Surla used to sit with me just like this when she was a child. She was very talented."

Peter nodded. "What about Mum?"

"No, she had her science." Nonna straightened her glasses. "Now let's see!"

Peter tried to stay as quiet as he could while Nonna stared into her crystal ball.

"I see the path is still open to you," she said finally, in a far-off voice. "But it's not completely secure, and you have to find the way yourself."

"Oh." Peter's face fell.

"Well, nothing in life is ever completely secure, Peter. You have to put in the effort."

"But what about Cleo Choat?" Peter asked, wrinkling his nose.

"Cleo Choat is bad – rotten to the core."

"We didn't need the ball to tell us that," scoffed Peter.

"She wasn't always like that, though," Nonna added sadly. "For some reason, she saw fit to cross to the dark side."

Peter didn't want to talk about Cleo Choat.

"Will I see you again, Nonna, after I leave?"

Nonna peered back into the ball. "You will see me again," she paused, peering into the ball.

Peter nodded, relieved.

"But it's not what you think."

"Oh...What about Dad, then? I have to deliver a message for him to Artiss Fleur at GAIA."

Nonna raised her eyebrows. "Have you been playing imagination games?"

Peter scowled at her. "No, it's true! I saw Dad while you were gone. He came through the jacket."

Nonna didn't seem at all surprised by this. "All right, let's ask him."

"What do you mean?"

"I'll see if I can tune in to Artiss Fleur through the ball."

"Nonna, are you crazy? It's not a mobile phone."

"Oh really? What do you think those silicon-chip thingies in mobile phones are, if not crystal?"

Peter hadn't ever thought about it that way.

"Look! He's coming through already."

A face peered up at them from deep within the glass.

"*Oooh!* He's much more wrinkled than I expected."

Peter stared into the wrinkly old face and tried not to shudder. "That can't be Artiss Fleur. He looks like a frog."

Nonna polished her glasses, then peered back in. "Oh goodness, he does have a lot of loose skin, doesn't he? I think it is a frog."

She held her fingers to her temples and closed her eyes. "Yes, and he's passed already, but he's reaching out from the other side to talk to us."

Peter stepped back fearfully. "What if we don't want to talk to him?"

Nonna opened her eyes held up a hand. "*Shh!* I'm getting something."

"But dead frogs can't talk," Peter protested.

"*Shh!*" Nonna smiled, then giggled. "Yes, I'll tell him."

"He said stop blabbing or he'll turn you into a toad."

Peter took another step backwards, feeling stunned.

"He's joking. Yes, Mr, ..." She paused. "Mr Quercus Croak?"

"Quercus Croak?" asked Peter, stepping closer again. "I think he's a famous frog. ..."

"He's got a very deep voice," whispered Nonna. "Oh! Says he's a singer in the Yang Chorus, does some solos. ... Yes, very masculine!"

"Nonna, are you flirting with him?"

"Croak," said Nonna, sounding unexpectedly like a frog.

Peter leant forward. He gulped nervously, then spoke. "Maybe he knows something about Spiral Hall."

Nonna nodded and listened.

"He does. He says he was one of the founding members of the school."

"Well, what about my invitation?"

"He says, 'It is written.'"

"Where?"

Nonna strained forward.

"On the wind," she said, shrugging her shoulders at Peter. "That's what I'm getting."

"Actually, that makes sense." Peter thought of the wind messing with the ink on Mr Biggs's newspaper.

"But will I get a real invitation?" Peter's voice faltered.

"Yes, but you have to find it."

"Where?"

Silence.

"I think we lost the connection."

"*Shh!* I'm going in deeper. Write down anything I say."

Peter sat silently, while Nonna concentrated.

"Look to where the guardian's treasure and yours become one," she said finally.

"What does that mean?" Peter wailed.

Nonna shook her head. "Maybe it's in Uncle Gorrman's safe; he's your guardian."

Peter sighed heavily. "Why can't we get a straight answer out of this thing?"

Nonna giggled. "Because the crystal's round, Peter! It's a ball!"

28

The Farewell Hop

That night, Peter's farewell dinner doubled as a wedding feast for Mr Dean and Ms Moth, with Peter as best man, and Pickles as bridesmaid. They ate Vegemite sandwiches made by Angel, and drank champagne supplied by Mr Dean.

After dinner, Nonna plucked five seeds from the nasturtium flowers in Pickles's bridesmaid coronet.

"You never know when you might need these," Nonna said cryptically.

As a farewell gift, Mr Dean gave Peter a solid gold wallaby pin to remind him of home, and one hundred British pounds sterling to put in his shoe for the journey – just in case.

A reporter from the *Jarra Jarra Enquirer* was at the wedding ceremony, to get the scoop on Mr Dean. The photo with Mr Dean, flanked by Peter on one side and Pickles in her wedding veil on the other, went viral on social media, with the tagline: "Wall Street's Mean Dean Becomes Green Dean!"

Everything was falling into place. Uncle Gorrman told Nonna on the phone that a special invitation had arrived for Peter from an invitation-only school. That could only mean one thing: Spiral Hall. There was more good news. Uncle Gorrman had also seen the news flash and the photo with Pickles, and called to say that he would be ready to have the famous wallaby come to London. Arrangements were quickly made: Pickles would travel by ship, and Peter would go by plane.

Then, came the most surprising news of all.

"Look!" cried Nonna, pointing out the window. "What luck for the bride!"

All heads turned as the drops began to fall. It was finally raining.

CHAPTER

29

To Wallaby or Not to Be

T he next day, it was still drizzling, and the air felt fresh. It was Pickles's last day at Gum Tree. Angel had made Spanish omelette for lunch; it was stringy and difficult to chew.

"Never mind," Mr Biggs told them kindly. "The Spanish probably have better teeth than we do!"

But nobody laughed.

When a rusty van with a trailer cage attached to it arrived for Pickles, everyone welcomed the chance to leave their omelettes and join the farewell.

Peter didn't like the look of the two animal keepers, who were smoking cigarettes and looking at their watches.

"Where's the kangaroo?" asked one of them.

"It's a wallaby," corrected Peter sullenly. "And look, the water bowl's empty."

While Peter was filling the bowl, the residents began, one after the other, to say their farewells to Pickles. It seemed that everyone had something special to thank her for.

The Trelawney sisters put two little packets of pickles wrapped in wax paper into Pickles's pouch.

"We would have given you more," they said, giggling, "but, thanks to you, we've let go of everything."

The two giggled even more when Pickles opened her pouch to Mr Witherspoon.

"*Ooh!* Something to eat?" he said, helping himself to one of the packets.

Tsk-tsk!

Mrs Weakes walked unsteadily from her wheelchair over to Pickles, and that was really thank-you enough. Pickles fumbled in her pouch and pulled out the blue notebook containing long lists of Mrs Weakes's health disorders, which had been lost for some time.

"You can use that to write down the feeding schedules for the joeys at the wildlife centre." Andy the vet smiled, indicating the notebook and loading a big bag of pellets into the trailer.

Mr Biggs was next. "Thank you, Pickles, for helping to calm my nerves after I lost my pipe and had to give up smoking."

The crowd clapped.

"She's been a real therapy pet," said Matron, admiration in her voice.

Tsk-tsk!

Pickles rummaged around in her pouch and pulled out something that Mr Biggs had been looking for: the missing pipe.

Nonna laughed. "Thank you, Pickles, for taking a hit for me from that evil Cleo Choat."

Tsk-tsk! Pickles looked up at Nonna, with moist brown eyes.

Peter was trying not to cry, so to take his mind off things, he asked Mrs Weakes for a blank page from her notebook. On it, he wrote a note to place on Pickles's pouch:

> To Whom It May Concern:
> Please be kind to my best friend.
> She likes pellets and pickles and bouncing on your stomach if you have time.

Tut-tut! Pickles approved.

Peter laughed. "Look, everyone! Pickles is pretending she can read."

"Nothing would surprise me," said Ms Moth, who, at the mention of reading, was suddenly alert. "Although, I must thank you, Pickles, for showing me there's more to life than my books."

Peter added, "Pickles even taught Mean Dean that there was more to life than m—"

"Don't say it," interrupted Mr Dean. "I still love money, Pickles."

Mr Dean then turned to Peter and said, "I love it because it's something I can use to do great and wonderful things."

Mr Dean also took a page from the blue notebook and wrote Pickles a share in Devlin Dean Holdings, which he put in her pouch. "Thank you for finding my true bride for me."

"Can we get this show on the road?" interrupted one of the keepers, clearly impatient. He had finished his cigarette and was waiting at the end of the gangplank for Pickles to hop up into the trailer cage.

While Matron was signing the paperwork and checking that Pickles's travelling conditions were in order, Mrs Millet stepped forward to offer her last goodbye.

Pickles stood staring at her, frozen to the spot.

"What?" Mrs Millet protested. "I don't really think I have anything to thank you for. I kept asking you to find me a man."

Tsk-tsk! Pickles directed her slender snout towards the back of the crowd.

"Oh right! Perfect timing," said Mr Dean.

Standing a little way from the group, a muscular man with a navy-and-white striped apron tied neatly round a large stomach smiled shyly from underneath a high chef's hat. He waved uncertainly at Mrs Millet.

Peter saw that Nonna's eyes had gone all twinkly.

Tsk-tsk! Pickles looked back from her position at the bottom of the gangplank.

"Has Pickles really found Mrs Millet a man?" asked Peter in disbelief.

"Not just any man. This is Gum Tree's new chef de cuisine," said Mr Dean. "Pickles and I hired him last week. Gave him a lifetime employment contract, and Matron approved it."

"Well!" said Angel. "If I'd needed an assistant in my kitchen, I would've let you know!"

"He's not your assistant. He's the new boss, and you're fired."

There were gasps from the crowd.

Angel opened her mouth to protest, but Mr Dean put his hand up, saying, "Put a cookie in it, will you? Let me finish."

He smiled out at the residents. "Angel is being offered a new, more highly paid position, doing something that she is actually good at."

He turned to Angel. "In Operation Green Dean, you will be my new Minister of Animal Welfare and Neville Biggs."

He turned to Mr Biggs. "Biggsie, if you're willing, you will be appointed to work alongside her as my new Minister of Forestry."

Everyone clapped, including the new chef, who seemed to have caught the eye of Mrs Millet.

Peter saw that he had a tattoo on his arm. He was the man from the table vision.

"Cecil? Is that you?"

"Hi, Vera!" The chef waved nervously.

"You can't be the new cook! You can't cook," she said haughtily.

"Oh great!" groaned the residents, disappointed.

The new chef walked over to Mrs Millet. "Well, actually, Vera … there's something I need to tell you."

Mrs Millet folded her arms and stood in steely silence. "What?"

Cecil Millet looked about him nervously. "Well, the truth is, I am a pretty good chef, from my navy days. 'Chef Cecil' they used to call me. I just never got around to telling you."

"But I cooked all those meals for you, for fifty years!" Mrs Millet exclaimed.

"Well, they were nice meals. And I was thankful for them." Cecil hung his head. "I just forgot to tell you that too."

"*Hmmph!*" Mrs Millet seemed unmoved.

"I also worried that you wouldn't think I was manned up enough. You always said you loved me because I was such a brave sailor."

"But you were brave," Mrs Millet protested. "What about that extraordinary service medal you got from the prime minister?"

"It was for culinary service."

Mrs Millet considered this for a moment, then surprised everyone by asking, "Can you make a good beef Wellington?"

"One of my specialties," said Chef Cecil, speaking with more confidence now.

While they'd been focused on the Millets' reunion, Pickles had hopped up the makeshift gangplank and taken her position in the travel cage. One of the men was strapping her in.

"What a girl she is!" said Mr Dean, clapping Peter on the shoulder.

"I'll see you in London, Pickles!" Peter called as the trailer bumped away, with Pickles standing steadfastly upright in her harness and staring back at them.

30

The Spirit of Fire

ust before bed, Nonna LaRosa tapped on Peter's broom-closet
door.

"Are you too old for a bedtime story?"

"No, never," said Peter, pushing his backpack off the narrow bed
to make room for her.

Nonna had lost weight with the illness and could now squeeze
rather easily through the space between the broom cupboard and the
secret cubby.

"What's the book?"

She showed him the cover of a colourful handmade booklet:
"*Thelma and the Flame* – by Thelma LaRosa".

"Mum wrote it?"

"Yep, when she was young. I found it hidden under the base of the
crystal ball. Strange, I remember now that Thelma brought it here on
the day of the fire and asked me to keep it safe."

Nonna perched her pear-shaped body on the edge of Peter's bed
and began to read:

> Once upon a time, in the sandy deep of the Australian
> bush, a girl called Thelma (that was me) met a tiny
> orange flame.

I was surprised when the Flame spoke to me. It spoke a language made of feelings, which my head somehow turned into words.

"Do you know who I am?" it asked in a friendly way.

"Yes," I replied, "you're Fire."

"You are right," said the Flame. "And do you know what I do?"

"Yes," I said, "you burn."

"Give me your hand," said the Flame.

"No!" I took a few steps back. Then, I said, "Today's my birthday. I'm nine. How old are you?"

"I am no age," replied the Flame.

"How come?"

"Because I am reborn in every moment."

I needed to think about this. "Does it mean that you die in every moment too?"

"No!" The Fire flared suddenly, spitting high flames into the sky around us.

I was scared and ran off down the path.

"Come back!" called the Flame. "I can't hurt you. I am Cosmic Fire."

I didn't really want to offend Cosmic Fire, so I decided to go back and be its friend again.

183

Then, Flame said, "I don't only burn things. Do you know what other things I do?"

"Um ... you warm things?" I found myself edging closer to its glow.

"Yes! I am Cosmic Warmth. I can even warm things to make them grow."

"What else do you do?"

"I also ..." Fire spirit paused.

"You also what?"

"I'll tell you later," said Fire.

"Well, I'm a nature scientist," I told it. "I collect things in the bush and study them."

Fire seemed pleased with this. "If you are a friend to Nature, then you are a friend to me."

"But you're not a friend to Nature!" I protested. "You burn the grass and trees and animals. You kill Nature."

"No!" Fire roared and made itself really big and high. "It is you people who kill! You poison the air with chemicals that make my fires burn longer and bigger."

Fire's words were heavy and breathy with anger. I should have been afraid. But the flame in me was also starting to get mad. My cheeks began to blaze.

"It's not my fault!" I screamed. "All I did was get born. What can I do?"

"That's what all people say. But you are free!"

"I don't know what you mean!"

"Well, I am Fire. I must burn. I have no choice. But you humans do have a choice."

"What choice?" I snapped.

I felt the Flame's words come through slowly and carefully.

"You can love Earth, or you can destroy it."

When I understood that Fire spoke the truth, I was madder than ever. I was mad at all people, especially myself. I was so mad that sparks began to fly from me. Fire must have found this funny, because suddenly it got small again – in the shape of a little Flame Girl with plaits in her hair.

Nonna turned the page to a beautiful wax-crayon drawing of the Flame Girl, in orange, red, and yellow, with not a speck of white left on the page. And beside her was little Thelma LaRosa.

"Keep reading," Peter whispered, leaning in closer.

"Okay, this is the last page." Nonna wiped her eyes behind her glasses.

Flame girl was the same height as I was, but her fiery plaits made her look much taller.

"How long are your plaits?" I asked.

"They are no length." Flame girl replied in an annoying way.

"That's hard to understand."

"No, it's not," Flame girl said. "It's just infinity."

"It's hard to imagine infinity."

"*Infinity* just means that, in the end, you and I are the same."

"No!" I said. "That can't be right."

"Why not?"

"Well, to start with, you have longer plaits than I do."

Fire girl sighed. "That's enough talking. Now we will play."

"Play?" I was surprised.

Flame girl's infinity hair started twisting and turning towards me. I stumbled back a few quick steps, but Flame girl moved with me. She flicked a fiery plait at me. I dodged, but it almost got me.

Flame girl giggled.

I giggled.

Then, we were leaping and circling the clearing.

She twirled; I whirled.

She dipped; I skipped.

She burned; I turned.

We both laughed till we needed air.

"Wait!" I begged. "You said you would tell me the other thing you do!"

Flame girl paused. "This is what I do."

"What? Play tag?"

"No!" She giggled.

Then, time must have stopped. Her light looked into my light. No words came, but she made me understand. Flame girl puts light into people, right inside of them. If she died, light would die. And that would be very bad.

I held my breath.

Flame girl tagged a fiery finger on my shoulder and said, "You're it!"

Holding the prized story in both hands, Nonna passed it to Peter. Nonna whispered, "Peter, now you're it."

BOOK V

The Journey of Trials

CHAPTER

31

The Plastic Flat

The next day, Peter Blue left Nonna and his home in Australia to travel right across the earth, to London, England, to meet Aunty Surla and Uncle Gorrman for the first time.

"Your uncle's very high up in the company, you know," the driver from Big Garbage Incorporated told Peter chattily as they pulled out of the airport terminal and onto the motorway.

They were heading towards Central London.

"He's even been tipped to be the next president of the company."

Peter nodded, then leant back into the spacious limousine seat. He felt tired from the flight but still strangely alert. *Just as a boy on a quest should be,* he thought.

It was early evening. For a while, everything around him looked grey, but as they got closer to London, Peter saw more colours: the sky above turned to neon orange, matched with vivid reds from telephone boxes and buses; there were pinks and purples from glossy ads on roadside billboards; patches of green showed on the verges or in walled off yards. Flashing through suburban neighbourhoods, the people seemed to change too – their skin shades, and also the styles and colours of their clothes.

Peter was a long way from Australia, and a long way from home.

As if echoing his thoughts, the driver said, "You've come a long way for a little boy."

"Yes," Peter agreed.

He found himself leaning forward to talk with the chatty driver, even telling him about the quest for Spiral Hall.

"It's a secret school where kids can learn how to save the world," Peter explained.

"Is that right?" said the driver enthusiastically.

I have to get there! thought Peter.

"You're almost there," said the driver, as if echoing Peter's thoughts again. "Leafton Street."

Peter was pleased to see that the street looked leafy and green, just like its name suggested. They passed by a line of white-fenced two-story row houses, all trimmed with grassy borders, and many with large shady trees in their yards. His heart lightened at the sight, then sank back heavily when the driver announced, "This is the place."

"Are you sure?"

They'd stopped outside the only flat on the street with no grass or trees in front – just slab after slab of grey concrete. And in the centre, like a beast lying in wait, a black plastic Dumpster filled the space. On its side, Peter made out the words "Big Garbage Inc".

The driver helped Peter carry his luggage down the concrete path leading to the front door and up the stone steps. He must have sensed that Peter was feeling anxious, because he gave him an encouraging smile and a pat on the shoulder before pressing the doorbell firmly. Nobody came. The driver pressed it again. Peter and the driver shuffled self-consciously from one foot to the other for a while. Still, there was no response.

Dusk gathered around them. The plastic garbage bin loomed largely behind them. The driver pressed the bell again. Then, he began to knock forcefully on the door. Peter felt his shoulders slumping.

Finally, footsteps were heard in the hallway, followed by some complicated key turning and rattling of chains. The door opened. It was Aunty Surla.

"Oh, Peter, you're here," she said loudly but flatly.

"Yes," said Peter, his voice suddenly croaky with emotion. His aunt was a much thinner version of his mother. Her brown, straight hair hung thinly against her shoulders, framing her thin nose and sharp cheekbones. Peter noticed straight away that her skin was very white, similar to the skin of the Gum Tree residents. Like them, she must stay indoors a lot.

"Goodness, you've grown," his aunt said, pecking him on both cheeks, then pulling quickly away.

"But, Aunty Surla, you've never met me before."

"Oh … but you know what I mean." She waved away the remark with her bony arm.

The sound of television laughter erupted from a room at the end of the hall. Aunty Surla looked nervously back over her shoulder. "Listen, Peter, Gorrman and I are just watching our show. It's nearly over."

"Uh-huh, no problem," said Peter, smiling insincerely, while his heart sank further into the pit of his stomach.

"Are you early?" Aunty Surla asked, looking vaguely at her wrist and finding no watch there.

"Um … well, I've been travelling for twenty-two hours now," Peter said, looking at his own watch. "I think I'm on time."

Even though he still hadn't been invited in, the driver began pushing Peter's luggage inside the flat.

"Good luck in London, then, lad – good luck with your quest." The driver laughed and winked at Peter.

Suddenly, Peter wished he could give the driver a hug. He seemed so much kinder than Peter's aunt. Instead, he and the driver shook hands. Then, the driver was gone.

Peter followed his aunt down the dimly lit hallway. Everything looked clean and new but somehow empty. There were no pictures on the walls, although there was some kind of tall statue rising up at the end of the hallway.

"Is that modern art?" Peter asked conversationally.

Aunt Surla looked at him strangely. "No!"

As they got closer, Peter saw that the statue was actually piles of brown, white, and cream plastic containers and bags.

"It's the rubbish waiting to go out." Her voice rose uneasily.

"Oh. ..." Peter giggled nervously at his mistake.

Maybe Aunty Surla had remembered he was on his way to a top eco-school and had left the rubbish for him.

"Did you save the recycling for me to take out?" Peter asked, suddenly pleased.

"Well, not exactly." Aunty Surla added her own nervous giggle to the conversation, and then said in a sing-song voice, "We don't recycle here. We're in the garbage business, you know."

Peter just stared at the pile of plastic, not even trying to hide his dismay.

"So, for us, you could say that all garbage is good garbage," she said.

Peter lowered his suitcases to the floor and allowed his eyes to take in the pyramid of plastic bags. The one on top contained plastic sweet packets, plastic crisp bags, plastic spoons, plastic forks, and plastic knives. It was piled on top of more plastic bags crammed with plastic milk bottles, plastic juice bottles, plastic soda bottles, and balanced on top of them were large brown plastic trays, overflowing with more plastic cartons, plastic carton lids, plastic ice-cream tubs, and plastic yoghurt pots.

Even though the thought of so much plastic going into the regular rubbish was sickening, Peter didn't dare say so. Instead, he just said politely, "Well, it looks like you've been waiting a long time for me to come from Australia to help you take out the rubbish."

Again, Aunty Surla gave him a strange look. "No, this is only from yesterday."

At the stairwell, she turned left, into another passageway that led to a small room with one window that faced out onto the street side. Not that he could see the street with the Dumpster blocking most of the view. The walls were bare except for one empty hook. There was no furniture except for a plastic night table next to a narrow single bed. He patted the bed, and it made a crinkly sound.

"The mattress is new, so I kept the plastic on, to keep it nice for visitors."

Peter lowered his head in dismay. Wasn't he a visitor? Then, he saw that the floor was made of nice-looking wood, and he felt instantly more cheerful.

"Come on, I'll show you the rest of the house," said Aunty Surla. She led him down another short passage and into a windowless room at the centre of the flat.

"This is my workspace." She indicated her computer on a desk in the centre of the room. There was not much other furniture in here either: just a few tables piled high with packages wrapped in more plastic bags. There were more packages on the floor too.

"What work do you do?" asked Peter. "Sell plastic things?"

"Oh no. These are just some things I've shopped for online. Things we need. I used to be a computer programmer, working from home, but I don't need to work anymore." Brightening, she added, "I quit last week. We have plenty of money now, thanks to your big inheritance."

"Am I rich?" asked Peter curiously.

"I'll say. At least your mum was. Who knew! That silly prize Thelma got for inventing that crystal thing came with millions of pounds attached to it – 'research dollars' they called it." Aunty Surla smiled at Peter for the first time since his arrival.

"It was called Chrysalite," said Peter. He wanted to add that it wasn't silly, but he didn't dare.

In the next room, a man's voice laughed loudly at the TV.

Aunty Surla said, "I'll just go and check on the show, and you can meet Gorrman as soon as it's over. He's dying to meet you."

Peter doubted that. He glanced dully about the room, until his eyes caught sight of something familiar. A vase of nasturtium flowers, Nonna's favourite. He waded through the sea of plastic packaging, moving towards the vase and thinking of the window boxes at home and the five nasturtium seeds from Pickles's wedding veil that were safe in his backpack.

Slowly, Peter picked up the vase and bent down to smell the flowers. He wanted the scent of home. But there was nothing. He took another deep breath, then saw with alarm that there was no water in the vase. At the same time, he realised the flowers were coated with dust. They were made of plastic.

CHAPTER

32

Vindaloo

When the TV in the next room was finally silent, Uncle Gorrman appeared.

"Well, well, Peter Blue, you made it to London." Uncle Gorrman shook hands with him in a grown-up way, but his eyes darted sharply about, avoiding contact.

He was the opposite of Aunty Surla in looks. Where Aunty Surla's hair hung limply and thinly, Uncle Gorrman's stuck upwards in short prickly points; where Aunty Surla was skinny and bony, Uncle Gorrman was big and bulgy; and where his aunt's lips were thin and her nose tapered, his uncle's lips were pudgy beneath a nose like an angry red stub.

A plump little boy waddled out from behind Uncle Gorrman's knee.

"Hello ... you must be Jimmy!" Peter crouched down to meet him.

"Gimme, Gimme," he repeated, wrenching at Peter's trousers.

Peter looked to Aunty Surla for help. "Is it Gimmy or Jimmy?"

"It's Jimmy, but he's saying 'gimme', as in 'give me'."

"Oh."

"Nonna told him on the phone that there would be a gift for him in your bag," Aunty Surla explained, as if it would be perfectly normal to demand a gift instead of saying hello.

"Oh well ... it's just something little we got at the airport." Peter reached for his backpack. It seemed like a long time ago now.

"Gimme!" repeated his cousin.

"He loves gifts," Aunty Surla said with a laugh, as if that explanation would excuse her son's rude behaviour.

Before Peter could properly hand the unusually shaped gift to him, Jimmy was tearing away at the wrapping.

"It's a boomerang," Peter told him kindly.

Instead of a thank-you, Peter received a stinging *thwack* from the boomerang as it hit his lower leg.

"Ow!" Peter waited for Jimmy to get in trouble, but Aunty Surla and Uncle Gorrman were laughing like proud parents.

Jimmy dropped the boomerang and latched his fist onto the silver pelican button on Peter's jacket.

"More present!" he demanded.

"Sorry, no more," said Peter, trying to loosen his cousin's tight grip on the precious pelican button.

Soon Jimmy had his teeth around it, making swift tugging movements.

"Hey, stop it!"

Too late. The threads snapped, and the button broke loose, sending Jimmy backwards to the floor.

"Where did it go?" Peter scanned the carpet desperately but couldn't see the button.

Then, one look at his cousin's firmly closed mouth and round eyes gave him the answer: he'd swallowed it.

Aunty Surla and Uncle Gorrman didn't seem to have noticed.

Peter wondered fearfully if it could it be dangerous. If so, would he be blamed? Jimmy seemed to be breathing normally. He was sitting quietly. *Digesting,* Peter thought grimly. By the look of the bulky padding around Jimmy's bottom, Peter guessed that he still wore nappies. Good, because one way or another, Peter was going to get that silver pelican button back.

Aunty Surla, in the meantime, was looking pointedly over at Peter's bag. "You've got gifts for us too, haven't you?"

"Oh yeah." Peter felt himself blushing as he rummaged around in his backpack for the other two packages. Trying to manage their expectations, he mumbled, "Well, more like souvenirs."

Aunty Surla ripped hers open in the same way Jimmy had, and pulled out a set of brightly coloured oven gloves and pot holders.

"What?" She didn't even try to disguise her disappointment.

"Um ... they have prints of Australian native flowers on them. See? This one's wattle." When Aunty Surla didn't smile, Peter added, "Nonna thought you'd like them."

Aunty Surla lifted her thin, twiggy leg and stamped her foot. "That woman's always tried to make me cook."

"I'll open mine," said Gorrman dismissively. He pulled out a stainless-steel flask with a map of Australia printed on it. "What is it?"

"It's a reusable water bottle," Peter said encouragingly.

Uncle Gorrman didn't reply.

"For going on nature walks," added Peter.

"And why would I want to do that?" Gorrman asked. He seemed genuinely curious.

"Um. ... Oh well." Peter was caught off guard. "Maybe you could take a reusable water bottle when you visit your garbage dumps. Nonna said that your company owns some really big ones. You might get thirsty when you walk around them."

Uncle Gorrman placed the bottle sullenly on a shelf. "So, you're one of those eco-nancy boys?"

Ignoring his uncle's tone, Peter sensed an opening to talk about Spiral Hall. "Actually, I can't wait to see the letter from the very special invitation-only school."

"Oh right," said Uncle Gorrman. "It *is* very hard to get into, but I managed to pull a few strings."

"You?" Peter was suddenly worried.

Uncle Gorrman then began rummaging energetically through a pile of papers. Aunty Surla, smiling her thin smile, stood by, looking unsure.

"Here's the prospectus." Uncle Gorrman passed Peter a thick glossy pamphlet.

Peter had expected anything from Spiral Hall to at least be on recycled paper.

But then, Uncle Gorrman shocked him by saying "The school's called Murksborne, and the chairman of Big Garbage sits on the board. You'll be pleased to know he's taken a very special interest in you."

Uncle Gorrman smiled to show small yellowy teeth, then squeezed Peter's shoulder to signal there should be no argument.

But Peter couldn't keep silent. "I want to go to a different school called Spiral Hall."

Gorrman screwed up his face. "Never heard of it."

Peter sensed a lie, but he couldn't be sure. He was too tired and too disappointed.

"So, instead, you're sending me to a *garbage* school?"

"Garbage!" cried Jimmy, looking happily up at his father.

"It's not a …" Uncle Gorrman looked at Aunty Surla, perplexed. "First of all, I'm not sending you. They only take a handful of new students each year, and you've got a special invitation."

"But I don't want it," Peter told him. "And, anyway, why does that chairman want to give me a special invitation when he's never even met me?"

Uncle Gorrman turned to Aunty Surla. "That's the one thing I haven't managed to figure out."

"Well, I won't go."

"I won't go." Uncle Gorrman mimicked. "Listen to him, Surla. A no-name boy from Down Under! You should be grateful to go!"

Angry blotches were forming on Uncle Gorrman's cheeks.

Peter lowered his head to stare blankly at the large *M* on the prospectus cover. Tears stabbed at the corners of his eyes, but he didn't want Uncle Gorrman to see them. *Just go along with it for now,* he told himself. *When you're alone, you can think things through.*

"When will Pickles arrive?" Peter said sullenly.

"Soon," said Uncle Gorrman. "Last we heard, the circus was headed to some place in Eastern Europe."

"Circus?" Peter's face showed uncontrolled shock. "But. ..."

"It's a travelling circus – Trod's Travelling Circus." Gorrman sounded out each syllable slowly.

"You gave Pickles to a circus?"

"There was no giving involved." Gorrman laughed. "I got a good price for it, thanks to that social-media campaign of yours with Devlin Dean."

"But she's supposed to be living here with us," Peter said meekly.

Now it was Aunty Surla's turn to step in. "You didn't really think we would keep a wild animal in a London flat, did you?"

"What is your nephew's problem?" interrupted Uncle Gorrman. "I find a good home for his pet, like I promised, and still he complains!"

Peter looked at Aunty Surla for support.

Her lips were moving, but no sound came. They were interrupted by a loud chiming of the doorbell.

Ding-dong! Ding-dong!

"Oh, lovely, the takeaways are here!" Aunty Surla found her voice. "Come on, let's talk about all this another day."

"Curry!" shouted Jimmy, scampering bow-legged out of the room, behind his mother.

Peter had never had curry before. In England, he'd been expecting to eat beef Wellington. As he followed his new family into their clean white kitchen, he tried to swallow his anger.

Even Uncle Gorrman seemed suddenly to switch to a better humour with the arrival of the takeaways.

Aunty Surla began unloading small plastic bags of hot food from a large plastic delivery bag. Peter watched as she dealt plastic trays, plastic cartons, and plastic plates round the circular white table.

Uncle Gorrman sat down first. He started dabbing thin bread pieces into a fiery red sauce and popping the pieces into his mouth.

Dab-pop! Dab-pop!

Jimmy, who'd managed to climb up, alone, into his high chair, banged his fist on the little table and cried, "Vindaloo! Vindaloo!"

"We're very adventurous here in London with our food," Uncle Gorrman told Peter through thick, moist lips. He seemed to have forgotten all about the disagreement.

Aunty Surla was now littering the table with plastic forks and plastic spoons, all wrapped individually in their own plastic wrappers; then straws in their own plastic wrappers; and, finally, water in its own plastic bottles – and all of this plastic stuff came out from still more plastic carry bags.

"Don't just stand there gaping, Peter. Sit down and try the vindaloo!" Aunty Surla smiled almost as brightly as she had earlier when she'd told Peter they were rich.

"Jimmy likes vindaloo, doesn't he?" Aunty Surla pushed large plastic plates piled with white rice and red curry towards Jimmy and Peter, handing them each a plastic spoon.

"I could just use a real spoon from the drawer instead of a plastic one," Peter offered, looking around the kitchen for a cutlery drawer.

"Oh, don't worry," said Aunty Surla, winking at him. "This is way more convenient. "No washing up.""

Peter tasted the curry, which was surprisingly good. It made his mouth and his throat feel warm. But after a while, it sank like a stone in his stomach, already heavy with disappointment.

"Try some yoghurt on top," offered Aunty Surla, passing him a plastic pot of plain yoghurt. "It makes it milder."

Peter took it gratefully, and with head bowed, ate the whole pot of yoghurt without stopping. As he ate, he caught sight of the bare threads on the GAIA jacket where the missing silver pelican button had been. He glanced over at Jimmy, who seemed to be eating well. Good, because this was one problem Peter was literally going to get to the bottom of!

"Thank you for the dinner," Peter said politely, when they were all done. "Would you like me to wash the plastic plates and things so you can reuse them?"

"No," said Uncle Gorrman flatly. "We're in the garbage business. Remember?"

Peter sighed quietly. "Can I at least reuse my yoghurt pot?"

Aunty Surla wrinkled her nose. "But it's dirty."

"It doesn't matter," said Peter.

"But what will you use it for?"

Peter was thinking of the nasturtium seeds in Nonna's handkerchief. "I can put dirt in it and plant something."

That thought made Peter happy. The jacket seemed to hum.

Uncle Gorrman, who'd been listening to the conversation, said, "And where do you think you'll find dirt here?"

Uncle Gorrman swept his hand around the steely white kitchen. "Do you think Surla keeps a house full of dirt?"

"I meant from the garden," Peter said with a sigh.

"The garden, eh?" Uncle Gorrman rose from his chair and beckoned Peter to the window facing onto the backyard. "First thing we did when we moved in here was fell all the trees and lay concrete, so no dirt; now it's clean and safe for Jimmy to play in."

"Play?" repeated Jimmy hopefully from his high chair.

Outside, alone with the garbage, Peter tentatively opened the door of the plastic Dumpster. He'd never been in a walk-in garbage bin before; the air inside smelt of stale takeaways.

Using the solar beam on his jacket sleeve, Peter picked out high walls of stacked white office paper next to piles and piles of stuffed plastic bags. He added the new plastic bags to the stash, then hurried out, exhaling as he went. Why would anyone want to walk into their bin, anyway?

With his yoghurt pot in hand, Peter wandered the yard, in search of soil for his seed. Finally, in one corner, he found a small crack in Uncle Gorrman's defence against nature. A long line of dirt had forced its way up between two concrete slabs. Using his index and middle fingers, Peter was gradually able to scrape up enough earth to plant with.

The sky cleared as he worked, and the seed, when he placed it into its circle of soil, sat edged with silver from the glow of the rising moon.

CHAPTER

33

Trapped in the Flat

The next day, Peter got up for a breakfast of cold vindaloo served on plastic plates, and orange juice in disposable plastic cups. When Aunty Surla came with a white plastic bag to sweep the table, Peter thought sadly of the walls of plastic lining the walk-in bin.

After Uncle Gorrman went off to work, Peter found himself floating around the flat, waiting for something to happen. He thought of Artiss Fleur's mailing address at Singlewood Lane. Where was Singlewood Lane? Jimmy must be going for a walk soon. Perhaps Aunty Surla would help Peter look for the street.

Jimmy was watching morning television, perched up on the plastic-covered sofa, wearing a disposable nappy and singlet. Peter wondered how long it would take for the pelican button to be digested. He wrinkled his nose at the thought, although he knew he'd have to keep a close watch for it.

In the next room, Peter found Aunty Surla at her computer screen. When she caught sight of Peter, she became the human equivalent of a Do Not Disturb sign, jiggling her computer mouse and making a great show of looking extra busy. Peter didn't dare interrupt her. Instead, he wandered up and down the hallway for a while; then he ventured halfway up the stairs, but they were so creaky he decided to turn back. What he really wanted to do was get outside and explore.

He ducked his head round Aunty Surla's office door, saying chirpily, "Just going out for a quick walk! To see where I am."

"Not on your own." Aunty Surla looked up, shocked.

"How about together, then, with you and Jimmy?"

"Sorry, Peter. I'm behind in my shopping."

"What do you need to buy? Peter asked politely.

"Oh, you know, we're always running out of things – groceries, stuff for the house, clothes. And I need to order tonight's dinner."

"Dinner? Like a mail-order dinner?"

"Yes, why not? London has lots of good takeaways, delivered right to the door."

Aunty Surla, staring forward at her screen, gave her mouse an impatient jiggle.

"Peter, why don't you watch television," she coaxed. "I bet there are lots of programmes you don't have in Australia. Go on, watch telly with Jimmy – keep him company for a while till the new sitter arrives."

Peter shrugged. "Okay."

In the TV room, he found Jimmy asleep, in a sitting position. Grotesque light images flashed over him like spectres reaching through the semi-darkness to slither across his smooth white skin.

"Jimmy's asleep," Peter called

"Oh good! Why don't you take a nap too, Peter? You must be tired from the journey."

Surprised by his aunt's reply, Peter shrugged again. He'd only just got up. Feeling unwanted, he wandered back to his empty bedroom and pulled out his treasures from the mother wallaby pouch. He laid them out on the bed: the frame of his mother at the podium, the little book *Thelma and the Flame,* his mother's shopping list for lollies, the four remaining nasturtium seeds, Artiss Fleur's business card, the gold wallaby pin from Mr Dean, and his mother's see-through pyramid with the bobbing spiral worm inside. He held the pyramid up in his hand and saw that, instead of bobbing, the spiral sat motionless and flat on the pyramid floor.

Later when Surla left her computer to take a shower, Peter was able to make a hurried search on her computer for Trod's Traveling Circus. A glitzy main page came up immediately, with a picture of a Big Top and Pickles as the star attraction. She was flanked on a circular stage by two men not much taller than her, both men dressed in red and white striped t-shirts and wearing blue berets. The caption read: The Singing Midgets, and, while the two midgets looked glum, Pickles appeared happy. She's probably forgotten me, Peter thought, letting his shoulders slump dismally over Aunty Surla's keyboard.

At noon, the new sitter, whose name was Mrs Levin, arrived. Peter stalked behind them when Aunty Surla took her upstairs to see Jimmy's bedroom. He watched very carefully at the nappy changing station, thinking of the silver pelican. Then, Aunty Surla showed the sitter all of Jimmy's toys. Mountains of plastic toys heaped up in plastic tubs.

"Play!" demanded Jimmy.

"Not now. We have to show Mrs Levin where everything is," Aunty Surla said soothingly.

She began opening and closing wardrobes stuffed with clothes.

"Play," demanded Jimmy again, latching both arms round his mother's thin, bare legs.

"Mrs Levin will play with you in a minute, Jimmy."

"No-o-o-o-o Levin. Mummy play." Jimmy's voice escalated into a high-pitched squeal, causing Mrs Levin to step back in alarm.

Aunty Surla gave Mrs Levin an embarrassed glance. "You see why I need help."

Mrs Levin followed Aunty Surla out. She was a biggish woman who swayed when she walked.

Peter hurried over to pick up his dejected cousin from the floor.

"Don't worry. I'll play with you," Peter told Jimmy kindly, and was rewarded with a pinch on the ankle.

"Ouch!" cried Peter.

Jimmy suddenly looked happy again.

Back in the TV room with Jimmy, Peter concentrated on the large screen that filled one wall. He was trying to stop himself from crying. Suddenly, he felt very homesick.

Mrs Levin swayed in to join them, a china teacup and saucer rattling in her hand.

Peter watched from the corner of his eye as she settled heavily into the sofa opposite Jimmy, to start her new job.

Mrs Levin began by directing a string of questions to Jimmy's profile, the kind of questions that didn't really require answers, which was good, because none came.

"You a good boy, then, Jimmy?" she asked. "You like watching telly, do you, Jimmy? Let's just sit here a while and get to know each other, shall we?"

No responses from Jimmy.

Mrs Levin took a few sips of her tea and, for a while, seemed content to just watch Jimmy watching television, but, gradually, Peter noticed her gaze drifting away from Jimmy and over to the cartoon on the big screen. Soon he saw that they were both staring forward at the television, their faces flat.

The cartoon was dull, with lots of high-pitched voices and not much happening.

"Change!" said Jimmy suddenly.

Mrs Levin said, "Oh, good boy for telling me." She started to raise herself up unsteadily from the sofa. "Did you do wee-wee or jobbies?"

"Change!" shouted Jimmy, pointing angrily at the screen.

"I don't think it's nappies," Peter advised. "I think he wants another programme."

The new programme on the next channel was worse. Peter felt hungry. No one had offered him a snack since the cold vindaloo for breakfast. He drifted over to the doorway.

"Aunty Surla, do you mind if I make myself a sandwich?"

"I'm afraid we don't have any bread and butter," Aunty Surla replied.

"Oh. That's okay. How about some cornflakes or something?"

"No. We don't keep cereal. What kind of sandwich?"

"I thought you didn't have any bread?"

She sighed impatiently. "I'll order in. Our Daily Bread does quick sandwich deliveries."

Aunty Surla made a few swift clicks with her mouse. "Here you go." She pivoted her computer the screen towards Peter. "Which looks good to you?"

"Wow, they all do."

"So, choose one." Aunty Surla's eyes looked alive.

Peter pointed at a big colourful picture of a giant sandwich and watched as his aunt clicked a checkmark in the box.

"But how do they know where to come with the sandwich?"

"I'm a returning customer."

Her movements were fluid, rolling with their purchasing power.

Peter had already noticed that his aunt seemed happiest when she was shopping.

"What about Jimmy's sandwich?" Peter asked as he watched the simulation of his own sandwich floating into a wrapper and into his aunt's shopping cart.

"He doesn't eat sandwiches. We'll get him some chips, shall we?"

"Yes, get him lots!" said Peter decisively. The more Jimmy ate, the quicker the pelican button was likely to get through.

"Do you want chips too?"

Peter was about to tell her that he was only allowed chips on special occasions, but he stopped himself. "Yes, please."

"Our Daily Bread does good chips," Aunty Surla said, looking pleased as she shovelled the chip icons onto a tray and then into her cart.

"Those desserts look good." Peter pointed at a tall chocolate sundae that stretched the length of Aunty Surla's screen.

"Have one!" said Aunty Surla, clicking and gliding with her wrist Add to Tray. "Let's get one for Jimmy as well."

Aunty Surla winked at Peter.

That meant Jimmy would only be having chips and pudding. Nonna would've never allowed such a lunch. Still, Peter didn't dare comment. He didn't want to risk upsetting his aunt, who could so easily cancel lunch with just one swift movement of her agile wrist.

Anyway, Peter didn't have time to worry about Jimmy. He had too many problems of his own – like how to find Singlewood Lane and Artiss Fleur, and how to get to Spiral Hall. He also wanted to get news of Pickles. He guessed if the circus had paid a lot of money for her, she'd be well cared for.

Peter watched, mesmerised, as Aunty Surla dragged and dropped a few more pictures onto her simulated takeaway tray.

Mrs Levin swayed out from the kitchen holding a tray. "Fresh tea for the workers," she announced, placing a steaming cup for Aunty Surla, next to the computer.

"Lovely, thank you," said Aunty Surla, her eyes still fixed on the screen. She was jiggling her mouse in the way another person might jiggle pocket change when they were about to make a purchase.

In the evening, when Mrs Levin heaved herself up from the sofa to leave, Peter saw why she was called a sitter. Her job did seem to involve a lot of it.

"We've had a lovely time," Mrs Levin insisted, even though Aunty Surla hadn't asked. "Tomorrow, I think we'll try some games."

"Games?" repeated Peter. "We could go to the park and try the boomerang I brought Jimmy from Australia."

"Hmm?" Mrs Levin asked, as if straining her ears not to hear him. Peter shrugged.

His first days in London continued in much the same way. The family ate hot takeaways at night and cold leftovers in the morning. Uncle Gorrman went out; Mrs Levin came in. Peter and Jimmy watched television, and Aunty Surla shopped.

On the third day, Peter stayed close to Mrs Levin when he saw that she was preparing to leave.

"Well, I'm off," Mrs Levin told Aunty Surla. "I'm just going to walk up the high street for my bus."

"Can I walk Mrs Levin to her bus?" Peter offered in his most polite voice.

Aunty Surla frowned and seemed about to say no.

"Just to give you enough time to finish your online shopping," Peter encouraged.

"Oh, all right then, but don't talk to strangers. Here, take the gate key." Aunty Surla hung a key round Peter's neck.

"I might have a little look around the high street while I'm there," Peter told her.

"All right," she said absently.

She's glad to be rid me, Peter thought sadly, then shrugged off the feeling. He needed to focus his thoughts on finding Singlewood Lane. The address on the business card was the only clue he had to finding Artiss Fleur and getting to Spiral Hall.

CHAPTER

34

The Shield

"**S**o how are you enjoying London?" Mrs Levin asked. Her breath was coming out in short puffs as they climbed the hill to the high street.

"This is the first time I've actually been outside," mumbled Peter.

"Oh. Well, be sure and go straight home," she cautioned.

Peter just smiled; he had other plans.

"That's my bus! Lovely, didn't have to wait. Well, then. ..." Mrs Levin's voice was lost in the engine noise as she wedged herself into a tight crowd of people and was sucked through the door.

Peter waved, then watched while the big bus rumbled away.

A man nearby, dressed in a suit, was also waving and shouting "taxi!" A black cab that looked like an old gangster car swerved up to the curb, and the man scrambled in.

Peter decided he could do that too and looked around for another taxi. It was only seconds before a taxi came, but by the time he'd raised his arm, the taxi had sped past. Another one came, and he raised his arm more quickly, but the taxi already had passengers in it. It took Peter a while to figure out that if the light on the roof of the taxi was off, it meant "occupied", and the light on meant "free". He saw one with its light on.

"Taxi!" he called with pretend confidence.

The driver leant out the window questioningly.

"Ah, excuse me, sir," Peter said with a gulp. "I'm looking for Singlewood Lane.

"Singlewood, Singlewood, …" the driver repeated the name.

"Number five … it's in Central London." Peter showed him Artiss Fleur's card. "Yeah, no probs." He tapped the address into his navigator device. "Here it is; looks like a pretty short walk: nine or ten blocks up, and on the left."

Peter watched him counting the blocks with his finger on the screen. Peter had 100 pounds in his shoe and was about to ask the driver to take him there when a couple jumped into the back of the taxi.

"Oh well … thanks," Peter mumbled shyly.

But the driver had already turned to his new passengers.

Peter set off along the line of stores, counting one block, then two. He found himself sniffing the air in circles, the way Pickles used to do. The smell of neighbourhood plants and flowers had given way to stronger smells: rusty metal from the wrought-iron fences, and stale pee rising off the concrete pavements. *Dog pee or human pee?* he wondered. All this was overlaid with a heavy smell of cooking smoke and many other aromas far more puzzling. *Pickles would like sniffing here,* he thought. But she wouldn't like the traffic noise, which seemed to rush at him in waves.

After Peter had counted three blocks, he reached a line of pavement cafes. It got harder to walk as he dodged the chairs and tables spilling onto the footpath. He passed a hairy man seated on the concrete, singing a very soulful song while playing a guitar, but his voice barely broke through the din. It was getting darker; Peter could sense that the sun was setting, even though he couldn't locate it on the skyline.

After six blocks, Peter thought it might be a good time to ask someone. He tried to catch the eye of a waiter in a white apron, but found that he couldn't make himself seen beneath the large tray the man was carrying. Then, he saw a nice couple coming towards him.

"Excuse me," he said a little too feebly.

But they were so absorbed in each other, they didn't even hear him.

Suddenly, he felt silly and hopelessly out of place.

He walked through a space between the restaurants, alongside a park railing. Up ahead a brightly lit yellow-and-red sign read: "Japanese food: The Seven Lucky Gods – stewed seaweed and fermented beans." Flashing above was a line of round-bellied old Japanese men. They seemed to be smiling down at him.

Peter decided he would ask in there, but before he could take a step forward, the jacket energy began to pulse. He felt unsafe.

"Gotcha!" said a harsh voice beside him.

Peter's arm was suddenly wrenched behind his back. A boy not much taller than he, but much stronger and older, held his face close to Peter's.

"Let me go!" Peter twisted his body angrily from side to side, trying to wrench himself free, but the harder he struggled, the more the boy tightened his steely grip on Peter's wrist.

The boy wore a black studded leather jacket and had a razor-sharp haircut.

Two more boys appeared from the shadows, dressed in similar jackets but with less-scary haircuts.

Despite his growing terror, Peter couldn't help noticing that one boy had a double nose piercing that went right between his two nostrils.

"Help! Help!" Peter screamed.

There were still a lot of people about on the footpath. But the short boy who had him by the arm clamped a smelly hand over Peter's mouth and dragged him backwards into the dark. Even the Seven Lucky Gods shining down from above couldn't help him now.

"What are you going to give us to let you go?" asked his captor menacingly.

"Hey, Vulcan," said the other tall one without the nose pierce, "he's only a little kid. Let's just get the garm and get out of here."

"Shut up, Nod. I want to have some fun first," said Vulcan. His breath next to Peter's cheek smelt bitter, like cigarettes.

"No!" repeated Nod. "Don't hurt him."

The one called Nod began pulling Peter by the jacket collar, away from Vulcan's clutches.

Peter felt momentarily relieved by this until he realised that Nod wasn't pulling him; he was pulling the jacket. He was trying to get it off him. He already had one sleeve out. Clinging onto the remaining sleeve, Peter wrenched his mouth free from Vulcan's grip.

"Help! Help!"

"Shut him up, will you!" snapped Vulcan to the third guy, with the nose pierce, who slapped a bigger and even smellier hand over Peter's mouth.

Vulcan began feeling around Peter's jacket and pants pockets. "Let's see if he's got any money."

Peter thought about the hundred pounds in his shoe. Perhaps he should offer to give it to them.

"Forget it, Vulcan," Nod said crossly. "That missus already offered us plenty of money to get the effing jacket. So, let's take it and get out of here."

Vulcan and Nod began to wrestle, with Peter wedged in between them. Nosepierce had to release his hand from Peter's mouth to try to break them up.

"I should go home," tried Peter weakly. "My guardians will be coming for me."

But the three boys continued scuffling with Peter stuck in the middle, struggling and kicking. He managed to twist his finger and thumb into Vulcan's neck, the way Gimme Jimmy had done to Peter's ankle.

"Ouch! You little—"

At the same time, Peter managed to wriggle his other arm back into the jacket sleeve.

"You think you're smart with your fancy jacket?" said Nosepierce menacingly.

Peter shook his head.

"Get it off him and let him go home," said Nod, who'd started puffing nervously on a cigarette.

"Shut up," said Vulcan. "Why don't you just go home to Mummy and suck a milk bottle too."

Think, Peter, think. He knew he could not lose the jacket. The jacket was everything. He must not let them take it. But he was too scared to think. Instead, he began to struggle uselessly again, crying, "Let me go!"

But Nosepierce had him in a vice-like grip.

Vulcan was fingering the fabric on the sleeve. "Wonder why that lady wants it so badly."

"Who cares! Just take it off him, and let's go," insisted Nod. "We'll have the cops on us in a minute."

Peter wished he could be back on the sofa with Gimme Jimmy, waiting for the takeaway bell.

"Okay," said Nod. "You two hold him while I get it."

Everything in the next few minutes happened very fast. Peter fought with all his strength as the boys began to wrench the jacket off him.

"Why's it so hard to pull … ?"

The three boys were straining and grunting.

Peter felt a holding force around, him but he knew it wouldn't last. The jacket was slipping away from him. Without thinking, he called into the jacket collar, "Invisible Bu-h! Are you there? Bu-h!"

He was surprised when he heard an answering crackling … then a voice: "Agent Blue! Is that you? Please respond! We have a copy on your distress resonance."

The voice was clear, masculine, and coming from a place of strength. The thugs didn't seem to hear, it but Peter stopped struggling and just listened.

"This is President Buchanan of GAIA. But you can call me Bu-h. Are you in need of help?" The voice was coming from inside Peter's head.

"Yes! Yes! Please help!" Peter sobbed into the air around him.

"Who's he talking to?" said Vulcan, peering suspiciously back behind them.

"Agent Blue, is your situation contained?"

"Ah … no, I don't think so," Peter replied shakily. "My situation contains three boys trying to steal my jacket."

"Who's he talking to?" repeated Vulcan.

"How the hell do we know?" said Nosepierce.

All three boys were looking around nervously.

"You think you can get smart with us?" Vulcan shook Peter threateningly by the neck again.

Then, Peter saw something flash in Vulcan's hand: a knife.

"How many assailants?" demanded the voice of Bu-h.

"Um … three."

"With arms?"

Peter paused. Of course they had arms! He was struggling to get free of them.

"I repeat, are they armed?"

"Oh … um … I see what you mean. Yes, one of them has a knife."

Peter could feel the cold steel of Vulcan's knife now at the side of his throat as he spoke. *A voice in my head isn't going to save me from a knife,* Peter thought, dismayed.

"No, I can't save you." The voice had read his mind. "But I can help you save yourself."

"How are you doing this?" Peter squeaked, sweat pumping through every pore of his body.

"Well, technically, the jacket's transforming electrical impulses from your brain into our GAIA radial receptors, but we can discuss that another time."

"Ow!" cried Peter, as Nosepierce twisted his arm painfully back behind him again.

"Agent Blue! Listen carefully. A knife has a very high frequency, but not nearly as high as your shield."

"My what?" Peter gasped.

"Keep your shield between you and the knife."

"But I don't have a shield."

"Your jacket … here at the agency, we call them shields."

"What's going on?" Vulcan squeezed Peter's neck more tightly.

"And do not enter the field of your assailant," added President Bu-h.

"Well, he has me in a headlock. So, I think I'm in his field."

"You're in his field physically, yes … but do not get into his field emotionally. Do not resonate with him!"

"I don't understand." Peter was choking for breath now. Vulcan smelt of sour sweat.

"What don't you understand?" Vulcan grabbed Peter by the hair.

"Now," instructed Bu-h, "you're going to disarm your assailant."

"How?"

"Relax. Consciousness creates all. Now, what emotions are you getting from the assailants?"

"Um. ..." Peter's voice was trembling. "I'm getting a lot of hate."

"Is he joshing with us?" Vulcan asked Nosepierce.

"I wanna get out of here," said Nod.

"Okay!" Bu-h's voice came through clearly again. "Tell me, Agent Blue, how well do you know your metaphysical sciences?"

"Um ... not so well."

"Got it. So, very quickly then, did you know that if you combine two perfectly opposite vibrations, you can cancel out the negative of the two?"

"Um. ..."

"You're experiencing hate. The opposing resonance waves for hate come from gratitude. Are you with me?"

Without waiting for a reply, the GAIA president said, "So, on the count of three, you're going to give them all the thanks you've got."

"Huh?"

"That's right: disarm the hate with thanks. Work with your inner fire power."

"Thank them?"

"Ready. ... Stay with your shield. Think of the spiral on your left pocket as the sight of a rifle, with the jacket as your weapon. Right! Go into your quiet place ... and ... one, two, three – *hit 'em!*"

Peter closed his eyes and tried to hit Vulcan with some thankfulness.

"Is that all you've got?" asked Bu-h, adding what sounded like a guffaw. "Here, let me help you with that."

It's not like I have anything to be thankful for right now, thought Peter.

"There's always something to be thankful for." The president had read his mind again. "I suggest you practise self-pity only after you've secured yourself and your shield."

Embarrassed, Peter searched his mind for something to be thankful for – Dad's jacket, of course.

"Good!" said the president. "Now, pack it up like a positive powerful punch, and send it off."

"Um ... okay. Like this?"

Using the silver GAIA spiral on the jacket dome like a rifle sight, he tried to imagine a lump of gratitude in his heart area shooting off towards Vulcan. He could feel the jacket helping him now. He tried again, this time, directing two more gratitude shots: one at Nod and then one at Nosepierce. He saw the visible impact as the three boys slackened their grip and their jaws. It was freaky but fun.

"What's happening? He's not talking to us," said Nod.

"He's a nutter," said Nosepierce.

"Vulcan scared him so much with the knife that he turned him into a nutter."

"Think so?" said Vulcan proudly.

"Stay calm," cautioned President Bu-h.

"Nah!" said Nosepierce. "He's up to something; he's joshing with us."

"Whatevs. Take the jacket, and we're out of here. I've had enough of this freak show," Nod told them.

Vulcan pushed the point of the knife back against the skin of Peter's neck.

At the same time, Invisible Bu-h's voice continued strongly and rapidly. "Disconnect emotionally from the resonance of the knife, and let the shield do the rest."

Peter tried to focus on disconnecting from the knife, but his mind kept screaming, *knife!*

"Now, for the biggest gun in your arsenal. ..."

"What's that?"

"Love, of course. Send them some love; start with the knife bearer, and you'll see that the knife won't penetrate your field."

Love? These guys? He had to be joking.

"The boys and I are going in with you!"

Peter felt a blast of energy suddenly shoot through him.

"And again!" commanded Bu-h. "Okay, one more. Give it all you've got."

The jacket field seemed to be gathering up the love energy from President Bu-h's team and shooting it out through the GAIA spiral. The first shot took Vulcan right across the footpath and into the gutter —then, *whoosh!* The knife flew from his hand and clattered to the ground on the second shot. Nosepierce gave a cry of disbelief, while Nod just stood gaping. Then, *whoosh, whoosh!* With two more shots of the same powerful force, he got them both down as well.

All three were struggling to get back on their feet, when Peter suddenly found his own feet and began to run.

Clutching the shield to his chest, Peter tore back through the streets the way he'd come; past the cafes and the Tube station, around the corner, down the hill, and back to the flat. No one seemed to be following him. He was running faster than he'd ever run before. His legs wobbled as he willed them to sprint still faster. He didn't stop till he'd reached the gate, where he began fumbling for Aunty Surla's keys.

"Is your situation contained?" asked Bu-h.

"Yes!" Peter said, weak with relief. "I don't think they followed me."

His voice came out in short gasps.

"Speak to me with your subtle voice, and save your breath," instructed the president. "Think what you want to say, then let the jacket transmute it."

"Um ... okay. ... Like this?" Peter was fumbling with the key in the gate lock now. At the same time, he tried to shape the words *thank you* in his head. He felt the message energy floating out from him and into the jacket.

"You're welcome," said Bu-h.

Peter giggled. It worked.

"Keep going, son. You're on your path."

"Thanks," Peter said again. "Thanks for being there."

"I've always been there for you."

Peter felt warm, even though the metal of the gate was cold. He was trying to see where to fit the key into the lock.

Then, he jumped at the sound of *click-clack, click-clack.* Someone was approaching. Gripping the jacket against his chest with one arm, Peter managed with the other to get the key into the lock. He turned it first one way, then the other. The gate latch yielded. He exhaled with relief.

In an instant, everything changed.

A dark shape pummelled against him, knocking him roughly into the iron gate. In the same moment, the jacket was wrenched from his tight hold. It was over before it began. The thief was gone. Peter's shield was gone. And worst of all, his connection to Invisible Bu-h was gone.

35

Bad News

Peter banged on the front door and rang the bell. "Aunty Surla! Aunty Surla!"

He fumbled with the keys but was too distressed to make any of them fit the lock; all the while, he was shouting, banging on the door, and ringing the bell.

He needed to be safely inside.

"Aunty Surla! Aunty Surla! Open up! Aunty Surla!" he repeated in between sobs.

There was a rattle of keys, and then the door finally opened.

Aunty Surla's face fell. "I thought you were the takeaways. Why didn't you use the key?"

Jimmy was scuttling bow-legged up the hallway towards them, naked and holding a heavy wet disposable nappy in his hand.

"He cry! He cry!" Jimmy shrieked.

Peter didn't care. He just continued sobbing and gulping for air.

"My shield!" Peter wailed. "It's gone."

"What? What? What's happened?" Aunty Surla asked irritably.

"My jacket's stolen!" Peter couldn't speak any more for crying. He thought he might cry for the rest of his life.

"Stolen? Where from?"

"Right here at the gate."

"What are you talking about – that old denim thing? We can buy you a much better one online. Come in now, quick, and stop making so much noise."

Aunty Surla peered over Peter's shoulder, towards the gate.

"She's gone! The thief's gone!" Peter howled, gulping for air and wrapping his arms around his aunt for comfort.

"Oh well. There are thieves around," said Surla, angling herself carefully away from Peter's hug and pushing him out to arm's length. She glanced once more towards the gate. "The takeaways are late too."

Peter tried to hug her again. He was feeling such a sense of loss that he had to anchor himself to someone.

"Never mind. You'll feel better soon," his aunt said, trying to push him away again. "Come on, stop all this crying. You're upsetting Jimmy."

Jimmy didn't look at all upset. He was staring at Peter with his television-watching face.

Peter didn't know what to do with the pain he was feeling.

"*Oooh!*" he wailed, unable to stop himself. "Aunty Surla, help me! Help me! I feel so bad."

"You'll be fine," she told him, patting his shoulder repeatedly in the same place. "Come on, let's go online and buy you a new jacket."

"No! No!" Peter stamped his foot, not caring how impolite he became. "I don't want another jacket. There is no other jacket. That was Dad's."

Peter followed Aunty Surla down the hallway, even though he already understood that she couldn't be there for him. There was no one here in London who could help him.

"I want to call Nonna. Please let me call Nonna," Peter pleaded.

"It's the wrong time."

"I don't care; she won't mind. We can wake her up. Please ... I need Nonna. Please, Aunty Surla. Please, please, let me call!"

"Look we can't call. All right?" Her patience was thinning.

Peter followed her into her workspace. There was the sound of a loud TV on the other side of the wall.

"I need Nonna to look into the crystal for me."

"Oh, what a ridiculous idea! Don't tell me you believe in all that nonsense."

"Hey, keep it down," Uncle Gorrman called through the wall.

The television volume increased.

"Look! Now you've upset Gorrman!"

Peter stood speechless. Jimmy was looking back and forth at them. Aunty Surla had an odd look on her face.

"I want to talk to Nonna because she loves me."

Aunty Surla looked uncomfortable, as if love wasn't a topic she felt ready to explore. She picked up a brown packing carton labelled "fragile" and decked with lines of coloured stamps. Peter wondered how she could think of opening her shopping right now. He saw that her lips were set in a straight thin line and her cheeks suddenly seemed more pinched than usual.

"I suppose this is as good a time as any to tell you."

"Tell me what?"

Aunty Surla pulled out of the package a cube-shaped box lined with red felt.

Peter recognised it at once, but his mind put up a block.

"This was all she left me," Aunty Surla said sourly.

Peter already knew what was inside, but he didn't understand how or why. His mind refused to connect the dots.

"Look, I'm not sure how to tell you this, but Mum went into hospital straight after you left." Surla spoke without emotion.

"Nonna went to hospital?"

"Yes, while you were travelling to London. 'Just for observation,' Matron said on the phone. And then … she went into a deep sleep … then she passed away."

"Passed away?"

"Died."

"But that's impossible; I was just with her last week."

"Well, she'd been sick for a long time. She'd been holding on for you, I think. Matron mailed this box. We got it yesterday."

Aunty Surla pouted at the box, which contained Nonna's most treasured possession: her crystal ball.

Tears were streaming in rivulets down Peter's already blotched and swollen eyes. He'd always had Nonna. How could she be gone?

"But ... but ... Aunty Surla. ..."

"Yes?" she said, stubbornly avoiding his eyes.

"Why didn't you tell me?"

"I was just waiting for the right moment. And I've been a bit busy."

"Busy? But Aunty Surla—"

"Yes?"

"Why ... ?"

"Why, what?"

"Why ... aren't you crying?"

"We weren't that close."

"Will there be a funeral?" he asked between sobs.

"They're going to scatter the ashes around some tree."

"The Great Gum?"

Aunty Surla shrugged and placed the crystal on the table next to her computer.

The pain was all around him. There was no place to be except in the pain. He would at least be alone with it.

"I'm all right now," said Peter untruthfully. "I'll go and rest in my room."

"That's a good boy," Aunty Surla said, brightening. "We'll buy you a nice new jacket tomorrow at my teleshopping portal."

In the empty bedroom, Peter looked at the empty hook where the jacket should have hung and where the jacket now was not. He desperately needed something to hold. He picked up the yoghurt pot where Nonna's nasturtium seed lay, still just a circle of dirt. Peter let his tears drip into the dirt. Sharing with another living thing gave him a tinge of hope – even though all he had to share was misery.

Peter's thoughts arched back to the day when he found out his parents had died. He must have cried a lot then, although three days in a fire without water would've made it hard for his body to make tears. He remembered that he'd slept – comforting sleeps on the ottoman. Everything at Gum Tree had been rounded by an endless comforting sleep.

But now, he was awake and adrift on the other side of the world. Nonna was dead, and he'd lost his most precious possession: Dad's jacket. He knew with rising alarm that there would be no comfort in sleep here, not in this empty room. He listened to the unfamiliar sounds in the flat. Uncle Gorrman was laughing loudly at something on the television. Jimmy was whining. The doorbell rang, and there were hurried footsteps.

"The takeaways are here!"

Peter turned off his light and curled himself up into a tight ball on the plastic bed. If only Pickles were here. He tried to relax his body and stop the unceasing sobs. He stroked the soft wallaby fur of the mother.

Why hadn't he chased after the thief? He recalled the smell of perfume and the sinister *click-clack* sound. It had been Cleo Choat, for sure. He could have run after her and snatched the jacket back. But he'd been too scared and too shocked.

Now he would do anything to have the jacket back in his arms, humming against his shoulders. Why had he gone off to find Artiss Fleur on his own? He kicked the plastic table leg. The jacket was his protection from Cleo Choat, and now she had it.

"Where power resides, evil must inevitably be drawn," Dad had said.

Now the jacket was alone with that evil. Peter hadn't protected it. But he was just a kid trapped in a grown-up world. What else could he have done?

"Oh!" Peter clutched his stomach.

"I've failed! I've failed!" he groaned out loud, then sobbed again for a long time.

An image of Pickles came into his mind.

Tsk-tsk!

Pickles! It gave him an idea. He sat up and rubbed his eyes. Despite the wet tears, his eyes felt dry. Dad had calibrated the jacket just for him.

Peter walked over to the window, focusing his mind on the jacket, and whispered, "P–i–c–k–l–e–s."

Then, out loud and with defiance, he said, "Release!"

From somewhere out there in the London night, Peter thought he felt a ripple of energy up his arms and chest. The ripple was very faint, but it brought a smile to his face. He felt almost certain that Cleo Choat wouldn't be able to break into the jacket's field now without the password. The jacket was locked. *Ha!*

When Peter woke up later, the room was dark. A shadow blocked the doorway. It was Uncle Gorrman. He closed the door and was gone. Sitting up on the bed, Peter felt empty and raw. His eyes were drawn to the hook where the jacket, his shield, should have been. Something else had been hung there. It was another jacket, a bit like Mr Dean's millionaires' club jacket, with a crest on the front pocket. Peter got up to take a look. It was a Murksborne jacket. Uncle Gorrman must have brought it in for him. After the terror of the three bullies and Cleo Choat, even Uncle Gorrman seemed ... well ... certainly not nice, but at least somehow safe.

With a heavy heart and sagging shoulders, Peter tried the Murksborne jacket on for size. Sadly, it fit him.

BOOK VI

The Fall

CHAPTER

36

The Lolly List

A
unty Surla was already tapping at her keyboard when Peter got up.

"Good morning, Aunty Surla."

"Morning," she said tonelessly, without looking up.

"What are you doing?"

She winced. "I'm a bit busy. … Catching up on my shopping."

Peter stood still beside her.

Aunty Surla jiggled her computer mouse impatiently.

"There's cold vindaloo in the fridge from last night," she said, still not looking at him.

His stomach ached with emptiness.

In the kitchen, Peter stood alone at the white bench edged with polished steel, and chewed dully on the cold, biting rice. He ate straight from a plastic container, using a large plastic spoon, then dropped the plastic container into the plastic rubbish bag with all the other one-time-use plastic. It made a dull plunking sound. No one else cared, so why should he?

His stomach was full now, but the emptiness had stayed. Why had he tried to find Artiss Fleur on his own? Why had he let go of the jacket? Why hadn't he chased Cleo Choat?

Overcome with a need to keep moving, Peter went back to the empty bedroom. The Murksborne jacket hung like an exclamation mark on the hook where Dad's jacket should have been.

Peter sat down to study the treasures under his pillow. His mother's photo smiling out at him from the podium; the book *Thelma and the Flame*; Mum's shopping list for lollies that Nonna had found in the secret jacket pocket; the little glass pyramid with the spiral; the four remaining nasturtium seeds wrapped in Nonna's handkerchief; the gold wallaby pin from Mr Dean; and the business card of Artiss Fleur.

Peter flicked through the pages of his mother's book, and for the first time, noticed that at the very back of the book, she had written a second chapter to the story under the heading "Ch 2". This chapter was written more in grown-up writing, and it was all in pencil; it was also full of strange symbols and equations that Peter couldn't understand.

Peter put down the book and picked up the pyramid, the silvery worm thing was still lying flat and lifeless on the base of the glass. Peter shook the pyramid vigorously, as if it were a snow globe, but the worm didn't budge. He put it back under his pillow, then pinned the gold wallaby into his shirt. He wondered what to do next. His eyes settled back on Mum's shopping list. The paper seemed to be telling him something.

I guess if I can talk to trees and tables, maybe one day I'll also be able to talk to paper.

He carried the list out to Aunty Surla at her computer.

"Do you think this is Mum's writing?"

"What is it?" She read the list out loud, one item after another. "Chocolate, licorice straps, jelly beans, salted peanuts, cream do-nuts. Yes, that's definitely Thelma's writing; she always used to do her *a*s like little *d*s falling backwards. Where did you get it?"

Before Peter could reply, Aunty Surla was pulling up a shopping site and typing in keywords. "Let's buy them, shall we?"

"Mum and Nonna hardly ever let me get sweets," said Peter.

"Well, I'm in charge now," Aunty Surla said tersely. "So, do you want them or not?"

"Um … yes, please," he said feebly.

"We can buy the first four items at the Lolly Trolley, and the cream doughnuts from Our Daily Bread."

His aunt became lost in her portals of power.

Less than an hour later, the doorbell rang, signalling deliveries of bulk cardboard boxes of sweets. By afternoon, Peter, together with Uncle Gorrman and Jimmy, had made multiple samples of everything on the list, including a six-pack each of cream doughnuts.

They sat for many hours in front of the big television screen, watching programmes with people in suits talking loudly about things and not listening to each other.

Later, Peter walked slowly around the house. The pain followed him like a rain cloud. In the bathroom, he got to work on Jimmy's disposable nappies. There were two in the bin. One looked like a ball of yellow snow. It was heavy, and he only needed to open it part way to see that it was pure number one, and a lot of it. He let it fall back with a *plop*. The other one was lighter and smelt bad. He fumbled for the wire coat hanger that he'd been keeping behind the towel closet, then, breathing strictly through his mouth, Peter went to work, raking through the poop.

Finding nothing, he passed by Aunty Surla's workstation again. She was nowhere around. He heard the shower running. Peter wanted contact with someone. He sat down quickly and began to type.

Email to: Devlin.Dean@Devlin.Dean
Subject: Help!

Dear Mr Dean,

I am still in London with the guardians in Leafton Street except our house doesn't have any leaves only garbage bins and I don't know how to find Spiral Hall and my uncle says he didn't get the invitation and that it's a nancy school and he wants me to go to a garbage school instead and nobody loves me and Jimmy my cousin is a biter he bit off a button from my jacket and swallowed it before I could stop him it was the pelican dome button the one that Dad said connects with my spirit which actually makes sense because my spirit feels like it really has landed in Jimmy's butt and I miss Pickles and I can hardly bear to tell you this but Cleo Choat stole my jacket I feel so bad I don't know what to do!!!!!!!!!

Peter heard the sound of the shower turning off. There wasn't much time. He reread the letter and saw that he hadn't remembered to use any full stops or commas. Also, it did come across as quite complaining, considering that Mr Dean was on his honeymoon, touring the world's great libraries with Ms Moth. On impulse, Peter pressed Delete and started again.

Dear Mr Dean,

I hope you're enjoying your honeymoon. Dreadful things have happened here. I lost my jacket, and I don't know how to get to GAIA. I've got no one else to ask. All ideas welcome.

Best regards,
Peter Blue

Aunty Surla was in the kitchen. She would be back any moment. Peter pressed Send and immediately started waiting for a reply.

By Sunday night, no reply had come. After the takeaways, Peter ate more sweets and watched more television. Then, he fell into bed without even bothering to check the yoghurt pot for a green shoot. He was already sure there wouldn't be one.

Lying in the dark, he thought of President Buchanan, saying, "I've always been there for you."

Well, he isn't here for me now.

Peter thought about the missing pelican soul of the lost jacket and tried to bring its silvery image into his mind. But, instead, he saw only Jimmy's curry-coloured poop.

37

The Betrayal

On Monday morning, Peter blinked open his eyes, only to find Uncle Gorrman in the doorway again.

"Quick, you, out of bed!" Gorrman ordered. "I'm taking you to the office. Chairman Dreeg wants to see you."

Peter frowned uncertainly. "Why?"

Uncle Gorrman shook his head. "His secretary didn't say, but it's obviously a good sign. He must be considering me for the top job."

Uncle Gorrman rubbed his big hands together.

Peter's stomach lurched. What could the top job at Big Garbage have to do with him?

When Peter didn't move, Gorrman spoke less patiently. "Well, hop to it, then! The car's leaving in thirty minutes."

As soon as his uncle had gone, Peter snatched up a half-eaten bag of jelly beans from the plastic night table and started cramming the coloured sweets into his mouth. In the bathroom, he gazed in the mirror at his tongue, stained a reddish-green colour. He needed water. In the kitchen, Peter stood at the open fridge. It was empty. There were cold takeaways on the table, but he couldn't face them. He walked past the delivery boxes from The Lolley Trolley and started loading up his backpack and the pockets of his shorts with licorice, peanuts, chocolate, and jelly beans.

At the front door, Gorrman reviewed Peter's appearance doubtfully.

"Why don't you put on the Murksborne blazer to impress the chairman?"

Peter looked blankly back at him.

"Come on!" Uncle Gorrman said. "Put it on, and be quick about it."

"Fine," Peter said through tightly pinched lips. Nothing mattered anyway.

The blazer sat heavily on Peter's shoulders. For comfort, he pinned the gold wallaby from Mr Dean into the lapel.

Out on the roadside, his uncle's driver greeted Peter with a friendly duck-bill smile.

"So, how are you enjoying London?"

"Fine, thanks." Peter couldn't help smiling back; it was like meeting an old friend.

"Lovely weather today, but hot for London," the driver told them as he cut expertly in and out of lanes of cars, pushing forward through the dense Monday morning traffic.

To Peter's relief, the driver didn't mention the quest for Spiral Hall. Maybe the slump of Peter's shoulders in the Murksborne jacket had steered him away from talk of secret eco-schools and kept him firmly on the subject of garbage dumps, which, of course, was where they were headed.

Peter settled back into the leather seat, blinking heavily into the morning sun. The quest had all been a silly trick of his imagination. Mr Biggs's newspaper couldn't suddenly have had a mysterious invitation. It was a newspaper reporting news.

It was a relief in some ways for Peter to finally be waking up. Just like Nosepierce had said, he was a nut job. He'd been hearing voices and seeing things; imagining some secret school, having no idea where it was, and yet thinking he could just go there. He was more delusional than Mr Witherspoon.

The car was entering a motorway and gaining speed.

Uncle Gorrman clicked open his brief case and began rifling through some white office papers.

Peter thought of Nonna and her crystal ball. In it she'd seen the path to Spiral Hall open for him; but according to Nonna's sight, Peter would see her again, and now she was dead.

The driver interrupted his thoughts. "Been seeing some of the sights, then, son?"

"Uh. ..." Peter wasn't sure how to respond.

"He'll be seeing some of our *sites* soon." Uncle Gorrman laughed. "As in, garbage sites."

"Are you looking forward to it, then, son?" asked the driver.

"Um—"

Before Peter could answer, Uncle Gorrman spoke to the driver.

"We're going to swing by the office first, then stop at Lot 17 on the way home. Give my nephew a taste of things."

As long as I don't have to actually taste anything, Peter thought grimly. He rummaged for a licorice strap to take away the acid flavour that had risen in his mouth. He followed the licorice with a bag of salty peanuts, then tossed down a few handfuls of jelly beans to complete the snack. Peter chewed hungrily on the lollies, even though he knew that, in the end, they wouldn't be satisfying.

Before long, the big car was exiting the motorway and turning onto a smaller tree-lined country road. As they bumped around the narrow bends, Peter began to feel slightly ill. He sucked and chewed on a few more sweets, handful after handful, to see if they would help him feel better. He even broke off half a family slab of chocolate and stuffed the whole lot in his mouth. Then, when the remaining half began to melt, he ate that too.

It was then that Peter remembered he hadn't brushed his teeth this morning. Uncle Gorrman hadn't mentioned teeth brushing. For a moment, Peter felt guilty, but if nobody else seemed to mind, why should he care? He chased down the chocolate with a few more jelly beans.

"Number 17's our best performing site," Uncle Gorrman told Peter, in a voice edged with enthusiasm. "Doubled its garbage capacity in the last five years."

Peter nodded solemnly, not sure how to respond.

Uncle Gorrman was sifting through a sheaf of papers in his lap. Some of them showed coloured bar graphs and pie charts. The skin on his uncle's face looked blotchy and red this morning. Peter tried to think of something about garbage that he could say to him.

"It'll be hot out there today," said the driver conversationally. "Don't you have cap?"

The driver was peering at Peter through the rear-view mirror. "Even though you're from Down Under, you've got that fair Anglo-Saxon skin."

Peter cleared his throat. "Actually, my dad was Welsh. His name was Byron Blue. He was a well-known adventurer."

Uncle Gorrman snorted unappreciatively.

"Is that so?" the driver said encouragingly to Peter, pausing and then adding, "Lovely singers, the Welsh. Did your dad have a strong voice?"

"Um ... yeah, I think so. ... My final memory of Dad is of him calling, 'Peter! Peter! Run! Run to Gum Tree!' He was shouting really loud."

"Is that so?"

"Anyway, I managed to get through the fire."

"You were running through fire?"

"Yeah." Suddenly, Peter was alive in the memory.

"And you made it to the gum tree?"

Peter was about to say that he had not made it to the tree, the Great Gum, but to the Gum Tree Rest Home; but, at that instant, he was hit with a flash of very strong memory. It was new memory. After all this time, and now sitting halfway across the world, five years later, Peter finally understood what had happened to him that day.

"Yes, I did run to a tree. It's all come back to me."

"Is that so ... ?" said the driver.

"I never made it to the Gum Tree Rest Home where my grandmother lived; I must have run to the actual gum tree. Then, even after I'd climbed inside it, I could still hear Dad's voice shouting and crying through the fire, 'Run, Peter! Run!'"

The driver's jaw had gone slack, and his head kept yo-yoing from the road to the back seat. Each time his head turned round to the back, he gaped at Peter.

"Yeah, that was the last time I heard Dad's voice, alive. Dad went back in to try to save Mum, but they both—"

"Whoa!" interrupted the driver, slamming his foot on the brake and almost crashing the car into a tree.

Uncle Gorrman, who'd shown no interest in Peter's story, gripped the back of the seat in front of him and said, "Steady on, speaking of running into trees."

"Sorry about that," said the driver. "Not really one for small talk, your nephew, is he?"

Uncle Gorrman didn't reply. He'd gone back to his charts. They were the same bright colours as Peter's jelly beans.

For a while, the three drove in silence, except for the purring engine and the crinkly sound of Uncle Gorrman sifting through papers.

Peter pondered his past. So, it was the Great Gum that had kept him safe for three days in the bush. The mystery was finally solved. Not that it really mattered anymore.

Uncle Gorrman began rubbing his hands together gleefully.

"Oh yes, I'm definitely in the right business," he said happily. "Fastest growing industry in the world. There'll always be more and more garbage – maximum growth potential."

Uncle Gorrman pulled up a page with a lot of coloured lines rising sharply like mountain ranges across it. "See, Peter? Profits going off the charts."

Peter nodded politely.

"More garbage, more gain!" He winked, then added with a chuckle, "More trash, more cash!"

Suddenly, Peter thought of something he could say about garbage. "But what about closing the loop, like nature does? You know, finding a way to recycle everything back to where it came from – compost and stuff ... ?"

"Closing the loop?" Uncle Gorrman looked stunned. "But that would entirely wipe out our business model. ... Close the loop? Loopedy-loo! All you eco-people are loopy."

Uncle Gorrman went back to his papers, while Peter opened another bag of jelly beans and began tossing them angrily one after another into his mouth. By the time they reached the offices of Big Garbage

Incorporated, Peter had eaten through two bags of jelly beans, a bag of salted peanuts, five licorice straps, and a mega family bar of chocolate. He patted his pockets. He still had two full bags of jelly beans and another chocolate bar for the trip home.

Big Garbage was a long, grey concrete building about ten storeys high and surrounded by parking lots. Peter followed grudgingly behind his uncle into an elevator and up to the chairman's office on the top floor.

"Hello, Clarice. You're looking lovely as always," Uncle Gorrman said in greeting to the receptionist.

"Morning, Gorrman," she replied, barely raising her head.

"Meet my nephew, Peter Blue. He's here all the way from Australia, going up to Murksborne tomorrow." Uncle Gorrman was full of extra polite flourishes.

"Well, hello there." She smiled crookedly at Peter.

"Peter, say hello nicely to Clarice Spartos, Chairman Dreeg's assistant."

"Nice to meet you." Peter's voice came out as a squeak, and he felt his face go red.

Clarice Spartos had long wavy blonde hair and might have been pretty, but it was difficult to tell because she had on so much make-up.

"Is Chairman Dreeg around?" Uncle Gorrman's voice had also developed a nervous squeak.

"He's on a call right now, but he won't be long."

"Okay, no probs," Uncle Gorrman gushed affably. "We'll wait then."

"Ah ... actually, the chairman wants to see the boy alone."

The assistant's manner, though outwardly sweet, made Peter feel uneasy.

Uncle Gorrman appeared to be thrown off guard.

"It's just a quick hello," said Clarice. "And then I'll have him right back down to you."

Peter sat alone on the squishy sofa outside Chairman Dreeg's office door. The voice speaking on the phone within sounded deep and self-assured. Nothing about this visit felt good to Peter, who didn't even dare to pop a comforting sweet in his mouth, in case he was suddenly called in.

Clarice Spartos left the reception area, carrying a bundle of papers. Now that he was alone, Peter stood up cautiously and leant in towards the door. The talking stopped.

Splish-splish! Splish-splish!

Was the chairman taking a bath in there?

The door opened suddenly, and Peter leapt back.

"Ah, Peter Blue, come in!" Chairman Elfhiss Dreeg was only a bit taller than Peter, and when he smiled, his blue eyes became two slits, squeezed in by the extra flesh on his face. "We're looking forward to having you at Murksborne. Your uncle thinks you'll be a good fit."

Peter smiled weakly and went into the chairman's office.

The chairman's iron-grey hair was pulled back in a ponytail that covered his neck.

"Come on, I want to show you something."

The chairman beckoned Peter to the other side of the office, opening large double doors to reveal a much larger, more lavish space. It was the size of a ballroom, glinting with gold-framed paintings and hung with crystal chandeliers.

Chairman Dreeg paused just inside the doorway to dip his pudgy hands into a marble font.

"Cologne," he explained as he splashed it all about his face and neck.

Splish-splish! Splish-splish!

"Do you like the room?" he asked, ushering Peter in and then closing the doors.

Peter nodded.

"Good, because I can see you in ten years in a room just like this, at a desk just like that." He pointed at the gilded table next to the floor-to-ceiling window. "I can see you picking up the phone, Peter, and asking for whatever you want."

Elfhiss Dreeg leant in close to Peter's face. "What is it you want, Peter?"

The cologne smell was making Peter feel dizzy. He didn't know what to say.

"What would you ask for if you could have anything? Come on, think big."

"Maybe a nice home," offered Peter meekly.

"Bah! A nice home!" the chairman scoffed. "Be bold and ambitious. Take ten nice homes; lavish mansions, luxury hotels – more than you could ever need."

Peter stifled a yawn. He wasn't sure what Chairman Dreeg wanted from him, but he was going to have to think big if he wanted to get out of here anytime soon. He thought of Mr Dean's scrolled list of assets. Peter had read them and written them out so many times, he could recite them. He started with Mr Dean's top-tier list, in alphabetical order by country.

"Well, maybe, I would ask for a luxury yacht in the Bahamas, or a rainforest in Brazil and a gold mine in Chile." He worked his way down the list, from memory. "Or a pine forest in Finland, a castle on the Rhine in Germany, a neoclassical house in Greece. ..."

Peter paused, seeing that Chairman Dreeg was looking staggeringly impressed, and then continued, "A Yugen mansion in Hungary, a Formula One fleet in Italy, a sea-view apartment house in Latvia, a sheep farm in New Zealand, um ... an ice hotel in Sweden, a beachfront villa in St John, and maybe a safari park in Zambia."

Chairman Dreeg's smile stretched wide across his doughy face.

He liked the list, Peter thought smugly, and then added, "Oh, and I want servants as well, who have to do just what I tell them."

Elfhiss Dreeg nodded thoughtfully, looking less convinced.

Perhaps I've overdone it, Peter thought worriedly.

"Well, well." Chairman Dreeg paced the room a little. "Your ambitions are admirable, and all this can be easily attained."

He picked up a purple-tinted glass bottle from his desk and poured a small amount of it into his open palm. "This cologne's more expensive than gold."

As Chairman Dreeg slapped the liquid on his cheeks and neck, Peter noticed that the nail on the little finger of his left hand curved into a hook and was much longer than the others. Gold rings flashed on all his fingers.

"But I don't sense that you're being truthful with me."

He was walking towards Peter now and leaning in close again. The smell of the second application of cologne was much more powerful than the first, almost hypnotic. Peter's eyelids felt leaden. Where had he smelt it before?

Elfhiss Dreeg indicated two gilt chairs. Peter sat down mutely on one, while the chairman took the other.

"I sense that there's something you want more than these things, Peter."

The cologne scent was reaching into Peter.

"A favourite friend, perhaps, or a lost loved one." The chairman's voice was soft and reassuring. "A special food, or a beloved toy – something, or someone, special to you, Peter, and only you."

Peter felt himself being lulled into thoughts of all the people and places he missed.

Chairman Dreeg's gaze shifted slowly to the little wallaby lapel pin from Mr Dean. "Well, now … what's this, a kangaroo?"

"It's a wallaby, actually." Peter smiled at the thought of Pickles.

"A wallaby? Of course. Well, well." Chairman Dreeg's voice had become even softer. "A special friend of yours?"

"Yes," Peter replied sleepily. "My one very special friend in the whole world, actually."

"And what do you call it?"

"Her," Peter corrected.

"And what do you call her?" Gold-ringed fingers floated gently across Peter's vision. "What was that? What did you say, Peter? What do you call her?"

"I. ..." Peter's head felt heavy and pulpy as he watched the waving fingers.

"Your one special friend in the whole world."

In his head, a blurred image of Pickles twitching her blue-grey snout appeared.

"I call her Pickles."

"Pickles?"

"Yes."

"P-i-c-k-l-e-s?" Chairman Dreeg's voice spelt the name out softly and patiently. "And that's your one special friend in the whole world?"

Peter nodded.

"And Pickles is your one special word too, isn't it, Peter?" The voice was dreamy but insistent.

"Yes," said Peter. "It's my most special word." He felt Pickles watching him from somewhere far away.

Tut-tut, she seemed to say.

The gold-ringed hand floated past Peter's eyes once more, then snap went the fingers. In that instant, he was hit by the recognition of why Elfhiss Dreeg's cologne smelt so familiar.

Psshht-psshht! It was the same smell that Cleo Choat had.

Dreeg was already back behind his desk, ignoring Peter now and speaking with calm efficiency into the phone.

"Clarice ... yes ... you can take Gorrman's little nephew back now. ... Yes, very good meeting. Yes, got exactly what we wanted."

It was then Peter knew that with one ill-spoken word, he had betrayed the jacket, his father's ghost, his best friend, and very likely the whole of GAIA.

CHAPTER

38

The Falcon

On the way to Lot 17, the car travelled past green meadowlands and through the quiet country villages, but Peter was barely able to glance out the window. Over and over in his mind, he replayed the scene with Dreeg. How could he have been such a fool? Giving away the password and betraying the jacket, instead of keeping it safe. He pictured Dreeg's pudgy fingers passing in front of his face. Peter had walked right into a trap. And Cleo Choat had been in on it too, for sure.

Peter slumped further into his seat. Beside him, in contrast, Uncle Gorrman was upright and chirpy.

"I heard Dreeg was pleased with you." Uncle Gorrman seemed to be looking at Peter in a new light. "I can feel that CEO position within reach; I can touch it … almost smell it."

Peter sniffed the air; suddenly, all he could smell was garbage.

The sign on the iron gate read: Lot 17; beyond it, stretching as far as his vision, Peter saw only garbage.

The driver jumped out to unlock the gate.

"Why do you lock it?" Peter asked the driver once he'd jumped back into his seat.

"Well, your uncle doesn't want his garbage escaping on him, now does he?" said the driver playfully.

As they bumped their way down the drive, Peter saw an old wooden signpost bearing a faded name: Green Chapel Hill. It was hard for Peter to believe this grey wasteland had once been green.

As the three of them walked a few steps away from the car and onto the site, Peter's head began to feel hot and heavy.

"Pretty neat, huh?" said Uncle Gorrman. "Private trash – the best kind of trash." He pointed off to an area of rising dust. "Over there, construction waste from a partner company of ours; they pay us by the tonne."

Peter watched Uncle Gorrman in his shiny grey suit rising up from the horizon of rubbish. In the sky above his head, a flock of gulls circled.

"Are they seagulls?"

"Garbage gulls," said Uncle Gorrman. "Dirty pests, all of them."

Well, it's not their fault human garbage is dirty, Peter thought. *I bet the birds preferred the days of the Green Chapel.*

Suddenly, the gulls began to scatter as a larger bird of prey with an immense wingspan flew in amongst them.

"A falcon!" Peter breathed with excitement.

For a while, the falcon was king of the sky, turning and tilting in wide spirals and clearing the blue space around it, before settling on top of a tall red smokestack.

"Stupid bird," Uncle Gorrman muttered.

"Why?" Peter protested angrily.

Uncle Gorrman shrugged. "There's a lot of landfill gas, methane mostly, coming off the site. The system collects it up through that pipe." He pointed to where the falcon was sitting, and added, "And then it shoots it up and sets fire to it."

"Fire? But what about the falcon? It likes to sit up there to look for its prey."

Peter's face began to feel flushed. He wished he hadn't eaten all those sweets.

"Are you okay?" The driver sounded worried. "I think the boy needs a hat for the sun."

"Please ... water!" Peter groaned.

The driver returned with two plastic water bottles: one for Peter, and one for Uncle Gorrman.

"Chilled from the car fridge in the back," the driver said, handing them each a bottle.

Peter cracked the plastic cap on his bottle, then winced when Uncle Gorrman said, "You don't mind plastic when you're really thirsty, eh, Peter?"

Peter drank down the water without stopping.

When they'd both finished, Uncle Gorrman dropped his own plastic bottle onto the ground next to Peter's feet. For some reason, it felt offensive. Peter willed himself to look away, but the plastic bottle lay between them like a gauntlet thrown between two warring knights.

As Peter bent down to retrieve it, the grey landscape seems to rise up to meet him. Groping forward for the bottle, his hand instead touched a bird. A dead garbage gull; its wings were singed, and its feathers spotted with blood.

Peter rubbed his eyes through the mirage of heat. Suddenly, he was finding it impossible to breathe.

"Spontaneous combustion!" shouted Uncle Gorrman. "Quick! The lot's on fire!"

Small fires were flaring up all around. Peter tried to stand up but couldn't. On his hands and knees, he lifted his head and stared up at the smokestack. The falcon was gone. He vomited – bold splashes of colour onto the bleak landscape. For an instant, it reminded him of the colours against the white background on his uncle's charts.

Then, the driver was carrying Peter to the car.

"The gas might have gone beyond safe levels," the driver said worriedly.

"Well, let's get out of here, then! What are you waiting for?!" Uncle Gorrman commanded.

Peter lay slumped on the back seat, and his uncle moved to the front. The Murksborne jacket reeked of sick. As they bumped their way back to the main road, Peter raised his head weakly.

"But what about the birds?"

"What about the birds?" Uncle Gorrman repeated sarcastically, his chest rising and falling into a chuckle. "Yeah, good one!"

CHAPTER

39

The Spirit of Water

Back at the flat, Peter hung the Murksborne blazer on the hook and climbed wearily into bed. He was almost asleep when he became aware of his aunt standing above him and sniffing the air.

"Are your bags all packed for tomorrow?"

"But I feel so sick, Aunty Surla."

"It's just nerves, probably. But you have to go; Gorrman doesn't want to upset Chairman Dreeg."

Wearily, Peter nodded and then closed his eyes. All he wanted to do was sleep; it was as if the plastic garbage fire from Lot 17 had moved into his head.

He must have slept for some hours because, when he woke, it was dark outside. The fire still burnt in waves pulsing into his ears from behind his eyes. The room smelt of sick. He must have vomited again. Peter pulled himself up slightly, then vomited some more.

Watching the runny sick draining down across the plastic mattress, Peter thought, *Aunty Surla was right to keep the plastic cover on.*

More candy-coloured sick gushed from his insides, then drizzled down the mattress cover and onto the floor. Using the Murksborne blazer like a towel, he mopped up the sick, then hung the reeking blazer back up on the hook.

He slept again. Much later, he woke to find the room full of chattering garbage gulls.

"How did you get in here?" he asked them.

We came through the fire in your head.

"Please keep it down," he told them, clamping his hands over his hot ears.

Peter staggered to the window and flung it open, then watched on weak knees as the gulls flocked to the ledge and launched off in flapping groups, flying into the night sky above Leafton Street.

It was then that Peter realised how thirsty he was. His tongue was so swollen with thirst that he couldn't swallow.

"Water," he croaked.

The garbage fire burnt on in his head; he needed water to put it out.

"Water, water ... please, someone, I need water!" he called.

But no one heard, and no one came.

Peter slumped his body back on the bed, and slept. When he woke again, it was to the smell of curry. Someone had left a takeaway tray on the night table. Just the smell of it brought a bitter taste to the back of his throat.

Peter wasn't sure if he was asleep or awake, but the room looked odd. The walls were wavy. The neon street light outside the window was making the room glow orange – fiery orange. He felt disconnected. Was he awake or asleep? He still wasn't sure.

He heard a shuffling noise coming from the folds of the Murksborne blazer on the hook. The big swirly *S* had slid away from its place between the *K* and the *B* on the pocket monogram, and was swinging pendulum-style from the pocket cuff. It seemed to be staring at him. Soon the whole blazer was swaying as the slithery *S* stretched and lengthened itself down from the bough of the jacket sleeve to the floorboards below.

This has to be a dream.

Peter sat powerless as the *S* slithered snake-like up the bed leg and onto the end of the mattress. Even in the semi-darkness, Peter could see its snake-like fangs preparing to strike. Suddenly, he found his voice.

"Help! Someone, help!" Peter's screams filled the room.

He closed his eyes, then opened them again. His bed had become a snarling mess of talons and fangs. It was the falcon from the landfill, fighting with the snake.

The snake retreated, protesting, *I'm only an S! I'm not what you think!*

"That was close," Peter whispered. He gasped, feeling wet with sweat, but managed to add, "Thank you."

It was nothing, said the falcon.

Peter saw that its wings were singed from the landfill fire. Teetering from side to side, the falcon fell from the bed to the floor.

"I'm so sorry about the fire!" Peter cried.

Don't blame yourself, the bird of prey said. *It was my journey.*

Peter took the vomit-soaked blazer from the hook, threw it violently into the wardrobe, and slammed the door firmly on it. He didn't want any more trouble from that *S.*

He turned back, to see a dark shape outside at the window ledge. It was Tollen from the hollow oak.

"You scared me," Peter said.

"I'm sorry. I was just looking for a falcon that might have come this way. Ah, there you are, my dear one."

Peter watched speechless as the old man lowered a heavy gloved hand towards the floor, just low enough for the injured bird to scramble onto.

Then, Peter found his voice. "Is it the bird that no longer flies?"

Tollen shook his head, then tied a cord carefully round the bird's talons, gently placing a hood on its head.

"You'll heal," he said kindly, looking first at the bird and then at Peter.

Peter understood that the remark was meant for him as well.

"Am I in your dream this time, or are you in mine?" Peter asked.

"Neither," Tollen replied, and when Peter frowned, Tollen added, "Consider one more possibility."

"Um ... could we both be in the falcon's dream?"

Tollen nodded and was gone.

Much later, Peter opened his eyes again. The fire in his head was trying to tell him something. It was the Flame Girl from his mother's book.

"Remember, you're it," she said aloud, tapping away at his shoulder.

"Go away," he told her. "I hate fire! You hurt the birds!"

But Fire stayed, burning him up from the inside.

"Go away!" repeated Peter.

"But I'm Flame Girl, the spirit of Fire."

"I don't want the spirit of Fire; I want the spirit of Water! I'm thirsty." Peter began to cry.

"I'm here," said a gentle voice. "I came through your tears. Now, tell me what's troubling you."

"I feel so sick, and I have to get to the GAIA Hub by the equinox and get a message to Agent Fleur. But the way is blocked; I can't get past my uncle. He's too big for me."

"Well, why don't you do what water would do?" Water spirit spoke in a soft musical voice.

"What would water do?"

"Simple. In a riverbed, if water reaches a boulder, it just rises up and flows over it. So, why don't you just flow over your uncle, like water would do?"

"Thank you," said Peter wearily. "I'll give it a try."

When he woke again, a plastic bottle of water had been left beside the bed. Peter drank the water down thirstily, even though it tasted like plastic landfill. It smelt like it too. It smelt like greed. Greed did have a smell, just like Dad had told him. Greed smelt like Uncle Gorrman's garbage dumps.

Then, there was daylight outside the curtain-less window.

Peter picked up the pot with the seed and held his face so close to the soil that he could almost taste the dirt.

"Grow!" he begged the seed. Peter might have been crying, or it might just have been the spirit of Water saying goodbye, but tears fell into the pot.

"Grow ... grow!" Peter pleaded.

The plant didn't reply, but the dirt left smudges on Peter's nose and chin.

He slept and woke again. How many days had he been like this? There were three plastic takeaway trays in a line now on the night table next to his bed. Three days? The seven lucky gods winked and laughed, clutching their bellies, rippled by the plastic delivery bags.

Peter smiled weakly back at them, thinking to himself, *I won't give up. Or will I?*

BOOK VII

The Hero's Leap

40

The Spirit of Air

Peter's eyes snapped open. A girl's face peered down at him. She looked like one of the thugs who'd stolen his jacket. The skin on her face was pierced with silver at the nose and the eyebrow. Peter shrank back against the wall. How had she got into the room?

The girl leant her pale face close to his and sniffed the air. "Were you sick?"

Peter nodded, his throat still too parched too speak.

She might have sensed this because she came back with cold water in a glass and carefully tilted it up to his mouth.

"Your mum said it was time to wake up."

"She's not my mum."

The girl nodded. Her skin shone unnaturally white against the black of her studded leather jacket and spiky short hair.

"I'm Jimmy's new sitter," she said.

"Where's Mrs Levin?" Peter asked, though he didn't really care. He coughed into the water.

"*Shh!* There, there … just lie still for a while." Her voice was soothing, nothing like the voices of Vulcan and Nod and Nosepierce. "The regular nanny didn't show up, and I was right here in the neighbourhood when the agency called."

Peter nodded.

"My name's Sylph. It means 'spirit of the air'." Her tiny face lit into a smile. She started sniffing again, wrinkling her nose at the line of stale takeaway trays.

"Shall I get you something fresh to eat?"

Peter nodded. His stomach felt achingly empty.

Sylph eyed the pot on the windowsill. "Would you like more yoghurt?"

Peter nodded again.

"*Ooh!* What's this?" She raised the dirt pot lightly in her hands. "Oh, a sweet little plant!"

"Let me see!" Peter sat up quickly.

The new shoot was no bigger than a pencil tip, but the nasturtium was finally growing.

A ray of silver-yellow sun beamed through the window, striking Peter's arm. It reminded him of the Fire in his mother's story: "I don't only burn," Flame Girl said. "I also warm things to make them grow."

Sylph was moving about the room.

"I won't give up," Peter said, in a voice meant only for the plant to hear.

Sylph looked over at him sternly.

"You've been a very sick little boy, by the looks, but now you're going be well again."

Peter nodded. Then, keeping his voice casual, he asked, "Do you, by chance, know the way to number 5 Singlewood Lane? It's in Central London."

Sylph pulled out a handheld device from the leather folds of her jacket and slid her finger across the screen.

"Yes!" She smiled to show a sparkling jewel attached to one of her top teeth.

Peter showed her Artiss Fleur's business card. Somehow, he felt that he could trust her.

"Spiral Hall?" She laughed lightly. "And this Artiss Fleur guy's a friend of yours?"

"No … not exactly." Peter hesitated. "Finding Artiss Fleur is part of my quest."

Sylph nodded thoughtfully. "Do you have any clues?"

"I can see things sometimes," Peter explained, "in trees and other stuff to do with trees. And I saw the invitation. But I need to find the actual invitation."

He looked away, feeling embarrassed.

Glancing again at the business card, Sylph tapped some more on her device, doing a keyword search for "GAIA" and "Spiral Hall".

"Nothing here," she said. "It must be a very secret school."

"It is," Peter said worriedly. "And I'm supposed to get there on the day of the autumn equinox."

Sylph consulted her device again. "The equinox is tomorrow. We'd better hurry."

Peter liked the way she said "we".

Sylph began sifting through a pile of Peter's clothes, moving soundlessly back and forth from the drawer to the bed, building him an outfit. She pulled open the wardrobe and wrinkled her nose at the vomit-soaked blazer, then gathered it up and carried it away.

Soon Sylph was back, throwing open the window at the end of the bed and expelling stale air from the room. Peter watched her lean out as far over the sill as she could, opening and closing her mouth to fill herself with air. It was as if the weight of her metal piercings and silver studded jacket were the only things holding her to earth. Without them, Peter imagined, she would just drift up and away into the London sky.

In the kitchen, Peter got cold curry and a cold stare from Aunty Surla.

"You missed the first day of school; your uncle was disappointed."

"Sorry," Peter said weakly.

Uncle Gorrman sighed self-importantly.

"You were out of it for three days. ..." He sighed again. "All kinds of carrying-on too; we could hear you calling out and thumping around in there."

When Peter didn't respond, Uncle Gorrman laughed, as if he thought Peter might have been enjoying himself.

Sylph appeared at the kitchen doorway, with Jimmy beside her.

"It looks like your nephew has been a very sick little boy," she told Uncle Gorrman.

"Hmm … well, no probs about the school," Uncle Gorrman continued. "I squared it away with Chairman Dreeg. We'll go up this weekend, and you can start next Monday instead."

He got up and wriggled his big upper body into his shiny grey suit jacket. "Dreeg even asked me to pass on a get-well greeting. Don't know what went on during that meeting of yours, but he seems to have really taken a shine to you."

Peter glanced over at Sylph, who'd begun spooning curry and yoghurt into Jimmy's mouth. It occurred to him that he could still just refuse to go to Murksborne. But then, Uncle Gorrman would stand up to him like a big angry boulder, and, despite the advice of the Water spirit during his fever, Peter knew he didn't have the strength to flow over Gorrman like water.

Sylph scooped up Jimmy and left the room.

"Who's going to go for a nice walk, then?" she said to Jimmy.

"No walky! Teebee! I want teebee-e-e-e!" Jimmy wailed.

"So, we'll go up Sunday then, Peter. Take Surla and Jimmy, and make a day of it," Uncle Gorrman confirmed.

Peter shrugged.

"What? You're lucky to be going."

Peter stared sulkily at Uncle Gorrman, trying to find the courage to stand up to him.

"You're not still on about that nancy boy school on an island in the middle of nowhere, are you?" growled Uncle Gorrman.

Peter's heart skipped suddenly with hope. He hadn't told Uncle Gorrman that the school was on an island. He hadn't known that himself. This was a breakthrough. Uncle Gorrman knew something. Peter shook his head uninterestedly. He needed to keep his uncle on his side while he figured out his next move.

"Good lad. Murksborne it is, then!" Uncle Gorrman was visibly relieved.

He's scared of Dreeg, thought Peter. *Otherwise, he wouldn't care where I went to school or what I did.*

The invitation might still be somewhere in the house, maybe in his uncle's office safe.

Look to where the guardian's treasure and yours become one. Peter recalled the words of Quercus Croak through the crystal.

The sound of Jimmy's sobs rose and fell from the front entranceway.

"Jimmy can watch more TV if he wants," Surla called from her shopping station. "No need to go out."

"This little boy needs air," Sylph called back firmly.

Peter heard the sound of the stroller belt snapping shut, accompanied by loud disagreement from Jimmy.

"I think I need some air too," Peter told Uncle Gorrman politely.

Peter flowed right past his uncle, out of the kitchen, and down the hall.

41

The Walk

Jimmy's cries gradually subsided into small whimpers as they strode at a fast walk up the high street. They were heading in the direction of Singlewood Lane and Artiss Fleur's mailing address. Peter had lots of thinking to do. Uncle Gorrman knew something. He might even have Peter's invitation locked in his office. All Peter had to do was break in and find it. He thought again about the message from the old frog in Nonna's crystal: *Look to where the guardian's treasure and yours become one.* Uncle Gorrman loved money, so the invitation might be in his safe.

There might also be a clue at Singlewood Lane, thought Peter. *Who knows? Artiss Fleur might even be there.*

They walked in silence for a while, then Sylph said, "My brother's just got a new job at the garden centre. How about we spy on him as we go past?"

"Okay," Peter agreed.

"I was worried about him for a while," Sylph continued. "You know, that he might turn out bad. But, like everyone else, he's just looking for some hope."

Peter nodded thoughtfully. Walking along at a fast pace, with a purpose, he could feel some of his own hope returning. People around them were also in a hurry, some of them in work clothes, some of them schoolchildren. If he hadn't got sick, he would be at Murksborne now, with Chairman Dreeg's narrow eyes watching him. But he wasn't. That was one very good reason to be hopeful.

Then, Peter saw something ahead that made him pull back in fear.

"What is it? Are you sick again?"

"No, up there … on the other side of the road." Peter pointed with one hand while dragging Sylph and the stroller backwards with the other. "It's one of the boys who tried to steal my jacket."

Peter could see already that it was Nod, the tall one, leaning his shoulders against a red brick wall.

"Where? What jacket?"

"My father's jacket." Peter pointed in the direction of Nod, who was calmly smoking a cigarette. The thumb of his free hand was looped lazily into the front pocket of his jeans.

Sylph squinted at him. "That guy?"

"*Shh!* Yes."

"Are you sure?"

"Yes. He's called Nod."

"Right!" said Sylph, snatching up Peter's hand and launching off towards Nod.

"Go! Go!" chanted Jimmy.

"Wait! Don't!" Peter winced, trying to rein Sylph in with his arm. "He could be dangerous."

"Dangerous?" Sylph laughed joylessly, then muttered, "I'll give him dangerous."

"Evander Hollings!" Sylph screamed across the high street. "I want to talk you!"

Blinking in surprise, Nod stood up straight and put out his cigarette.

"Why aren't you working?" Sylph challenged as she bumped the stroller up the curve.

Nod seemed to be studying something in the tar seal of the footpath. He mumbled, "I'm on a break."

"No, you're not! You're slacking off." Sylph snatched Nod up by the collar, then directed his face roughly towards Peter. "Is this one of the jacket thieves?"

Peter nodded reluctantly, all the time avoiding eye contact with Nod.

Sylph made an angry gesture, as if she were about to spit, then thought better of it.

"What do you have to say for yourself?" she demanded.

"Nothing!" Nod whined.

"What did you do to this little boy?"

"Nothing," Nod croaked.

Sylph glanced up at the sign above their heads: Good Gardening Store.

"And what are you doing standing out here smoking? Why don't you get inside and do your job?" she said.

"Ah ... okay." Nod made a move towards the shop door.

"Come back here!"

"Make up your mind," he said petulantly.

"What were you thinking?" Sylph shook him by the elbow, warming to her subject. "Picking on a little boy, a guest in our country. Wants to make something of himself, and you and your lazy, useless, layabout friends attack him and steal his clothes. I'm ashamed to have you as a little brother."

Nod looked so dismal now that even Peter began to feel sorry for him.

"Actually," Peter interrupted, "Nod was the nicest to me of the three."

Sylph seemed momentarily gratified to hear this, then her face clouded. "The nicest of three boys who mugged and robbed a little lost boy?"

"I wasn't lost," Peter protested.

"Mum's going to be so proud," Sylph continued.

Nod winced, and Peter saw that, to his credit, Nod did look remorseful.

"Don't tell Mum; please don't tell Mum. I'll do anything."

"Is that so? Where's Vulcan, then? I'm sure he was in on this, and I'm going to give him a piece of my mind too."

"Please, no! Not Vulcan!" wailed Peter, gripping the leather on Sylph's jacket. "Don't get him!"

Jimmy sat forward in the stroller with his TV face on, watching them.

"Don't worry," said Nod, talking directly to Peter for the first time, "Vulcan's in hospital."

"What happened?" asked Sylph in a voice slurred with suspicion.

Nod grimaced. "Stabbed himself by accident with his own knife. It was just a superficial flesh wound, so don't worry."

"I wasn't worried," Sylph snapped. "How did it happen?"

"How do you think?" Nod indicated Peter. "This poor little boy of yours took us all on, and, I'm telling you, it was us that came off worst."

Nod then demonstrated the action of bending and straightening his elbow. "Still can't move my arm properly after he slammed me into the iron fence."

Sylph looked at Peter thoughtfully. "You did that?"

"Well … kind of." Peter smiled self-consciously.

"And you took on Vulcan?"

Peter nodded.

Sylph shook her head in wonder for a moment, then snapped her attention back to her brother. "But that still doesn't explain what you were doing stealing a boy's jacket."

Nod mumbled his reply. "Some lady wanted the jacket … said she'd give us a big load of money if we got it for her. But in the end, when we went back to her, she didn't even pay us! Just kept ranting about the jacket being locked and that it was no good without the boy. Like, how could a jacket be locked … ?"

"Um … did that lady stink of perfume?" Peter asked.

"Yeah, I think so. …" Nod sniffed the air, as if to reactivate the memory in his nose. "Yeah, now that you mention it, she didn't smell too good. Come to think of it, I wouldn't call her a lady either … old witch, more like it, hanging round this burnt-out building."

Sylph took her brother by the scruff of the neck again. "So, keep talking. Why'd she want a little boy's jacket?"

Nod looked sulky.

"Tell me!" Sylph shook him by the collar again.

"She talked about doing some kind of weird lab experiments on it. I think she was a bit barmy."

259

"But why?" Sylph persisted.

"She kept raving on about some guy … said she was going to get the jacket and bring down this guy, and everyone would pay." Nod shuddered.

"Would that guy be your dad?" Sylph asked Peter gently. "You said it was his jacket."

"Well, my dad's dead."

Both Sylph and Nod looked uncomfortable.

"It's all right." Peter wasn't looking for sympathy; he was looking for information. "Are you sure she said 'a guy', not 'GAIA'?"

Nod frowned. "Yeah, maybe that's what she said. What's GAIA?"

"Never mind. Did she have black frizzy hair and a pointy chin, wear square glasses, and have a kind of triangular face?"

"Yeah, yeah – that's the ticket."

"My shield!" Peter gasped. The traffic seemed to stand still around him. He could feel his heart pounding a steady beat. "It might still be there. Can you take me to the place?"

"Not likely," said Nod. "Never going back there again."

Sylph squeezed Nod's bad arm.

"*Youch!*" he protested. "All right, all right."

He started heading off down the footpath.

"Where are you going?" screeched Sylph.

"I'm taking you there!"

"Aren't you forgetting something?"

Nod looked blank.

"You'll first go in and tell your employer that you're stepping out to take care of an urgent family problem."

"But it's not a family problem."

"It will be if Mum finds out."

"Yeah, okay. All right," he grumbled and turned to go back into the Good Gardening Store.

"Good boy," Sylph said forgivingly.

As they set off together, Peter suggested it would be quicker to take a taxi.

"I can pay," he told them. "I've got money."

"How much money you got?" asked Nod, interested.

"Money, money!" Jimmy chanted, causing passers-by to look around sharply.

"I have a hundred pounds in my shoe," Peter confided.

"Then, I believe the phrase is 'well heeled'!" said Sylph with a laugh. "But you keep your money. Nod's a working boy now. It's his turn to pay."

42

The Prospect

"Shame about your place," said the taxi driver, looking out at the house, which had been gutted by fire.

"Well, actually—" Peter was about to explain when Sylph kicked him.

"Yes, it is a shame," she said sadly. "We're just here to pick up some things."

"Well, if you're not going to be long," the driver told her amiably, "I could turn off my meter and wait for a bit. I'm due for a break."

"Oh, thank you!" Sylph's facial piercings flashed like silvery stars. "That makes us feel so much better. We've heard there might be thieves about."

As they turned down the path along the side of the house, they heard muffled voices inside.

"Stay back," ordered Nod, barring their way. "I'll go in first."

Sylph nodded and guided Peter and the stroller behind a scraggly bush. Fortunately, Jimmy had fallen asleep.

They watched Nod kneel down to look into a lower window, almost at ground level. He turned and gave a thumbs up.

"They're in the cellar," Sylph said, interpreting the gesture.

Nod then climbed through what was left of a ground-floor window frame and disappeared inside.

"Let's get to the cellar window and cover for him," whispered Sylph.

Peter's knees shook as he crept behind Sylph to the burnt-out house.

From the empty window frame, they had a clear view of Cleo Choat, who sat facing away from them with her neck stooped, tapping into the keypad of a triangular device. Peter was sure it was her; he recognised the sharp slant of her profile against her tight curly hair. He sniffed the air and knew her for sure by the smell. Sadly, Peter saw no sign of the GAIA jacket. Cleo Choat raised her head and turned suddenly, startling Peter and Sylph. They pulled themselves quickly from view. A *click-clack, click-clack* noise started up. Sylph frowned over at Peter. It was as if the room were full of tap dancers, but Cleo Choat was alone in there, sitting down.

"Malodor! Quiet down the clackinations!" Cleo Choat screeched.

"Yes'm," replied a wheezy voice from another room.

Cleo Choat rummaged through the pockets of her spiny black coat until she found a gold cylinder.

Psshht! Psshht! She directed spray from the cylinder to the back of her neck.

Her regular bad stench was now overlaid with the scent of perfume. Peter shuddered, recalling the *splish-splash!* of Chairman Dreeg's cologne.

Cleo Choat stowed the gold cylinder carefully onto a high ledge, not far from where Peter was positioned. Dare he reach down for it? Sylph was nodding and pointing at it. Peter's heart thumped as he snatched up the cylinder soundlessly and stuffed it safely into the pocket of his shorts. Having possession of something of hers gave him some small satisfaction. Mr Dean might call it *leverage*.

Then, the clackinations, as Cleo Choat called them, started up more loudly than before.

Peter couldn't figure out where they were coming from.

Sylph must have been fearful of Jimmy waking up because she went over to gently rock the stroller.

"Malodor!" Cleo Choat shrieked again.

"Yes'm."

They heard footsteps approaching. A small round man, only the height of a child, hurried into the room. He was dressed in high platform black boots and grey trousers that buckled just below the knee. As he clip-clopped past the window, Peter saw unmistakably that the little man was wearing the GAIA jacket – Peter's jacket. Peter tugged Sylph's arm, and pointed down at the jacket. She smiled, but then her face fell. They were both thinking the same thing: stealing it back wouldn't be easy.

Cleo Choat stamped her foot, bringing a new eruption of *click-clack, click-clack, click-clack.* "I told you to shut up the clackinations! I can't hear myself think!"

Malodor said, "I can no longer control them."

There was silence as Cleo Choat glared up at him.

"Well, why is it taking so long, ma'am?" he asked defensively.

"I'm connecting to the field," she said tiredly. "But I just can't hold the space long enough to make the power transfer over to you."

She glanced down at her triangular device.

"Wait a minute, what's this?" She straightened quickly.

Malodor leant over her shoulder, keeping a polite distance.

Peter stared at the high platform boots. The man's plump moon face reminded Peter a bit of Elfhiss Dreeg's.

"I can't understand it," Cleo Choat was saying. "Something's suddenly changed. Look, I can hold it now."

"Hold what, ma'am?"

"The electromagnetic field, you idiot! Now stand still; this could be a breakthrough!" She laughed throatily.

"Well done, ma'am," Malodor said with a wheeze.

"Although it is puzzling." Cleo Choat glanced suspiciously round the space.

Once again, Peter was only just able to duck out of sight in time. Peter knew enough about the jacket to guess that it was his own personal field making the difference to the experiment. The thought worried him. He didn't want to help her.

"Stand still while I plug in," Cleo Choat commanded. "Do you remember the password?"

"Yes'm." Malodor licked his lips distastefully.

Click-clack, click-clack, click-clack, click-clack!

"Why are the clackinations so strong now?" She rubbed her neck. "And the fetor too!"

"The hatchlings are excited," Malodor said darkly. "I have a strong sense there's a prospect nearby. They'll be sensing it too."

Click-clack, click-clack!

"A prospect?" Cleo Choat sounded interested. "How advanced?"

"Seeping with greed. It would be an easy conversion." Malodor sniffed the air. "Very close, if I'm not mistaken."

Peter pulled back from the window and flattened himself against the wall. Were they talking about him? Was he a prospect seeping with greed? Or was it Nod? He was in the house; he was also greedy enough to want to steal a jacket for money. A fussy whimpering sound cut through the silence. Could they mean Jimmy? He was as greedy as they came, but a prospect for what?

Down in the cellar, Cleo Choat said, "Forget the prospect. It's taken me three days to get this far. Now stand still, and let's try again!"

Having issued her command, Cleo Choat bent down to Malodor's waist.

"Prepare to have your secrets unlocked," she said.

"I've no secrets from you ma'am."

"Not you!" she snapped, "The jacket! It's the key to bringing down the GAIA kingdom and, with it, that smug so-called Sleeping King."

Cleo Choat clipped her triangular device through the empty buttonhole where the pelican dome had once been. This gave Peter an idea. Pulling the stroller closer, he placed a hand on his sleeping cousin's big tummy, then focused on connecting with the pelican dome, the soul of the jacket. He sensed quite strongly that the dome was still there and that he'd made the invisible connection. *Good.*

Click-clack, click-clack!

"Malodor! Stop the clackinations. I need silence for this!"

Malodor mumbled something under his breath, and the *click-clack* sound softened.

Meanwhile, Peter directed his inner focus towards the jacket, putting all of his thought energy into opening a space that included the pelican, the jacket, and himself.

Yes! He was doing it!

Quickly, Peter floated the password P-i-c-k-l-e-s across his mind's eye. *Fuse!* He felt the jacket energy connecting effortlessly into the space. It worked!

He repeated the process to release the connection. It worked again.

But would this remote ability be enough to prevent a transfer to Malodor, who was physically wearing the jacket?

"Right!" snapped Cleo Choat. "Put the password into your mind, and hold it there. Once we're connected, we'll change to the new password, and the power will be ours."

She arched her neck forward, filling the air with a waft of breathy stench. The smell made Peter drowsy.

"Are you thinking of the password, Malodor?"

"Yes'm."

Cleo Choat consulted the triangular device, then shook it roughly. "Are you sure?"

"Yes'm."

"Okay, on the count of three, we're going to fuse."

While Malodor stood squeezing his face in concentration, Peter, a few feet above, put his energy into reopening a competing space. He floated the password so vividly that it even included a visualisation of the real Pickles hopping through his head.

Cleo Choat began to count slowly. "One ... two. ..."

Fuse! Peter got in one beat ahead of her. *Fuse! Fuse! Fuse!* He repeated and felt the word shooting rapid-fire through his head and out into the universe beyond.

Cleo Choat commanded, " ... Three, and fuse!"

But Peter had control. He could feel the jacket energy all around him, almost as if he were wearing it. It was his jacket, and he had the home advantage.

"Fuse! Fuse!" Cleo Choat repeated, stamping her foot and glaring at the triangular gauge.

"Fuse!" Fuse!" she cried between foot stampings. "It should have worked!"

"Please don't agitate yourself, ma'am. It's bad for the—"

"I'll agitate myself if I want to! Now concentrate! I hope we're in, but it's not as clear as I would've expected. We're going to input the new password, and release. If that works, the transfer will be complete, and we'll have possession. All right, here goes; think of the new word. Are you focusing?"

"Yes'm." Malodor's face was red with exertion.

Above them, Peter focused again on holding the space. He still had possession with the old password.

"On the count of three!" Cleo Choat commanded. "We're going to release with the new password. One ... two—"

Release! interrupted Peter, with the same silent intent as before. Yes! The jacket was with him. He knew it. His heart sang.

Cleo Choat screeched, " ... Three, and release!"

She glared at the triangular device, then screamed with rage.

"There's no response!" She ripped it from the buttonhole and threw it skidding across the stone floor, towards the fireplace. Malodor wheezed nervously.

"You weren't focusing hard enough, you worthless, greedy Anthrog man-baby!"

Peter smiled and quickly put his hand back on Jimmy's tummy to reopen the jacket. But this time, he sensed its remote energy waning. They would have to act soon. The problem was that Malodor was still wearing the jacket, even though Peter had control of it.

Click-clack! Click-clack!

"Find some way to shut them up!" Cleo Choat was rubbing at the back of her neck.

"I'm afraid I can't, ma'am. You see, they're hungry, and they sense a prospect is close."

Cleo Choat picked up her triangular device. "I don't care. Stand still, and let's try again."

She paused, then, as an afterthought, asked "How close?"

"Hard to say, because they're so agitated from the forced starvation of the last three days, and you yourself are so agitated. ..."

"Oh, shut-up!"

Cleo Choat looked up at the empty shelf near the ledge, then began rummaging through her pockets. "The fetor's getting too strong. Where's my redolence?"

Peter smiled over at Sylph and held up the gold dispenser.

"Perhaps you are ready for your prospect now, ma'am."

"Yes," Cleo Choat said tiredly. "Find me the prospect while I go and rest, then we'll get straight back to work. And find my redolence too!"

Malodor tripped out of the room.

The Jacket Rescue

"**M**alodor's coming," Peter hissed.

He and Sylph scooted with the stroller behind a jutting garden wall with a view of the front doorway. They crouched there, waiting for the little round man to appear.

They swung around in shock when a wheezy voice behind them said, "Well, well, who have we here?"

"I could ask you the same," snapped Sylph bravely. "This is not your house, is it?"

Malodor seemed at a loss for a moment, but then his eyes settled on sleeping Jimmy. A gluttonous look came across his face as he stumbled towards the stroller.

Sylph winked at Peter, then glanced almost imperceptibly upwards. In one swift movement, Nod dropped from the roof onto the unsuspecting Malodor, throwing the little round man to the ground.

They wrestled for a few seconds, then Nod quickly lost his advantage as the air around them filled with a foul stench.

The fetor, thought Peter grimly.

Everyone except Malodor began to cough and gasp for air.

Nod fought on weakly, but Sylph, who was so much smaller, fainted into the stroller, on top of Jimmy.

Peter felt his senses slipping away too. He needed an idea, and quickly.

Next to his foot, a narrow open gutter sloped across the concrete to an open drain. Using the last of his strength, Peter crawled the length of gutter, all the way to the drain, on his hands and knees, then pushed his whole face into it. An open sewer had never smelt sweeter. He breathed in deeply.

Behind him, Nod was groaning with defeat. Malodor would get Jimmy.

Think, Peter, think. He felt in his pocket for the cylinder containing the redolence. Cleo Choat had sprayed her special perfume on the smell. Peter leapt up and began spraying liberally over the huddled bodies of Nod, Jimmy, and Sylph.

Psshht-psshht! Psshht-psshht!

It seemed to instantly revive them, and Nod sprang back into action, dragging Malodor backwards from the stroller and into a tight headlock. At the same time, Peter made a grab for Malodor's legs.

"I never thought I'd hear myself say this, Nod, but could you steal my jacket?" Peter gasped, adding, "And don't mess up this time."

Nod laughed appreciatively and began wresting the garment from Malodor's pudgy upper body, while Peter held tightly to his legs.

Inside the house, the sound of clackinations picked up again, rising to a pitch. It was as if hundreds of people in tap shoes were now dancing desperately across the floorboards. Cleo Choat was on the move.

But Nod had the jacket in his hand, and they were home free.

Sylph released the stroller brake.

"Run!" she cried.

Too late, Peter felt himself being wrenched backwards.

"Not so fast!" snapped Cleo Choat.

"Let me go!" Peter put all his strength into wriggling free, but she had him in a vice-like grip, pulling on his shirt collar, so he could barely breathe.

"Hand over the jacket – now!" Cleo Choat shrieked at Nod.

"Nah, not today," Nod said firmly.

"Hand it over, or I'll hurt the boy!" Cleo Choat threatened.

"I don't care about that little sod," said Nod.

Is this a trick? Peter wondered with a pounding heart.

His hopes were dashed when Nod said, "I've got the jacket now, and someone's going to finally pay me the money I'm owed."

"You'll get your money," Cleo Choat said hastily.

"Oh yeah? That's what you said last time. Now you're going to have to pay triple. No, actually quadruple the first offer, because you said you wanted the boy, and now we've brought him to you as well."

"Okay, okay ... whatever you want. The money's yours; just give me the jacket." Cleo Choat was snatching at the jacket with one arm and gripping Peter by the throat with the other.

"Nah! Not falling for that one. Money first," insisted Nod.

"Malodor, give him what he wants. Then, take the boy and lock him behind the soot door in the chimney. Hurry! The hatchlings are turning in on me."

"Yes'm." Malodor's pudgy fingers counted out bank notes.

Peter was struggling for breath. He tried to catch Sylph's eye, hoping for a sign, but none came. Surely, she was still on his side.

But his conviction weakened when Sylph said to Malodor, "Wow, that's a lot of money! Tell you what, Nod: I'll take the cash, while you pass the lady her jacket, to make sure it's a fair exchange."

"I knew you'd see it my way, Sis." Nod smirked at her.

Could Sylph have even gone to Aunty Surla and Uncle Gorrman's house as part of this elaborate plan? Peter didn't want to believe it. Somehow, he felt sure he'd seen some goodness in both of them earlier – especially Sylph.

"All right, on the count of three, we make the exchange," snapped Cleo Choat. "Do this well, and there'll be more high-paying gigs."

"That's what we were hoping," Sylph gushed.

Peter's heart tightened with a mixture of disappointment and fear.

Nod was holding the GAIA jacket slightly out of Cleo Choat's reach, while Malodor held a big wad of money just short of Sylph's outstretched hand. There was a silent stand-off as they stared suspiciously at each other.

Peter noticed that Jimmy was awake now, with his television-watching face back on. Even though Sylph had one hand out for the money, her other hand still clenched the stroller handle tightly. There was something in the way her knuckles showed white that gave Peter hope.

"Ready – one, two, and—"

Peter knew he had to stop them, but he couldn't move. He remembered Cleo Choat's fear of Matron's injection at her neck. If only he had something sharp to go for her neck with. He looked wildly around him for something sharp. An image of a wallaby flashed into his mind. Pickles couldn't help him now. No, not Pickles, the wallaby pin from Mr Dean! The fingers of Peter's left hand found the pin easily. He pulled it from his shirt and, without hesitating, reached up and gently pricked the back of Cleo Choat's neck.

Then, a lot of things started to happen.

Cleo Choat screamed and released him. This caused Nod to pull back with the jacket and Sylph to push forward with the stroller and mash the money into Malodor's round face.

"Help!" Cleo Choat buckled over, clamping both hands to the back of her neck. "The hatchlings are escaping. They're going for the prospect!"

Jimmy's shrill cries began to pierce the air. His arms and legs flailed, as if fending off an invisible swarm of bees.

Peter pulled the redolence from his pocket and began spraying it over Jimmy, while Nod again managed to pin Malodor to the ground. The air around them quickly cleared, but not before Cleo Choat had grabbed Peter back into her iron neck grip.

Peter groaned, but then he remembered that he still had leverage. It was almost too easy. He held the gold cylinder at arm's length, where Cleo Choat could see it, then he dropped it casually into the open gutter. Her face froze as the redolence made one low bounce, then began its slow roll down the slope towards the open drain. In a few seconds, the redolence would be free-falling into the London sewer system.

Click-clack, click-clack!

Cleo Choat struggled only briefly with her choice. She flung Peter aside, dropped forward onto her hands and knees, and moved in the direction of the drain.

"Run, Peter! Run, Nod!" Sylph cried.

Nod and Peter tore off behind Sylph, bumping the stroller through the rubble. Malodor chased off behind them, but he must have stumbled in his platform boots, because they turned to see him face down in the dirt. Malodor did manage to hit them, though, with a parting shot of Anthrog fetor. And by the time they reached the taxi, all of them were gasping and choking for air.

"Sounds like some nasty coughing," the driver said worriedly as they shovelled each other and the stroller inside the car.

"It must be the soot," Sylph told him breathlessly.

As the taxi pulled away from the curb, Nod tossed the jacket onto Peter's lap. His smile was as wide as his face.

"Had you going there, didn't we?"

Peter laughed and tried to hug him.

"Steady on." Nod laughed too.

"So, where to now?" asked the taxi driver amiably as they sped away.

Peter, filled with the energy of victory, found his voice first.

"Number 5 Singlewood Lane!"

44

The Garden of Ashes

I n Singlewood Lane, they stopped outside a high stone wall embedded with a large mailbox.

"Number 5," said Peter.

"Let's go in," suggested Sylph, her eyes sparkling. "I like this place."

"What do you mean? There's not even a gate."

"Never mind. It's a very big mailbox." Sylph pushed it open and they saw there was enough space to get in and through to the other side.

"Wait!" insisted Peter, not wanting to be rude. "Isn't there a bell?"

"On a mailbox?" Sylph giggled as she sailed right through with the stroller.

Peter and Nod followed after her. They stepped out into an enormous garden exploding with plants, flowers, and tall trees all blazing with autumn reds, fiery oranges, and bright yellows. There was no house, but the garden expanded endlessly out ahead of them, just like an invitation.

Peter watched Jimmy tumble across the uneven grass.

"Flower," Jimmy said pointing at a clump of yellow wild flowers. Sylph nodded.

"Tree," Jimmy said and smiled.

"All these taller trees are mostly ashes," Nod told Peter.

"Nod failed all his exams at school," said Sylph. "But he knows a lot about nature."

"You're a wasted resource," said Peter.

Nod scowled.

"Peter's right," said Sylph. "It's a compliment. Now get back to work."

After Nod left, Peter wandered around a bit, hoping to find Artiss Fleur, but his home, though exploding with nature, was empty of people.

"Did you notice how Jimmy hasn't fussed at all since we came here? And now, he's sleeping like an angel!" said Sylph.

Peter thought Jimmy did look peaceful, maybe not like an angel, but at least almost like a human being.

When Sylph took Jimmy home for lunch, Peter stayed alone in the garden to think. A tall clump of trees seemed to wave out to him. As Peter walked towards them, he considered how far he'd already come as well as how far he still had to go. He hugged the jacket in close to himself.

Suddenly, he really wanted Artiss Fleur to come and find him and feel sorry for him and tell him what to do. In order to finish his quest, Peter would have to get to the GAIA Hub by tomorrow evening, but he still had no clue where the GAIA Hub was.

Peter chose the tallest ash tree in the garden, then sat down and leant his back against its broad trunk. A shaft of sunlight reached through the canopy and caught him between the eyes. For a moment, the brightness brought him a surge of hope, but then it got to be too much, and his eyes began to water, filling him with self-pity again. Finally, he lay back and slipped into a deep and dreamless sleep.

Peter was startled awake when his body was thrown forward. A man wearing a bow tie and a cardigan lay beside him, sprawled on the grass, the contents of his briefcase spilling out around him.

"I do apologise," the man said, jumping up and dusting himself off. "I must have tripped right over you there."

In stunned silence, Peter hurried about, collecting the man's papers, which he hastily crammed back into his case.

"I do tend to lose myself in this garden," he told Peter.

Peter nodded. He felt drowsy and had a pain in the small of his back.

"How long have you been here?"

"Ah. ..." Peter looked at his watch, and gulped. "About three hours."

"You've done a great job."

Peter looked at him, perplexed.

"Oh yes! The garden looks splendid! These ash trees love being with children."

Peter smiled at this.

"The ashes are leaving us though, leaving our world."

"Where are they going?" asked Peter, swallowing sorrowfully.

The man didn't answer straight away. He just looked Peter up and down.

"But we'll find a way, forward," he finally said. "Now I really must hurry; an auditorium of impatient climatologists awaits me."

Peter nodded and looked around blankly.

"I'm Theodorus Meriwether," he said, reaching out to shake Peter's hand. "Peter Blue."

"Hope," said Theodorus, "is the way forward."

And, after taking one last look at Peter, then the garden, he walked quickly away, briefcase in hand. Peter watched as he bent over and left through the mailbox, as if it were the most normal thing for a man on his way to a lecture to be ducking through Artiss Fleur's mailbox.

Peter walked thoughtfully back to the big tree. He felt his face redden with embarrassment at the sight of the scuffle marks where the man had tripped right over him. Still, it wasn't as if Peter had been lying in the middle of one of the paths; he'd been leaning against a giant tree trunk.

Peter noticed one leftover rectangle of paper from the spilled briefcase, and he snatched it up, scanning it quickly:

Professor Theodorus Meriwether
Date/Time: 21 Sept. – 3 p.m.
Task: Keynote speech
Venue: Royal Albert Hall
Travel: GAIA Hub to TP SW London (TP: two minutes) / to venue (On foot: twenty minutes)

Theodorus was from GAIA! He'd travelled from the GAIA Hub to SW London today. Peter's hands were shaking. A big clue had just fallen, literally, right at his feet. It didn't matter that he still couldn't make sense of it. He had until tomorrow to figure it out.

CHAPTER

45

The Garbage Gives Back

B y the time Peter left the garden of ashes, there was a storm brewing. Rain clouds were gathering, and the wind was gusting around him as he hurried back to the plastic flat, where he planned to go treasure hunting for his invitation.

It was only when he found himself in front of Uncle Gorrman's heavy and imposing office door that he realised he didn't actually have a plan. He tried the door handle; it was locked. Perhaps he could offer to clean the flat. Then, Aunty Surla would unlock the door for him, giving him a chance to snoop around.

While he was deciding what to do, an image of Pickles came into his head. She seemed to be showing him something. He watched in his mind as Pickles leapt through the air towards a big slab of wood and moved right through it. Peter thought it must be a sign that he should try to force the door open.

"Okay, here goes, then." He took a few steps back then charged against the door. *Thwack!* The door stood firm, but, with a heavy thud, Peter hit the hall floor. He raised his head to see the office door opening, then Uncle Gorrman standing above him.

Now he would be in for it!

But, surprisingly, Gorrman flashed him a rare smile, showing small, yellow teeth.

"Ah ... I was just doing some dusting," offered Peter lamely. He felt into his pocket for a handkerchief, but, finding none, began rubbing with his jacket sleeve on Gorrman's office door. "I was going to polish it up for you."

Instead of disbelieving him or accusing him, Uncle Gorrman did a little stepping dance, then said, "You must have read my mind, Peter, because from now on, my office must be spic and span, the reason being that you are now looking at the new chief executive officer of Big Garbage Incorporated!"

"Oh ... congratulations," said Peter with pretend enthusiasm.

"Thank you. Come in! Come in! Dust away! Polish away! You can take out the garbage while you're at it." Uncle Gorrman pointed expansively at the overflowing wastepaper basket.

"Um ... should I dust the safe? With all your money in it?" asked Peter.

"I suppose so. You like money, then, do you?"

Peter shrugged. He knew Uncle Gorrman did. *Look to where your treasure and the guardian's become one.* Peter felt a glimmer of hope. "Can I see inside?"

"All right, no probs." Uncle Gorrman knelt down at the safe under the desk. "Turn your back while I open it."

He showed Peter the inside of the safe.

"Wow, there's a lot of money in there!" Peter exclaimed.

"Well, I don't want to be left without cash, do I?" Uncle Gorrman pulled out a pile of hundred-pound notes, while Peter craned his neck to see if he could see anything other than money inside the safe.

"Don't you keep your important papers in here too? I mean, letters and invitations and stuff." Peter was trying to hide his disappointment.

"Nope, only money."

Uncle Gorrman was skipping in a circle now, in front of his desk, and Peter's efforts to sidestep his uncle's heavy-footed manoeuvres resulted in him falling backwards against the wastepaper basket. The large red slogan on the side of it read: No Garbage, No Gain!

Suddenly, Peter knew exactly where he would find the invitation.

Down in the backyard, the storm was getting closer. The sky was darkening, and Peter was being battered by the wind. He would have to hurry. Breathing only through his mouth, he climbed onto the plastic Dumpster and dragged opened the top hatch. His heart lurched. The space was crammed full with trash.

How was he going to find one, single invitation in there?

Leaving the hatch open, Peter climbed down to the side entrance of the walk-in Dumpster, to investigate the magnitude of garbage from a different angle. He had to battle with the wind to get the door open, but when he did, a dreadful, unthinkable thing began to happen.

A sudden extreme gust of wind tunnelled past him, through the door, and up out of the open hatch, spewing up stinky garbage like magma from a volcano vent. In desperation, Peter hurled himself up onto the bin, trying to contain the outflows of paper, plastic, and food waste, but nothing could be done until the big bin was spent.

"Thank you very much!" he told the wind sarcastically as he began the uninviting task of returning every stinking scrap of garbage to the bin.

Shoo-ster! The wind seemed to reply.

When Peter entered the bin with the first armload, Peter saw that one piece of paper had escaped the blitz. He would have trodden on it if something in the colour and texture of the paper hadn't made him stop. It reminded him of Artiss Fleur's business card. He picked it up and turned it over. Peter's hands shook as he stared down at the paper.

He smiled and looked up into the London sky. "Thank you very much," he told the wind again, this time, in a voice charged with gratitude and amazement.

In his hands, Peter held the invitation:

Dear Peter Blue

You are cordially invited to join the new autumn intake of

Spiral Hall: School for the Ecodemically Gifted.

Initiates must assemble at the GAIA Hub for departure by 5.55 p.m. on the afternoon of the September autumn equinox. Latecomers not accepted.

Eco-adventurers and frog lovers of the highest order only need accept and attend.

Tad Pollings
Head of Junior Admissions

(This invitation is not transferable. Travelling directions available to bearer on request.)

It was all real. The school was real. Uncle Gorrman had known all along, but it wasn't worth confronting him, because he was never going to let Peter go to the GAIA Hub. Peter would have to get himself there, and, luckily, he had Theodorus Meriwether's clue to work with.

He looked around him and sighed. But, first, he had a yard full of garbage to attend to.

Back inside, the doorbell was ringing.

"Stir-fry from the Happy Dragon!" Aunty Surla called in that sing-song voice she reserved only for takeaways. "Spring rolls for dinner!"

After nearly three days without much food, Peter couldn't stop himself from wolfing down his dinner.

Uncle Gorrman was talking to Aunty Surla about his new promotion.

"Dreeg's vote on the board today was the deciding one, you know."

Aunty Surla nodded and smiled. "The donation helped, of course; the others couldn't possibly match it."

Uncle Gorrman laughed in a way that sent fragments of spring roll spitting from of his mouth.

Peter saw that this clearly impressed Jimmy, while Aunty Surla just pretended not to notice.

Donation? Peter considered this. The thought of his mother's prize money being spent on bribes to Elfhiss Dreeg, that king of cologne, sent Peter into a fit of coughing and choking. But he had so much food in his mouth that rice grains and vegetables started flying across the table from Peter as well. Instead of reprimanding him, Uncle Gorrman shot him a look of admiration. Greed was something that Uncle Gorrman respected and appreciated.

Aunty Surla said sourly, "For three days, I couldn't get him to eat any of those good takeaways."

"Well, he's hogging in now," said Uncle Gorrman.

They spoke as if Peter weren't sitting there choking right in front of them.

It was only after he'd washed a full glass of water down his throat that he managed to breathe normally again. But there was no time for self-pity. He had more important things to worry about, such as, what did TP stand for on Professor Meriwether's travel paper?

"Excuse me, Uncle Gorrman. Do you happen to know what the letters TP stand for?"

Uncle Gorrman paused chewing and thought for a minute.

"From where I sit now as the CEO of Big Garbage, the letters TP would stand for top profits." He showed his small yellow teeth for the second time that day, then actually winked at Peter.

"On my shopping site, TP stands for teleshop portal," Aunty Surla said.

Theodorus Meriwether hadn't looked like much of a shopper. But Peter decided he did like the word *portal*.

Uncle Gorrman raised his glass proudly. "Let's drink a champagne toast to me, the new head of Big Garbage!"

Aunty Surla smiled encouragingly and clinked glasses with her husband.

Peter saw that she was quite pretty when she smiled. The sharpness of her face was less noticeable.

"Congratulations, Uncle Gorrman," said Peter. "It must be an honour."

"Thanks. Here, have a few more spring rolls." He nudged the plastic tray towards Peter. "Come on, we've got extra."

"Thanks." Peter piled a few more onto his plate. The trip to the garden of ashes had given him a good appetite.

He sensed Uncle Gorrman watching him.

"What makes you so chirpy all of a sudden?" his uncle asked in a voice friendly but suspicious. "What've you got up your sleeve?"

Peter smiled, unsure of what to say. The invitation was not in his sleeve but safely tucked in the secret pocket at the back of the GAIA jacket. He wasn't taking any chances.

Suddenly, Jimmy, holding rice in his pudgy little fists, started pelting the grains at Peter. When Peter didn't react, he started to spit the grains at him.

"Jimmy, don't spit the rice," Aunty Surla reprimanded him. "That's the expensive kind with the egg noodles in it."

Peter wondered who Jimmy would spit his exotic takeaways over tomorrow while he was gone to meet his new friends at Spiral Hall. He smiled over at Jimmy, who was now leaning forward in his high chair, all the fight suddenly out of him. He had an extreme look of concentration on his face. His body twisted, his face contorted, and his eyes popped with shock. It reminded Peter of the night he'd arrived.

Could it be? Jimmy was sitting up very straight now, perhaps sensing that he was delivering something important and rising to the task.

Peter scooped his little cousin from his high chair, and, trying to keep the note of triumph from his voice, said, "I think Jimmy needs changing!"

That night, Peter wore the GAIA jacket to bed. Things had really started to move, literally, with the return of Peter's pelican spirit dome, which was now in the secret pocket, well washed and shiny.

As he lay still on the pillow, Peter thought of President Buchanan telling him, "I've always been there for you."

"I got the invitation!" Peter called weakly into the darkness.

Closing his eyes, he suddenly wanted to try something. Using all the strength and imagination he could manage, Peter fired a shot of thank-you energy from his heart out through the silver GAIA spiral on the jacket. He couldn't tell if the shot was weak or strong, but he aimed it at Bu-h.

"That's all of I've got!" he whispered, imitating President Bu-h and then giggling self-consciously.

Saying thank you had made him feel good, so good that he added one more gratitude shot to a place he'd never imagined thanking – he fired off a heartfelt shot of *thank you* to Uncle Gorrman's garbage bin.

CHAPTER

46

The Plant Speaks

eter woke and sat up nervously in bed. He still didn't have a plan. All he knew was that, somehow, he had to get to the GAIA Hub by 5.55 p.m. *Latecomers not accepted.*

Pulling Professor Meriwether's transportation details out from under his pillow, he studied them again. *Think, Peter, think.* He checked his watch: 9 a.m. Somehow, he just had to keep moving.

He got up and finished his packing, then stared around the room, all the time searching his mind for a big idea. His eyes settled on the yoghurt pot.

"Can you help?" he whispered to the little green shoot. "I'm collecting ideas."

Peter patted the tiny leaves with his finger. He had talked to trees and wooden tables before, so why not to a tiny sprout? The plant didn't seem very talkative, though. Peter tried to clear his mind and make a better connection, but nothing came through.

Before he knew it, his watch read: 10 a.m. He still didn't have a plan.

"Oh, this is hopeless," Peter told the plant moodily.

Not as hopeless as you might think, the plant seemed to say, suddenly communicative.

"Well, somehow, by 5.55 p.m. today, I've got to get to a place called the GAIA Hub, and I just don't know where it is or how to get there.

I do have an invitation, though!" Peter fluttered the paper above the yoghurt pot.

The plant didn't seem to have anything to say to this.

"Do you think it's too late for a miracle?" Peter asked, hoping to impress the plant with his positive outlook.

Looking down at the tiny sprout that had once been a seed wrapped in Nonna's handkerchief, it occurred to Peter that being alive in this room was already miraculous.

The plant seemed to agree: *Look at the miracle I'm being.*

The plant seemed to have a lot more to say now: *In order to grow, I have to convert the knowledge of the universe into something beautiful, living, and breathing. I have to go all the way to the cosmos for my information, while all you need for your transformation is right in front of you. So, stop chattering, and do it!*

For a tiny sprout, the plant was getting bossy. Peter put it back gently onto the sill and stared down at his treasures scattered across the bed. Sylph had brought him a London transport map, which he opened out next to Professor Meriwether's transportation details.

"So, what I know," Peter told the plant, turning his head towards the windowsill, "is that the professor travelled from the GAIA Hub on a TP to SW London. He checked the map for South-West London, but it was so big, and there was no mention of a TP anywhere."

The plant was silent again.

"Help me," Peter groaned.

The door opened, and Sylph entered.

"I'm going to help you as much as I can. But there's one thing I stand firm on." She lowered her voice to a whisper. "I can't help you run away from home; it would be a breach of my professional ethics as a nanny."

Peter pouted disappointedly.

"I'm sorry, Peter, but you have to find a way to get permission from Surla."

Great, thought Peter after she'd gone. *Now I have two impossible tasks instead of one. Aunty Surla will never let him go when Uncle Gorrman is so determined about Murksborne. If only I could talk to Pickles.*

Peter closed his eyes and tried to conjure up an image of the wallaby in his mind.

"Tsk-tsk," he whispered softly to himself, then panicked when no image appeared. He squeezed his eyes tight. *Pickles, where are you?*

Oh no! thought Peter. *I'm so anxious now that my imagination is shutting down.*

This was not good. Peter was experienced enough to know that *if* he was going to get to the GAIA Hub today, it would be his imagination more than anything else that would get him there.

He had to pretend that this was all already happening. Trick his brain into thinking everything was on track. He found a piece of paper and wrote a note, which he propped up next to the yoghurt pot:

Dear Aunty Surla,

I've gone to school. Please keep this plant as a thank-you-for-having-me gift.

If you water it and give it sunshine, it will become a nice flower.

Yours sincerely,
Peter Blue

PS: Thank you for the takeaways.

He smoothed out the travel paper and studied it again. There was something about that garden that held a clue. The tall ash, the one he'd slept against, stood up in his mind. Theodorus Meriwether had tripped right over Peter, and the paper and fallen to the ground in front of him.

Suddenly, the paper seemed finally to open up to Peter. *I didn't just fall there.*

Dah! added the plant.

Peter's heartbeat quickened. His imagination was reopening. Could Professor Meriwether have dropped the paper there to help him?

Suddenly, Pickles was back, leaping across Peter's mind and jumping through the wooden door again. "No thanks, Pickles. I tried that yesterday."

Nonna's crystal had said that the way to Spiral Hall was open to him. Nonna had been so sure too. But, then again, the crystal had also said that he would see her again.

He heard Aunty Surla leaving her office and climbing the stairs for her morning shower. Now was his chance to check her computer for a message from Mr Dean.

Peter's heart skipped when he logged on and saw one. This would be the miracle he'd been waiting for, the missing information to help get him to GAIA. Even though Mr Dean was on his honeymoon touring the world's famous libraries, he had somehow managed to come through for him.

Peter scanned frantically through the message lines, in search of something he could use.

Dear Duke of Wellie,

Sorry for the delay; I've had technical issues. Actually, at a library in Venice, I was walking and working on my handheld device, and I ended up wading right into a part of the library that had become submerged in water from the Adriatic Sea. Luckily, Hester was able to fish me out, but not before all my devices had floated off into watery darkness, along with a few old mouldy books.

But enough about me. I'm told that today's the equinox. So, you'll be on your way. I know it. Sorry I couldn't help you with coordinates on this secret school of yours. It's all very hush-hush. No one in my circles can get access to the information you need.

So, I'll leave you with the advice I always give myself: Extraordinary outcomes require extraordinary thinking!

Your friend and supporter,
Devlin

Peter looked at his watch: 1 p.m. Soon there'd be no time left. He had to think some extraordinary thoughts.

In the living room, with the television on, he found Sylph chasing Jimmy in circles.

"Teebee! I want more teebee-e-e-e-e!"

Sylph snatched up Jimmy and hurried out of the room.

Peter was just about to switch off the TV when he looked at the screen and saw a man with a familiar face. The man was talking to a big audience.

"We in the garbage generation have a lot of figuring out to do!" the man said.

It was the smiling face of Professor Theodorus Meriwether. "R*efuse* all that *refuse!*" he commanded. "It's the only way!"

An announcer's voice came on: "'If you think that the rise of the garbage generation has nothing to do with weather disasters, then think again!' celebrity weather host Professor Theodorus Meriwether yesterday warned experts at GOWD, the Global Organisation for Weather Disasters. 'But we can fix things,' Meriwether promised, predicting that children would lead the way."

The news clip finished, but the professor and his smile stayed frozen on the screen. Peter felt a shot of static crackling through his head and shoulders, then, strangely, Professor Meriwether's comments continued.

"Look for signs; look for ways to see the world around you differently." He seemed to be looking straight at Peter now. "Sometimes a tree is more than just a tree. And sometimes you might even wake up to find the truth stumbling right over you."

The professor chuckled, and then the TV screen went dark.

Inside Peter's head, Pickles chose this moment to romp through on her big hoppers again. Peter watched with his mind's eye as she leapt into the piece of hardwood again, but this time, she didn't reappear on the other side. Suddenly, Peter made a leap of his own: a quantum leap, in his thinking.

"That's it." The truth had fallen right over him. *Sometimes a tree is more than just a tree.* These must be the kind of extraordinary thoughts that Mr Dean was talking about. The wood that Pickles kept leaping through was not Uncle Gorrman's office door. It was a tree, the one from Singlewood Lane yesterday.

Peter ran back to the bedroom. Even though he'd been leaning his back against the trunk of the tall ash tree, Professor Meriwether had fallen right over him. And there'd been footprints leading away from the tree, but none going up to it. The only possible conclusion was that the professor had come straight out of that tree.

That meant that the path to the GAIA Hub had something to do with the trunk of that tree, so if *P* stood for *portal*, then the *T* must stand for *tree*.

Tree Portal?

Peter liked the sound of it, but then what about SW? Singlewood Lane was in Central London not South West London. Of course! SW: Singlewood.TP SW meant Tree Portal at Singlewood Lane.

Peter looked at his watch: 2.30 p.m. He was going to get there, after all. He had plenty of time to figure out how to get into that tree once he got to the garden. And according to the professor's travel paper, the trip to the GAIA Hub only took two minutes. Peter's stomach churned nervously. What kind of journey out of London took only two minutes?

Peter decided to use the remaining time to figure out how to get Aunty Surla to let him leave. He just needed one more extraordinary thought. One came to him almost immediately. It was a long shot but not impossible. All he would need to do was persuade Aunty Surla, somehow, to open up Nonna's red felt–lined box with the crystal ball in it.

47

Cleo Choat Returns

H is thoughts were interrupted by a loud hammering at the front door, followed by the dreaded sound of a voice he knew.

"Let me in!!!!"

"What's that awful noise?!" Aunty Surla called.

This could ruin everything, thought Peter as he tried to think of the best way to escape.

The pounding on the door grew louder.

"Why doesn't she use the bell?" Aunty Surla emerged from her office, looking worried.

"Where's the boy?" screeched the voice.

A window on the side of the flat would do it, thought Peter. But Aunty Surla was barring his way.

"Is that someone you know out there?" Aunty Surla asked him.

"I think it's Cleo Choat," Peter mumbled.

Jimmy ran behind his mother and started to cry.

"Choat!" he chanted. "No Choat."

Aunty Surla ordered Sylph to take Jimmy upstairs.

"Tell me right now what's going on, Peter!" his aunt demanded.

Knock, knock! Thump, thump!

"Um. ..."

When he didn't offer an answer, Aunty Surla began stamping the feet of her twig legs like an angry marching girl.

"Tell me! Who is Cleo Choat, and why is she trying to break into my house?"

Peter shrugged.

"All you've ever brought us is trouble." She took a step towards Peter and shook him roughly by the elbow.

"I'm sorry!" cried Peter.

"Sorry doesn't help!" Aunty Surla screeched. "You're nothing but trouble!"

Wham, wham! Thump, thump! Click-clack! Click-clack!

"We never wanted you here in our house, bringing us trouble!"

Listening to his aunt's tantrum, Peter suddenly saw a way out. It was like seeing a path to freedom unfold right in front of him.

"You're right Aunty Surla," he said firmly. I've been way too much trouble for you."

Surla nodded, sniffing.

The hammering at the door stopped.

"I understand what a burden I've been to you, especially when you've got Jimmy to take care of and all that shopping to do!"

Aunty Surla continued to nod.

"And every night, you have to order one extra portion of takeaways for me," Peter continued.

Thump, thump! The hammering was starting again.

"And that's why I'm going to do the right thing, and leave," Peter told her decisively.

"Leave?"

Thump, thump!

"Yes. I'll go with Cleo Choat. She wants to take me away."

"She wants *you*? Why?"

Ignoring the rudeness implied by the question, Peter decided to continue. He would tell the truth, but only the suitable bits.

"She's a scientist friend of Mum's. She came to Australia … told Nonna she wanted to pay for my education and take me travelling."

Peter was aware that he'd left out Cleo Choat's plan to use Peter and the jacket to bring down GAIA and fill the world with the invisible clacking maggots, but that was a lot to explain. It was getting late.

"Wait," said Aunty Surla. "This crazy maniac outside the door has met Nonna?"

"Yeah, she came to Jarra Jarra and the rest home and everything. Kept saying Mum would have wanted me to be with her and that she'd get some adoption papers. I guess she has the papers now, so I'll just go with her," said Peter, stepping towards the front door.

"Wait!" Aunty Surla pulled him back by the shirt. "What papers? There can't be any papers. We're your legal guardians."

She's thinking about my money, thought Peter. *Good. Everything is going according to plan.*

Ding-dong! Ding-dong! Thump, thump!

Aunty Surla looked questioningly at Peter.

"I guess she's mad because I chose you and Uncle Gorrman instead of her."

"You chose us?" Aunty Surla sounded surprised.

Peter nodded. "Yes!"

It's working, he thought.

Aunty Surla looked through the peephole. "She's holding some kind of metal fireplace poker. She looks crazy."

"People always look strange through those peepholes, even the takeaway people." Peter reminded her.

"Anyway, Cleo Choat's a serious scientist interested in GAIA." He didn't mention that she was only interested in GAIA so that she could bring down the human race. "So, it'll work out well for me. Hey, and I can even get to the school I want to go to."

"Is that what this is all about?" interrupted Aunty Surla. "That silly school?"

Peter tried to arrange his face calmly. "Well, I do have to be there soon; today, actually." Peter looked at his watch, adding, "And I'm already packed, so Cleo Choat could just take me there."

"Wait. What do you mean? I could take you. ..." Aunty Surla stopped herself. "It's just that Gorr's job and Chairman Dreeg. ..."

Peter watched her considering things in her head – damage control, fear counselling – she was turning purple. If only this would work!

"I get it," said Peter. "I've known for a while that you didn't want me. ..."

"Oh no, it's not that," Aunty Surla lied.

"But I do want to get to the GAIA training school," Peter continued, watching her reaction.

"Well, if you really want to go that badly. ..."

Aunty Surla was coming around. Now for the final push.

"What's that bumping sound coming from your office, Aunty Surla? Has Cleo Choat broken in?"

Peter ran in ahead of his aunt and snatched up the red felt–lined box. He opened the box carefully and pulled out the crystal ball. He remembered Nonna telling him that his aunty Surla had been gifted in using the crystal as a child.

This had to work.

Peter hefted the crystal ball into his hand, pretending to study it.

"Why would it bump around like that, Aunty Surla? Could it be trying to get your attention?" he asked innocently.

Aunty Surla looked at the ball and then at Peter.

"What are you up to?" she asked, some of her anger returning.

Peter's plan had been to pretend to see Nonna in the ball, but he could see now that Aunty Surla was on to him. Then, he was surprised to feel a faint shifting of energy from the ball to his hands. Something really *was* happening. He almost dropped the crystal when Nonna's face really did appear. She was about the size of a ten-cent piece and waving her arms a lot. Peter smiled down at her, then thrust the ball at Aunty Surla.

"Oh, is that you Mum? Yes, it's me Surla. ... Yes, he's leaving soon to Spiral Hall. ... Yes, a very good boy. ... No, there's no need to turn me into a toad. Yes, we'll make sure he gets there. Fix it with Gorrman? Yes, I will. ... tell Croaky Quirk it's all arranged? Yes, that's what I meant. ... Quirky what? Yes, he's just leaving. ... We're saying goodbye now, Mum! We're saying goodbye."

Aunty Surla dropped the crystal ball back into the box, and, while she was reaching for the lid, Peter had just enough time to glimpse

Nonna's face, eyes smiling behind her black-rimmed glasses. Nonna blew Peter a kiss.

With tears in his eyes, Peter remembered Nonna's voice, from another time and place, saying, "You will see me again, but it's not what you think."

The Leap

Sylph lowered Peter out the back window, then tossed down his bags.

"Thanks for everything." Suddenly, Peter didn't want to leave.

"Don't talk to strangers," said Sylph with a sniff.

"You mean anyone dressed like you," Peter said jokingly.

Sylph laughed. "Don't worry about those guys. You'll never get trouble from them again."

"Why do you say that?"

"Because Vulcan fell in love with a nurse, and now we can't get him to stop smiling."

"What about the nose-pierce guy?"

"Vill? He's completely transformed too. I saw him yesterday, in hospital, and didn't recognise him," Sylph said, adding lightly, "He's started doing his art again, and some of it's very good."

Peter's jaw dropped at the thought of Nosepierce doing art. Bu-h's love must have done it.

"He fell in love too." A smile twitched at the corners of Sylph's tiny mouth.

"With a nurse?"

"No, with me."

Standing in the garden of ashes, with only twenty minutes to spare, Peter studied the area around the tallest tree, where Professor Meriwether had landed on him. The only place he could have stepped from was the inside of the tree. Standing on tiptoes, he saw that a GAIA spiral had been etched into the bark. When he touched it, an automated voice spoke: "Singlewood Tree Portal. State your destination."

"Um ... GAIA Hub," said Peter, his heart pounding with a mix of fear and excitement.

"Please state your password, or place ID onto activation pad," the automated voice continued.

"What ID? Who said anything about ID?" Peter cried.

The tree voice didn't reply.

What now? He jumped at a sound on the other side of the wall. *Click-clack! Click-clack!*

"I know you're in there, Peter Blue!" screeched Cleo Choat.

There was a new sound – *clang, clang, clang!* – the fireplace poker against the wooden fence. She was moving along the fence line, towards the mailbox, looking for a way in.

"Preparing to shut down," stated the automated voice in the tree.

"No, wait! Let me in! Let me in!" Peter pounded the tree spiral with his wrist.

"Shutdown in thirty seconds."

Cleo Choat was at the mailbox. *Clang, clang, clang!* went the metal poker.

"I hate you, stupid tree!" Peter punched it again, this time, with the flat of his fist. "I'm just a child! This is too much for me. Help me! Help me, you dumb tree. I don't know what to do!"

The automated voice of the tree stated, "Eight ... seven ... six. ..."

Click-clack! Click-clack!

Peter heard the mailbox open and close.

"I'm going to get you, Peter Blue!" shrieked Cleo Choat.

In frustration and desperation, Peter banged his fist against the spiral on the tree, over and over again, ignoring the pain in his hand and wrist. Cleo Choat was going to get him!

"Five ... four ... three. ..."

"Let me in! Let me in!" Peter cried.

There was a loud beeping sound.

Peter paused.

"ID accepted. Prepare to embark."

Peter sniffed warily; he didn't have an ID.

Click-clack! Click-clack!

The jacket wrist was beeping too.

Dad's ID must be embedded there. It must have activated while I was beating up the tree, Peter thought.

The tree voice repeated, "Prepare to embark."

The sound of Cleo Choat grew louder. *Click-clack! Click-clack!* Any minute now, she would find him.

How was he supposed to embark? The bark on the tree trunk was becoming shimmery and grainy. Peter thought of Pickles leaping into wood.

"Final departure call in five seconds," said the tree voice. "Destination: GAIA Hub Oak. Estimated travel time: two minutes. Five ... four ... three. ..."

Cleo Choat had entered the clearing.

Peter took two running steps forward on legs that shook with fear and doubt. Then, with one more step, Peter Blue leapt right into the tree.

CHAPTER

49

The Royal Jelly

The Top Drone stumbled along the underground passage, a few steps behind the Anthrog Overlord. When they reached the cave of the inner sanctum, three grey-robed, hooded attendants stepped out to meet them. One of them took the Drone's arm, guiding her towards a triangular slab of stone in the centre of the candlelit room.

"Don't fear, milady, it will be very quick," the attendant whispered.

The Drone knelt shakily onto the ceremonial cushion, leaning her forehead against the cold stone so that her neck was laid bare.

"It's time to atone for your mistakes," the Overlord said in a voice that betrayed no emotion. Standing to one side, he extended his left-hand little finger, sharpening the hooked fingernail that he kept unnaturally long for this purpose.

The hooded attendants chanted an incantation while the final preparations were made:

Long live the Overlord and his most potent Drone;

Long live the warriors born from this sacred stone.

The Overlord bent over towards the Drone's neck. "Your Anthrog hive is ripe for picking."

The chanting grew louder as the Drone's cries began to fill the crypt-like space.

"No!" screamed the Drone over and over.

Ignoring her pleas, with one deft movement, the Overlord pierced his long, hooked nail into the smooth white skin of the Top Drone's neck.

"No get away from me!" she cried, as he wielded his fingernail like a surgeon's scalpel, cutting the flesh into a triangular aperture.

The Drone's cries continued, and her breath laboured close to his ear. The incantations grew faster. Suddenly, the surface of the triangular cut began to darken and separate with slow wavy movements.

The Overlord could wait no longer. He began to work his fingernail along the grey maggoty lines of the firstborn hybrid Chrysalite killers.

"You're so minuscule," he mused, speaking directly to the newborns. "Yet, each of you can carry etheric nectar more than one hundred times your own body mass."

"Just get on with it!" ordered the Top Drone through gritted teeth.

"Although perpetually in gestation, you are anything but motherly." The Overlord chuckled to his Drone. "Still, this is a very good crop indeed; you are commended."

He marvelled at the tiny transparent bodies of the new hybrid species folded in and over each other, delighting in their sharp, seeking noses that arched out over lines of snapping teeth.

Working his hooked nail along the rows, the Overlord began pulling the weightless, lightless bodies apart from each other and releasing them up through a roughly hewn hole in the rock ceiling above. As the first Chrysalite-killing warriors were released, the voices of the attendants launched a new chant:

Up spring the newborns like see-through slugs of flight;

For whom the stink of human greed will keep us free from light!

When the last of them had hatched, the attendants retreated, leaving the Overlord to stare greedily at the grey jelly-like remains of the incubation.

"And now for my birthright," he told the Drone, who was collapsed and past caring. "The Anthrog royal jelly."

Saliva dripped from the corners of the Overlord's mouth as he stirred his fingernail into the wobbling, shimmering mass, then began stabbing at the most fulsome of the maggoty blobs. One after another, he tucked them neatly into his mouth. But, as he settled into his feast, the Overlord became less discriminating, slurping and sucking greedily with his whole mouth at the triangular trough in the Top Drone's neck.

BOOK VIII

Spiral Hall

50

Into the Light

The GAIA Hub was a strange mix of nature and super technology. Glass elevators shot up, down, and sideways inside glass walls, carrying people to the transparent floors above.

The atrium was brightly lit and full of students, some talking loudly in groups, and others alone and just gazing about. Even though Peter didn't know anyone, he immediately felt part of things.

He looked down at the GAIA jacket. He'd brought Dad's shield home; that was definitely something, he decided. And now, he would find Artiss Fleur, deliver Dad's message, and properly finish his quest. Tears stood up suddenly in Peter's eyes, but he pushed them back. He was certainly not going to cry in front of the kids in his new school.

He turned back to the tree that had just delivered him onto the hard, wooden floor. He'd never seen a tree growing inside before. Its sturdy branches reached all the way to the highest point of the vaulting ceiling glass.

What a ride! Peter thought. *Like a high-speed slide.* He wondered how fast he'd been travelling. Maybe faster than the speed of sound, because he remembered screaming at one stage and hearing nothing. But now, despite jelly legs and popping eyeballs, Peter didn't feel bruised at all; instead, his body was buzzing.

Peter leant against the trunk. The tree was silent, but it was a comfortable silence.

Quite a few of the students, he noticed, were carrying animals in transfer cages: dogs, cats, hamsters, and geckos, a monkey with bug eyes; there was even a pony.

Peter's mood clouded slightly when he remembered Pickles, alone somewhere in a far-off country. *We should be here together,* he thought moodily.

His thoughts were interrupted by a *thump* in the small of his back that sent him sprawling forward to the floor.

"Oh, sorry!" came a familiar voice beside him.

Theodorus Meriwether, the famous meteorologist, was pulling himself up and dusting at the knees of his corduroy trousers.

"It's you, Peter!" The professor seemed happy to see him. "I was hoping to *bump* into you again!"

"I saw you on television." Peter said.

"Ah well. ..." The professor straightened his bow tie modestly and smoothed down his well-groomed hair.

"At one point, it felt like you were talking just to me," Peter said.

"Well, I was." Professor Meriwether smiled; it was a slow crinkly smile that moved up from his mouth, to his cheeks, and then his eyes, taking its time to fill up his whole face.

"Selective broadcasting," Professor Meriwether continued. "I'm experimenting with transmissions to targeted centres of consciousness."

Peter nodded without understanding and was relieved when the professor said, "But enough with the science lecturing. How was the tree portal?"

"Amazing!" Peter gasped. "How does it work? Is it some kind of magic?"

"Well," the professor said, looking thoughtful, "I've always thought any technology that totters at the edge of human reason is approaching the idea of magic. Don't you agree?"

Peter shrugged.

"Well, I'm sure you know from your science studies that this trunk is really just a bunch of spinning electrons," the professor continued, "so if you can convince those electrons to kindly spin a bit more slowly, that's where the cooperation with Nature comes in. It's then the space will open up – space that you can leap right into."

"And that's exactly what I did," said Peter, dizzy with relief all over again.

The professor's eyes gleamed at Peter.

Before they could finish their conversation, Professor Meriwether was mobbed by a group of students, and Peter set off across the room, in search of Artiss Fleur. Pausing at the far floor-to-ceiling window, he looked down and saw with shock that the GAIA Hub was built right on the edge of sheer cliff face. Like the end of the earth, it seemed. The sea stretched endlessly out in front, and Peter saw fingers of foam rising up from the surface, as if beckoning him towards his new life.

Over on Peter's left, an African-looking girl stood straight and tall despite being weighed down by a seriously big backpack. Her hair was drawn into big buns like pom-poms, one on either side of her face. She seemed to be standing alone by choice.

Just behind her, Peter noticed a man wearing a GAIA jacket, scrolling with one finger on a handheld tablet and scanning the faces around him. Peter watched him gaze out at the sun in the way another man might look at his watch. Slanting shafts of gold from the early evening sun seem to crown the top of his head.

A tall older boy approached him. "Excuse me, Agent Fleur."

Peter's heart stood still. This was Artiss Fleur? The man whose name had sat for so long in the top pocket next to his heart; the man who Dad had said Peter could trust with his life.

Peter started edging closer. As soon as Artiss Fleur finished talking to the boy, he turned towards Peter, as if sensing he was there.

"Is that you, Peter Blue?"

Peter nodded shyly.

"You look so much like Byron!"

"So do you," said Peter, giggling. Even though Artiss Fleur's hair was the colour of gold sand, and Dad's had been black, he stood about the same height as Dad, wearing his GAIA jacket in a way that reminded Peter exactly of Dad.

Suddenly, Peter's knees felt weak. Artiss Fleur's hand flew to Peter's elbow to steady him.

"You're not going to be sick, are you?" Agent Fleur crouched down to Peter's eye level.

Peter wasn't sure. He was suddenly feeling the shock of having actually arrived.

"I'm fine now, thank you. Um. ..." Peter giggled self-consciously. "What is it?"

"Well ... um ... I'm supposed to give you a message from Dad, but it's only for you." Peter said, adding, "Dad made me promise we would be alone when I delivered it."

Artiss Fleur smiled kindly at Peter. Despite the high-tech surrounds of the GAIA Hub, Artiss Fleur's skin was tanned, and he smelt of the outdoors.

"Tell me, is it something he told you when you were small?" Artiss Fleur's blue eyes were studying Peter intensely.

"No, I um. ..." Peter's voice trailed off. He was embarrassed to find himself choking up again. "I met his ghost."

"His ghost?" Artiss Fleur repeated.

"Well, kind of. It was in a dream of sorts."

"Right." Artiss Fleur seemed suddenly more at ease. "Well, we can talk anytime. You know, Byron wasn't just the best agent GAIA's ever had, he was also my best friend."

Peter nodded and felt his lips quivering.

"So, when should I give you the message, then?"

"Anytime." Artiss Fleur stood up and patted Peter's shoulder benignly.

Suddenly, it occurred to Peter that Artiss Fleur didn't believe him. *I shouldn't have mentioned the dream,* he thought, in dismay. A sob rose in Peter's throat.

"But when exactly?"

Seeing his distress, Agent Fleur crouched back beside him.

"Tell you what, Peter. Let's meet on Saturday morning, and talk. Okay? That's a promise. I'll come find you."

His smile was kind and fair, unlike Uncle Gorrman's, which was always twitching with irritation and sarcasm.

"Now come and meet the gang!" Artiss Fleur was leading him towards the African girl with the pom-pom hair.

"Riva duLac, meet Peter Blue."

"Hi!" Riva said in a strong confident voice.

"Hi!" replied Peter and cringed at the squeaky, shy sound of his own voice.

"Spiral Hall has high hopes for both of you," Agent Fleur enthused.

Riva's smile faded into a frown. "But where is Spiral Hall?"

Artiss Fleur pointed at the sea. "Over there."

Peter and Riva looked out across the endless empty horizon ahead. "Where?"

"Hmm?" said Agent Fleur in a way that grown-ups did when they weren't going to give any more information.

"Well, how do we get there?" Riva pressed.

"We'll take the Fusca!"

"What's the Fusca?" asked Peter.

"It's an undersea transport system, one of Professor Meriwether's new prototypes."

Peter felt a sudden rush of nerves.

"Is it a long trip?" he asked.

"Yes, but it takes a surprisingly short amount of time." Agent Fleur let out a loud spontaneous laugh.

Riva grinned at Peter. "That means hold onto your eyeballs!"

Then, the tall boy from before was back. Agent Fleur introduced him. "This is Junior Agent Jukes, one of our top adventurers."

Jukes was thin and spotty and didn't look much like an adventurer, which made Peter feel less self-conscious about his own unmanly appearance.

Agent Fleur scanned his handheld tablet.

"We're waiting on the Blott brothers, Otto and Ben," he told Jukes. "We'll give them five more minutes."

Artiss Fleur seemed suddenly mindful of time. Beckoning Peter and Riva, he walked purposefully to the centre of the room. Remarkably, when he raised his hand for attention, about a hundred excited initiates and their animals fell into a hush of silence.

"Listen up, everybody. My name's Artiss."

The initiates broke into a cheer, but he continued talking, and the din fell quickly into silence again.

"Congratulations, all of you, on being selected for this year's Spiral Hall intake. Give yourselves a big round of applause."

There was clapping and more loud cheers.

"Listen up, newcomers! Some of you have had more difficult journeys than others, but you've all made it to the GAIA Hub." Agent Fleur was speaking in a normal voice, soft and low, but it was as if his words were able to hold the space just with his personal power. "Do you all know what GAIA stands for?"

A short blonde girl next to Peter raised her hand. Agent Fleur pointed at her.

"Yes, Wanda Shore."

"It stands for the Global Advanced Intelligence Agency." Wanda spoke loudly, with a strong American accent.

"*Ya-a-a-a-ay!*"

More loud cheers arose from the crowd.

Wanda celebrated the moment by pulling out a cube-shaped camera. "Selfie time!" She clicked a quick photo of herself with her back to the crowd.

Artiss Fleur cleared his throat. "Now, the September equinox sun is preparing to slide out of our grasp, and it is very important for our departure, so I'm going to be brief." He paused to smile at two boys entering through the main door. "Otto and Ben Blott, you're just in time!"

The two brothers were shoving each other roughly, and neither looked very happy, but Artiss Fleur pushed on with his remarks.

"Now, some of you know that in addition to being a GAIA agent, I'm the science-adventure mentor at Spiral Hall."

"Science adventure," whispered Wanda to Peter, "as in, oxymoron."

Peter frowned at her. He wasn't sure what *oxymoron* meant.

"Two opposites," whispered Wanda, covering her mouth as she faked a yawn, "as in science is *bo-o-o-o-o-oring* and adventure is *coooool.*"

"Can anyone tell us what GAIA has to do with the school of Spiral Hall?"

A big roundish boy said, "GAIA people are going to teach us there."

"Nice try, Roland Portogalo." Artiss Fleur gave a twinkly smile. "But it's actually the other way around: you kids are here to teach us."

There was a chorus of quiet gasping.

"We grown-ups are your mentors, but it's the kids at Spiral Hall who take the lead."

There were more cheers.

"Hands up if you love earth!"

Hands flew up, including Peter's.

"Who loves adventure?"

All the kids were waving their arms and cheering, except a sullen-looking Asian boy who was holding a metal case tightly in both arms.

"Some of you might be wondering why you're here. Some of you didn't choose to come here."

The Asian boy with the box scowled.

Agent Fleur continued.

"Spiral Hall is an invitation-only school for the world's most advanced eco-science kids. What does that mean?" Agent Fleur paused, then answered his own question. "It means that all of you, in your short but important lives thus far, have already proven yourselves as agents of Nature. Nature is ready to reward you for your service by providing you with knowledge – or what we call 'eco-intelligence'. Some of this knowledge will come from mentors; some from books and high-tech devices; and still more will come from Nature itself. By middle school, you'll be so in touch with Nature that you'll be writing your homework assignments on the wind."

Peter laughed uncertainly.

Artiss Fleur continued, "You will learn from stories told to you by trees. Or from the trip codes of birds, or even from the sound of the sea at sunset."

He looked out the window. "And right now. the sun is telling me that this is not a time for poetry; we have to push on."

Junior Agent Jukes nudged him.

Artiss Fleur added, "Oh, but before we head down below earth to the Fusca teleport, I need to make a few quick introductions. Your principal, Erthia Halowell, will give you a formal audience tomorrow at noon, but here in the room we have Junior Agent Sinta, our head girl at the academy."

A tall, dark, serious Latino girl stepped forward and waved.

"And Junior Agent Jukes, the head boy," Artiss Fleur said.

Artiss Fleur's eyes were scanning the room. "Another key figure for you to meet is Professor Theodorus Meriwether, the smartest man in this room and probably in all the world – inventor, and world-renowned meteorologist and climatologist."

A smiley Professor Meriwether turned in a circle on the spot, waving out while Artiss Fleur glanced again at the setting sun, standing now on the horizon like a circular plate of gold.

"Just one more quick introduction," said Artiss Fleur hurriedly, "because the equinox sun will not wait."

"Actually, it usually does wait," interrupted Professor Meriwether with a chuckle, "if we ask it nicely."

The crowd laughed, then Agent Fleur said, "We have one more very new GAIA agent on site today, a recruit. Now, where is she?"

Artiss Fleur's eyes scanned the room until they settled on Peter.

Why was he staring at him?

"She's a very sensitive type," Artiss Fleur explained.

Whispers rose and fell about the room.

Agent Fleur was laughing now, and all eyes seemed suddenly on Peter.

"She's also a very successful therapist, available for counselling in the coming weeks if anyone gets the 'new-school blues'."

Peter couldn't figure out why Artiss Fleur was smiling at him.

"But where is she?" Agent Fleur was striding through the sea of kids towards Peter. "She's only four feet tall."

Tsk-tsk!

Peter heard the familiar sound at his elbow.

"Pickles? Pickles!"

"That's *Agent* Pickles to you!" corrected Artiss Fleur.

And, suddenly, Peter and Pickles were mobbed by a laughing wallaby-loving crowd. It was all so miraculous that Peter's own emotions didn't know how to respond.

"Pickles?"

The crowd laughed encouragingly.

Inevitably, Peter burst into tears.

"It looks like she's found her first therapy patient," said Professor Meriwether delightedly.

"Okay," said Artiss Fleur, "let's give Peter Blue a little space to catch up with his friend Pickles. Meanwhile, all the rest of you, prepare to board."

Junior Agent Jukes shouted, "Everyone else, let's queue up in the west corner."

Peter buried his face in Pickles's neck fur and cried and laughed, then cried again.

Riva said, "Can I meet her?"

Peter nodded. He liked the way she said "meet her", as if Pickles were someone you would really want to get to know and not just pet for a while. He didn't even care that he was still crying a little in front of Riva.

"But how did you find this place, Pickles? How did you get here?" Peter kept asking Pickles. *Tsk-tsk.* She nudged the silver dome on her GAIA vest.

"The traveller dome?"

"It's a GAIA tracking device." Artiss Fleur was standing beside them. "Every jacket has a GAIA positioning signal, and you gave yours to Pickles. That's why we couldn't track you, but we had no trouble finding her."

Tsk-tsk. Pickles nuzzled her warm snout into Peter's palm.

Professor Meriwether bent down to shake a paw with Pickles.

"What a wallaby!" he said. "I was on her interview panel. She was a shoe-in for the animal intelligence job – or a 'hop-in', you might say. In her previous job, she successfully rehabilitated a team of depressed midgets and transformed a circus into a wildlife centre."

He patted Peter's shoulder before his eyes settled on the grumpy Asian boy, who still hadn't gone to join the queue.

"And you must be Chu Lee Wong, our science prodigy from Hong Kong. We know your grandfather well."

Chu nodded nervously.

Professor Meriwether crouched down to meet him at eye level and shake his hand. "Glad to have another top scientist aboard," he told Chu. "Would you like to meet Peter Blue?"

Chu shrugged in a non-committal way.

Professor Meriwether gave them both one of his never-ending crinkly smiles. Peter noticed the silvery crystalline blue of the professor's eyes. His long cardigan carried a scent of something familiar. Was it salt?

"The sea," said Professor Meriwether, as if reading Peter's mind. "The sea awaits us."

CHAPTER

51

The Fusca

In the blazing light of the setting sun, the procession of new GAIA initiates followed Agent Fleur through a circular hatch that had mysteriously opened up from the floor.

"To the Fusca!" he called as he led them, stumbling off down a sloping passageway towards sea level.

The light grew dimmer as they zigzagged down and around, and the air felt damper and cooler. Eventually. the passage straightened out towards a distant, winking silvery light.

"The Fusca!" cried one boy, and the initiates hurried forward.

A strong wind whistled eerily from the Fusca tunnel, bringing with it a clear bubble-shaped pod labelled number one. It was surrounded by silvery light and carrying Professor Meriwether, who waved out at them. From his place towards the back of the queue, Peter saw with a thrill of pride that Agent Pickles was being helped onto the first pod by Agent Fleur, together with the head boy and girl. Then, he was shocked to see that blonde girl Wanda jump into the first pod too.

Artiss Fleur's voice broke through the rising chatter: "Okay, kids, you're now approaching the Fusca launch tube. I need you to form an orderly queue, in groups of five; we're boarding one bubble pod at a time. Once you're on, you're going to strap yourselves into a seat immediately, so we can move you on and board the next pod."

As instructed, the initiates began shuffling into groups. Peter stepped closer to Riva and Chu, then two girls moved in next to Chu, to make up five. As they approached the boarding zone, Peter saw streams of water washing up the clear curved walls of the Fusca tunnel.

When Peter's group, led by Riva, reached the front of the queue, a clear bubble pod swept to a standstill just for them: pod number eighteen. Peter watched nervously as the curved see-through hatch slid sideways and Riva stepped onto the transparent floor. Chu and Peter followed, then the pod lurched violently to one side as the two girls who were supposed to board next were knocked back by the Blott brothers, pushing their way through instead and knocking Chu and his metal box to the floor.

Riva glared at them, while Peter helped Chu and his box into his seat. He wondered what was in the box but didn't dare ask.

Captain Meriwether's voice on an overhead asked, "Is there a hold-up in Pod 18?"

Everyone, even the Blotts, hurried into their seats, and the pod moved forward.

Ahead and behind in the Fusca tunnel, bubbles just like theirs bobbed at equal distance from each other.

"Hey, Ben, I wonder if these pods go upside down," said Otto, the shorter but stronger-looking of the two brothers.

Ben was fiddling worriedly with his shoulder straps and didn't reply.

As the pod moved forward, a high-tech whirring sound from a circular ceiling device was followed by the drop-down delivery of mini control panels for each seat, while headsets popped out from the seat backs.

"Wow!"

Like the bubble walls, the equipment was made of a clear jelly-like substance that felt springy but also firm to the touch.

An oxymoron, thought Peter, trying out the new word from Wanda.

An image of the smiling head and shoulders of Professor Meriwether appeared on everyone's personal screen.

"Hello again. This is Captain T coming to you from the front control bubble. Welcome to the Fusca, our new GAIA prototype."

"Do you know that *prototype* means 'test'?" Chu asked them shakily.

A shadow of fear passed across the face of Ben Blott.

"We're ready to start cruising down to about thirty-five metres below sea level," Professor Meriwether continued. "Then, if the winds are favourable, we'll be able to start picking up speed towards our island destination."

"It is an island! I knew it!" Riva's dark eyes shone at Peter.

"Now, on your dashboards, you should each have one red button and one green button," the professor continued. "Stay away from the red button, except in emergencies, but feel free to press your green one anytime you have questions."

As soon as the professor had spoken, Peter was amazed to see Riva fearlessly lean over and press her green button.

"Do we have a question out there in Pod 18?"

"Yes," Riva said confidently into her mouthpiece. "How can the winds be favourable if we're underwater?"

Professor Meriwether laughed, throwing his head back.

"Good question! Glad one of you is awake!"

An image of Riva's face appeared on everyone's screens.

"The answer's simple, Riva. The Fusca's a wind-powered vehicle, quite literally. In fact, now would be a good time for you all to meet Agent Etheron."

The indoor wind, thought Peter, smiling to himself. *I know that wind.*

"Agent Etheron, known affectionately as the Shooster, is a very intelligent quantum of wind, who will double as our engine today."

Suddenly, everyone had to grip their armrests as a shuddering *whoosh* of energy charged through the line of pods, causing them to lurch deeply, one after another, from side to side.

"Anyone out there scared?" Professor Meriwether's smiling face replaced Riva's on the screens.

"The Fusca runs on simple pneumatics. Just imagine a peashooter. … It's the same thing, really, just on a bigger scale. Any one of you could've invented it!" the professor said modestly.

Peter laughed disbelievingly, while Chu stared sullenly forward.

Then, suddenly, the Fusca pods were gaining speed, and Professor Meriwether had to shout above the noise of the wind.

"Hold on tight, we begin with a bit of a dip!"

The Fusca lurched off into an ear-popping free fall, which, at first, was met with cries of "whee!" "whoa!" "woo-hoo!"; but by the end of it, most of the Fusca occupants just sat petrified in their seats, trying to hold onto their lunch.

When the sharp descent finally levelled out, Professor Meriwether informed them that they had reached a cruising speed.

Peter was just leaning back with relief when a girl's voice came through the speaker system.

"*Oooh!* Captain T." It was Wanda Shore's face on the screen. "Can I have a go at driving?"

If Peter hadn't been strapped into an over-shoulder harness, he would have fallen off the seat when he heard Professor Meriwether chuckle gleefully and say, "Okay, Wanda, take it away!"

Beside Peter, Chu groaned and clutched his metal case tightly to his stomach.

When Wanda took the controls, only the top of her head appeared on the personal screens, but her voice came through at full volume.

"Woo-hoo!" she called as they began to increase speed.

"How did she get into the front pod anyway?" asked Riva resentfully.

The Fusca had begun to swing violently from side to side.

Chu and Ben looked ill, but Otto seemed impressed.

"You're a natural, Wanda." The professor chuckled gleefully over the airwaves.

"Yee-haw!"

The Fusca pods were spinning out at neck-buckling speeds. Screams pierced through the tunnel as the front pod flipped right over, causing a chain reaction of more flipping pods.

Wanda hollered through the sound system, "360!"

Peter wondered if there were vomit bags. The stream of water on the tunnel floor had grown to a churning crashing force, lifting the Fusca bubbles to the tunnel ceiling, then dumping them down and around again. *Now I know what it would feel like to go through a washing machine!* Peter thought.

"Okay, Wanda, thank you!" Professor Meriwether's voice had lost some of its enthusiasm.

"Hit the brakes! Hit the brakes!" They heard him cry.

"What a riot!" Wanda chirped.

"What a relief!" Riva groaned.

Then, just as the churning began to subside, Professor Meriwether was heard asking if anyone else would like to take a spin at the controls.

Chu's face looked green, and his jaw dropped.

"Okay, have a seat, and take it away!"

The professor's image disappeared, leaving an empty screen in front of the driver's seat, but, at the same time, the Fusca engines were powering up again.

Peter strained to see. Could someone even shorter than Wanda have taken the controls?

"You'll be fine; it's very intuitive," the professor's mentoring voice said reassuringly.

Slowly, the Fusca began jerking forward with a series of fast stops and starts.

"Hey, who's kangaroo jumping?" complained Otto.

As if to answer his question, a pair of pointy ears bounced briefly into view at the base of the screen, then disappeared again.

"Wallaby jumping, actually!" Peter choked back a laugh.

"Okay, mind the brakes with those big bouncers of yours, Agent Pickles," the professor said with a chuckle.

Chu was scowling in dismay, but, in no time at all, Pickles surprised everyone by hitting her stride, and for a while they coasted along at a smooth and comfortable pace. Peter felt his eyeballs start to relax and his eardrums loosen. Then, without warning, the Fusca jolted to a sudden stop.

Chrrkkk-chrrkkkkkkk!

"Oh, I'm sorry. Was that your tail?"

Then, the wind dropped, and the Fusca sat silent beneath the sea.

CHAPTER

52

The Spirit of Water

Peter was relieved to see the unruffled head and shoulders of Professor Meriwether back at the controls.

"Just a temporary glitch," the professor assured his passengers. "But it'll be a good opportunity to get to know some sea life."

Beside him on the left, Riva duLac pointed out into the distance at something vivid and red.

"Look, Peter!" she cried.

The two watched closely as the thing expanded and contracted gracefully with the current. It looked like a slow-moving jellyfish.

"My old enemy," Riva croaked prophetically.

Peter squinted more closely.

"It's a plastic bag!" he said.

Two large sharks cruised past, and Peter watched the smaller fish scatter. The plastic bag disappeared with them.

Then, Professor Meriwether's voice was back on the speaker system.

"So, who fancies a swim?" he asked.

Chu sat forward, still clutching his metal case, and gasped loudly in disbelief.

Peter was certainly not going to push the green button on his dashboard to volunteer.

Nobody else did, either.

"Don't worry, kids!" Professor Meriwether was laughing and talking at the same time. "We're going to play a new game – it's an invention of mine, very high-tech. Now listen carefully. With the help of some special equipment, you're going to feel like you're jumping into the sea, but your bodies will actually be staying safely here inside the Fusca."

Small silver devices like cameras started popping up from the armrests of everyone's seat.

"Now," continued Professor Meriwether, "you should have all just received your playing pieces. They may look like cameras, but, let me be clear: they are not for taking pictures. I repeat they are *not* for taking pictures!"

Peter noticed that Otto and Ben Blott, sitting opposite him, weren't listening. Ben was already training his device on the sea outside the pod.

"Hey, take a photo of that shark," Otto told him.

"Wait!" Riva cried. "Didn't you listen? It's not a camera; it's something else!"

But it was too late. Ben pressed the blue button on the top of his playing piece. Immediately, a large headset that looked like a diving mask sprang from Ben's seat back and slid snugly over his head. Then, in almost the same instant, Ben's body sank limply into his seat.

"Ben, wake up! You idiot!" Otto shouted.

Otto slapped and punched at his brother's arms and legs, but they stayed motionless. Ben's eyes stared out at them from inside the mask, open but unseeing.

A shark approached the wall of their see-through pod.

The shark began making violent body slams against the Fusca tunnel, sending shudders against the pod walls.

"That's him out there!" Chu's voice quavered.

Peter and Riva both gasped in agreement.

Riva leant towards the green button on her dashboard, but Otto pushed her hand roughly away.

"No need to go blabbing to the teacher. I'm going to go get him."

Otto adjusted his seat belt, then trained his device in the direction of a second approaching shark.

"Be careful," Peter said kindly.

"No, it's you who'd better be careful!" Otto snapped back nastily. "Or at least watch out for sharks."

Otto clicked his blue button. The headset lowered into place, and he was gone.

Outside the pod, two sharks now loomed close to the wall. One was long and thin, and the other short and strong looking.

The Blott brothers for sure, thought Peter.

Professor Meriwether continued to give instructions over the speaker system. "These camera-like devices are actually the brains of the game. All you have to do is train your sights on something that you'd like to become, then click through with the blue button."

"How long does the game take?" asked one initiate from another Fusca pod.

"The whole simulation lasts fifteen minutes," Professor Meriwether informed them. "And don't worry; you'll all be perfectly safe. So, let's get out there!"

Peter saw that Riva was already directing her device out to sea. Peter was about to ask her what she was going to be, but she clicked her blue button and was gone.

"What are you going to be?" Peter asked Chu.

"I'm not playing," he mumbled. "I need to guard this."

Chu gripped the large metal case even tighter than before, holding it close to his chest.

Chicken! thought Peter as Chu curled up in his seat for a nap.

Peter turned his attention back out to sea, wondering what he should try to be. All the colourful fish looked so small, especially compared with the size of the two Blott sharks. Peter saw a sea horse bobbing by. It could be fun to be a sea horse, but it was also very small. He'd have to decide quickly, or the game would be over.

Suddenly, the walls of the Fusca pod were shuddering. Something was pushing against it.

Peter saw a small girl, no bigger than the sea horse, out there in the sea, her tiny white hands rocking the pod. She was dressed in a funny old-fashioned swimming costume and cap.

She must be some kind of optical illusion, Peter thought.

The girl was waving and beckoning.

"Do I know you?" Peter asked, leaning closer to the wall.

"Yes. It's me ... Edilene. We met during your fever."

Peter looked blankly at her.

"I'm a saltwater spirit. I came through your tears."

"I wasn't crying," protested Peter.

"Oh well!" She giggled. "Maybe it was your sweat."

"I remember now," said Peter. "You gave me advice."

"Did it help?"

"I think so." Peter grinned. "I'm here."

"Are you?"

"Um ... yes, aren't you?"

"I'm not sure; take a photo and see."

It was a trick. As soon as Peter clicked the blue button on his device, he found himself out in the sea next to Edilene. Up close, Peter saw that she wasn't wearing a swimming cap; her head was actually bald. Peter raised a hand to check for his own red hair, finding his scalp was smooth too. But the shock of losing his hair was nothing compared with the sight of his hands and feet, which were webbed like duck feet.

Behind Edilene, Peter saw tens of other little boy and girl swimmers, twisting and somersaulting through the currents, and all somehow managing to breathe underwater. They were all dressed in old-fashioned striped swimsuits of all colours.

Edilene smiled. "We're called Nixies. Come on, Peter, swim with us!"

Peter tried paddling his webbed feet through the water, copying the other swimmers. It was fun! He found he could move long distances, riding the currents with very little effort. As the Nixies twisted and turned together, Peter began to notice coloured lines like rods of different lengths hanging all around them in the water.

"What are they?" Peter asked Edilene.

"Water," she said, surprised. "That's what water looks like to a Nixie."

Edilene darted in an out among the coloured rods, pushing them in ways that made them tinkle and jingle like chimes.

"And this is water music." Edilene laughed. "We're swimming in music!"

For a while, Peter, swimming beside Edilene and imitating her moves, felt nothing but joy. But the feeling faded when he spotted the two Blott sharks swimming nearby. They must have seen Peter, because, suddenly, they were coming right towards him – making a rush on him.

Just in time, Peter managed to dodge both of them, using the turning speed of his webbed hands and feet. But now they were circling round and coming back in for the kill. He was going to be eaten this time, for sure.

"Help! Edilene!"

Edilene darted quickly in beside him and took hold of his hand. Peter would've been embarrassed in front of the other Nixies if he hadn't been so scared.

"Relax," Edilene told him gently. "Just let the sharks swim through you."

"What?!"

"It's okay. Sharks are actually very high-energy beings."

The sharks were getting closer.

"They can fill us with positive power, if we let them," Edilene continued.

What are you talking about? They'll eat us!" Peter cried fearfully.

Edilene shook her head, smiling. "No, they won't. Just tread water, and wait. You'll see."

Peter had never expected to play chicken with a shark. But there was no time left to pull out. It all happened quickly. The shorter, stronger-looking shark struck first. Peter waited for the pain as the lines of sharp white teeth plunged into him, but, instead, he felt a strange rush of excitement, like an energy charge, as the shark passed right through him. Next, the longer and thinner shark shot through him in the same way.

Whoosh! Peter got the same big rush of positive power.

Then, the sharks were gone.

Peter was shaking all over, but the pale smooth skin of his little Nixie body had not one single scratch on it.

"How come?" he asked Edilene.

"Because we're Nature spirits. Our body energy is on a different vibration compared with the other sea beings."

Peter wasn't quite sure what she meant, but he was glad not to have been eaten.

Then, Edilene and her friends showed Peter how to move through rocks and seaweed, and even through little fish. A turtle swam past him.

"Can I move through that turtle too?" asked Peter.

"Of course!"

Peter swam onto the turtle's back, dropped through its hard shell, and swam out from underneath it. The energy Peter got from the turtle was different from the sharks' power. The turtle energy felt tired.

Probably exhausted from travelling the world so many times, Peter thought.

Then, his eyes caught something red and see-through drifting towards him. As it got closer, Peter recognised the big red plastic bag from before.

"Can the Nixies move through that bag?" Peter asked Edilene.

"Yes," she said hesitantly. "We can, but we won't."

"Why not?"

"Because Nixies wouldn't like to absorb the energy of its field; it will fill us with too much sadness."

"Oh."

As the bag approached, the Nixies darted clear of it, but Peter stayed, circling it and studying it. He found himself feeling quite sorry for the red plastic bag.

"Are you sad?" Peter asked the bag.

"Yes." The bag sighed.

"Why?"

"Because I don't fit in here."

The Nixies were calling Peter to come away.

But Peter ignored them. "Why not?"

"You don't want to know." The bag was being lifted by a passing sea current and was starting to drift away.

"Yes, I do; tell me!" Peter swam to keep up with it.

Edilene and the other Nixies followed along too, though still keeping their distance.

"Tell me!" Peter repeated.

The bag swung around. "Because I'm not part of Nature! And I'm dangerous. If I play with the fish, I could kill them."

Peter didn't know what to say.

The bag continued, "And the worst thing is, I know I must stay here forever."

Behind him, the Nixies were crying salt tears. Peter also felt like crying. He began to feel pain on both sides of his head. It was the headset digging into his temples. The Nixies were waving now, and Peter felt himself being drawn away.

He was back in the Fusca pod. Riva was back too, taking off her mask. Otto and Ben were sitting opposite him, talking excitedly about the game. Only Chu seemed strangely absent. Was he still sleeping? He had his headset on now, and Peter saw with alarm that Chu's sleepy head seemed to have slumped forward against his blue button.

Professor Meriwether's voice came through: "According to my master system, everyone should be back by now!"

Gently, Peter reached over and shook Chu's shoulders, but the boy didn't stir. Then, Otto Blott kicked Chu's ankle with his foot; still, nothing. Chu must have joined the game without realising it.

Peter would have to alert Professor Meriwether.

Somehow, he found the courage to press the green button on his dashboard. Peter then immediately went red with embarrassment at the sight of his own face on the intercom screen.

"Excuse me," Peter said nervously, "but I think Chu Lee Wong may still be out there in the game."

"Okay. Thanks, Peter, we'll look into it."

After only a few tense moments, Professor Meriwether's voice was heard again. He sounded relieved. "It looks like there's a loggerhead turtle out there with Chu's name on it. Okay, we're bringing him in."

As Chu slowly sat upright, Peter thought his tiny face inside the big headset made him look more like a giant fly than a turtle.

"Chu, can you hear me?" It was Professor Meriwether's voice again.

Chu nodded sleepily and pulled off his headset.

"It looks like you dived into the system a little outside the game. That means your experience may have been calibrated differently, in terms of time."

Chu nodded again.

"How long do you think you were out there Chu?"

"Um ... seemed like years," Chu said wearily.

"You were out for a lifetime simulation, about fifty years, almost an entire turtle lifetime."

Laughter rang through the pods as Chu's dazed face appeared on the screens.

"Great," mumbled Chu. "Fifty years at school already, and we're not even there yet."

More laughter followed, and Chu sat speechless for the rest of the journey.

Just before landing, Peter said to Riva, "That was you in the plastic bag, wasn't it?"

Riva nodded.

Otto must have overheard them.

"Why would you want to be a piece of stinky trash?" he asked rudely.

Riva scowled at him for a long time, as if deciding whether or not to reply. Finally, she said, "Because ... I want to know my enemy. Get inside my enemy's skin."

CHAPTER

53

Welcome to the Field

One after another, the Fusca bubbles pummelled out of the transparent tunnel like peas from a shooter, and then sped through the shallows towards the beach. Unfortunately, only a few reached the sand. Most bubbles, including Peter's, rolled just short of the shore and landed with a *plonk* back in the water.

"Sorry about the botched landing, kids." Professor Meriwether's voice over the intercom sounded unconcerned. "Welcome to the Field!"

"What field? We're still in the sea!" cried Wanda.

"The GAIA Field. It's all around you now!"

They were interrupted by a whirring sound as the transparent hatch doors on the Fusca bubbles were activated. Soon the students started piling out of the pods and into the foamy knee-deep surf.

It was a bit of a wobbly finish to the journey, but Peter didn't mind. He saw that even Professor Meriwether's control bubble had rolled back down the beach and into the surf.

"You'll have a chance to wash up as soon as you get your room detail!" the professor announced.

Peter rolled up his long pants to his knees. Then, holding his backpack high, he jumped out of the pod and into the water to join the other initiates wading forward through the gentle breakers, their eyes on the sand dunes ahead. Peter couldn't resist pausing to look back in the direction they'd come. He could still see the speck of the GAIA Hub rising up like a glass cathedral from the sheer cliff face overlooking the sea. But something about what he saw wasn't quite right.

He yelped when an incoming wave spilled over the knees of his rolled-up pants, but he managed to keep his backpack clear of the water.

Beside him, Chu wasn't so lucky. He made a strange wailing sound as the force of the water dragged the metal case from his arms.

"Is it waterproof?" Peter called, pushing through the surf to get it for him.

"How do I know?" Chu said sarcastically. "It's not like I would've ever thrown it in the sea before!"

Chu's childish face contorted into a sob.

Peter carried the case onto dry land and waited while Chu opened it and inspected the contents.

"Looks good," Chu said finally, gazing at his precious science kit. He gave Peter a half-smile.

Up on the sand dunes ahead, they heard the unmistakable voice of Wanda Shore.

"Over here! Come get your free backpacks!"

She was standing next to some older kids, looking all official, handing out bags to the initiates as they headed up the beach.

"Solar–lunar backpacks. Free! Over here!" Wanda shouted.

The Blott brothers, in their hurry for the free gifts, stumbled right over Chu, roughly kicking the contents of the open science kit into the sand.

"Hey!" Chu shouted angrily.

"Stupid place to sit!" grumbled Otto, without stopping to apologise, while an incoming wave picked up some of the strange objects and pulled them off into the shallows.

"The salt water will erode my cathodes!" Chu raged as he leapt back into the sea, wetting his clothes completely now.

When Peter and Riva jumped back in to help him, Chu scolded both of them, saying, "Be careful! It's very sophisticated equipment."

Riva raised her eyebrows at Peter but carried on snatching up the curiously shaped objects.

Soon nearly every piece except for one was back in its proper place.

"Oh no!" Chu groaned. "My bubble spirit level. It's made of glass, so it's going to be very hard to spot."

The tall thin shadow of Professor Meriwether paused in front of them, while the three scanned the sand.

"Are you children cleaning up the beach on your first day?"

They laughed politely as the professor held a small glass object out to Chu.

"I'm guessing this is yours."

"My spirit level!"

Peter saw Chu smile for the first time since they'd met.

"A very high level of precision, by the look of things," said the professor, and Peter noticed that he was peering not at the object but at Chu. "It reminds me of a Chinese proverb your grandfather taught me: 'If you stand straight, you do not fear a crooked shadow.'"

Chu nodded and seemed to stand a little straighter in response.

Peter thought of Cleo Choat and her stooping neck, with her jagged profile and triangular jaw. Now that was a crooked shadow.

"What does that spirit level do?" Riva asked.

"Good question, Riva. As Chu knows well, it's for measuring surfaces and finding the lines that are straight and true."

The bouncing bubble inside the level reminded Peter of the floating spiral in the pyramid from his mother's lab that he'd been carrying around with his treasures. He quickly put down the mother wallaby pouch and rummaged for it.

"Is that everyone?" Junior Agent Jukes called down from further up the beach.

"These are the last!" Professor Meriwether called back, pointing at Peter, Riva, and Chu.

"Um ... excuse me, Professor." Peter held out the glass pyramid. "But this looks a bit like the spirit level, except it's got a spiral instead of a bubble in it."

One glance at the tiny object, and Professor Meriwether's eyes showed disbelief.

"Do you know what it's for?" Peter asked uncertainly.

"Yes, I do Peter," the professor said quietly. He reached out for it. "May I?"

Peter nodded, handing it to him.

"There are only three of these in existence," continued the professor.

"How do you know?" asked Riva.

"Because I made them," he said, "some years ago. I gave two of them away to two top scientists." Professor Meriwether turned to Peter. "One of them was your mother."

"What about the other one?" interrupted Riva.

"A-a-ah ..." was all the professor said, with a note of sadness in his voice.

"Well, what about the third one?" Riva persisted.

"Oh that? It's a much larger version, which I kept for myself, up in my weather tower." He indicated a rising edifice at the edge of a rocky peninsular in the distance, then handed the pyramid carefully back to Peter.

"But what does it measure?" interrupted Chu, looking jealously at the object.

"One could as well ask, what doesn't it measure?" Professor Meriwether crouched down on the sand. "But let's take an easy example. What's the weather like this evening?"

"Fine," said Riva, glancing at the clear dome of cloudless orange-gold sky.

"Good. Now, Peter, place your device onto this flat piece of sand, and let's see what it can tell us about the weather."

The wiggly spiral inside the see-through pyramid flattened out parallel with the sand and started to spin slowly.

"What direction is it going?" Professor Meriwether asked Peter.

"Um ... anticlockwise."

"Correct. What does that mean?"

"Anticyclone high pressure," replied Chu.

"Huh?" said Peter and Riva at the same time.

"Good weather," Chu explained absently.

Riva frowned. "Well, I just told you that."

Then, the spinning spiral began to sink to the base, where it slowly changed direction.

"Meteorological changes coming. ..." The spinning got faster. "Coming soon!" Professor Meriwether took a handkerchief from his trouser pocket and sneezed. "Rough weather."

The spiral began to tilt and bounce across the edges of the transparent walls.

"The device also works as a measure of earth's health, kind of like taking her temperature. As you can see, she's been ill lately. She's out of balance, and she's definitely running a temperature." Professor Meriwether spoke as if he were discussing a beloved family member.

Peter saw the professor was still holding his white handkerchief close to his face, and hoped he wasn't going to cry.

Instead, Professor Meriwether sneezed again.

"But how does it work?" asked Chu, who still couldn't take his eyes off the spiral device.

"Ah … well now," said Professor Meriwether, looking past Chu and out to sea. "Here, at the wild shores of science, these are the questions we must continually ask ourselves."

A queue had formed further up the beach, at the place where Wanda Shore was handing out backpacks. She greeted them in a fake friendly voice.

"Welcome to Spiral Hall. Here are your solar–lunar survival packs; one per student. Enjoy!"

"Thanks a lot," gushed Peter, looking over the gift. "Wow!"

"It has all kinds of survival items inside," Wanda chirped, flicking her blonde hair. "Gloves, food packets, fire starters, miniature tools."

"Survival from what?" asked Chu nervously.

Ignoring Chu, Wanda said to Peter, "You can follow me if you like."

"Why? Where are you going?" Peter asked.

"No, I mean follow me online. Hashtag Shore Thing." She turned to Riva. "You can follow me too if you want."

"Why would I want to do that?" asked Riva, narrowing her eyes.

Wanda shrugged, looking slightly taken aback. "Just, you know, to see what I'm up to." She smiled another fake-looking smile.

"I can already see what you're up to," said Riva darkly. "It's called buying friends. These gifts aren't from you; they're from the Global Advanced Intelligence Agency."

"So what? I'm giving them out on behalf of Artiss Fleur."

"But you're using GAIA's goodwill to try to make people like you and follow you on social media."

Wanda pouted. "Well, it doesn't seem to be working, does it?"

"Whatever!" said Riva, taking her bag and striding away.

"I'll follow you," said Peter kindly. He was happy to get a new bag and happy that Wanda was helping Artiss Fleur.

"Great!" Wanda handed Peter a card with a big picture of herself in the middle. "Any personal device will do. Time tablets, personal organisers, cell phones, laptops."

"Oh, I don't have any of those things," Peter told her.

"What about your jacket?" interrupted a roundish boy with a friendly open face, who Peter remembered as Roland.

"What about it?"

"It's a wearable device."

"How do you know?"

"I can tell by this little icon here at the sleeve pocket. Look! This one that looks like a GAIA spiral stretched out into a radio wave."

A few initiates coming up the line behind them started looking over at Peter's sleeve.

"*Shh!*" Peter told Roland, pulling him to one side and whispering, "It does have Wi-Fi."

"That's just the beginning," Roland said. "I know this kind of jacket; it has its own field, and you can pair it up with any known device."

"Like what?" asked Peter. "Do you mean with a laptop or something?"

Roland giggled. "Or with a rocket ship if you want to. That's how powerful they are."

Roland fingered the jacket lapels enviously.

"Well, nothing will surprise me any more, after travelling to the GAIA Hub in a Tree Portal," Peter said.

Peter waited for Roland to ask what that was, but he just shrugged again and said, "Cool."

"Do you know what a Tree Portal is?" Peter asked.

"Yep, my dad took me in a T-Port for my fifth birthday. He was on a business trip. We went from the Netherlands to New York in nine and a half minutes."

"Were you sick?"

"Only on the way back. Too many pancakes." Roland fingered Peter's jacket sleeve. "Can I try on your jacket? I promise to give it straight back."

Peter took it off reluctantly and let Roland pull it on.

"I'm Roland Portogalo, by the way. You're Peter, right? The guy with the kangaroo?"

Peter nodded. "Wallaby, actually. She's gone to start her field training with Artiss Fleur."

"Wait a minute. Peter who?" Roland asked suddenly.

"Peter Blue."

"You're Peter Blue?"

"Yes."

"*The* Peter Blue?"

"Well, I'm *a* Peter Blue."

"The Sleeping King?"

Peter wondered if Roland was making fun of him, but he didn't seem the type.

"That's your GAIA name," Roland explained.

"My what?"

"All the high ones at GAIA get a name – kind of like a code."

"You mean like President Buchanan is Invisible Bu-h?"

"So, you do know something, then."

They were distracted by three tall pretty girls at Wanda's table who'd started to giggle and squeal. "We'd like to become followers," they were saying.

"Oh … well, great!" Wanda chirped, reaching for her name cards.

"No," said the girls. "We want to follow him." They were pointing at Peter.

"Oh, that's okay … thank you," Peter said politely. After Cleo Choat in London, the thought of being followed by anyone terrified him.

He turned back to Roland. "I kind of need the jacket back now."

"Okay. Yep, sure." Roland took it off slowly and passed it to him in a regal way, with both arms extended full-length in front of him and his round shoulders stooped into a slight bow.

"How do you know so much about these GAIA jackets?" Peter asked.

Roland pulled him down into a dip in a sand dune, then looked around cautiously, as if to check that they were properly alone. "Because I'm a spy," he whispered.

Peter didn't really know how to respond to this. "What kind of spy?"

Roland burst into gleeful laughter. "'Course I'm not a spy. I was joking. Man, you'll believe anything."

Peter laughed too. "So, that stuff you said about my GAIA name, the Sleeping King, was a joke."

"Oh no! That's true."

"How do you know?"

"From my dad."

"Your dad's a GAIA agent?"

"No not likely!" Roland laughed again. "If you met him, you'd understand. He fixes the jackets and the transport devices and stuff. My dad's a GAIA geek."

A loudspeaker announcement resonated around the beach: "Calling all initiates! Please make your way to the green flag for your luggage pickup and room assignments."

"I wonder where we'll sleep," Peter said to Roland.

"We've got mini dormitories rammed right into the hillside."

Peter squinted over at the hills. "I can't see anything."

"Exactly," interrupted Roland. "It's rammed earth; a great feat of GAIA engineering."

Wanda was already up at the green flag, standing importantly with the older students. Behind them, the sun was still somehow not quite setting.

"So, if I'm the Sleeping King," Peter challenged Roland, "what's your GAIA name?"

"I don't have one; none of the other initiates do."

"How do you know?"

Roland giggled. "Promise you won't tell?"

Peter nodded solemnly.

"Because," Roland whispered, "I actually am a spy."

CHAPTER

54

Into the Earth

"Y ou will now be divided into groups and assigned to your dorm pods. Listen carefully for your names, and follow all instructions."

Wanda's and Riva's names were called out for the same pod. Peter noticed Riva didn't look pleased. They were led off by a junior agent called Kaito.

"Everyone stick together behind me," Kaito told the girls as he moved towards a meadow trail that headed in the direction of a high sloping hill.

"Don't we have golf carts or something?" asked Wanda. "I don't usually walk that far."

"Well, you can fly there" said Kaito, "as long as you use your own energy – that's what this school's all about."

With a pouty look, Wanda scooped up her backpack, along with a large open carry bag.

"Hey," said Riva, pointing into the top of the bag, "Aren't those plastic bottles? Didn't you know that single-use plastic is banned at Spiral Hall?"

Peter thought he saw a momentary flash of panic in Wanda's eyes, but she quickly recovered. "They're not mine. I was just taking them to the recycling for someone."

"Time to go," Kaito told them.

Wanda looked around nervously.

"Here," she said to Peter and began stuffing the bottles hastily into his new solar–lunar backpack. "Could you take these to the recycling for me? I don't have time; I'm being called."

Peter took the bottles politely. "Um … okay … but where is the recycling?"

Wanda stepped onto the trail and didn't reply.

"That looks like a long way," he heard her telling Kaito. "Are you sure we don't have transportation? Has my pony arrived yet? Horsepower would do it."

Kaito was speeding up, and Peter saw that Wanda hurried to keep beside him.

"I don't know if you know, but my dad's a big donor here? I'm talking huge sums of money! This whole place would probably go under if it weren't for my dad," Wanda said, now jogging behind Kaito as they disappeared over the crest of a small rise.

"Do you have a room assignment yet?" one of the other junior agents asked Peter.

Before he could answer, Otto Blott was beside him, snatching up one of Wanda's empty plastic bottles.

"Hey, look!" Otto cried. "This guy's got plastic!"

"Quick! Grab him!" Ben said.

"What are you doing with that plastic?" the junior agent demanded, taking Peter by the arm.

"Um … just going to the recycling bin," said Peter innocently.

"There is no plastic recycling. The island's plastic-free," said Junior Agent Jukes, the head boy.

The sun was finally setting now, creating a shadowy light in the space around them.

"Didn't you read the rules before you came?" Otto Blott scolded him imperiously, in front of the others.

"No," said Peter.

Junior Agent Sinta, the head girl, joined the conversation.

"We have a closed loop on our garbage here, which means it's a zero-waste school."

Peter felt very glad to hear this. "My uncle's in the garbage business in London and doesn't recycle or reuse anything, so I'm really—"

"So, it runs in your family!" Otto interrupted unfairly.

A small crowd was now staring down menacingly at the pile of empty plastic bottles spilling from Peter's bag onto the sand.

"They'll end up in the sea before we know it," said Ben.

"So, where shall I put them?"

A grown-up voice behind him said. "We'll start by putting you and your plastic pollution into detention."

With that, Peter was led away.

The detention officer was a grey, tired-looking man with thinning hair. The nameplate on his narrow, dark, wooden desk read: Administrator Arun Drufus.

"Detention on your first day; not a very good start."

Peter said calmly, "Well, if you'll just let me explain—

"Name?" Mr Drufus interrupted.

"Peter Blue."

"I know exactly who you are."

"Why did you ask, then?"

"Standard detention procedure, and don't answer back. You're lucky to be here, you know."

"What, in detention? When I've done nothing wrong?" Peter was suddenly having trouble keeping his temper.

But the detention master's eyes snapped up from his paperwork and stared him down so piercingly that Peter felt suddenly afraid. Mr Drufus was right: he was lucky to be here at school.

"Don't know how you did it, actually," Drufus muttered under his breath. "Just slipped in here against expectations, didn't you? Slippery type, aren't you?"

"If you say so."

Everyone had been so kind and welcoming so far that Peter felt confused by this sudden meanness. Still, it didn't matter; Artiss Fleur and Theodorus Meriwether were happy that he was here. And even Pickles had just slipped in. *She must be a slippery type too,* thought Peter.

"What are you smirking at? Think you're some kind of big rising GAIA star, do you?"

Peter gulped and shook his head. "No, not at all. I agree with you that I'm lucky to be here."

Mr Drufus seemed taken aback by Peter's unexpected humility and switched to a new theme. "Is that a genuine GAIA jacket?"

"Um … yes."

The detention master scribbled a sidebar note on the detention paper. "Where did you get it?"

"From my father, Agent Byron Blue. …"

"I know exactly where you got it," Drufus grunted. "And he had no authorisation to give it to you."

Peter didn't have the courage to answer back this time. …

Mr Drufus sighed. "So, please tell me exactly why you felt so incumbent to break the rules on your first day at Spiral Hall."

"I didn't know the rules," protested Peter. He then went on to explain, "I didn't have a prospectus or anything – not even a proper invitation."

Mr Drufus scribbled another sidebar note, this time, reading aloud in a sharp voice, "No proper invitation; question mark over legitimacy of admittance to Spiral Hall."

Peter sighed. "That's not true. I had a proper invitation, but my uncle—"

Mr Drufus glanced up sharply at Peter. "But you admit that the plastic was yours?"

"No, of course not!"

"If you don't admit it, it'll get harder for you later."

"The plastic bottles weren't mine."

"That's what they all say."

Peter saw weakness and disappointment in the man's small grey eyes.

"The fish are very sensitive here," Mr Drufus continued. "They don't expect to be poisoned by plastic."

"Can I please talk to Agent Fleur?" interrupted Peter.

"What, that cowboy scientist? He can't help you now."

There was a knock on the office door, and they were interrupted by a woman's voice.

"Working late, Administrator Drufus?"

"Just a small matter, Principal Halowell. Nothing for you to worry yourself about."

Principal Halowell, dressed in a purple gown, pushed the door open and seemed to fill the room with her presence. "Thank you, Drufus, but why don't we let *me* decide?"

"Well, it's just a rule breaker on his first day. He seems also to be a liar."

"Oh dear! And the offence, Drufus?"

"Possession of six single-use plastic soda bottles, and suspicion of being about to throw them into the sea."

Principal Halowell clutched at her stomach, looking suddenly ill.

"They weren't mine! And I was looking for the recycling bin," protested Peter.

The principal took a step backwards. "Where are the bottles now?"

"Sinta sent them to the GAIA Do-tank for experimental purposes," Mr Drufus replied.

Principal Halowell turned to Peter. "Do you know where plastic comes from?"

"Um ... yes ... from petrol."

"Correct. And where does petrol come from?" she asked.

"Um ... from fossils in the ground. ..." Peter was suddenly extra glad that he'd been seated next to Riva on the Fusca trip.

"And do you know how long it takes for earth to dispose of plastic?" asked Drufus, with a smug glint in his eye.

Peter nodded. It was a trick.

"Earth can't ever dispose of plastic," Peter answered, thinking of Lot 17 and the plastic wasteland. "Every bit of plastic that's ever been created still exists — even the stuff that gets burnt at the landfill turns into tiny poisonous pieces."

The principal said, "I'm impressed."

Mr Drufus, on the other hand, just looked depressed.

"All right," said Principal Halowell. "I'll take it from here. Thank you, Administrator. You're dismissed."

"But this is my office."

"Dismissed!" she repeated in a no-nonsense voice, and Drufus shuffled out.

Laying a hand gently on Peter's shoulder, Principal Halowell exclaimed, "Goodness, Peter, your clothes are all wet!"

Peter shivered involuntarily.

"Another one of Meriwether's botched Fusca beach landings, was it?" She frowned good-humouredly, as if they were old friends. "Now, I'm presuming you haven't got your room detail yet."

Peter shook his head.

"Good, because you're just what I'm looking for."

A few minutes later, as she led Peter through the tunnel entrance to one of the rammed earth dormitory pods, Principal Halowell said, "You'll learn that life at Spiral Hall is all about balance, which is why you're going to make a perfect roommate match for another lost initiate I just rounded up wet from the beach. He's a nice earthy scientist to offset your airy philosopher type."

Principal Halowell entered one of the circular dormitory rooms, and there, sitting sulkily in his canoe-shaped bed, was Chu Lee Wong.

"I thought I'd have the room to myself!" Chu stepped off the bed and stared down at the floor.

"Come now, that's hardly a warm welcome," said the principal breezily." Well, I'll leave you two to get acquainted."

As an afterthought, she added, "You'll find a geothermal whirlpool bath down the hall and snacks in the family room – including unlimited hot chocolate during Orientation Week."

"Thank you," said Peter as he gaped around the space.

The room was like a circular cave, but the ceiling above the canoe-shaped beds was made of glass. On each side of the room there was a workstation with a large screen and all kinds of devices.

The principal pulled a brightly coloured book from her pocket and passed it to Peter.

"Welcome to Spiral Hall," she said.

"What is it?"

"A copy of our prospectus." She smiled wide and was gone.

Peter had to force Chu to take a bath, but he had no trouble convincing him to eat the sandwiches and hot chocolate. He was still not very talkative, though, so Peter, who sensed he was probably homesick, began to read to him from the prospectus.

"It says here we can program cosmic musical tones and therapeutic aromas to pipe through our living, breathing walls."

Chu grimaced as he polished his science pieces.

"And our canoe beds have mini planetarium glass domes above them, for star watching."

After Chu had fallen asleep on the other side of the sleeping screen that separated the beds, Peter lay staring up at the night sky and thinking. He couldn't sleep; too much had happened.

He tiptoed outside in his pyjamas and perched on the side of the hill facing out to the beach. Towards the mainland, he caught a distant wink of light. It was coming from the GAIA Hub. There was definitely something wrong with that view. He would get it in a minute.

For a while, Peter thought about Pickles and wondered where she was with Artiss Fleur, training to be an agent. Peter couldn't wait for his own meeting with Artiss Fleur on Saturday, when he would finally be able to deliver Dad's message: "Never capitulate!"

Artiss Fleur would know what that meant.

Peter stared out across the sea. The GAIA Hub stared back at him. Suddenly, he realised what had been bothering him about the view. From the big window of the GAIA Hub, there'd been no view of this island – just empty sea. His heart began to thump. That meant this island must be invisible!

The Tree Tenders

The day was breezy, with only patches of warmth coming from a weak autumn sun dodging in and out of the fast-scudding clouds.

Principal Halowell brought the initiates to a halt in a small orchard where the air was laced with the scent of ripening apples. No one knew why they were here or what was going to happen.

The principal positioned herself beneath a towering apple tree, the largest by far in the entire orchard, and raised her purple-robed arms like branches.

"A tree. … What is a tree?" she asked expectantly.

Hands shot up everywhere.

"*Ooooh,* Miss … a tree is a plant – like a tall big plant."

"Yes, very good. Anyone else?"

"Um … it has a trunk, and branches and leaves on it."

"Yes, good. Anyone else?"

"It gives us oxygen," said Roland.

"Good. How?"

"Photosynthesis!" shouted Wanda.

"Oh goodness, you're all very smart," Principal Halowell enthused.

Then, after a brief pause, she asked again, "But what *is* a tree?"

"We just told you!" said Wanda, not even trying to hide her annoyance.

The principal gazed up into the dappled apple leaves.

"A tree," she intoned, "is the human being of the plant world. Or, if you like, what we are to the animal kingdom, a tree is to the plant kingdom."

Nobody spoke.

She continued, "Except they're an upside-down version of us. Is that clear?"

The initiates nodded uncertainly.

"That is, the brains of a tree are in its roots, and the feet are in the leaves, waving when the breezes blow."

When nobody spoke, the principal lowered her voice to a whisper.

"Now, in this world, there is one special tree that grows for each person – and only that person. Sadly, most people are never aware of their one special tree; they never meet it or even know it exists."

"Are we going to get a test on this?" whined Roland.

"No, dear, but in a moment, you will get a chance to talk to the experts."

Everyone looked around for some experts. A boy with the sticking-up hair who was unloading gardening gear onto a long table smiled over at them, but, otherwise, the orchard was empty.

"Who will we talk to?" asked Roland.

"Why, the trees, of course!"

"This is stupid," Otto Blot mumbled.

"How are we supposed to talk to trees?" grumbled another student.

"Well, there are no rules; that's up to you and your baby trees."

On the table in front of her, she placed a sign that read: Baby Tree Drop.

"Baby trees? Our trees?" A ripple of excitement zapped through the group like a surge of electricity.

All Peter could think about now was getting his own tree to talk to. This was going to be his best subject ever at this school. He'd already had so much practice with the Great Gum and the kitchen table. If he got good enough at talking to trees, he might one day be able to talk to his mother's shopping list.

"Are you ready to receive your tree?"

"Yes!"

"And tend your tree?"

"Yes!" cried everyone.

"Your tree will forever be your connection to the school and this island! Talk to it, shape your life around it, grow with it." The principal's voice rose up like that of an opera singer. "Graft your very soul to your tree. With your tree, you will never be alone at school."

A hush had fallen over the initiates. No one had ever heard a grown-up speak like this before. But then, the moment passed.

"All right! Quick, smart, everyone! Take your equipment from Elvin, one planting pouch per person, and fall into line."

The principal's voice rose above a new round of happy chatter.

"No pushing, no shouting, no chewing gum, no littering, and no cutting in line," she cautioned as the initiates made a rush on the planting gear.

"But where are the baby trees?" whined one girl.

"Patience, please!" Principal Halowell gently sniffed the air. "*Ahh!* That's more like it. ... The weather's turning."

A few drops of rain brought the beginning of a light shower.

"Excellent. Well done." She seemed to be directing her praise to the sky.

While the initiates were complaining and pulling up the hoods of their raincoats, Principal Erthia Halowell left her place at the baby tree drop and strode right out into the open meadow, as if to meet the shower.

"Very refreshing!" she exclaimed. "And perfect for planting."

"But won't the rain ruin the outing?" whined someone.

"Tell that to the trees!" Principal Halowell cried. "Because, for a tree, there is nothing in the world better than a light afternoon shower!"

"And if the weather turns strongly enough, we may yet be joined by Mr Tollen, a great expert on trees," the principal added.

"Is Mr Tollen a teacher?" asked Riva.

"Well, yes and no; he's difficult to pin down. Comes with the storms and leaves with the calm."

The name Tollen sounded familiar to Peter, who hoped they would get to meet him.

But by the time everyone had picked up the planting pouches, the rain had almost stopped.

In the meantime, Peter noticed Riva scowling watchfully at Wanda, who was snapping a series of quick selfies, posing with her mini watering can and personal fertiliser sack.

Peter tied the belt of his own planting set like a pouch around his waist, then began to carefully read his instruction card.

"Can we keep the planting pouches?" asked one girl hopefully.

"Of course," said the principal. "You *must* keep them – you're tree tenders now!"

By the time Peter was ready with his equipment, the queue at the baby tree drop snaked halfway round the orchard.

Roland was at the head of the queue.

"Step onto the circle, Roland, and stand still," said Principal Halowell as she indicated a thick, circular wooden plate in the ground at her feet.

Roland stepped nervously onto the wooden plate.

"I shall now *intend* a tree."

"Don't you mean *tend* a tree?" corrected Roland.

Principal Halowell gazed good-humouredly at him.

"I shall now *intend* a tree," Principal Halowell repeated pointedly.

This time, Roland didn't correct her.

The principal raised both arms up into the boughs of the great apple tree.

"One, two, *tree*," she said.

"Don't you mean one, two, *three?*" Roland couldn't resist interrupting her again.

Principal Halowell sighed theatrically. "I shall try once more."

"One, two, *tree!*"

In her hands, she held a perfect little tree sapling, complete with a ball of compact soil around its roots. The ball clearly resembled a newborn baby's head.

"Oh, look how darling!" Principal Halowell cradled the baby tree in her arms. "Our firstborn for this year."

They all watched, barely breathing, as the principal gently patted its tiny baby leaves. "Count the fingers, Roland."

"Five?" Roland guessed, looking at the leaves.

"*Ooh,* five," she cooed. "It's a maple tree."

She glanced down at Roland, then back at the tree. "Mm-hmm ... this will do just nicely for you. The maple tends toward heaviness at the trunk, but there's light-filled sweetness within."

The principal passed the baby tree carefully to Roland, who just stood rooted to the spot, gaping at it.

No one could figure out where the baby tree had come from.

Maybe she pulled it from one of the sleeves of her gown, thought Peter.

"How did you do that?" Wanda called, without even raising her hand.

"*Easy-treesy!*" said the principal in a pleased voice. Then, she clapped her hands and called, "Next!"

As Peter's turn came closer, he began to feel fluttery in his stomach, wondering what kind of tree he was going to get. To calm his nerves, he concentrated on trying to figure out where the baby trees were actually being dispensed from. Standing on tiptoe, he watched as, time after time, Principal Halowell put her hand up behind the broad apple bough and then, once again, brought down a brand-new little tree, a different one every time.

Students continued taking turns standing on the circular plate.

"A cherry tree for you, to bring more sweetness to your life," the principal said in her strong melodic voice, handing the tiny sapling to the girl standing on the plate.

"A pine tree for you; shallow roots will let you spread your warmth," she told another student.

Peter recognised the three tall pretty girls who had asked to follow him the day before. They stepped up together, and all got the same: apple trees.

"Very apt," said the principal. "The tree of this island, bringing a rosy gift of health and wisdom to each of you."

There was a growing bulge of students already holding their baby trees but still muddling around in the baby tree drop area.

"As soon as you have your tree, you may proceed directly off," instructed the principal, her slender hands waving away the confused students.

"But where to?" asked the group. "Where do we go?"

"To start planting, of course," she said. "You've got your equipment and your planting instructions."

They began moving slowly away, except Roland, who stayed rooted to the spot.

"Are you still here?" Principal Halowell asked admonishingly.

"Where's the planting place?" Roland persisted.

"*Oooh,* I see that's what's troubling you." The principal clapped her hands to get everyone's attention, then addressed her remarks loudly to the whole group. "On the matter of location, please let your trees decide."

A breakout of giggling arose among the initiates, but the sound quickly faded when they realised she was actually serious.

"If you're finding it difficult," Principal Halowell advised, "hold the tree in your left hand, which is more sensitive than the right, then straighten your arm, and let your tree guide you."

A ripple of disbelief ran through the remaining group as they watched tree holders with outstretched arms being pulled along.

The principal didn't seem at all surprised as she resumed handing out baby trees to the next students in the queue.

"A baby olive for you," she said to a serious-looking boy. "It will protect you from the cold in winter and the heat of summer."

Peter looked around for Riva, who stood just a few places back from him, with her chin raised expectantly. Riva rolled her eyes meaningfully in the direction of Wanda, who'd begun posing for more photos and still hadn't bothered to join the queue.

At the front, Principal Halowell's voice rang out like crystal.

"Marvellous! Only the gingko tree will do for you; the oldest living tree on earth, and one of the most special, to my mind."

Otto the bully rolled his eyes over his shoulder at his brother. There seemed to be a lot of eye-rolling going on.

Now it was Otto's turn. He stepped confidently onto the wooden circle, pulling Ben along with him.

"Ben and I need to have the same kind of tree because we're actually non-identical twins," Otto instructed.

"Is that so? Well, we'll see about that, won't we?" Principal Halowell closed her eyes and raised a hand behind the apple branch. "For you, Ben," she said, pausing to study the sapling, "I have a grey poplar. Yes; perfect. They stoop at the crown but are very enduring." She passed the baby tree to Ben.

Everyone was surprised to see her rummaging down at the foot of the apple tree.

"And for your brother—"

"What? What is it?" asked Otto in a stunned voice.

"Swamp grass."

"But you said there was a tree for everyone!"

"And, indeed, there is – all in good time."

Peter wondered if this might somehow be a punishment for yesterday's bullying.

Meanwhile, Otto was regarding the swamp grass sullenly.

"I know what you're thinking," continued the principal. "You're thinking that swamp grass is very important for purification of water here at the island. And it is. You'll be doing us a great service, and we thank you for that."

Otto was about to protest, but Principal Halowell looked right over his head and pronounced, "Next!"

When it was almost Peter's turn, he watched in amazement as Wanda cut into the queue, right in front of him. Actually, she asked a boy to give up his spot for her, so, technically, it wasn't cutting in. Peter decided not to say anything because he was curious to see what kind of tree Wanda would get.

"Ah, Wanda Shore! Step up and let me take a good long look at you."

Principal Halowell stood still, with her fingers to her temples, while Wanda flicked her hair and arranged herself with one hand on her hip as she stood on the wooden plate. Wanda's face fell when she saw that the principal had closed her eyes tightly.

"Principal Halowell! Hello! How can you look at me with your eyes closed?"

The principal made no reply, and her eyes remained closed. The remaining initiates were getting restless. Still, the principal didn't open her eyes.

"Why's mine taking so long?" Wanda wailed.

Still nothing.

Wanda stamped her sneakered foot.

"Principal Halowell! Why's mine taking so long?" she repeated." It's taking forever!"

Principal Halowell's eyes snapped open. "How does one of eleven years old speak so knowingly of forever?"

The principal reached one arm upwards, into the boughs of the tree. She lowered her arm, holding in her hand a lovely, floaty-looking tree with a slender trunk.

"A silver birch; graceful, vital, and dedicated to the sun. With the silver birch, you'll never lose hope." The principal bent her face close to Wanda's as she passed her the tree. "It may look frail, but its resilience comes from its flexible character and a trunk that bends with the wind. Which way will you bend, Wanda Shore?"

Wanda, who was not very tall, took the silver birch sapling and displayed it like a trophy above her head, posing for the remaining crowd.

"Wow! I love this tree!" Wanda tried to push her camera cube into the principal's hand. "Can you take a picture of us?"

"Why do you need a picture?" Principal Halowell asked irritably.

"To share. ..." Wanda's voice faded slightly.

"But your friendship with this tree is a very personal thing. One does not need pictures to remember that which can be grafted on your very soul." Principal Halowell sighed tellingly.

Wanda, for once, didn't seem to have a reply.

"Next."

Peter was next.

"Ah, dear Peter Blue. You might be a middling academic, but. ..." Principal Halowell paused to look up, then added, "You'll be prince of the forest with this tree!"

Then, without even closing her eyes, she reached both arms straight up into the tree boughs, held them there for a few moments, then pulled them back down – empty!

The remaining students in the queue gave a collective gasp, while Peter felt his heart thumping with a mixture of shame and disappointment.

"How strange. ..." The principal swung herself athletically up onto a lower tree branch. She reached up again. "No tree?"

Peter was determined to hide his disappointment. His eyes caught a flash of purple high up in the branches. Principal Halowell was climbing the tree. The winds blew up from nowhere. He saw her clinging to the centre trunk, as if it were a ship's mast.

Then, the principal was down once again, standing behind him and holding a massive tree sapling.

"I'm afraid you'll have your work cut out for you with this one," she said with a sniff. "Always the same with these princely types. Big for a newborn too."

Elvin the helper appeared, and, together, they heaved the oversized sapling onto the table.

"Wow!" said the crowd.

"The dawn redwood! I've never seen a better specimen." Principal Halowell paused to stare at Peter. "And I see now that nothing else will do."

"Thank you," said Peter, needing all his strength to take the redwood from the table. It was almost as tall as he was. He was about to leave when he noticed that something strange had happened to Principal Halowell's hair. "Excuse me, Miss. Has your hair changed colour?"

She smiled appreciatively and patted her long hair, which was usually grey but had now turned to the colour of brown apple bark.

"Thank you, Peter, for noticing. Yes, it has. Very rejuvenating – that climb."

CHAPTER

56

Tollen

eter left the orchard at a fast walk. The redwood was heavy,
and he was looking around for a close-by place to plant. To
one side, he saw a narrow rising mountain path, and to the
other, a path that twisted down to the sea.

"It might be nice place to plant down there," he told the redwood
conversationally, pointing towards the sea.

But the tree had a different idea, because it began tugging at his
wrist, pulling him in the direction of the steep trail.

"I should have guessed you'd want to go up – princely type!" Peter
told the tree, mimicking Principal Halowell.

For a while, they puffed along, sun-baked pine needles crunching
underfoot.

Peter talked to the tree, making polite remarks, such as, "It looks
like the weather's beginning to change, after all."

Every time Peter tried to pause to start planting, the tugs became
more insistent, and the tree directed him to keep on climbing, higher
and higher up the trail.

Finally, the steep trail ended. With sweat pouring and knees aching,
Peter emerged from the woods at the mountaintop. It was a circular
summit, bare of trees except for a tall, ancient-looking oak right at
the cliff edge. It felt like the top of the world. Below, the whole island

spanned out in rolling forests of bright autumn gold that sloped all the way down to the silvery sea. At the foot of the mountain, he saw the circular-shaped Spiral Hall. It was definitely the same dome roof that his father had shown him in the vision at the clearing. A shiver of excitement rippled down Peter's spine.

Then, the redwood tugged at his arm, demanding attention.

Peter could hear a stream running nearby, and the earth felt soft underfoot. This was the place to plant. He could feel it. Thankfully, the tree seemed finally to agree.

Chu was the last of the initiates to get his tree. As a serious scientist, he didn't believe in anything that he couldn't see and explain, so, instead of joining the queue, Chu had stood watching from the other side, trying to figure out the trick of the tree drop. Unfortunately, though, the principal's hands had just been too quick for him.

Now, like all principals, Erthia Halowell also seemed to have eyes in the back of her head.

"*Ahh,* Chu Lee Wong. Step up, please," she said without turning around.

Chu circled back to the wooden plate. This would be his last chance to figure out her trick. Arching his head backwards and training his eyes diligently on the tree branches above, Chu waited for Principal Halowell to raise up her purple-robed arms, but, instead, she surprised him by bending down to rummage in her pocket.

"Here you are," she said brightly. "This is for you."

Chu extended his arm out to Principal Halowell.

The principal placed an acorn onto Chu's outstretched palm, announcing, "The common oak."

Even though Chu didn't care that much about nature, he found himself suddenly speechless with disappointment.

It's not even a tree, he thought, miserable.

"No, it's not a tree," Principal Halowell said, as if reading his mind. "But, inside this tiny acorn, is something truly amazing."

"Like what?" Chu asked sullenly.

She leant her face close to him. "It's the *idea* of a tree."

Principal Halowell seized back the acorn from Chu's little hand and raised it high in her fingers to catch a fleeting ray of sun. "It's an idea that expresses itself with every fibre of its being."

She gently pressed the acorn back into Chu's hand. "My dear child, this is a very special seed. I've been holding it a long time, waiting to give it to just the right person."

Chu sniffed the acorn suspiciously. *How long?* he wondered, still miserable.

High on the mountain, Peter was gently tramping down the soil of the fresh mound around his tree when he realised that the weather was changing. A fog had rolled in, and, suddenly, he could barely see in front of him. He was also no longer alone.

Voices rose up from further down the slope. One of them sounded like Wanda's.

"I told you to quit following me," she snapped.

"I'm not following you; I'm going with my tree," replied another voice that Peter recognised as Riva's.

As the wind tore at the mist, Peter glimpsed them stooping down to plant, just a few metres away.

"I can't see anything. Ouch! Watch out!" Wanda wailed. "I told you to quit following me!"

"I thought you wanted followers," Riva told her sarcastically. "And, anyway, I'm trying to plant here too, so watch out, yourself!"

Lightning crashed, and Peter found himself diving to protect his tree. Thunder rolled, rain fell, and wind gusted. Then, just as quickly as it started, the storm blew itself out, and the sky began to clear.

"Hi!" Peter called out to Riva, feeling very pleased to see her. "What kind of tree is yours?"

"Elm. She's going to grow blossom bunches just like mine." Riva pointed to her pom-pom side buns.

Peter couldn't stop smiling.

Wanda joined them.

"Strange that the three of us ended up in the same place," she said.

A strong burst of sunlight shone through a patch of clouds, brightening the sky.

Wanda wrinkled her nose at the sight of Chu, kneeling just across from them. "What's he doing here?"

"Forget Chu!" Riva hissed. "What's *he* doing here?"

Riva pointed at a large shadowy figure behind Chu, right at the cliff edge. His silvery-grey beard fell to his waist. Despite his obvious very old age, the man stood tall and imposing.

"That must be Tollen," whispered Peter. "The one who comes with the storms."

Chu turned to see what they were looking at, then hastily stepped to one side.

"He looks like some kind of wizard," Riva remarked.

"Look how wrinkled he is!" Wanda added rudely. "And all that stringy hair. ... *Ugghh!* Aren't wizards supposed to wear hats?"

"Excuse me! Are you Tollen?" Riva called out bravely.

Instead of answering, the old man peered out to the west, in the direction of the afternoon sun. Then, without any greeting or explanation, he approached them. In his hand, the old man held a wooden staff. Using its pointed end, he began etching a circle that extended around all four children. His long grey robes dusted the ground as he went.

When the circle was done, he took a few paces towards its centre, where he staked his staff decisively into the ground.

Peter watched, mesmerised, as the old man then picked up a shorter stick and dug it into the ground at a sharp angle next to the upright staff. What was he doing?

The old man cleared his throat to speak. "Yes," he said, turning towards Riva. "I am Tollen."

His voice sounded gruff, rather from lack of use, it seemed to Peter, than from bad temper.

"And you must be the four." Tollen paused to train his gaze on each of them in turn.

"Which four?" asked Riva.

"The four who found their way to the highest point of the island."

Wanda spoke out.

"I'm not one of *the four!*" she corrected. "I'm *the one!* Look, my tree is planted a little higher than all these others."

Tollen didn't reply.

Chu also took the chance to speak out.

"Excuse me, Mr ... um ... Tollen. I'm pretty sure I'm not part of the four either. I was just up here looking for my acorn, which I lost in the storm." He then added, "It somehow forced me up here, even though I don't actually like heights."

Tollen bent his tall frame down towards Chu and spoke matter-of-factly.

"My dear boy, your acorn is now quite exactly where it should be." With his large sandaled foot, Tollen nudged gently around the soil to uncover the seed.

Chu was surprised at how pleased he was to see the little acorn again.

Then, Tollen pulled a thinner, smaller stick, like a wand, from the folds of his robe and, using it like a gardener's dibber, planted the acorn decisively down deep into the earth.

"Tend it well," he told Chu. "This seed has long dreamt of becoming a mighty oak."

Without giving Chu time to argue, Tollen turned his attention back to Riva – or more precisely, to Riva's tree.

"A very old tree is the elm, known for its generosity of spirit." His remark seemed to please Riva, who smiled shyly up at him, then back at her tree.

Tollen raised a gnarled and purplish hand in warning. "But, with all the elm's generous outflows must also come generous inflows. You must water this one well."

Tollen glanced tellingly over to where a tiny spring bubbled downward into a stream flowing over silvery-grey rocks. "You did well to plant here; your elm tree feels good when there's water close by."

Riva was beaming with joy now at her tree. "I will always water you well, my dear little elm. I promise, I promise, I promise!"

Riva's outpourings were interrupted by Wanda.

"What about my birch?" she demanded.

"Do you always have to be speaking?" snapped Riva, who wanted to hear more about her elm.

Tollen turned his gaze away from both girls and looked towards Peter's tree.

"Ah, the dawn redwood! Now that is a hard-wearing tree. Survived the last ice age, you know. The redwood also likes the water. It will grow and grow and grow." He was staring at Peter now, a wrinkled smile filling his face. He seemed to whisper something that was swept up by the breeze, then gone.

Peter wanted to ask what Tollen had just said, but Tollen had already shifted his attention to Wanda's birch.

"What do you think of it?" Wanda stood with a hand on her hip, her voice rising proudly. "Not bad, eh?"

"Nice birch," Tollen remarked absently before switching his viewpoint to somewhere above Chu's head, far off in the western sky.

Late-afternoon sun was breaking free from a long stretch of cloud. The four children watched curiously as Tollen repositioned himself about one arm's length from the two sticks at the centre of the circle, and studied the ground.

A shadow from the stick appeared in the dust and flickered there as the sun faded in an out of view. Tollen stood so perfectly still watching it that all four children held their breath. Then, a golden shaft of sun held strongly on the stick and cast a clearly defined shadow across the clearing.

"What is it?" Peter asked Tollen.

"Time will tell."

The shadow seemed to be pointing towards Wanda.

"Look!" she squealed. "I told you. I'm chosen. This is such an honour."

Wanda bounced up and down on the spot. "Look, Mr Tollen! The sun chose me! And my tree," she added as an afterthought.

"About 120 degrees," Tollen mumbled to himself. "The sundial is telling me that it's four o'clock. I must leave you; it's time to feed my frogs."

Without another word, Tollen set off down a narrow path leading into thick forest. When they caught the sun, his dull grey robes shone like rocks in a glittering stream. Peter couldn't help noticing what an enormous shadow the old man cast on the ground behind him. Then, as quickly as it had come, the sun passed back behind a wall of clouds, and Tollen was gone.

Peter turned his attention back to the clearing, and it took him a few moments to realise that the old grey oak he'd seen standing at the side of the cliff was also gone. The others didn't seem to have noticed.

"Nice birch!" mimicked Wanda, in an annoyed tone, once she was sure Tollen was quite out of hearing.

When nobody replied, Wanda turned her irritation on Chu. "So, you didn't get a tree," she said spitefully.

"No." He folded his arms, and scowled. "I just got *the idea* of a tree."

"But it's the idea of a *mighty* oak," Peter said reassuringly.

"You'd better mark the spot where Mr Tollen pushed it in. Use a stick or something," said Riva.

"I don't actually need to," said Chu. "I can just use mathematics. Look. If you take Tollen's sundial as a guide, you'll see we're all planted equidistant from each other on a circular continuum."

"How strange," said Riva.

"Wait a minute! You won't even need maths to find it." Peter fell to his knees, adding with excitement, "Look, Chu! It's already got a tiny oak leaf growing from it!"

Riva and Chu bent down to study it.

"This is too weird," Riva told them excitedly.

"Well, I think I'm freaked out enough for one day," said Wanda, disregarding Chu's miracle shoot. "Come on, let's go down."

She headed off, towards the trail, and then looked back, surprised to see none of them following her. "Come on!" she urged.

Again, none of the three moved.

Finally, she shrugged and turned around.

"Fringe dwellers!" Wanda called back scornfully as she set off without them.

The Combination Room

Back at the foot of the mountain, Peter found Artiss Fleur waiting for him.

Smiling, Artiss Fleur extended his hand to shake Peter's, as if Peter were a grown-up.

"We're convening the Council of Five, and you, Peter Blue, are personally invited."

"Just me, not the other initiates?" Peter asked nervously.

"Yep, but you can bring one friend to help make the numbers."

"Um ... okay, thank you. Who are the Council of Five?"

"You'll see." Agent Fleur's smile deepened. "But you might rather ask, what's the occasion?"

"Why, what is it?"

"It's the official GAIA swearing-in ceremony of Agent Pickles."

Peter's heart skipped. "I'll get to see Pickles?"

"Yep, we're going to be in the Combination Room. I'll send Doris, my assistant, to pick up you and your guest in thirty minutes."

Peter nodded uncertainly, looking down at his muddy pants.

"Just come as you are," Agent Fleur told him kindly. "The occasion is solemn, but the dress code isn't."

A short distance away, Wanda was frowning at them.

She's annoyed to see me talking alone with Artiss Fleur, Peter thought.

"Would you like to bring Wanda as your guest?" asked Agent Fleur.

"No," said Peter decisively. "I'd liked to bring my new friend Roland."

"Will there be doughnuts?" asked Roland, once Peter had explained where they were going.

"I don't know. Why do you ask?" Peter couldn't stop grinning at the thought of seeing Pickles.

"Well, when Dad goes to GAIA Council meetings, he usually gets doughnuts."

They were interrupted by the sound of a dog barking outside Roland's dormitory.

"So, are you going to be my guest or not?" Peter asked.

"Are you kidding? I wouldn't miss it," Roland replied.

Woof, woof, woof!

The boys ran out onto the grassy hill, headed in the direction of the barking. They found a little sausage-shaped dog, with an unusually big snout. As soon as the dog saw them, it started running down the hill, towards the sea.

"Quick, follow that dog!" Roland instructed.

"Why?" asked Peter, setting off at a jog behind Roland.

"Because she's Doris, Artiss Fleur's assistant."

For some minutes, the two boys followed behind, sometimes having to jog to keep Doris in sight. The woods gradually opened up into an area of coastline, and the ground became sandy underfoot. They followed Doris up and down a series of pathways until, suddenly, she sped up. Both boys set off at a fast run in pursuit, but they quickly lost sight of her.

"She's gone!" Peter gasped.

They were almost at the sea.

Puffing for air, Roland pulled up behind him. He pointed at some animal tracks on the path. "Look: two sets. One belongs to Doris, but what about the other?"

"It's not Pickles; she has long thin stompers."

"I bet they're badger tracks," said Roland.

"How do you know?"

"I just know that Doris likes to track badgers."

They started off again, following the paw prints, until, in the distance, up on a grassy sand dune, they spotted Doris, galloping feverishly in tight circles, nose to the ground. But when Peter and Roland reached the spot, there was no longer any sign of her, and the springy grass held no tracks.

"Now what?" Peter frowned at Roland.

As if in reply, a muffled barking broke out. It was coming from below ground.

"Over there!" Roland pointed to a narrow rock opening, nearly hidden from view.

They squeezed through into a dimly lit tunnel, then crept cautiously in the direction of the barking. After a few twists and turns, they reached Doris, parked outside a heavy wooden door, scratching and whining to get in.

"I guess this is the place."

Peter knocked a little too timidly, and when no one came, Roland boldly leant past him and turned the heavy knob. The door creaked open into a large circular rock cave with a high ceiling.

Doris bolted ahead and disappeared into the shadows.

It was difficult to see. Flaming torches attached to the stone wall gave out a kind of wobbly light that made the whole place seem eerie and mysterious. In the centre, Peter saw two lines of rocks, arranged like seats facing each other. At one end, was a speaker podium, and at the other, a stone chair like a throne. The cave felt damp and smelt of salt.

"I wonder where that badger got to." Roland glanced around.

"I wonder where Artiss Fleur and the Council of Five have got to."

Peter couldn't wait to see Pickles. His gaze was drawn beyond the seats, to a strange, oval-shaped blue light on the cave's far side. He was about to go and investigate when he spotted Doris galloping back towards them, with Artiss Fleur behind her.

"You made it! Welcome to the Combination Room!" He gave them each a sturdy pat on the back, adding, "The soon-to-be Agent Pickles is a little nervous."

Peter's heart jumped at the sight of Pickles hopping towards them across the roughly hewn stone floor. Peter fell to his knees, squeezing the wallaby into a too-tight hug.

Chrrkkk-chrrkkk, Pickles protested while nuzzling Peter's ear with her slender snout.

"Sorry ... I'm just so pleased to see you!"

Pickles was dressed in the blue GAIA vest that Nonna and Angel had made for her, and on her paws, she wore a tiny pair of white reception gloves. While Peter was introducing Pickles to Roland, Doris engaged her oversized nose in some polite sniffing along the span of Pickles's tail.

Tsk-tsk, Pickles said graciously.

Woof! Woof! added Doris, her barks echoing through the cave.

Then, Doris trotted off across the cave, nose and belly to the ground, with Pickles hopping along behind her. They were heading towards the blue light on the far side when, suddenly, Doris came to a stop and began to whine, shuffling backwards on her stubby paws.

"Doris is not a swimming dog," observed Artiss Fleur.

"Huh?" Peter said.

He went over to them and saw that the whole floor fell away in a curved line across the room. Water. The blue light, he realised, was actually a patch of open sea and sky at the cave's furthest point.

"Is that why this is called the Combination Room," Peter asked, "because half of the room is on land and the other half is sea?"

"Not exactly," Artiss Fleur said with a chuckle, "but it's as good an explanation as any."

"Wait a minute, I've heard about the Combination Room from my dad," Roland said. "Isn't this the place where animals can talk to each other?"

Ah-choo!

A sudden sneeze made them all jump. It was Tollen, who'd been sitting still on the stone throne all along.

"That's not entirely correct, Roland." Tollen spoke in a voice that was deep and gravelly. "Animals talk to each other all the time through body language, scent, and behaviour, but the Combination Room is a place designed to let humans join their conversation."

Tollen waved his robed arm in the air above the two lines of rock seats. "In this case, using a shared lexicon of words, which our language unscrambler cleverly decrypts for us."

"Wow!" Roland and Peter stared up at the space, looking for the unscrambler, but saw nothing.

Still, Peter's heart thumped with excitement. Would he actually be able to talk to Pickles? What would he say to her? Everything in his life had changed for the better since the wallaby's arrival. *Thank you* would be a good place to start. Peter bit his lip. He'd also need to say he was sorry for letting Uncle Gorrman sell her to the circus.

Agent Fleur was looking at his watch.

"Okay, Pickles, you'll sit here." He indicated the first of the five rocks, to the left of Tollen. "And Rani will sit there." He pointed at the second rock.

"Who's Rani?" interrupted Roland.

A small frog popped its head up from Tollen's top pocket and, with one large leap, landed neatly onto the second rock, next to Pickles.

"She's the great-granddaughter seven generations removed of Quercus Croak, a founding frog of this school," Artiss Fleur told them.

Rani the frog was staring at Peter. She looked familiar, and Peter was about to say so when he was startled by the sight of the fifth rock beginning to move on its own. Stepping back in fear, Peter would've fallen into the sea if Roland hadn't grabbed him to keep him on safe ground.

"It's a giant turtle!" Roland said with a gasp.

"Quite right." Tollen pointed his staff towards the turtle. "Meet the oldest living member of the Council of Five: Odysseas Geopolis."

The turtle raised its hooked snout in their direction.

"Nice to meet you," said Roland and Peter shakily.

Artiss Fleur turned to Tollen. "How about we test the equipment while we wait for the others?"

Tollen nodded and stood up heavily. From his sackcloth pocket, he pulled a lump of rough crystal. He showed it to the boys. It was an orange-gold colour and about the size of his fist. The old man knocked the crystal gently against the stone arm of the throne until a small slither the size of thumbnail fell away.

"Thank you," he told the larger piece, and then returned it to his pocket.

The group watched in silence as Tollen placed the crystal fragment onto a low stone pedestal, centred halfway between Tollen's throne and the podium.

"It doesn't look very high-tech," Roland said disappointedly.

"Wait and see," Tollen told him gruffly.

Next, Tollen took a flaming torch from the wall and held it to the crystal. After a few seconds, a tiny flame began to fizz and pop before erupting into a much larger, high, pointed flame.

The two boys stared in alarm as the flame broke away from the pedestal and expanded up and out, into a volatile blob of burnt-orange light.

Then, with a pleased sigh, Tollen sank back into the stone throne as if it were a cushiony armchair.

Artiss Fleur signalled for Peter and Roland to take their seats on two rocks opposite the animals. And as they did, the orange-tinged, cloud mass arranged itself around them.

"The arcus cloud formation is ideal for these purposes," Tollen told them. "Which is why the official name for the unscrambler is the Arcus Decryptor Cloud."

Peter dipped his head in and out of the cloud, which was kind of misty but still see-through. Even though the cloud had come from a flame, it wasn't hot, and it didn't seem to have any particular smell.

Next, from his belt pocket, Artiss Fleur pulled a circular steel device that looked like a hand-held flying saucer.

"This is Poco," he told the boys.

Releasing the device upward and into the cloud, Artiss Fleur commanded, "Poco, hover!"

The tiny machine whirred about the cloud space before circling towards the centre.

"And stay!" Artiss said.

A series of beeps and red flashing lights followed as the mini flying saucer centred itself in the air directly above the pedestal where Tollen's crystal lay.

"Does Poco decrypt the animal languages?" asked Roland.

"No." Agent Fleur seemed to find the question funny. "Poco's a super-smart machine, but he'll never reach that level of intelligence. He's more of a command-control centre."

Agent Fleur pointed at Tollen's twinkling fragment of crystal. "That's the master power there – the intelligence of fire."

Peter thought of Flame Girl in his mother's book. *Fire doesn't only burn.*

"So, how does the Arcus Decryptor Cloud work?" asked Roland.

"Simply put, it unscrambles all the different animal communication modes, and their wavelengths, then floats the correct translations around the space to the correct brain bearers."

Roland nodded uncertainly.

"Everybody in the Combination Room gets a voice," Artiss continued, "and an individual length of wave to communicate on."

"Can we try it out?" asked Peter, smiling over at Pickles.

"Sure, but quickly, before the other council members arrive."

"Who are the others?" interrupted Roland, staring over at the two vacant rocks?

They were interrupted by a low growl from Doris, followed by a flash of black-and-white stripe. Peter caught a glimpse of a long animal with loose skin and a smallish head.

"A badger! I knew it!" said Roland in a pleased voice.

Doris charged off across the cave, kicking up dust in pursuit of the badger. The two animals circled the seating area round and round in a high-speed chase until Agent Fleur finally managed to snatch up Doris. He placed her on the rock in front of the podium.

"Doris takes the teasing a bit far sometimes."

Then, Peter spotted a hedgehog, shuffling in and out from the shadows.

"Are the badger and that hedgehog the other council members?" asked Peter

Artiss Fleur chuckled. "No, this is First Secretary Badger, who works for the Council of Five, and this is Hedgepig, his helper.

Woof! said Doris, pushing her brownish-black snout into the horizontal cloud.

"Do you want to help us test the system?" Artiss Fleur asked Doris.

Woof!

The badger hopped up onto the second rock, below Doris, leaving the lowest rock free for the fretful-looking hedgehog to crouch on.

"Poco, activate!" Artiss Fleur commanded.

Poco spun a few times, this time, flashing green.

Then, Artiss Fleur put his head into the cloud and said slowly and clearly, "Testing, testing – one, two, three."

Everyone waited. After a slight pause, they heard a faint barking sound – *woof woofrrrrrrrf rff rffrf rrrrr* – transmitting into the cloud.

Artiss Fleur seemed pleased and signalled with his index finger to Doris, who made an answering bark.

"Testing, testing – what's for tea?" interpreted the Arcus Decryptor.

Peter and Roland giggled.

"Now she's teasing me!" Artiss Fleur laughed.

Odysseas the turtle let out a loud *hoot.*

Tsk-tsk, said Pickles.

Squeak, squeak, added Rani.

The Arcus Decryptor interpreted all the animal sounds as "ha ha ha!" in human speech.

Then, everyone started talking at once, and Peter saw his chance to speak directly with Pickles. Leaning towards her into the middle of the cloud, Peter whispered, "I'm so glad we found each other again."

Tsk-tsk. "Me too."

"And, sorry about Uncle Gorrman sending you to the circus."

Tsk-tsk; chrrkkk-chrrkkk, Pickles replied. The Arcus Decryptor translated, "Nonsense; it was my path. And, besides, I had the time of my life."

She threw back her tapered snout and made a sound like *hssht, hssht, hsssssssht,* which the Arcus Decryptor interpreted as breathy laughter.

The sound reminded Peter of the winds of Jarra Jarra moving through the spinifex grasses, and for a moment, he'd never felt so happy and so homesick at the same time.

Then, First Secretary Badger's voice rose above the conversation, with a series of long, drawn-out badger yelps, followed by a barrage of shorter *keck, keck, keck sounds.*

"I really think I should take over the testing, because I'm a more official member," he said.

"Okay, Doris, you've had your fun." Agent Fleur directed the little dog down to the floor, her tail sagging reluctantly.

"So, what *is* for tea?" asked Roland with a giggle.

Woof! said Doris encouragingly.

Grunt, grunt; chitter, chitter, said the badger turning his snout to the hedgehog. "Speaking of snacks, it was your job to bring the savoury offsets."

Hedgepig put her snout into the cloud and made some snorting, snuffling sounds, which the Arcus Decryptor interpreted as "I couldn't get any meat, but I did manage to rustle up some pickled herring."

"Herring will do nicely," interrupted Tollen with a smile.

Snort, snort; snuffle, snuffle; hiss. "Thank you, Tollen. You see, living in a hedgerow, it's not easy to put together a snack for a bear. I only managed to get the fish with the help of a seagull."

Peter and Roland looked at each other questioningly.

The badger grunted.

"And by the way," Hedgepig continued, "why can't I be the second secretary instead of just an assistant?"

"Stop complaining," snapped the badger, "or we'll offer the bear some nice hedgehog stew instead."

Peter couldn't stop himself from laughing.

"What's so funny about my career ladder?" Hedgepig glared defensively at him.

"No, it wasn't that," Peter stammered. "I just thought you said something about a snack for a bear."

"I did!" Hedgepig's snout jerked upward, sniffing the air, while her small circular eyes searched the water. "He'll be here soon."

She scuttled over to the fourth rock and began using her mouth to lay out long strips of fish.

"Eleven strips, well done," Tollen told the hedgehog, who was already scuttling back towards the shadows.

Behind them, Peter heard a loud splash. Both boys turned to see the head of a big brown bear rise from the water.

Keck, keck, keck, added badger. "Toivo Toivonen, late as usual."

Peter and Roland sat frozen with fear.

The big energy and strength of the bear was suddenly all around them.

"It's perfectly safe," Artiss Fleur advised, although he took a seat protectively on the rock next to Peter.

On all fours, the big brown bear lumbered up the stone steps, his fur sleek and heavy with water.

"Wait for it," whispered Roland.

The bear paused, then savagely shook himself dry – water droplets curling through the air and spraying both boys, who couldn't help giggling.

Somehow, the moment helped Peter relax. Although the idea of sitting calmly in a circular room with a bear seemed unthinkable, if Artiss Fleur found it normal, then Peter would too.

He watched as the bear paused, seeming to bow his head towards Tollen, before padding on all fours around the speaker podium and over to the fourth rock. There, he rose up on two legs to take his seat like a human. Peter guessed that the bear was twice as tall as he was, even in a sitting position.

The bear sniffed at the strips of herring.

"Toivo's always served the right number of savoury offsets, to match the right number of guests," Tollen explained.

"Why is that?" asked Roland.

"Shall we say, it's a safeguard against the unlikely possibility that he might wish to ... how can I put this delicately?"

"Eat someone," suggested Roland, a nervous flutter his voice.

"Quite right," Artiss said, chuckling. "If Toivo gets a sudden urge to eat one of us, he simply snaps up one of the savoury snacks to offset the need."

Tollen cleared his throat meaningfully. "It was Toivo's own idea, actually, for dealing with any possible unsociable behaviour."

"But it is very important," the badger warned, "that no one else touches the offsets during the course of the meeting."

"So, how many are we now?" asked Artiss Fleur.

Grunt, grunt; chitter, chitter; grunt, grunt, began First Secretary Badger.

"Participants include the Council of Five, with its newest member-to-be, Agent Pickles." The badger looked pointedly at the wallaby. "Plus Chairman Tollen, makes six. The badger nodded his black-and-white snout in a formal way. "Agent Artiss Fleur makes seven, plus guest of the honoured guest, Peter Blue, and his honoured guest, Roland Portogalo, that's nine; then Doris the assistant makes ten. ..." The badger sniffed once, as if to show disapproval. He looked at the needy hedgehog squatting two stones below him. "Assistant to the First Secretary makes eleven, plus my humble self, makes twelve. We have a perfect quorum."

"Except Esther Purler, the pelican, is not here yet," Agent Fleur reminded him. "So, we're only eleven, and we need a quorum of twelve to start the meeting."

Tollen sighed and looked out towards the sea. Rani the frog, who must have tired of sitting still, chose that moment to jump off her rock and go sniffing at the herring strips. Toivo the bear raised a large paw to bat her away, but Rani was too quick, finding refuge inside Pickles's pouch.

Peter watched, mesmerised with fear, as the bear leant over towards Pickles. Would he hurt her? Toivo pawed inside Pickles's pouch like a bear scooping for honey in a tree hollow, but Pickles retaliated, giving Toivo a swift kick in the shin with one of her long bouncers.

Aoooh! Toivo the bear moaned, but the Arcus Decryptor couldn't translate it because, with the force of the blow, the bottom-heavy bear had toppled right off his rock. Rani the frog saw her chance to hop quickly out of hiding and back over to the safety of Tollen's pocket. The turtle raised his head supportively while the bear settled himself back onto his rock.

Peter watched, in alarm, as the bear helped himself to the first of the herring strips: *hrrrmph,* then a second one, *hrrrmph.* He followed this with some brief grunts, which the Arcus Decryptor translated as "Excuse me, all; just nerves."

"No problem," Tollen said absently. "But, tell us, Toivo, why does Esther not come?"

The bear sat silent, as one who knew the reason but wasn't saying.

"You know what this means." Tollen turned to Artiss Fleur.

367

"The prophecy?"

Tollen nodded.

They both glanced at Peter, then looked quickly away, leaving Peter to wonder what he could possibly have to do with a missing pelican.

They were interrupted by a loud knocking at the door.

"Come in!" called Agent Fleur.

Peter had been expecting Esther the pelican to fly in from the open sky, not arrive through the door. But, of course, it wasn't the pelican.

The door opened, and a voice now familiar to Peter rang through the cave.

"Hello-o-o-o-o!"

CHAPTER

58

The Party Crasher

It was Wanda.

"Hi! I'm a friend of Peter Blue," she called.

Friend? thought Peter resentfully.

Roland frowned at Peter as Wanda bounced cheerfully over to join the group.

"I made it!" she said to Peter, as if he had been anxiously awaiting her arrival.

The badger cleared his throat with a low-pitched rumbling sound. "Very rude arriving without an invitation," the Arcus Decryptor interpreted.

"Okay, no problem," Artiss Fleur said calmly. He stood up and shook Wanda's hand.

"Did you invite her?" Roland hissed at Peter.

"No!"

"Well, never mind. I've got a good idea how we can get rid of her," Roland whispered.

"Put your head out of the cloud if you want to speak in private," Peter warned.

"Oh, right."

Wanda had begun taking selfies. "Just a few snaps to post later."

She leant over to Peter, with her head in the cloud. "Why did you bring Roly Poly here when you could have brought me?"

"Roly Poly!" the turtle repeated and began to hoot again. "Ha ha ha!"

"Are you calling me fat?" said Roland defensively.

First Secretary Badger leant over the podium and directed a series of keckers at Wanda. *Keck, keck, keck!*

The Arcus Decryptor translated, "Actually, Roland's not fat. He carries a lot of loose skin, just like we badgers do. See? We look bigger than we are." The badger turned to show his profile.

Wanda didn't say anything. She seemed momentarily stunned by the Arcus Decryptor and the talking animal channels.

"For example," the badger continued, "if a predator, *such as a bear,* were to get hold of Roland – or me, for that matter – all that loose skin makes it much easier to wriggle free."

"That's right," said Roland, squeezing at some of his excess tummy area and hoping that Toivo was paying attention.

"All right," Artiss Fleur interjected. "Let's move on with the informal part of the ceremony while we wait for Esther to arrive."

The badger cleared his throat noisily. "Ah ... well ... quite. Despite one missing council member, I do have a long set of prepared remarks to get through."

The turtle made a groaning sound which the Arcus Decryptor translated into English as a groan.

But the first secretary seemed happy to ignore it. First, he let his gaze settle on Tollen for a few moments. "Dear Grand Master Tollen of the trees and frogs—"

Tollen raised a hand for silence, interrupting the badger.

"Not to worry about your speech," Tollen said kindly to the badger. "Even though the pelican's not here, why don't you just introduce our guest of honour?"

Wanda stood up. "Wow, thank you! I'm so glad to be here," she said. "Can all the animals here talk?"

"You're not the guest of honour," Peter hissed at her, a little more roughly than he'd meant to. "Pickles is having her swearing-in ceremony."

"Oh sorry!" Wanda giggled, showing no sign of remorse.

Rani the frog couldn't sit still any longer. She began bouncing around on her rock.

"Peter Blue, watch me do a somersault!" Rani called.

Peter cringed, embarrassed.

"Sit down," Tollen admonished the frog, "or you won't be able to attend in the future."

The sight of Rani hopping about must have made Toivo hungry again.

Hrrrmph! he snorted, devouring another strip of pickled herring.

"What's that he was eating?" Wanda asked.

Roland pulled Wanda out of the cloud and whispered something in her ear, to which she nodded and smiled. Before Peter could stop her, she was bouncing around the seating area, headed towards the remaining herring strips.

"Did you explain what they were?" Peter asked Roland.

"Yes," he said with a giggle. "I said there was one fish savoury for each participant."

Unfortunately, before anyone could warn her, Wanda had snatched up a strip of the salty herring and lowered it into her mouth.

Toivo sprang from his rock with agility that belied his bulk, rising to his full height before letting out an explosive roar. The sound filled the cavern.

All the animals except the turtle scattered clear. Peter and Roland both dived into the water and began swimming for their lives towards the open sea. But Toivo's roars quickly subsided into passive grunts. Peter paused to tread water. Looking back, he thought he saw two bears wrestling each other, but it must have been a trick of the flickery light because, when Peter swam back a few strokes, he saw that it was Tollen standing over the bear, his robed arms raised at full height.

Grrrwl, grrrrrrrwl! growled Toivo.

"It's all right. He's calm now! Artiss Fleur called out.

Tollen lowered his arms and sat back down heavily on his stone throne.

Peter and Roland shuffled back slowly to their seats, feeling wet and subdued.

"We were just testing the water," mumbled Roland, pulling off his shoes.

"Quite nice for swimming," agreed Peter, wringing out his shirt sleeves.

It was then that Odysseas the turtle started to laugh. *Ha ha ha! Ooo-hoooo-hooo!* His flippers flailed around, limp and useless with mirth.

Peter leant into the cloud. "What's so funny?"

Ha ha! Ooo-hoooo! "I haven't laughed so much since I was tickled by a squid in the East Timor sea!"

Toivo the bear gave Odysseas the grizzly eye. *Grrrr-grrrr-gruuruur! …* "I can't see the joke."

Toivo ate another herring strip. *Hrrrmph!*

Only six strips left, Peter noticed.

"Where did Wanda go?" asked Artiss Fleur.

He and Tollen both seemed concerned and began searching the cave.

Peter didn't like Wanda much, and she shouldn't have crashed a private party, but he didn't want her to get eaten by a bear on her second day of school.

The turtle was laughing so hard now that he flipped off from his rock and fell upside down. Peter hurried over, knowing this could be the death knell for a turtle. But Odysseas only chuckled harder.

Peter tried with all his strength to flip the turtle back onto his feet, but he was too heavy. So, instead, he slid the turtle across the wet stone floor and heaved him into the water. Now Odysseas would be able to right himself.

It was from that low vantage point that Peter saw a terrible thing: Wanda lying face down behind the brown bear's feet.

"Agent Fleur, look! Wanda! She's … not moving."

Artiss Fleur dragged Wanda's little limp body up from the cold stone floor and laid her on a nearby bench. Everyone seemed to be holding their breath as he patted her cheeks and took her pulse.

Suddenly, Wanda's eyes snapped open. "I'm all right," she said defensively, sitting herself up and stepping shakily onto the floor.

Wanda walked over to where the bear sat hanging his head and she ducked her face into the language cloud. "Is this thing still on? Can you all hear me?"

Without waiting for a reply, she continued, "Didn't you all know that if you ever meet an angry bear, the only safe response is to lie prone on the ground and play dead like I did?"

Wanda looked over at Peter and Roland. "Escaping into the water won't save you from a bear at your back. Bears are excellent swimmers."

She smiled smugly as she called out to Badger, Hedgepig, Doris, and Pickles, "Running away won't save you either."

"Climbing the wall is not even a safe bet," she said to Rani, who was still quavering up on a high rock. "Bears are actually quite good climbers too, you know!"

Wanda glanced up at Toivo, towering above her. The bear was watching her in a calm, gruff sort of way. Then, Wanda did quite a brave thing. She held up her little pale arm, fearlessly extending her hand towards the bear. "My name's Wanda," she said.

Toivo put out his paw, and the two shook hands.

Even Tollen looked mildly impressed. "We are looking for a quorum of twelve," he muttered, "so your presence will serve that purpose, as a stand-in for Esther the pelican."

"Great!" said Wanda. "I'll sit over here next to the bear."

The animals were watchful, but no one spoke.

Peter couldn't stop himself from snapping at Wanda. "You can't just sit on the pelican's rock!"

"Why not?"

"To start with, you're not a member of the Council of Five," protested Roland.

"And you weren't even invited to this meeting," added the Badger.

Toivo raised a paw and growled something that the cloud interpreted as "Let her stay here so that we can begin."

Peter nodded obediently and sat back. He wasn't going to argue with the bear, especially now that he was so calm. Right now, Toivo Toivonen reminded Peter of Mr Biggs, although in his earlier rages, the bear had reminded Peter more of Mr Dean when he first arrived at Gum Tree, before he became relevant.

"So, what *is* the ceremony?" Wanda demanded to know, as if everything and everyone was there just for her.

"Actually, Wanda," Artiss Fleur said with a chuckle, "the ceremony begins with a character reference of our honoured wallaby. And that should come from you, Peter Blue."

"What?" Peter was caught by surprise.

"Speech, speech!" called Wanda annoyingly.

Roland elbowed Peter in the ribs.

"On your feet, Peter," Artiss Fleur said kindly.

Peter stood up reluctantly and glanced over at his dear friend Pickles.

"Just tell us a little in your own words about the wallaby's character," advised the badger.

Peter leant into the cloud. "Well, Pickles is—" Peter paused, his voice was squeaky with nerves, but even so, he made himself continue. "Pickles is ... always courageous and always kind. She's also very sensitive. She helps people wherever she goes." He paused again. "Actually, she doesn't just help people; she changes them."

Peter felt tearful watching Pickles sitting calmly on her rock. He couldn't think of anything else to say.

"What kind of things does she like?" asked Artiss Fleur.

"Oh, she loves vinegar cucumbers. That's how she got her name."

Everyone laughed supportively.

"Any weaknesses?" inquired the badger.

"*Ahh.* ..." Peter was caught off guard. He was about to say no, but then, he remembered that he and Pickles shared the same fear.

"Tell, tell!" begged Rani.

"Well, we're both afraid of fire."

Peter saw Wanda roll her eyes condescendingly, and, suddenly, he felt so much dislike for her that he couldn't resist an unfair comment. "You see, both our mothers were killed by fires."

The audience sighed.

Hedgepig sniffed and choked on her condolences.

Then, Odysseas the turtle actually did begin to cry, making loud howling sounds.

"Sorry. I laugh really easily, and I cry easily too."

Peter saw that Wanda really did look sorry. So did the bear, who snuffled up two more of his herring offsets, perhaps to console himself. There were four herring strips left. He then took two more, so there were only two left. Then, he ate those as well. The rock was empty. Peter hoped the meeting would end soon.

"Well, all animals are afraid of fire," said Roland supportively.

"Actually," said Tollen, "it's not that animals fear fire; it's more that they revere it."

"Revere? You mean like worshipping it?" asked Wanda.

"Well, no, it is more like reverence, in the sense of holding it in great awe," Tollen explained. "As well we all should."

Tollen clapped his hands and stood up. "Now it's time for the formal swearing-in ceremony. Where is the Book of Promises?"

Artiss Fleur passed a heavy book to Roland and Peter to hold together.

"The book contains all the promises ever made through all time," the badger told them.

"Your promise might be in there," Rani said impishly to Peter, who scowled, not knowing what she was talking about.

"Proceed with the oath," instructed First Secretary Badger.

Pickles placed her gloved paw directly onto the heavy book. She'd obviously rehearsed this.

"Do you, Pickles, solemnly swear your allegiance to the Global Advanced Intelligence Agency, in the service of all living things and in pursuit of the light of GAIA?"

Tsk-tsk. "I do."

"I shall now dub you." Tollen produced a short, wand-like stick. "This is made from the wood of lignum vitae, only for very special occasions" Tollen explained then standing before Pickles and holding the wand high, he remarked, "Your shoulders are quite sloping, aren't they?"

Roland and Peter giggled.

"Silence!" ordered the badger.

Tollen solemnly tapped Pickles on both her furry sides, then smiled. "I now pronounce you Agent Pickles, Animal Intelligence Agent of GAIA and new member of the Council of Five."

Everyone was silent.

Tollen bowed his head towards Pickles, and the others did the same.

Then, Tollen raised his wand and his face to the cloud. He spoke again, more powerfully, this time. "May the Force be you!"

"Don't you mean, may be the Force be with you?" interrupted Roland.

Tollen looked flustered by the interruption. He lowered his wand, then raised it again.

"May the Force be you!" he repeated.

"May the Force be you!" repeated Agent Fleur and all the animals, in a cacophony of support.

Then, Rani hopped onto Pickles's shoulder. "It is quite sloping! *Whee-e-e!*"

Chrrkkk-chrrkkk-chrrkkk! Tsk-tsk! Pickles said, catching the little frog and pulling her up to ear level, as if she were a mobile phone. "*Ooh! Funny frog*," interpreted the Arcus Decryptor.

"What's the Force?" Peter asked Agent Fleur.

The top agent looked surprised. "The Force is Nature, of course."

Keck, keck, keck! the badger called loudly. "We're not done! We haven't raised the formal toast to Agent Pickles."

Wanda raised her hand. "*Ooh!* Can I make the toast?"

"No," said Agent Fleur. "That's Peter's honour."

"Me?" Peter gulped.

"Of course."

Artiss Fleur lifted a tray of water glasses from a side table and passed them around. They smelt faintly of herring.

The audience waited expectantly.

"Ah. ..." Peter didn't know what to say. He stared at Pickles. What would Mr Dean have said? Then, it came to him.

"To Agent Pickles, the best wallaby I ever knew!"

Tsk-tsk-tsk! "He hasn't known that many wallabies," said Pickles modestly.

The turtle hooted with laughter and the meeting was adjourned.

CHAPTER

59

The Spiral Hall

That evening, Peter was out walking when he spotted a greenish-brown frog on the path ahead. The frog looked just like Rani. Keeping his distance, Peter followed the frog all the way to a cobbled courtyard, then up some stone steps and through an arched entrance into the Spiral Hall.

The sky outside had darkened, and Peter wondered if it would be all right to go in. The frog stopped and turned around, as if to check that Peter was there.

She's leading me here on purpose, Peter thought.

Still, he couldn't stop himself from taking a few steps into the massive circular hall. It was empty of people. His eyes were drawn first up to the high dome ceiling and then to the enormous spiral table that filled the space beneath it.

Peter felt drawn to it. There were no lights, but the silvery glow from a rising moon shining through the upper windows was enough to see by. Peter wanted to try sitting on one of the table's spiralling corridor of chairs. Instead, he found himself leaping beneath the table with the approach of grown-up voices.

Principal Halowell entered the hall, in close conversation with Agent Fleur and Professor Meriwether.

"Well, Captain T, I trust you're feeling better?" the principal enquired.

"Thank you, but no." Professor Meriwether sneezed loudly. "I had one of my regular turns with the storm this afternoon."

"Well, we'll certainly try to keep our meeting short so that you can get back to bed with your fever," the principal said kindly.

She turned to Artiss Fleur. "Tell me, Dr Flower, what do you think of the new batch?"

"Very green but lots of promise," Artiss Fleur said, chuckling.

"And what about our Sleeping King?" Professor Meriwether asked. "I heard he was very popular with the trees today."

"Well, I certainly had to go out on a limb for the boy, I must say." Principal Halowell's high-pitched laugh rang through the domed hall. "All the trees of the island babbling at once, everyone wanting to be his tree."

"Erthia nearly went out of her tree herself," Artiss Fleur told the professor with a laugh.

"But, I must say, that boy shows a lot of promise," Principal Halowell told them.

"Maybe there's some truth in that old Sleeping King legend after all, Artiss Fleur pointed up to a block of old fashioned writing on the high-domed wall and read one piece aloud:

The Sleeping King's promise made lifetimes before
When the world needs him most, he'll awaken once
more

There was silence for a moment as the three gazed up at the writing on the wall.

Then, Peter heard a slight rustling sound from somewhere else in the hall. *That pesky frog,* he thought.

Agent Fleur must had heard it too. "What was that?"

"Let's continue the Secretariat meeting in here," Principal Halowell told them, and they disappeared into an alcove room, closing the door firmly.

Peter sat, straining his ears. Was there someone else here? If so, who was it? And what was all this Sleeping King stuff again? He would have to see if Roland had more information about this.

From his hiding place under the table, Peter strained to read the legend on the high wall, which was lit only by the light of the moon. He found the title, "The Legend of the Sleeping King", and saw that one of the verses was about fire:

> This King's true mark comes not from name,
> But from the boy who bears the Flame.

Why would anyone think that was he? Peter felt the back of his neck beginning to itch. Just as he stood up, he heard footsteps. It was Roland, hurrying towards him.

"Peter, quick, you have to get out of here!" Roland hissed. "You'll get in trouble."

"Were you spying on me?" Peter said, more roughly than he intended.

"No!" Roland retorted. "I was spying on the Blott twins, who were spying on you."

There were footsteps in the entranceway. Roland scooted safely under the table, but Peter hesitated a moment too long and came face-to-face with Administrator Drufus, flanked by two triumphant-looking Blotts.

"Your second day at school, and here you are, back in the detention room. What have you got to say for yourself?"

Peter sighed and said nothing. He already knew that Drufus would have no sympathy for his story about following a frog.

"Speak, boy! What were you doing in the sacred hall, some kind of sabotage?"

"No, I only wanted to glance at some of the wall inscriptions," Peter explained, adding hopefully, "It was extra orientation."

"Well, my sources said you were in there for some time. Initiates are not allowed in the Spiral Hall unaccompanied."

Peter couldn't resist asking, "So, what were your sources doing in there?" He was thinking of the Blott twins.

"I'll ask the questions." Drufus ran a hand through his limp grey hair, then scribbled something energetically across the subject line of the detention slip.

Peter felt his face burning with irritation. Ever since he'd been in the hall, the back of his neck had begun to itch and bother him. The more he scratched at it, the worse it felt.

"Who are you working for? What are you really doing at Spiral Hall?"

"What are you talking about? I'm a kid at school."

Peter touched the skin on his neck. There was something there – a welt of some kind.

"You're just like your father," Drufus said sneeringly.

"What's that supposed to mean?"

"Going off on your own to the sacred hall, behaving like some kind of a maverick."

Drufus put down his pen and picked up a wooden stick.

"Bend over!" he told Peter.

For a moment, Peter didn't move. He didn't feel like getting whacked. Surely, it was illegal. He needed an idea.

Think, Peter, think.

Administrator Drufus had stepped away from his desk and was walking around behind him.

Peter connected with the energy of the wood in the stick, but he could only get the word *cruel,* so he pulled back.

"I said, bend over!" Drufus growled.

Reluctantly, Peter bent over and braced himself for the blow. But Drufus was still circling. Why didn't the man just hit him and get it over with?

Peter felt the stick at his head, parting his hair at the back, then the detention master's breath on the back of his neck. He waited fearfully for the blow.

Suddenly, he sensed Drufus was stepping back.

"The glyph!" Drufus cried. He sounded frightened.

"Shall I stand up now?" asked Peter, relieved.

"Of course, of course! Stand up."

Drufus put the stick into his desk drawer, while Peter stood up, rubbing at the skin on his neck, which was tingling.

It might be some kind of nervous rash, Peter thought and wondered if the school had a nurse.

Meanwhile, something had changed in the detention officer's behaviour. He was back behind his desk, far away in his thoughts. Peter noticed how limply his suit jacket sat on his shoulders, covering a greyish-coloured shirt that might once have been white.

Drufus still didn't speak.

Shuffling nervously from one foot to the other, Peter wished he could leave.

Finally, the silence was broken by approaching footsteps in the hallway. Drufus jumped back into action, reaching for the detention paper and scribbling hurriedly in the margins. He was back to his old self. The footsteps were almost at the door.

Drufus forcefully pushed the slip into Peter's hand. "Dismissed."

There was a loud knock at the door. Agent Fleur entered the room.

"Evening, Agent Drufus." Agent Fleur's voice was polite but without warmth. "I heard Peter Blue's been giving you trouble."

Roland shuffled in behind Agent Fleur.

"Oh ... no. Just a little misunderstanding." Drufus began to laugh in an unnatural way.

"Take him away," said the administrator with a wave. "But just so you know, Fleur, this golden boy of yours has already had two consecutive detentions. You know the rules. One more detention tomorrow, and he'll be out!"

CHAPTER

60

Byron Blue's Message

On Saturday morning, when Agent Fleur came to find Peter, he looked worried. "You'll have to promise to keep out of the way of Drufus for the next twenty-four hours. It could get very tricky on the administrative side if you get three detentions in a row during your first three days of school."

"But I wasn't doing anything wrong!" Peter wailed.

"Of course you weren't. We know that. Drufus has issues with you that go way back."

"But I only met him yesterday!"

"Let's just say that a lot of GAIA people have been angry with Byron for a long time."

"But you said he was your best agent."

"Come on. Let's walk."

They walked side by side towards the beach, and, after a while, Agent Fleur spoke again.

"The agency is strongest when we work as a team, and some people think Byron acted recklessly when he took on the Anthrogs alone."

Peter's mouth quivered with emotion. "But ... wasn't it just a fire?"

"It was much more than a fire, Peter. Byron lured them to Australia."

"You mean Dad wasn't a hero, then? He just died because he was reckless?"

When they reached the beach, Artiss Fleur stopped and put a hand on Peter's shoulder.

"To me, your dad will always be one of the greats — a hero of the highest-possible calibre."

They were both silent for a while, gazing off towards the horizon above the sea.

Agent Fleur continued, "The stupid thing is that *I* could've helped him. *Tollen* could've helped him. But Byron didn't tell any of us what he was planning. ..."

"Wait. Dad knew Tollen?"

"Of course. You knew Tollen too when you were small." Artiss Fleur drew his arm round in a circle to indicate the entire island. "None of this exists without Tollen."

Peter was silent.

"But then, your dad had to go off alone and take on the darkest force this world's ever known. It was all such a stupid waste." Agent Fleur kicked moodily at a stone.

"So, he *was* brave — at least," mumbled Peter.

"Oh yes. Braver than all the rest of us put together, but he died because of it ... and Thelma with him."

Agent Fleur added grimly, "Losing Thelma, one of the best scientists we've ever had, right at that time when she was so close to cracking the formula for the next-generation Chrysalite, was even harder to bear. Some people can't forgive Byron for that."

"Do you forgive him?" asked Peter, terrified he might say no.

"Of course. There should never be any doubt."

"Why?"

"Because of why he did it, of course."

They stared at each other, eyes suddenly locked.

"Why?"

"For you, Peter, of course. Byron sacrificed himself to the darkness to try to save you and your mother. But the enemy was more than he'd bargained for."

Peter stood in shock. He didn't want to be told that Dad and Mum were gone so that he could be here. Seagulls screeched, and a gentle wave rose towards the beach, then retreated again.

They had almost reached the water's edge. Peter took a deep breath in.

"Agent Fleur, I think, now that we're alone, I'd like to deliver Dad's message."

"Is this the one from the ghost in the dream?"

"It wasn't a dream, actually. It was real. I know because, when I woke up, I actually found the spiral that Dad had traced in the sand."

"Exactly," said Agent Fleur in a voice that was gentle but firm. "When you woke up."

Peter could feel himself getting irritated.

"Well, do you want to hear the message anyway? Dad said it was mission critical."

"Okay, sure. Peter, please tell me if it makes you feel better." Smiling patiently, Agent Fleur pulled out a notebook.

"Okay, here goes." Peter took a deep breath inward. "The message contains just two words: Never capitulate!"

"Never capitulate," Agent Fleur repeated the message back while scribbling it down.

"Dad said you'd know what he meant."

Agent Fleur was already closing the notebook and putting it back into the pocket of his GAIA jacket.

Peter felt disappointment washing over him.

"I'm sorry, Peter. I wish I could make this easier for you. But I don't understand any particular meaning that I could get from this message that others couldn't. I presume you mean never give up the fight against the Anthrog forces."

Peter shrugged and hung his head.

"But that doesn't take away from the blessing you received, Peter, from seeing your father in a dream."

"It wasn't a dream!" Peter persisted, stamping his foot in the sand. "Dad said he wouldn't have even been able to get through to me if I hadn't taken off the jacket."

"What was that?"

Suddenly, Peter saw he'd regained Agent Fleur's attention.

"Well, I hadn't taken a bath for a quite a long time, so when my grandmother took the jacket off me to fix—"

Artiss Fleur interrupted him. "But what did you say about your dad getting through?"

"Oh … well, Dad told me that the jacket coordinates were still imprinted on his brain, even in death, and that was how come he could come back and give me the message."

Now Peter had Artiss Fleur's full attention.

"Are you telling me you saw Byron inside the GAIA jacket?"

"Yes," said Peter, nodding excitely. "But the jacket was too small for him by then, because my grandmother had resized it to fit me. And he wasn't like himself exactly – he was all wispy and see-through, which was how I knew that he was a ghost."

"And you're telling me the absolute truth?"

"Yes!" Peter nodded solemnly, and, somehow, he could tell that Artiss Fleur believed him.

Agent Fleur looked at Peter, then looked away, pacing out a small circle in the sand, hands on hips, expelling air noisily.

Peter, standing and watching him, wondered what had changed.

"What?" Peter heard his own voice shaking.

Agent Fleur took two steps towards Peter and grabbed him by the elbow, gripping so hard that it hurt his arm. Peter bit back tears.

"I'm not sure I should say," Agent Fleur said.

"Say what?" Peter cried. "Do you understand the message now?"

Agent Fleur nodded and said gravely, "Yes."

A wind was blowing up, and the waves seemed to crash more loudly than before.

"Remote jacket projection is a security trick the top GAIA agents are taught in advanced esoteric training, and I know Byron had mastered it, because we trained together."

"So, Dad managed it, even after he died?"

"Well, not quite. Your father was a great adventurer, but he was never very good at physiology class." He chuckled. "What I'm trying to say is that if Byron really did manage to project himself into his GAIA jacket, then—"

"Then, what?"

"Then, it means, Peter, that he must still be out there somewhere on this earth! Your father must be alive!"

Peter felt his whole insides turning over. His knees got so weak that he would've fallen to the sand if Agent Fleur hadn't taken hold of both his shoulders.

"But he can't be alive!" argued Peter.

"Yes, he can. That's how the top agents do it if they get separated from their jackets. We project a part of ourselves from the physical body into the jackets – this is classified, by the way, Peter – during emergencies, using the power of our subconscious memory, where the coordinates are stored. So, what you saw was not a ghost but a projection of your father from somewhere on the earth plane. He's alive! I'm telling you, Peter!"

"He's not!" Peter snapped angrily.

"Why not?"

"Because if he were alive, he would have said so. He would have told me where to come and find him. He would have wanted us to be together."

Some of the exuberance seem to drain away from Artiss Fleur's face. He pulled out the notebook again and frowned down at the message.

"They've got him," said Artiss Fleur finally. "Probably in a state of distended consciousness."

Agent Fleur put his hands on Peter's shoulders and looked down at him solemnly. "The Anthrogs have him. He may even have offered himself to them in order to give you the chance to run free. They'll be keeping him in an etherised state, a kind of life in death. So, in that sense, he didn't lie to you. If anything, he would have wanted to spare you. He's warning GAIA through this message never to capitulate to his captors."

"Huh?"

"They plan to use Byron as a tool to bring down GAIA. Do you know what leverage is?"

"Yes," said Peter in dismay.

"They'll be expecting to leverage Byron's life in return for victory. But Byron won't allow it. He planned all along to sacrifice himself for the greater good."

"But you won't let him! You will capitulate to save Dad, won't you?" said Peter.

Artiss Fleur's eyes narrowed. "Well, if I have my way, we'll be going in with bells on; the whole team, this time – but only when the time is right."

They were both silent for a while.

Then, Artiss Fleur frowned. "But what I can't understand is why the Anthrogs have waited so long to use their leverage. They've been holding Byron captive more than five years."

In a moment, he answered his own question. "Of course! With Thelma gone, and the Chrysalite generation 2 formula off the table, there was no hurry."

"Is that what Mum was inventing when she died?"

"Yes. So, the Anthrogs have been busy cracking Chrysalite generation 1. They've done it too. There was news this morning of an unusually big and vicious attack on one of GAIA's global defences. I'm afraid we may have very dark days ahead of us."

Peter frowned sadly.

"But let's not think about that now. Peter, your father's alive. My best friend's alive!" Artiss Fleur surprised Peter by picking him up and swinging him through the air. "And we've still got the light on our side. Or at least what's left of the light."

The Sleeping King

T he weather in the afternoon was clear and calm. Pine needles crunched and slid under Peter's feet as he hiked upwards. Now that he'd learnt the truth about himself, he was acting on a hunch that he'd get more answers back up at the mysterious mountaintop tree.

When he reached the plateau, his eyes settled straight away on the giant oak tree at the edge of the cliff. It dominated the space. Peter was so focused on the oak that he almost stumbled on his own baby redwood sapling.

Look at me, not that old oak, the redwood seemed to say.

Riva's elm, Wanda's birch, and Chu's acorn shoot also waved out to him in the breeze. Feeling guilty, Peter tried to ignore the oak, giving water to his tree and to the others in the group.

Just as he was finishing, Peter was surprised to hear voices rising from the trail below; Riva appeared, followed by a red-faced Roland, puffing a few paces behind.

"Hi!" they both said with fake surprise. They weren't very good actors.

"Were you following me again?" Peter said accusingly to Roland, even though he was actually pleased to see both of them.

"I told you it wasn't a good idea!" Riva snapped at Roland.

But, before Roland could answer, they both caught sight of the enormous oak tree.

"Where did that come from?" Riva searched the ground for her own little elm sapling, checking that it was where she thought it should be, then gazed back at the tree.

"Remember, Tollen only comes out in bad weather, and today it's fine, so his oak is here." Peter swallowed nervously. "And I'm guessing he's in."

"What are you talking about?" Roland strode across the clearing and ran his hand across the scraggy bark of the giant tree.

"What he's talking about is that this wasn't here yesterday," Riva said incredulously.

"I'm going to try to get in," Peter told them.

Riva and Roland looked nervously at the tree, then each other, and didn't offer to join.

"Well, since you both went to the trouble of following me this far," said Peter, suddenly feeling miffed, "you might as well come with me."

"We'll come," Roland said, swallowing. "But is there a door?"

"There doesn't seem to be." Peter knocked uselessly against the bark.

The three circled the broad trunk until they found a small opening.

"Hello in there!" Riva called fearlessly.

A frog hopped onto the ledge. It was Rani from the Council of Five, the same frog Peter had followed last night to the Spiral Hall.

"And who might I say is calling?" squeaked the frog.

Riva gave a start at the sound of a talking frog, but Peter quickly found his voice.

"This is Roland Portogalo; you met him in the Combination Room yesterday. This is our friend Riva duLac. And I'm Peter Blue, the one you led into trouble last night."

"I'm Rani. I'm learning to croak," the frog told them, ignoring the bit about leading Peter into trouble.

"Good for you!" Riva said encouragingly. "But how did you learn to talk?"

"This tree has its own language unscrambler cloud inside and around it."

Riva frowned without comprehending. "Well, that's very nice. May I shake your paw?"

"Of course!" Rani offered one of her little paddy paws. "It has opposable fingers."

"Did you say 'disposable fingers'?" asked Peter, who was still mad at Rani.

"It wasn't me last night," said the frog.

"It wasn't you last night, where?" interrupted Peter.

"You know, hopping ahead at the Spiral Hall," she said, giving herself away completely.

"Well, you got Peter into a lot of trouble!" Roland reprimanded her.

"But I only wanted to show him his destiny," Rani said dolefully.

"It's okay." Peter patted the frog's tiny head forgivingly. The skin felt rough.

"Can we please come in?" the three peeped over the frog's head into the large circular room, then drew back in surprise.

Tollen of the forest and frogs was seated just a few metres from them, hunched over a thick book.

Rani had to cough squeakily a number of times before Tollen finally raised his head. He then hurriedly made a great show of welcoming his guests.

"Well, well! Please come in!" he urged. His strong voice resonated through the tree.

Roland looked dubiously at the narrow window. "We won't fit."

"But you must use the door!" Tollen indicated with his robed sleeve.

The three circled back and were surprised to find a door there, after all.

"Now how can I help you all?" Tollen asked once they were inside. Roland and Riva both looked at Peter.

"Um ... do you have a Book of Legends?" asked Peter.

"*Aaahh!*" Tollen's eyes twinkled. "As it happens, I have the Book of Legends open, right here on my desk."

"So, you were expecting me?" Peter glanced nervously at Roland, who just shrugged unworriedly.

"Well, let's just say I've been waiting for this day for some years."

Rani hopped onto the desk and peered at the gilt title on the book cover.

"But, are you sure this isn't the book of recipes?"

"Well, if it is, do you have one for frog legs?" joked Roland Tollen leant over the open book.

"Here it is: The Legend of the Sleeping King."

"But legends aren't really true," suggested Peter nervously. "They're just stories people make up about other people, you know, to give them hope."

"But this is the book of *true* legends," interrupted Rani annoyingly.

Ignoring the frog, Tollen pushed the big book towards Roland and asked him to read aloud.

One glance at the old-fashioned writing, and Roland staged a few coughs. "Um. ... Actually, I have a frog in my throat," he said. "Why doesn't Riva read?"

"As you wish. The first three verses, please, Riva."

Riva began to read in a bold, clear voice:

The Legend of the Sleeping King

I

From times of old, the legend holds,
Earth's darkest days must yet unfold.

Till such a time when earth's bright spark,
Shines lesser light and greater dark.

II

The pelican soul that keeps the light,
Will contemplate its final flight.

And when this bird no longer flies,
The Sleeping King again must rise.

III

This King's true mark comes not from name,
But from the boy who bears the Flame.

His light that Nature holds devout,
Shines within and shines without.

"That's it! That verse – that's what I want to explain." Peter stepped up to the book and peered down at the text. "I think you've been confusing me with someone else."

"Oh?" Tollen's whole face crinkled upwards into a smile.

"Yes! That's why I wanted to come and clear things up," Peter told him. "I think I understand why people here at GAIA might think that I'm this King boy in the legend. It's because I survived the fire when I was five, right? You thought I was the one who could bear the flames."

When nobody spoke, Peter continued.

"But what you're forgetting is that I was wearing Dad's GAIA jacket, which carries a protection against fire."

"Well, what about your head and your legs?" squeaked Rani. "Why didn't they burn?"

Peter sighed patiently. "Well, okay, I only just remembered this bit, but it turns out that the jacket protected me while I was running to the Great Gum, which is this kind of legendary tree that never burns down."

"But I thought you said that legends weren't true?" Rani interrupted even more annoyingly.

"But you do bear the Flame," Tollen told him quietly and kindly.

"No! That's what I wanted to tell you. Look!" Peter's swiped his finger through the candle on Tollen's desk.

"Ouch!" He screamed, extra loudly, shaking his fingers to make the point. "See? I can't bear it."

The wizard Tollen chuckled, shaking his head, then shuffled across the dirt floor to the doorway, where a tall pot of wand-shaped sticks stood. He selected the most colourful of the sticks.

"The Flame that we speak of is symbolic, my dear child – symbolic of a light you carry with you from another time. Now, if you will, bow your head slightly please."

Using the soft rounded point of the wand, Tollen gently parted the hair at the base of Peter's head, just above the neck.

"There it is, at the nape of the neck. The glyph!" Tollen said with a note of triumph.

There were surprised intakes of breath from Riva and Roland.

Then Rani plonked her froggie legs onto Peter's shoulder. "Let me see!"

"It's that triangle thing," Riva said with a gasp.

Everyone was breathing down Peter's neck now.

"The upwards-facing triangle," Tollen confirmed. "It is as the legend decrees: the true mark of the Flame."

Tollen guided Peter over to a tall hanging wall mirror, then angled a smaller hand-held mirror behind his neck to show him. The triangular mark about the size of a thumbprint sat up like a raised welt against his skin.

"Why haven't I seen it before?" Peter asked, disbelieving.

"Well, how often do you look at the back of your neck – or behind your ears, for that matter?" Tollen chuckled again. "You might want to give the whole area a good scrub one day."

Then, his voice became more serious.

"A true mark of greatness is not for you, the bearer of it, to gaze upon, but to show the way for those who come behind you."

Peter frowned doubtfully. Suddenly, he couldn't stop scratching and rubbing at his neck.

Rani, who'd been silent for a while, squeaked, "If Peter Blue really is a king, does that mean I should have to curtsy to him? Or, do you think that, since I'm the seven-times great-granddaughter of a famous frog, I shouldn't have to?"

Tollen laughed. "Well, I, of course, should kneel, except my old knees have been troubling me lately."

Everyone laughed, then Tollen said, "Rani, what do we have that's nice to offer our guests?"

Rani smiled widely. "Let's see, we have some fresh silverfish scones made with fly-blown buttermilk, served with slow-brewed worm tea, or plain fresh water."

"Just water, thank you!" chimed the three guests.

After they'd all taken seats on little wooden stools, Riva said, "Why do you stay here in a tree, Mr Tollen?"

Tollen laughed. "Actually, for many years, I had no choice. I was trapped here against my will; tricked by a woman who used one of my own spells to imprison me in the tree. But, after a while, it began to feel just like home. One day, I realised I wasn't trapped at all."

Tollen paused. He had a faraway look in his eyes. "I realised that all I had to do was just relax and become the tree, and therein lay my freedom."

The three children gaped at him.

Then, Riva said, "You're not planning on becoming the tree while we're still in it, are you?"

"Goodness no, child!" Tollen's chest heaved with laughter. "I usually only leave when the weather turns."

Roland looked nervously out the window. "It's still fine out there."

He took three more helpings of water from Tollen's glass jug.

"It doesn't matter how much I drink," Roland told them. "I'm still thirsty."

"Well, perhaps it's not you who's thirsty," suggested Tollen. "Perhaps it's your tree."

Roland frowned. "My tree?"

"That's right," interrupted Riva accusingly. "I bet you haven't even been back once to water that baby maple of yours. Remember what Principal Halowell said: you and the tree are connected now."

Roland gulped the last of his water without replying, then jumped up guiltily.

"Well, thanks for having us."

Riva jumped up too, turning towards Peter. "You coming?"

Before he could answer, Tollen said, "Why don't I keep Peter here for a bit, in case he has more questions?"

"Okay. Do you want to hang out tomorrow?" Riva asked.

"Ah yes ... yes please!" Peter didn't even try disguise how thrilled he was by her invitation. He'd never just hung out with other kids before.

"Don't worry," Roland explained to Riva. "Peter's friends in his last place were mostly old people and trees."

"Well, speaking of trees," Riva said, pulling Roland by the arm. "Do you even remember where you planted yours?"

After they left, Rani hopped onto Peter's shoulder. "You don't even remember, do you?

"Remember what?"

"I was the frog in your dreams," she said breathily.

"Tollen and this tree and me – we were all in your dreams."

"Is that true?"

Tollen nodded.

Peter wandered over to the desk and placed the frog on the table where the book still lay open. Suddenly, he couldn't fight off a wave of irritation.

"I didn't ask for any of this Sleeping King stuff, though, you know!"

"Nobody ever does," Tollen replied mildly. "It's your gift for this lifetime, to do what you want with."

Peter pushed the book aside, a little too roughly.

"But I don't know anything about lesser lights and darker days and pelican souls!" He suddenly felt flushed, and the more he scratched the mark on the back of his neck, the more it irritated him. "I really don't. ..."

"It's all right." Tollen raised a hand. "Don't say anymore; it's no matter. Most people turn their backs on the light of their true potential. Why should you be any different?"

The old man sat back down at the desk, with his back to Peter.

Rani said, "*Humph!* ... Now he'll need to start looking for a new legend."

"Wait!" Peter protested. "I didn't say I wouldn't—"

As Peter paused, Tollen turned his head wearily towards him.

"I didn't say I wouldn't do my best!" Peter managed.

The corners of the old man's mouth twitched into a smile, and Peter couldn't stop himself from smiling back.

Then, Peter felt guilty. "The Pelican is Esther the pelican, isn't it?"

Tollen nodded solemnly. "I fear so."

"But how could I possibly help?"

"Well, Peter this may surprise you, but as new events unfold, the most important thing you can do on behalf of humanity is *hope*." Tollen turned fully in his chair to face Peter. "All our hope once lay in your mother Thelma's next-generation Chrysalite formula, you see."

Peter didn't really see, but he nodded anyway.

"Thelma was so close to success, and then all her hard work was lost – destroyed."

Peter deliberately didn't speak, hoping Tollen would continue talking about his mum.

"The Chrysalite generation 1, which she so famously invented, was enough to keep the Anthrogs contained for some years, but now we know for certain that its code has been cracked and a counterforce created."

Tollen stood up and began to pace the room. "I fear I shouldn't be telling you this. It may upset you too much."

"Please. I want to know."

Tollen sighed. "Well we all feared that this would eventually happen, which was why President Buchanan commissioned your mother to come up with a new, second-generation Chrysalite formula, one that would be so sophisticated as to be undecipherable by the Anthrog intelligence."

Peter shook his head in amazement.

"But why Mum? Why couldn't Professor Meriwether have invented it? Isn't he the best scientist in the world?"

"Well, so they say." Tollen laughed in an oddly self-conscious way. "But your mother had one special link with Nature intelligence that no one here at GAIA could come close to."

"What was that?"

"You mean, you don't know? Think, Peter," said Tollen in a way that almost mimicked Ms Moth.

Peter frowned. "Um. ..." He thought of her book, *Thelma and the Flame*. Mum had insisted it was a true story. "Was it something to do with the Nature spirit of Fire?" asked Peter.

"Precisely!" Tollen smiled. "You see Peter, the ability to cooperate fully with Fire intelligence, the highest of the elemental Nature spirits, was imperative for the creation and widespread application of the Chrysalite 2 formula."

He leant his face close to Peter. "The plan for Ch 2 was to infuse it directly into the soul field of the earth itself, to the place where the extreme weather comes from—"

"Wait!" interrupted Peter. "What did you just say?"

"Which part?" Tollen smiled tiredly.

"What did you call Mum's second-generation Chrysalite?"

The old man seemed about to reply, but Peter was already heading for the door. "Never mind! I'll be right back. I think there is still hope."

62

The New Dawn

eter flew into the rammed-earth dorm room that he shared with Chu. He had a strong hunch he was going to find just what Tollen and the rest of GAIA had been looking for, right here among his belongings. He pulled up his pillow, where he'd been keeping his treasures, but the book was missing.

Where is it? Peter fumed as he scrabbled through his backpack, pulling things out and tossing them to the floor. He rummaged through the cupboard of his night table and across his desk.

Chu barely looked up at him. He was bent over his own desk, scribbling in a notebook.

Then, the back of Peter's neck began to prickle. Could the book have been stolen? His mother's book that he'd carried across the world with him?

"Hey, Chu, has anyone been in here touching my stuff?" Peter demanded roughly.

Chu shrugged without looking up. "I don't think so, but I've been busy."

Peter thought of the Anthrogs. Could they have finally got to GAIA and stolen his mother's formula, just when he'd finally figured things out?

Nothing else seemed to be missing – just the precious book, Mum's prized story.

"Did you smell anything strange?" Peter demanded.

Chu shrugged again in a way that was so passive and uninterested that it suddenly made Peter's blood boil. The back of his neck felt hot and tingly, and it was as if his pulse were leaping about his body.

"I'm talking to you!" Peter hollered. "Did you smell something so cosmically bad that you could never wipe it from your memory, even in death?"

Chu shook his head, clearly alarmed by both the question and the way Peter was speaking.

There was something bubbling in a flask on his tripod above the burner, and Chu's desk was littered with piles of crystals, beakers, test tubes, and half-scribbled notes.

"Actually, there was this one annoying man who came looking for you."

Peter groaned. "Who?"

"I can't remember," said Chu unhelpfully. "But he told me to tell you to report to his office ASAP."

Peter grimaced. "Did he have tired eyes and a crumpled shirt?"

"I don't know about the eyes, but the shirt sounds right."

"Did he touch my stuff?"

"I'm not sure. I told you: I was busy," said Chu nervously.

"He wants to give me another detention, to make three in a row so that I'll be expelled."

"Lucky you!" Chu said sullenly.

Peter started rummaging on Chu's side of the room now. He pulled up Chu's pillow, then looked under his bed, then opened Chu's cupboards and rummaged through his shelves. Chu didn't seem to mind until Peter began pushing things around on the desk.

"Hey, watch out!" he told Peter rudely.

"No!" Peter snapped back. "I have to find my book."

"What book?"

"A book written by my dead mother! Okay?!"

"Could it be this?" Chu calmly pulled the little hand-drawn storybook from under his notebook pile.

Peter snatched it up with relief.

"It was actually very hard to understand" said Chu. "Even for me."

"It's a story about a little girl who meets the spirit of Fire. What's not to understand?"

Chu giggled. "I didn't read that part. I'm talking about the scientific stuff at the end. If it's yours, then I obviously misjudged your intelligence."

"Why?" Peter couldn't resist asking.

"Well, I thought. ..." Chu blushed slightly and scratched through his spiky black hair. "I thought that you might, you know, be a bit simple."

"Thanks very much." Peter laughed and decided not to be offended. "Why?"

"Well, you know, the way you stare off into space with that empty kind of look."

"I'm philosophising!" protested Peter.

"Well, anyway ... so far, the entire formula's got me beat."

"Formula?" Peter's heart was beating hard against his chest. So, his hunch was right.

"It's genius," added Chu respectfully.

Peter flicked through his mother's book to the pencil-written part at the back, with all the strange symbols and equations. His eyes found the heading "Ch 2".

Not Chapter 2, as he'd thought, but Chrysalite generation 2.

"Can I borrow it?" asked Chu, but Peter was already closing the book and running for the door.

As he puffed back up the winding path towards Tollen's oak, Peter clutched the booklet tightly to his chest.

It wasn't stolen, and now I'll be able to hand it safely to Tollen – before Drufus expels me, he thought in dismay.

Peter's legs felt weak, and his chest ached from the exertion of the climb, but still he continued hurrying upwards. It was hard to believe that he might be holding something that could actually help save the world. He couldn't wait to show it to Tollen.

Finally, Peter stepped free of the trees, into the clearing at the top, where the old oak stood lit by a bright afternoon sun.

When Tollen opened the door, Peter was too exhausted to speak. He could only hand the wizard the book and then sink onto a stool.

Tollen sat down next to him, flipping with interest through the handwritten story by nine-year-old Thelma LaRosa.

"Do you think it's a true story?" Peter asked him.

"I have no doubt of it," Tollen replied in a way that made Peter's heart feel warm.

Then, the old man turned to the page headed "Ch 2". Almost at once, his hands began to shake as he turned page after page, taking in the strange equations and scribbled symbols. The wrinkled spokes in the corners of Tollen's eyes grew damp with tears.

Then, Peter jumped up in fright as Tollen's robes began to sway and sink towards the dirt floor. Peter wondered if he was having a heart attack. But then, he saw that the old man was lowering himself purposefully onto his knees in front of Peter.

"You've done it, Peter Blue!" Tollen raised the book upwards, clutching it in both hands in a gesture of victory, and never taking his eyes off Peter, who just stood gaping with embarrassment.

It was only when Tollen began clutching at his knees and groaning in pain that Peter bent down swiftly to help him.

"This is indeed a big day for GAIA," Tollen told Peter repeatedly as he pulled the old man up unsteadily by the arm.

Tollen rummaged in a drawer for some large sheets of thick paper, and then he pulled out an old feather pen and an ink bottle from the clutter on the top of his desk.

"I'll need to make a copy immediately, of course. Two copies are safer than one. Then, later on, when the time is right, we can start to try to make sense of it all. It's unfinished but still very far along."

Peter nodded. "Can I help?"

"No, but you've done well, child. More than I ever could have hoped for."

Tollen sat down heavily at his desk, his back to Peter, and started working on the new copy.

Peter shivered and suddenly felt very tired. He looked round the large circular room. "Where do you sleep?" he asked curiously.

"Oh, on a mat on the floor beside the fire."

"Where's the fire?"

"There." Tollen pointed to the centre of the oak room, where flames suddenly leapt from a circle of stones.

"Hey! That wasn't there a second ago!"

"It's warm, though, isn't it?"

"But how did you do make it appear so suddenly?"

"Oh, it's nothing. One of the first tricks I learnt as a boy."

Peter found it hard to imagine tall, wrinkly faced Tollen as a boy. He wondered if he'd ever been given a detention for lighting fires in the classroom. The thought reminded Peter of his own detention problem.

"I've got two detentions in a row from Administrator Drufus, and I'm afraid of getting a third," he confided. "Agent Fleur told me it would be a tricky administrative manoeuvre to get me out of that kind of trouble, even for him."

Tollen, not taking his eyes away from the formula, said, "Well, it shouldn't be too hard to stay out of trouble just until Sunday morning, should it?"

"No, except that Mr Drufus seems to be against me, for some reason – like he's trying to set me up or something."

Tollen looked up at Peter.

"Ah, yes ... well, that's a problem, isn't it?"

Peter shivered again. "What shall I do?"

Tollen laid a mat out by the fire and directed Peter to lie on it.

The warmth of the flames felt soothing to Peter.

"For now, I'm only going to let you do one thing," Tollen muttered.

"What's that?" Peter said drowsily.

"Something you asked me a long time ago. I'm going to let you sleep."

There was a plate of warm rolls and berry juice waiting for Peter when he woke up.

"Now you'd better hurry home and do your homework."

"But I don't have homework; it's orientation."

"Then, hurry home and orientate." Tollen smiled.

"What about Mr Drufus?" Peter hung his head nervously.

"Oh, I wouldn't worry about him. Your future at Spiral Hall looks secure."

"But, how ...?"

"Let's just say that our friend Arun Drufus occasionally takes an early rest on a Saturday and sleeps right through until well into Sunday, especially after a long week in his detention room."

Peter smiled gratefully, although he wasn't entirely sure what the old man was telling him.

"Sleeping potions." Tollen winked at Peter. "The second trick I learnt as a boy."

On the way back to his room, Peter paused, alone in the meadow at the foot of Tollen's mountain. He thought about the Sleeping King legend and all the things he didn't understand about the future.

Suddenly, he wanted everything to stay still for moment. But nothing would; a sudden gust of wind spiralled round him, tugging at his jacket and whipping his hair.

Shooooooo-ster!

"I know you," Peter told the wind.

Then, he heard a voice from another time and place say, "Someone from this new generation will have to fix things." And a circle of wrinkled watchers nodded, looking straight at Peter.

The jacket hummed gently. Peter thought he heard the voice of Devlin Dean say, "I couldn't have done it without you, Peter Blue."

Tsk-tsk! The new Agent Pickles sounded her agreement from her animal-intelligence training camp across the way.

Then, Artiss Fleur's voice exclaimed, "Your father's alive. This changes everything!" And from somewhere deep in his captive sleep induced by the Anthrogs, Byron Blue's eyelids flickered in a way that said, "Never capitulate!"

Then, far across the meadow to the west, caught in the orange-gold rays of the setting sun, Thelma LaRosa, in a white dress, waved out to him. She wasn't running from the fire; she was running with it, leaping and circling in the flames. And behind her, high on the hill, a little redwood tree couldn't help but shake its new leaves just from the joy of it all.

Finally, the Great Gum Tree of Jarra Jarra wanted to add its voice to the conversation. Pulling itself up to its highest possible self, the Great Gum said, *Silence!*

It was almost a perfect silence until a sinister sound came and went so quickly that Peter wondered if he might have imagined it.

Click-clack, click-clack.

ACKNOWLEDGEMENTS

Writing a book is always a team effort. My first thanks go to Jay Quinn and the CT, who listened tirelessly to my tales and critiqued and co-created my characters and storylines. I will always be grateful.

Thanks also go to Tina Colbert at Balboa, who called me in the Finnish countryside and persuaded me to take this journey, and to all the Balboa staff for your professionalism and positivity. Thank you Dr. Georgina Spyres for your science and nature advice, and for continuing to believe in this project. Thank you Michelle Roche for your honesty around my earlier work. Thank you Tim Upperton for your help on style. Thank you Julie Garman Kolokotsa, Marie Ridder, Sarah Hamilton, Liz Hogan and Laura Lee Williams for telling me to keep writing. Thank you Teo Soon Kwong for helping me realize my characters with your illustrations, and Zoe Nikitaki for giving your energy through 'the colours' with your cover artwork. Thank you to Helen and Brian Colless, my carbon busting parents, who taught me to respect and love nature.

My highest thanks go to my husband Pekka, who shouldered the family burden while I was away with my laptop, and to my daughters Olivia and Julia for giving up mummy time and always encouraging me to keep going.

The final thank you goes to my characters, especially my beloved Peter Blue, whose childish light will inhabit my heart always.

ABOUT THE AUTHOR

Through storytelling Laurel Colless inspires children to take the lead on big world problems like climate change, extreme weather, and plastic pollution. That means drawing wisdom from all the intelligences available: from super-technology to trees, and even from the croak of an occasional frog. Laurel brings a background in environmental business and literature to create a new kind of myth-making that reflects the reality of today's children – separating from nature and from each other. Laurel Colless is an Al Gore Climate Reality Leader and founder of the Carbon Busters Club.

Made in the USA
Lexington, KY
10 December 2017